# THE
## *Storyteller*
## BY THE
## SEA

ALSO BY PHYLLIDA SHRIMPTON

*Every Shade of Happy*

# THE *Storyteller* BY THE SEA

## PHYLLIDA SHRIMPTON

*An Aria Book*

First published in the UK in 2023 by Head of Zeus,
part of Bloomsbury Publishing Plc

9 7 5 3 1 2 4 6 8

A catalogue record for this book is available from the British Library.

ISBN (PB): 9781803281414
ISBN (E): 9781803281384

Cover design: Emma Rogers

Typeset by Siliconchips Services Ltd UK

Printed and bound in Great Britain by
CPI Group (UK) Ltd, Croydon CRO 4YY

Head of Zeus
First Floor East
5–8 Hardwick Street
London ECIR 4RG

WWW.HEADOFZEUS.COM

For my family and friends and anyone who loves Shelly, Exmouth, Devon as much as I do.

Thank you Exmouth and Shelly (or Pirate's Cove as it is now known) for finding a place in my heart all those years ago when I was just a child. Shelly has changed a lot over the years but it is still beautiful – it's just a different kind of beautiful.

# PART 1

# 1

## Exmouth, Devon

Melody's life was a simple life. She'd never asked for anything more from it. Until now.

She always wished, of course, that she could hold Milo's hand again, or once more feel the softness of their mother's cheek against hers, but those kind of wishes were born of love. This was different. Now, there was desperation in the air. A kind of grief growing in the place where she lived in the community of Shelly, a little corner of Exmouth on the south English coast. Her simple, *beautiful* life had finally found its way to the summer of 1988 and the days were almost banging against each other in their race towards the summer of 1989. Days that were giving her so little time to hold on to each one before the next arrived.

The dipping sun threw Melody's long shadow across the sand where she stood, casting a shining cloak of golden light over the windows and rooftops of the bungalows behind her. These little seaside dwellings had hugged Shelly beach for a hundred years, Victorian weatherboarding and wooden balustrades giving a quaintness to each one, their white paint bright against the yellow sand. Her own home, Spindrift, was right in the middle of a row of them, looking out, in its ageing wisdom, across the sea. She'd been born in Spindrift and had lived all of her thirty-four years there, never wanting more than she had.

The little homes smelt of salty damp from years of sea spray and their single-glazed windows barely kept the winter chill at bay. But the people who lived there didn't mind any of that. They wiped the condensation from their windows and cooked their meals in the tiny kitchens. They opened their doors in summer and put logs on their fires in winter. They were at one with the coast. No, Melody had never asked much from life, but now she wanted the impossible. She wanted time to stop.

A rogue wave swept along the sand, caressing Melody's toes with cold sea foam, leaving tiny bubbles on her bare feet as she stooped to pick up a music cassette. Her long blonde hair, caught by the wind, whipped around her shoulders and across her face as she teased at a whirl of tape escaping from the plastic casing.

'Motown,' she mused. 'Who left you here, I wonder?' Pulling seaweed from the tangle and poking her finger in the reel hub, she turned it until the length of tape wound back inside the case. Melody knew it would never play again but the music, heard many times before, lived on in her mind. The easy rhythm imprinted forever within the strands of twisted, shiny film didn't need the mechanics of a tape recorder to remind her of it. 'Being broken can't silence you,' she said, putting the cassette in her old wicker basket. Her words, spoken out loud, were swooped up by a gust of sea air and she imagined that, even though they'd left her mouth, Milo could still hear her voice, like the music on the tape. He was there somewhere, her younger brother, listening to her from his other world, still waiting to hear stories about all the things she'd gathered in her basket.

Finding an oyster shell, she brushed the sand from it, running her fingers around its contours to feel the deep ridges along its edge and the smoothness of its centre, loving how the creamy white of it caught the evening light. Like an old man's ear, she thought, inhaling the salty scent of the coast that rose from it. Placing the shell in her wicker basket, she tucked loose tendrils of her hair behind her ear and walked for a while before picking up a discarded lolly stick. The dried remains of pink ice-cream clung to the wood and it smelt of strawberries and sugar. She popped it in her basket alongside the tape and the oyster shell, a large pebble shaped like an egg and a worn piece of pottery shining with dusky tea rose. Buckets and spades were now abandoned for the day, two rowing boats slumbered on the beach and the halyard of a Mirror dinghy tap-tapped in the breeze. Melody absorbed the loveliness of it all and, making her way home along the beach, did her best to swallow down a sense of rising fear.

Putting her basket on Milo's bed, she sat down in his wheelchair and scooted it closer to his empty mattress. His room was small with a single bed and many shelves on the walls to display all his things. Above the headboard hung a large canvas painted by their mother, a likeness of the two of them when they were children, along with their younger cousin, Juliana. In the painting, Milo knelt in the sand, placing a flag in the top of a sandcastle, and Melody was beside him holding a yellow bucket. They wore hand-knitted swimming costumes of lemon and green and Juliana, wearing little blue shorts and a sun hat, was crouching nearby, hunting for shells. Melody's pale hair hung in a straight, blonde ponytail down her back, Milo's fell around his shoulders in long blond curls and Juliana's was a glowing crown of strawberry blonde. Spindrift, shouldered by the other bungalows, was painted behind them, recognisable by its white fence, complete with a wooden ladder leading down to the beach.

Opening a packet of marshmallow tea cakes, Melody devoured all six of them while removing her treasures from the basket and describing each one out loud. 'This, Milo...' she said to the empty room, holding the pebble shaped like an egg and taking a moment to align her thoughts, 'is a phoenix egg. It's extremely rare and we're very lucky to find such a treasure. The phoenix egg symbolises renewal. Soon, it will burst into flames and a new phoenix will spread its golden wings and rise from the ashes.' Melody smiled as she placed it on his bed. The pebble had cracks radiating from a dent in the side and Melody thought that, later that day, she would paint an eye peeking through it as if the mystical creature was hatching from inside.

Licking her fingers to remove a residue of chocolate, she dipped her hand into the basket again and pulled out the cassette tape. 'You used to love Motown,' she said. 'Remember, Milo? How we would play Dad's records before cassettes were a thing?' She placed the cassette on the bed next to the pebble, singing one of the tracks to her brother while the story behind how it came to be washed up on the beach formulated in her mind. Milo, she believed, waited silently and patiently for her to bring the treasures of their beach to life.

Each item had a scent and a texture and a reason for being and she couldn't bring herself to throw anything away once their story had been told. After reading that day's newspaper, she removed the covering with its date and headlines and neatly folded it.

'Goodnight, my lovely,' she said, as she smoothed down the pale blue and creamy white stripes of the woollen over-blanket that hid the rubber sheet beneath it. Then, standing up, she raised her chin and straightened her back in the way her mother had always taught her. Finding a space on Milo's shelves, she placed her gatherings on the folded front cover of the newspaper alongside all the other treasures and stories she'd brought him over the years. Keeping the headlines from each day was a new thing for Melody because every single day was now more precious than the last. She was determined not to forget a single one.

Today belonged to Wednesday, that Wednesday belonged to June, and that June belonged to 1988.

# 2

'His name is Milo.' Melody's mother, Flora, flushed and sweaty, brushed her daughter's cheek softly with the back of her hand then tugged gently at a soft, yellow, knitted blanket. There, peeking out from the blanket in her arms, was the face of a tiny baby.

Melody peered closer, taking in the damp hair, fanned lashes and soft breaths that puffed from a little button nose. At three years old, Melody had no real understanding of how the baby came to be, only that he'd somehow appeared after an unholy amount of yelling behind the closed door of her parents' bedroom. A stout woman had arrived wearing a wool coat and felt hat, carrying a large leather bag, and she'd slipped into the bedroom where her mother lay in bed. She'd closed the door firmly behind her, reappearing only to boil a large pan of water on the hob in the kitchen which, Melody assumed, was because her mother liked soup. Her father, Daniel, had paced the rug outside the bedroom and proceeded to circle the sitting room so many times he was making Melody dizzy, repeatedly forbidding her to investigate the goings-on. Once, he stopped to call through the door, 'Breathe through it, you're doing grand,' but her mother had shouted something very rude at him about what he could do with a watermelon. It seemed to Melody as though her mother was furious at him, and it confused her because her mother had never been furious at anyone. And now she was shouting that there was a *ruddy thing* inside her that she needed to get out. Out of where, Melody wondered.

When her father had finally flung open the doors to Spindrift and stood on the terrace outside, calling to anyone who would listen, 'It's a boy! It's a boy. My son, Milo, is here,' she'd followed him outside, staring at a rare grin on his face, the likes of which she'd never seen him with before. It was so wide it almost broke his face in half with the joy of it.

There were huge white clouds in a blue sky that day, a salty wind blowing across the sea, and the tide was so far out she could see right to the end of the rocks that edged the beach. The air had a frosty bite to it and, out of season, the beach was quiet. Soon, however, with the noise her father was making, neighbours began to appear on their bungalow terraces, shouting back at him with voices that sounded equally as cheery. Then, her father had picked her up into his arms and spun her around until the world blurred into colourful ribbons. He'd been so very happy in that moment that the feeling of it had flowed right through Melody and into her insides, making her feel so very happy, too.

Now, breathing in deeply through her nose, Melody smelt the sweet warmth of her brother's skin and a milky scent on his breath. She loved how his downy hair tickled her lips when she kissed him and how he squeaked and mewed like a kitten. The winter was harsh that year and the coldness of it was finding its way into Spindrift so, being the big sister that she now was, she tucked the soft, yellow blanket close to his body.

'He should hold your hand if you place your finger into his palm,' Flora said serenely, smiling at her precious newborn and removing his blue mitten so that Melody could see a tiny hand. Such little fingers he had and with tiny nails as delicate as the mother-of-pearl buttons on his suit. She traced the outline of his hand with the pad of her finger before gently pressing it into his palm, murmuring softly to him as she waited for his fingers to curl around hers. His hands, though, remained open, pink and wrinkly and soft as a butterfly kiss.

'I'm your big sister,' she said, leaning closer and introducing herself to her brother. She felt such pride to belong to this little person that when he opened his eyes, shining like two dark, polished stones, it was as if she was falling into the depths of them. 'He likes me, Mumma,' she whispered.

'He *loves* you,' Flora rectified, running a gentle hand down the length of Melody's hair. 'You're going to be a wonderful big sister.'

Melody knew that something amazing had happened. She knew that a brand-new person had arrived at Spindrift. And, when she kissed the soft cheek of the little boy in her mother's arms, she knew, in a moment, that she loved him right back.

# 3

By the time Melody had placed the remaining flotsam and jetsam on a pile in the sitting room, put her basket away and cleared the wrapping from her marshmallow tea cakes, it was getting late. The sun had long since scooped her fiery colours from the sea and taken them with her as she sank behind the distant skyline. Melody sat alone in her old sun chair on the terrace of Spindrift, drinking boxed zesty white wine from a mug and painting the finishing touches to the mystical yellow eye which now peeked through the cracks in the pebble shaped like an egg. Three candlelit lanterns offered a rosy hue to the unseasonably chill evening air by the time she had finished and, when a sharp wind blew across her shoulders, she simply arranged her thick woollen blankets around herself and settled into the embrace of the night. Lights glowed from the bungalows around her and twinkled in the distance where the land across the water formed the yawning mouth of the River Exe.

The rain had blown east that morning and wasn't due to return for two days so, long after the lights and the candles had flickered and waned, Melody continued to sit outside. The moon, gaining majesty over his indigo sky, hosted a waltz of gauzy thin clouds just for her, while rhythmical waves coursed along the beach, halyards tinkled in the bay and gulls called into the darkness.

When sleep came it brought with it a quiet gift. She dreamt she was a child again. It was summer. Milo was playing on the beach in front of Spindrift making pies out of sand and their cousin, Juliana, was with them.

A subconscious feeling of happiness filled Melody's dream with light as if the sun was shining inside her mind. She and Juliana were holding hands, wading into the sea together, the clarity of the water turning their feet a pale green, the cold water reaching Juliana's knees long before Melody's. They jumped over each incoming wave together, squeezing each other's fingers tightly to keep their balance, their long hair lifting in the breeze as they leapt. Then, they looked into each other's eyes for a silent command and, still holding hands, they ran, crashing through the waves, laughing out loud and squealing with delight until they fell belly down into the water. By the time they made their way back along the beach, collecting Milo along the way, their hair plastered to their shoulders, their skin shimmering with drops of sea water, Flora was putting three glasses of homemade lemonade on the table, each with a different-coloured straw.

When a fat seagull cackled its early morning greeting from the fencepost next to Melody she woke with a start, the sleepy residue of her childhood days so clear in her mind that she felt she could simply reach out to drink the lemonade her mother had made. She wallowed in the feeling of it, keeping them all close in her thoughts before the need to pee made her fidget. Cold air in a pale dawn sky hung in misty layers over the water and, regretfully, letting go of the dream, she threw off her blankets and made her way inside. Returning with a mug of tea and two toasted waffles, she ate while watching the sea mist lifting to reveal calm waters which moved in silken sheets of lavender and battleship grey. Her rowing boat, *Serendipity*, listed on the damp sand, a solitary seagull perched on her bow. Early mornings were special as far as Melody was concerned. Her corner of Shelly, hugged by its crescent of seaside bungalows, slept on, and with the soft sound of morning waves against damp sand, and the call of seagulls wheeling in the sky, Melody bathed in the loveliness of it all.

She tried to ignore the harsh reality that another day had yet again pushed its way forward on the calendar, nudging the old one behind it. She also tried to ignore the fact that Juliana had now left five messages on the telephone answering machine, an ugly modern contraption that gathered dust as a result of rarely having to perform the task it was designed for. Juliana had bought it for Melody after complaining that it was almost impossible to get hold of her by telephone and, although she was the only person who ever called Melody, her calls had become steadily fewer and further between. For two days, however, the answering machine had taken to flashing its red light, alerting her to the fact that Juliana's voice messages were inside. Although Melody had every intention of ringing her back at some point, today wasn't the day to speak to her cousin. Then again, nor was yesterday, or the day before that, but it was the fact that Juliana had rung at all after such a length of time that had sent Melody's equilibrium into spirals.

She eyed the flashing red light of the answering machine where Juliana's most recent message waited, already knowing what it was going to say because it would be the same as the others. Juliana wanted to visit.

Once upon a time she would have been thrilled that her cousin was coming to see her. Ever since they were both little, Juliana had visited each summer, staying for six glorious weeks at a time while her parents left her, escaping to the busy lives of their thriving business. Those visits had formed some of the sweetest of all Melody's childhood memories. They'd been so close, she and Juliana, filling their summer days with all the freedom a seaside life had to offer children. Her cousin now, however, was comparable to one of the treasures she gathered while beachcombing along the shore. She was part of a story that belonged to another place, in another time, when life was simple. Melody thought that, perhaps, she should stay that way.

'Gosh, it's... it's getting even *busier* in here,' Juliana had exclaimed last time she'd visited. She'd breezed into Spindrift with a hamper of food and a case of wine, her eyes darting here and there as she entered the sitting room. Putting her gifts on the dining table, they'd both watched as the wheel from a boat trailer tumbled from the table and rolled along the floor. Juliana's smile had become fixed and the lines on her brow deepened at the doorway of Milo's room where she'd paused for a full five minutes before she could speak. 'All Milo's things, Mel – his wheelchair, his *commode*. It's all *still* here... and more! More shelves, more *stuff*, bits of newspaper. You were going to clear it out. What happened? We agreed...'

'*You* agreed,' Melody had said.

Still at Milo's doorway and now examining the extra shelves laden with beach treasures and newspaper covers,

Juliana had an expression of horrified fascination. 'Mel, come on, *really*? It's time to…'

'Remove all evidence?' Melody had interjected. She'd felt challenged, a flash of irritation swelling in the pit of her stomach, threatening to burst out and pepper them both with the stains of her pique. She'd spent all day cleaning and getting everything ready for Juliana. She'd put fresh towels and a vase of flowers in Flora's room ready to greet her and now she wished she hadn't.

'You know I don't mean that… as such.' Juliana had done her best to explain. 'It's just that I thought we'd agr… I mean, I thought we'd *talked* about things. Talked about how you live with ghosts, Mel. We talked about how you need to *let those ghosts go*.'

She'd put a soft hand on Melody's arm and Melody had moved her arm discreetly away.

'Anyway!' Juliana had smiled brightly then, holding her arms open wide. 'Come here, cousin, it's been too long.' They'd tucked themselves inside each other's arms and gradually, as their disagreement melted away, they'd hugged each other tightly, allowing the memories of all that they loved about each other back into their hearts. The scent of perfume and clean hair had filled Melody's senses with a familiar, delicate loveliness which, for a wonderful, comforting moment, she'd lost herself in. She'd wondered if her own hair and skin held the scent of sea spray and hoped that it did. When Juliana broke away she'd left part of herself imprinted in the cavity of Melody's beating chest.

Taking one of the bottles of wine from the case she'd brought, Juliana had held it high in the air, calling over her shoulder as she entered the kitchen, 'Come on, it's over the yardarm!' She'd taken a bottle opener from the drawer and two small glasses from a narrow wooden shelf then made her way past bags stacked on the floor in the sitting room to get outside to the terrace. Melody had followed her with a small platter of cheese and grapes.

'How are you really? Honest answers only.' Their fragile peace had been shattered. They'd been sitting in the sun chairs, their bare feet propped up on the white fence of the terrace, the second bottle of wine already lined up. Melody had been studying the carefully applied fuchsia-pink nail varnish on Juliana's toenails, thinking that they, along with the on-trend vivid blue eyeshadow Juliana wore, looked horribly garish.

'I'm OK. Honest answer.' Melody had torn her gaze from the overbright toenails and laid it to rest on a small boat chugging its way down the estuary and out into the sea. She spoke into the bowl of her glass then took a sip. She'd been living and she'd been surviving and, until questioned about it, had thought she'd been doing a pretty good job at both. There hadn't been enough time... or wine... to articulate how she *truly* felt. 'I'm OK, *really*.' Melody had taken another sip. 'Good even.' She'd switched her focus from the small boat to a larger fishing boat coming in from the sea towards the dock. It was followed by a flurry of excited seagulls, the marker buoys tied to its side beaming orange against the shades of watery slate and platinum it coursed through.

'You say that, but to be honest I'm getting worried now.' Juliana all of a sudden had sat forward and planted her pink toenails on the ground in a moment of determination and Melody inwardly cursed that they were managing to steal more attention from her than the sea view. 'I'm going to come right out with it, Mel. You've added to it... the stuff,

I mean... It's everywhere now! More than last time.' Juliana had jerked her head in the direction of the open double doors of Spindrift, her face contorting again into disapproving lines. She'd been exasperated, seeking an explanation that Melody knew there was no point trying to offer. How could she put into words that it was *not* just stuff?

'It isn't everywhere,' Melody had defended. 'The sitting room has a few more bags in it admittedly, and Milo's room has a lot more shelves on the wall, I suppose, but Flora's room is perfectly tidy.'

'Flora's room is a shrine,' Juliana had said, quietly.

Melody, humiliated by such an accusation, felt herself burn with pain, but then, just at that moment, the sun had peeked out through the cumulus clouds that were lumbering lazily across the sky. It had splashed Shelly with a warm light and kissed each ripple in the sea with sparkles. Melody believed that it was as if Flora was giving her a private hug. She'd closed her eyes and, tilting her face to the heavens, had said a silent *thank you.*

# 4

'Oh, Daniel, how lovely, Isobel had her baby two days ago, a little girl, Juliana. What a lovely name.' Flora held a letter in her hand and beamed at it. 'They want us to be her godparents because they're godparents for us.' She read the letter again quietly to herself before sliding it back inside the envelope and into the pocket of her apron. She sighed contentedly. 'I'll write a nice long reply after lunch. I need to get this finished if Juliana's going to wear it before she outgrows it. I wasn't expecting her to come so soon.'

She resumed her knitting, where soft white wool was now growing from thin knitting needles into the recognisable shape of a matinee jacket. Milo was asleep in his pram on the terrace and Melody was sitting at the table working on a puzzle, a wooden picture of a circus, listening to the conversation between her mother and her father.

'We should get a telephone,' Flora said. 'Isobel might want to ring me. She might have lots of questions that I could help her with.'

'I think it's about time your sister and Gordon learnt for themselves, don't you?'

Her mother, she noticed, didn't reply to his comment.

Melody saw that her father didn't lift his gaze from the book he was reading but she could tell he didn't sound too pleased that her Aunt Isobel and Uncle Gordon had just had a brand-new baby. She looked over at him and wondered why, this time when a baby had arrived, there was no whooping for joy or lifting her into his arms to spin her around.

'The telephone lines are up now and Mr and Mrs Morris have just bought one. The Modern Telephone, it's called. Theirs is green. I like green for a telephone.'

'Isobel is the one that's green,' Daniel answered, snorting from behind the pages of his book.

'She's green?' Melody imagined that her stern, and rather unapproachable, Aunt Isobel had somehow changed colour. She secretly thought it might suit her.

'It means she's inexperienced with children,' Flora clarified kindly. 'She's got a lot to learn about looking after a baby, that's all. But she'll be fine.'

'You can say that again.' Daniel snorted again, making Melody wonder if perhaps he didn't like Aunt Isobel much either.

'Hush now,' Flora tutted. 'You're just being mean. It is what it is and she is who she is. Little Juliana is here now and that is all that matters. They *need* this.' Her father, she noticed, did hush then. But before long, he looked across at Flora as if thinking about something else he wanted to say but seemed to decide better of it. Instead, the sound of the clickety-clackety knitting needles filled the room until Flora called over to Melody.

'You and Milo have a gorgeous little cousin, Melody.'

'Will she come to play?' Melody asked. She held a piece of wooden tiger in her hand, and although she didn't understand what the word 'cousin' meant she did understand that, like Milo, another new person had arrived in the family.

'I'm sure she will, Melody.' Flora smiled at her, her fingers still working the knitting needles without stopping a beat. 'Aunt Isobel and I will make sure you'll come to know Juliana very well indeed.'

# 5

Melody continued to stare at the flashing light where the familiar voice on the answering machine held a hidden truth. Perhaps it was a hidden lie, or perhaps it was both, but, regardless, it was something that for years had been *so* well hidden, even Juliana didn't know about it. Melody had discovered it twelve years ago while sorting out her late mother's things. In an old book she'd noticed that the pages bulged with things that had been placed within them. There was a twist of hair, a yellowing envelope and a photograph which slipped between the pages and onto the floor. Picking up the photograph Melody had studied the grainy image, her hands beginning to tremble when she noticed something odd. It was a photograph of her parents, Flora and Daniel, looking happy and young. When she'd turned the photo over and seen the date stamped on the back, however, her hands had begun to tremble and her heart to beat so fast she had to sit down. Flora had been keeping a secret, and it was a secret she'd taken to the grave.

Whenever Melody thought of her mother, she ached for her. The ache, visceral and raw, still threatening to overpower her with just the same intensity as it had the day she'd unexpectedly passed away, hooked up to a monitor that beeped away the last moments of her extraordinarily kind heart.

Melody had removed the damning evidence from the old book and placed the items in a blue folder, filing them away in the hope that she could forget all about them. The truth bound within her discovery, though, had eaten away at her ever since, worming around her brain, sliding in and out of her waking thoughts and crawling into her dreams.

Now, pressing the button on the answering machine, she listened to Juliana's latest message.

*'Melody! Are you getting my messages? I know it's been ages since I called, and I know I was mean about all your stuff last time I was there… and I'm sorry, but can I come to stay for a while? I'll mind my own business this time, promise. Spindrift will be perfectly perfect, I know it. Say you're going to be there and not out gallivanting somewhere, living the kind of wild, decadent life a gorgeous thirty-something should be? Please ring me back.'*

Melody pressed the 'stop' button and rewound the tape, pressed the 'play' button and listened to the message again. Of course she was going to be there, she never went anywhere else. Never *wanted* to go anywhere else. And did she believe that Juliana would mind her own business? No, she didn't, because Melody's gatherings – '*clutterings*' Juliana had taken to calling them – had grown again since she was here last.

Lifting the telephone receiver with one hand and gripping tightly at the cord with the other, she dialled Juliana's number. Grime had settled within the looped curls of the cord and she picked at it with her finger, the dirt collecting in her nail while she listened to the steady hum of the dialling tone. She swallowed hard when she heard the *click*.

'Hello, Juliana speaking.'

'Jules? It's…'

'Mel! You're there! I was beginning to think you'd died and forgotten to tell me – sorry, that was insensitive. You know what I mean. How are you? How is Exmouth and is lovely Shelly still the same?' Juliana machine-gunned a succession of questions at Melody as if expecting her to fill a gap of months in just a few minutes.

'Yes, it's me. Yes, I'm here. And yes, I'm very much alive, thank you. Everything is good.' She tucked the truth carefully behind her answers and tried to imagine what would happen if Juliana were here. Would she still say that Spindrift was 'perfectly perfect'?

'And lovely Shelly is just as lovely as the last time you were here.' Melody bit her lip until it hurt. *Until next summer*, she said silently to herself. In her mind's eye, she reread her eviction notice and her heart squeezed with pain.

> This letter serves as notice that the lease for the land where your property stands is to terminate on 30th September 1989. The Dock Company has applied for planning permission for the development of the area known as Shelly, Exmouth, Devon…

Juliana breathed a happy 'ahhh' into her receiver and Melody listened to the crackle of it as it issued out through her own. She sounded as familiar as she always did. Same cultured voice, same casual upbeat tone, just perhaps, if Melody wasn't mistaken, the slightest hint of something that sounded like desperation. 'I'm sorry it's been so long since we last spoke, Mel. Time flies so fast. You know how it is?'

'I know how it is,' Melody agreed. Not so long ago she wouldn't have understood this at all, believing that time must surely fly faster in Juliana's world than it did by the coast. Now, however, the dates on her newspapers were moving forward with such rapidity that each one she bought alarmed her more than the last.

'I was hoping to come and see you. It's been too long. Are you free… at the moment? Like, tomorrow?'

*Tomorrow?* Melody bit her lip again and felt her heart race so uncomfortably that the waffle she'd just eaten turned over in her stomach. She'd known Juliana would want to stay, of course she had, but so soon? So immediately? She fought for something, *anything*, to fend Juliana away, just for a bit longer. Something that would give her a little more time to prepare.

'The weather has taken a horrible dive,' she began. 'It's forecast to be like this for a good while. In fact, there's a squall out at sea right now. Wouldn't you rather come in July or even August when it's likely to be warmer?'

'It's you I'm coming to visit, silly.' Juliana spoke with a tinkle of laughter, the high notes of it betraying her. 'I don't care if there's hail and thunder. I'll bring a coat.'

'And an umbrella… possibly some galoshes,' Melody pressed.

'And an umbrella… but never galoshes.' Juliana fell into expectant silence as she waited for Melody to play her part in the conversation. 'Say you're free. Please, Mel.'

'Yes, Jules, I'm free. That would be lovely.' Melody heard her own words come out as if they were traitorous, speaking on her behalf, while all the while the inner workings of her mind were saying something different. *Ask her to book a room in the Cavendish... or the Devoncourt... or better still, ask her not to come at all.*

'You can have Mum's room,' she said.

Melody replaced the receiver in its cradle and looked slowly around her home. The sitting room had more flotsam and jetsam now than when Juliana was here last. There were bags containing broken fishing nets and abandoned crab lines, and more bags containing plastic bottles that floated in from the ocean in ever increasing amounts. She constantly worried that all these things would endanger marine life. There were also piles of driftwood, shells and sea glass everywhere that she thought would make interesting pictures or works of art.

Milo's bedroom still had his wheelchair, his rubber mattress cover and the commode that Juliana had complained about last time. It still had his belongings in it and the shelves had become so full of all the beach treasures she'd found for him that she'd had to put up several more.

And then there was Flora's bedroom. Still as the day she had died. Her clothes were in the cupboard, her underwear in the drawers, her shoes in a neat row and her old towelling dressing gown still hanging on the back of the door. She could still hear Juliana's accusation. '*It's not a guest room, it's a shrine.*'

Melody chewed on a nail and took a deep breath.

Her little bathroom at least was clean and tidy but, compared to what Juliana was used to, it was horribly dated. The toilet flush system was dodgy these days and the shower was temperamental. Her kitchen was the same, tiny and shabbily old fashioned, with a tap that had dripped for nearly two years. They were minor things, simply the foibles of an old Victorian seaside bungalow. But, for Juliana, all these things screamed of Spindrift's failings.

All her life, Juliana had walked a very different path from Melody's own. She had cruised through life, eating out in restaurants, attending West End theatres and holidaying abroad, all the while with her hair styled into fashionable shapes and her body draped in the fashion of the moment. She'd attended a private boarding school, gone to university, built her own interior design business and landed a marriage deemed 'highly suitable' by her parents.

Flora and Isobel, two sisters with the same upbringing, had raised their own children so very differently. Melody had experienced none of the things that Juliana had. Local school, no marriage and only a handful of failed romances starting with Clive, a holiday-maker to Shelly. They'd both been fourteen and he'd wooed her down by the pier, with a bag of chips and a bottle of Cream Soda, overzealously kissing her, sucking at her face until she'd pushed him away to wipe at her mouth. Some boyfriends had lasted a few months but most, only weeks. Her 'career', despite gaining excellent grades in her O and A Levels at school, had been to work in the Pier Head Stores, the 'everything' shop near the dock. It hadn't required a three-year degree and a gap year spent in Paris, just an ability to handle cash and eat copious doughnuts from the bakery shelf. It also meant she could be near home to help her mother with Milo.

She'd loved working at the Pier Head Stores. It was the kind of shop that sold crab lines and coloured fishing nets on sticks, buckets and spades, holiday souvenirs, bread, milk and general groceries. To Melody, it was a little shop with a big heart that offered excitement. It smelt of sandy feet and salty wet hair and it had a bell on the door that gave a clang when children came in clutching their pennies.

When she and Milo were very young, they'd go to the Pier Head Stores to buy sweets every Saturday morning, their sandalled feet slapping against the iron floor of the swing bridge over the dock entrance, a sixpence from Father in their hands. Milo always wanted more than his sixpence could buy and she'd have to carefully steer him away. 'We have shells at home, Milo,' she'd say, sensibly replacing netted bags that bulged with shells of all shapes and colours. Or as he held on to the wooden handle of a spade, shining with bright red gloss on its metal blade, 'We don't need another spade today. We have two at home which are perfectly fine, it's just that the colour is all scratched by the sand.' On one occasion he had wanted to buy the polished shell of a giant sea snail, holding it to his ear, his free-spirited smile spread across his face.

'Ocean,' he'd said.

Melody had put it carefully down on the shelf with all the other shells. 'We can hear the sound of the ocean anytime we wish, Milo,' she'd said.

That shell, or the shell of a giant sea snail just like it, bought from her wages at the Pier Head Stores, was now in Milo's room, given to him years later by Melody so he could still hear the sea from his hospital bed.

'She's arriving tomorrow, Milo.' Melody sat in Milo's wheelchair by his empty bed. 'One more sleep.'

She would explain time to him like this when they were children, especially when Juliana's long-awaited summer visit was imminent. Today, however, there was trepidation rather than excitement in her voice.

'She's promised to keep quiet about the way I live but I know she won't be able to. She's bound to have something to say about it.' The room fell into a hush as Melody strained to hear the echoes of her brother's voice transcending not just years but a whole other world. Satisfied that he was listening still, she continued. 'I've cleared a space for her – enough for her suitcase and a quantity of shoes even Ivana Trump would be proud of.' Melody laughed a little, knowing that Milo would be laughing too as Juliana had never once arrived at Spindrift without a volume of belongings that could keep an entire travelling circus going. Melody remembered how, when Juliana was a child, she would always turn up with bows in her hair, shiny shoes on her feet, a choice of sun hats, a case of shoes, a case of clothes and yet another of books and toys.

'So, I'm going to have to tell Juliana about the eviction,' she said, straightening up and pausing uncertainly at Milo's door. 'But is it time to tell her about the secret?'

Normally when she talked to Milo she imagined him answering her but, after this question, the silence in the room was impossible to read. It was the first time she'd ever asked him this, but it was not the first time she'd asked it of herself. It was a question that had gone around and around in her mind, ever since she'd found the things hidden in the old book. Now, with the impending visit from Juliana, the ongoing argument with herself as to whether to share such a burden weighed even more heavily on her mind.

For the twelve years since Flora's death, she'd often raised her eyes heavenward to ask her for help on the matter, whispering to her in the dead of night, straining in the dark to hear answers that never came.

'I don't know what Mum would want me to do, Milo,' she said sadly, her words lingering, unanswered, in the empty room as she closed the door behind her.


Melody lifted the curtain and peeked out of the front window of her bungalow again. Juliana had said she would arrive late morning but it was nearly lunch time and there was still no sign of her. Melody was as ready as she was ever going to be but, even so, she felt trepidation in the pit of her stomach as she scanned the road outside waiting for the beeps of a horn.

When Juliana had turned eighteen she'd passed her driving test and had been indulged by her parents with a brand-new, bright orange Mini Clubman. The Mini would announce Juliana's arrival with two beeps of the horn each time she completed the journey from Cheltenham to Exmouth without her parents in tow. She would pull up outside Spindrift, the paintwork of her car vibrant and glossy against the ageing backdrop of the Shelly bungalows. At some point, the orange car had been replaced with a blue something or other that was bigger and faster but just as shiny as the Clubman. It also hailed her arrival with two beeps of its horn. In recent years, however, the visits had become further and further apart and Melody now had no idea what Juliana drove.

There were, Melody knew, two reasons that the pair of them had begun to drift apart. One, the things she'd discovered in the old book could never be *unseen*. Two, Juliana herself had changed and, no matter how pleased they were to see each other, these days they could never quite seem to rekindle the easy friendship they'd shared in their youth.

Juliana's criticisms from her previous visit still hung in the air as if she'd physically hooked them from the ceiling in every room like butchered carcasses. Melody still couldn't believe that Juliana had accused her of living with ghosts. She'd survived grief, that's what she'd done.

When a red sports car pulled up outside Spindrift, Melody raised an eyebrow. It was a sleek curve of a car with an extravagantly long bonnet. It looked brand-spanking, hot-off-the-production-line new, and even Melody could see that it was a car worthy of satisfying any male menopause. It was a modern beast of a thing and, set against the peeling bungalows of Shelly Road, it was even more out of place than her other shiny new cars had been.

'Will my car be all right here?' Juliana asked, by way of greeting, sweeping her hand towards the road, screwing her shiny glossed lips together with uncertainty. Most of the bungalows in Shelly had no drive or garage, or any back garden to speak of, and the road that weaved its way through them was narrow. Melody thought of the dusty cars that occasionally went past, or boats on trailers, or canoes being dragged on wheels. She thought about how the closest thing she had to a vehicle was Flora's old bike which she kept round the side of Spindrift by the dustbin. It had probably got rotten tyres by now. She didn't mention that when it next rained, which was forecast, a veil of yellow sand would dump itself on the bright, red paintwork.

'I'm sure it will be fine,' she answered, smiling brightly and opening her front door wide enough to let Juliana's shoulder pads through.

Juliana heaved her cases inside with a grunt then gratefully dropped them down again in the hallway. The fact that there were more than usual was not lost on Melody and her chest constricted at the realisation that this was not to be a fleeting visit.

'Hello, you,' Juliana grinned, hugging Melody tightly and with genuine pleasure. She let go only to make herself immediately at home by taking her jacket off to reveal a buttercup-yellow shift dress. Her gaze travelled up and down Melody's own attire and Melody knew, with hot certainty, that Juliana would be finding the long skirt and woollen jumper she was wearing positively Amish by comparison. In her defence, it wasn't a warm day, and when the forecasted wind and rain blew in from the sea later it would feel even colder. As they set about dragging the suitcases into Flora's old room, Juliana was audibly shivering. 'Gee, it's cold in here. In fact, it's cold everywhere. What happened to flaming June?'

'British summer at its finest!' Melody declared as Juliana slipped her jacket back on.

'Let's not waste any time and go straight out!' Juliana grinned, her glossed lips offering a wide smile. 'This visit, cousin of mine, we're going to have some fun, so how about I treat us both to lunch? What do you say?'

Melody swallowed her anxiety as if it were a lump of gristle and, catching Juliana's enthusiasm on her breath, she inhaled it until she could feel it tickle her insides with a pleasant kind of hope.

★

Linking arms, they set off along Shelly Road towards town, past the huge grain silos and across the iron swing bridge of the dock entrance. The bridge clanged beneath their feet as they walked through the familiar, heady smell of the working dock which served to separate Shelly from the rest of Exmouth. A huge cargo ship was being loaded with wood and the cranes on the wharf edge were hauling in a shipment of coal. When Melody was a child, she and other children were sent to salvage pieces of scattered coal for their fire. Everyone knew not to hang their washing out on those days for the black dust that carried in the air.

Out of the corner of her eye, Melody could see that Juliana was trying, but failing, not to wrinkle her nose, her heels clip-clopping as fast as she could go to get away from it. She'd almost reached the corner of Victoria Road before she took a deep gasp for breath.

'Bloody hell, Mel, how do you stand it?' She blew her nose into a thin hanky and checked it discreetly for any dirt or grime she may have inhaled. 'Anyway,' she said, brightly, dropping her hanky into her handbag, 'which pub does the best lunch these days?'

The Beach pub was just behind them and the esplanade in front and a decision over which direction they were to take had to be made.

'Don't say the Pier Café.' Juliana masked a groan, noticing Melody gazing in the direction of the old café building near to them. 'It's not a pub, it's a *café*. It only sells food that's been plunged into a deep-fat fryer. Plus, there appears to be some building work going on.' Melody nodded wordlessly, eyeing the jaws of machinery that had arrived, waiting like huge insects to devour the café. She felt a little piece of her heart break away.

'It's closed,' Melody said, shrugging it off as if the café shutting for good wasn't all that important to her. Like the first tooth to be pulled, she thought sadly. She and Milo had been going there ever since they were little and so had Juliana. As Milo got older, he could be easily wheeled inside its wide doors for knickerbocker glories and ice-cream sodas. This café was one of the few places that would let him in, the staff ready to ignore the cruel comments of ignorant customers. On special days with Flora and Daniel they would have a complete meal there – something with chips followed by a slice of apple pie and custard.

'They do good chips,' she said wistfully. '*Did* good chips,' she corrected, realising that it was as if the café, like her family, had already gone.

'We don't want chips anyway,' Juliana said. 'We want something *nice*. Real food that doesn't slide off the plate on a river of grease.' She laughed carelessly and Melody tried not to care as she tugged on her arm. She turned away from the café where it still stood, for now, looking out to sea, like an old gent whiling away his final days reflecting on a good life. 'We want somewhere we can have a grown-up drink with our food instead of Cresta or Panda Pop or whatever they served in that café. We're starting my visit off with a kick! OK?'

'OK,' Melody agreed, turning away and leaving her memories inside the café's empty windows. 'The Beach pub?' she suggested tentatively. She thought she already knew the answer as Juliana had never been keen on it. It smelt of cigarettes and old upholstery, the yeasty scent of beer and the sweat of a decent day's work, and a piano was frequently played to the sound of people singing along. Melody loved it.

'It's a bit *shipyard*, Mel,' Juliana complained. 'Come on, think further afield. Somewhere *nice*. Somewhere you like to go for a drink when you go out.'

'It *is* where I like to go for a drink when I go out.' Melody's despair was beginning to show. She always enjoyed propping up the public bar with the dock workers and sailors. She even knew who would be drinking there just from the line of grubby boots outside that were covered in molasses or coal from the cargos they'd been working with, taken off before stepping over the threshold. The captains, custom officers and boat pilots washed away the toil of their day still with their shoes on in the carpeted lounge bar.

She glanced at the line of boots outside and recognised one of the pairs, larger than all the others. Big Joe Wiley, her neighbour, was in there. He was a docker and would be having his lunch break with all the other dockers, the scent of hard work on his skin, a cold tankard of beer in his hand. Her heart missed a beat at the thought of him and of her unrequited love.

Big Joe lived in a bungalow called Pebbles, only a few bungalows along from Spindrift, and from time to time he'd bring her gifts of fresh mackerel or bass if he'd been out on his rowing boat, *Wild Rose*. Sometimes he stopped to talk before he went about his business and stayed for a while, accepting a drink on her terrace. The flames of candles in her lanterns would shine golden beams in his eyes while they watched fishing boats coming in to dock at night, their lights beaming a bright path against the dark sea. Although girlfriends had come and gone, she had once overheard him telling the other workers drinking in the pub that the only real girlfriend he would ever have was his boat, *Wild Rose*.

Juliana tugged at her arm again and Melody turned her attention regretfully away from The Beach pub trying, instead, to think of some other place that might meet Juliana's approval. 'The Cranford? We'd have to take a bus but, if you remember, they serve good food?'

'We went there last time.' Juliana groaned, making it sound as if eating somewhere more than once was a bad thing. 'Maybe not a pub then. Maybe somewhere different? Where do you go with your friends?' She waited expectantly, pushing her sunglasses onto her head, wedging them into the volume of her over-sprayed hair while Melody pretended to think hard. 'You do *have* friends…?'

'Of course I have friends.' Melody laughed, but the sound of it was too high, too eager to please.

Juliana breathed a sigh of relief. 'You had me worried there for a moment, it took you so long to answer I thought you might have gone the full hermit or something. I'd hate to think that you weren't partying your way through the best years of your life and being poured into taxis at the end of the evening like the rest of us.'

As Juliana joked, Melody felt the half-forgotten pang of regret whisper its sadness in her ear. Several of the bungalows in Shelly were rented to the young people from Exmouth Rolle College. They could frequently be heard holding parties and playing their music on the beach round by the sailing club until the early hours of the morning. For a very short time she had been a student too. A few short, carefree weeks at Rolle College hanging out in the student bar well into the evening with her new group of friends. She'd been invited to a party and had a couple of dates when she realised just how much Flora was beginning to struggle with Milo's increasing needs plus doing her best to make ends meet. She also saw how terribly Milo missed her on the days she stayed out late.

Melody left college in the middle of her first term, pretending that student life wasn't for her. On the very same day she'd got herself a job in the Pier Head Stores.

'I am far from a hermit, thank you, Jules,' she insisted. 'But, equally, I don't need to get poured into a taxi at the end of the evening after a night on the town either. I'm part of a terrific community here and even when the holiday-makers arrive, most of them are annual returners so I know them too. There's Mrs Galespie in Spinnaker; then there's Mrs Johnson in Mud Larks, the corner bungalow; the Franklins in Traveller's Joy; and Old Tess and Old Albert in Westward Ho! Most of the dock workers who drink at The Beach are my friends too, of course, and…' she counted on her fingers as she spoke, watching Juliana's face ripple uncertainly; a raised eyebrow here, a tug of a frown '… and there's Big Joe Wiley in Pebbles.'

At the mention of Joe Wiley, Juliana gave a knowing smile. 'He's a good-looking guy to be fair… but he's a beach dude. He sleeps in his rowing boat for goodness sake!'

'Sometimes.' Melody felt her cheeks go pink and wondered if they were giving her feelings about Joe away. 'He only *sometimes* sleeps in his rowing boat. When the weather is warm and the stars are at their brightest.' She could feel her heart skitter as she thought about his long pale hair which hung loose down his back and how a black tattoo of a nautical compass encircled his shoulder; how sometimes, late at night, she would see him walk across the beach to his boat, his feet bare, a rug over his shoulders, and how she wished she could join him and look at the stars, too.

Juliana waved a dismissive hand. 'Whatever. All the people you've just mentioned are neighbours, workers and visitors. I'm talking *friends*. People you go out with, share secrets with, go drinking and dancing with.'

Melody felt awkward under the deep brown eyes which challenged her. 'They *are* all my friends,' she insisted, secretly admitting only to herself how her social life sounded when out in the open. Her close school friends and the students she'd briefly known had drifted away a long time ago, going off to lead what they claimed were more exciting lives. They'd travelled abroad or moved to other towns, and the ones who'd returned had found love. They'd married and were growing families of their own.

'What *do* you do then?' Juliana pulled a half smile. 'I've always assumed that when I visit you, you just put your social life on hold or something. I didn't realise there wasn't anything much to put on hold. Don't you want more? A friend? A boyfriend?… A lover?'

Melody blushed again. She'd had boyfriends but she'd never had a lover.

'But don't you, Mel?' Juliana pressed. 'Don't you want more from life?' Melody thought Juliana looked almost sad when she asked this, as if she'd unearthed something terrible. What could be so awful about being part of a community? Part of a group of people who lived and breathed the same life she did? The people of Shelly who knew each other inside and out understood each other and were there for each other. She would miss it too much when it was all bulldozed and flattened to the ground.

'You said *let's have some fun*, and now you're giving me the Spanish Inquisition about my life,' Melody complained. She tried to hold Juliana's gaze but the frosted blue mascara put her off. She wiped fidgety, cross hands on the fabric of her skirt and wished she was at home – her feet pinched in the stupid wedged shoes, and the strap of her handbag kept sliding off her shoulder.

'You're right. I'm sorry.' Juliana looked momentarily shamefaced. She popped Melody's handbag strap gently back on her shoulder and, linking her arm affectionately, she steered her into Victoria Road. 'Come on you. Onwards and upwards. We'll walk into town and jolly well sniff out the best place to eat!'

At the table of a little bistro in the centre of town, Juliana looked crestfallen.

'No oysters! They're out of rock oysters and I didn't even know that there was a season for native oysters. There I was positively drooling over buying us a whole platter of them for lunch when we found this place and there isn't a single one to be had.' As Juliana looked across at her over the menu, Melody couldn't help noticing her eyebrows. They'd gone all Brooke Shields since her last visit, full and fluffed and worked to perfection. They used to be plucked and pencilled, making her look permanently startled as if she'd sat on something sharp. Melody hated how fashion and make-up could change a face so drastically, and she missed the softness of the Juliana she used to know; the strawberry-blonde eyebrows and lashes that shone pale against her freckled skin. 'You've got stuck – you're doing a *starey*,' Juliana prodded. 'What are you thinking about in that head of yours?' A hand waved in front of her face and Melody blinked.

'I was thinking that there's no R in June,' she answered hastily. 'You can't eat native oysters in the summer months... months without an R in them... because they'll be in the middle of a spawning frenzy.' Melody saw the full and fluffed eyebrows rise as if they didn't understand what she was saying. 'Busy having oyster sex,' Melody clarified.

'Oh! And how do they...?' Juliana crinkled her lips, amused and disgusted at the same time. 'Never mind, Mel, I don't think I want to know. Let's just hope they're good at it however they do it. Do you mind terribly?'

'Do I mind terribly whether they're good at it?' Melody asked.

Juliana flapped a playful hand at her. 'You know what I mean. I saw how disappointed you looked when the waitress told us they're off the menu.'

Melody shrugged as if she didn't much care one way or the other. 'I'll eat anything. I'm just happy to be having lunch with you in a bistro.' She beamed across the table.

The first time she had ever tasted an oyster she was seven years old. She and Milo were outside the fishmonger, their mouths open like those of two hungry chicks, Flora scooping an oyster into each. Milo had immediately spat his out where it landed on the ground by his feet like the worst part of a chest infection. He'd pulled a face and stuck out his tongue as if it were coated in poison, while Melody had just discovered what the ocean tasted like. Sea foam and sea breezes on her tongue rode her high on the delicious crest of a salty wave until, at last, the oyster slipped down her throat and was gone.

'Can I have another, please?' she'd begged, her nose almost

touching the shop window. Fish of all varieties were on the other side of the glass, nestled in ice, wide-eyed and open-mouthed, their scales shimmering under the strip light. Next to red crabs, smooth round clams and fat pink prawns was a display of shucked oysters bathing in their briny pools. Melody pressed a finger against the glass, pointing at them.

'They're a luxury, I'm afraid,' Flora had said, reaching for Milo to steady him as he stumbled. 'We can't really afford them but I wanted you to try one – just so that you know what luxury tastes like. When we can't have something very often it makes it extra special when we do.'

'Luxury,' Melody had repeated. The bumpy grey shells of an oyster, she thought, looked unremarkable from the outside but, on the inside, within their porcelain white interior, they captured the very essence of everything she loved about living by the sea. She saw that her mother was biting her lip as if she'd changed her mind. Delving into her purse, she dropped some pennies into Melody's hand and ushered her back into the shop.

'There's just enough for one more,' she'd said as Melody looked anxiously up at her. The oysters were expensive and Melody hadn't realised they might not have the pennies to spare. She tried to give the pennies back but Flora gently pushed her hand away saying, 'Go on, darling girl. Buy yourself another moment of luxury.'

Juliana closed her menu, placing it decisively down on the table. 'I think I'll have the crab then… unless they're *at it* too. It comes with a fresh salad and bread – but I won't have the bread.' She patted her stomach as if congratulating herself for gaining mastery over her body in a way that Melody had no intention of doing with her own. Melody hungrily eyed a basket of bread on a nearby table, where a dish of butter curls lay inviting themselves to be spread thickly upon it.

'All the more bread for me, then,' she said, and placed her own menu decisively on top of Juliana's as if she dined like this every day.

'I'm so sorry, we don't have any crab either,' the waitress apologised, going a little pink when Juliana deflated in front of her eyes with dismay.

'This is going well,' she sighed.

The waitress pointed helpfully at the specials board. 'We do have the catch of the day. A choice of fresh plaice or bass today. Beautiful fish, and both dishes come with buttered new potatoes and salad.' Melody felt her mouth water at the sound of the plaice although she wondered if perhaps she should ask for a sandwich, such was the price of the food.

'I'll have the tenderloin, please. Blue, thank you.' Juliana closed her menu decisively and looked expectantly across at Melody.

'Same, please,' Melody blurted, hastily placing her own menu down again and trying not to think about the plump white plaice with the buttered new potatoes.

'Blue?' Juliana and the waitress looked at her, waiting for a decision, but Melody didn't know what *blue* meant. 'Do you like it medium, medium rare, or still mooing?' Juliana asked. Melody's palms moistened as she battled to think how she best preferred her steak, but all she could think of was that the rump steak they served in the Pier Café was *cooked* and no one ever questioned as to what degree. 'Medium,' Juliana said kindly, smiling at the waitress and thereby saving

Melody from her agony. 'It's not still breathing, yet not totally buggered either.'

The steak, when it arrived, was delicious, although even cooked to medium, Melody thought a good vet could have brought it back to life. 'This gravy is amazing. Do you think they'd bring me some more of it?' She harpooned a chunk of steak, pushing it around the plate to scoop up as much of the flavour as she could. There was still bread and curls of butter left just begging to mop up more gravy.

'It's not Bisto, Mel. It's *jus*. It's posh gravy – not something to be slurped at. Wash your food down with this instead.' Juliana handed Melody a glass of wine, deep and red and poured by a very attentive waiter. She clinked her own glass against it, tipping it to her mouth to drink what appeared to Melody to be enough to quench the thirst of a camel. As the bottle couldn't have been cheap, she wondered at the speed it was disappearing down Juliana's neck and it wasn't long before a waiter was being summoned again. Juliana held up her empty glass to catch his attention for another bottle and Melody feared that, at this rate, they'd both be crawling out of the bistro on their hands and knees.

'How's Alastair?' she ventured, studying Juliana's face closely for any kind of reaction. She was rewarded. The merest flicker of a worrisome twitch tugged at the skin on the corner of Juliana's mouth.

'He's good,' Juliana replied. Her answer, however, echoed its way through a tunnel of unshared meanings. Melody poured water from a fat glass jug into two tumblers and took a cooling sip as she toyed with how best to proceed.

'Is he still a banker?' she probed.

'Oh, he's definitely one of those,' Juliana said under her breath.

Melody squashed a laugh. Alastair, much to her relief, rarely featured in her life. He didn't make trips to Exmouth other than for funerals and she hadn't made trips to Cheltenham, apart from for their wedding. He was part of the rugby crowd; he played hard and partied hard and, on the few times they'd all been in the same location together, Melody knew she didn't like him. She observed that he'd always had a strong arm around Juliana's shoulders. Possessive rather than protective, she'd always felt. Life with Alastair, by all previous accounts, was busy and glitzy and very much in the fast lane but it was a life that, by the sound of it, had flaws.

'He's climbing promotional ladders quicker than...' Juliana continued, pausing trying to think of what Alastair could be quicker than.

'Than you can drink wine?' Melody interjected.

Juliana, who was taking a sip of her wine, responded by theatrically checking how much liquid she had left in her glass then downing it in one. 'Not quite, but definitely quicker than he can spend money – hence buying me a surprise new car.'

'Lucky you,' Melody replied, in truth thinking no such thing.

'Aren't I!' Juliana's answer was laced with sarcasm.

'Is everything OK?' Melody asked, knowing instinctively that it wasn't because she had a strange grin on her face.

The strange grin immediately slipped from Juliana's face and her shoulders sagged. 'He wants me to be pregnant.' She blurted this out as if Alastair wanting her to have a baby might be a problem and Melody was confused.

'But it's not happening?' she asked carefully.

'No,' Juliana answered.

'Oh, I'm sorry,' Melody sighed, her voice soft with sympathy.

'Don't be! It's not the best time to bring a baby into the mix.' Juliana unzipped her handbag and flashed a foil strip of contraceptive pills. 'Thanks to these little things, I have a choice in the matter.' She put the foil strip back and zipped up her handbag. 'Alastair isn't happy about it. He doesn't like the fact that I'm establishing my own design career and turning into a pretty damn good businesswoman. He would rather I was at home pumping out babies and making his dinner.'

'You don't want children?' Melody couldn't disguise her surprise. Time was moving so fast along with Melody's biological clock that she was frightened a family of her own might never happen. She would love more than anything to have a baby.

'I do,' Juliana nodded. 'At least I *think* I do – but not yet.'

'Hence the pills,' Melody commented.

'A necessary caution. Until recently Alastair was, how shall I say... *energetic* in the trouser department... in the pantry, up against the shower, over the washing machine, if you get what I mean.'

Melody's cheeks blushed at her own lack of experience. She couldn't fail to understand what Juliana meant and tried to hide her embarrassment over the details of it. 'So why did all that *activity* happen only until recently?' she asked.

Juliana pushed a forkful of green beans into her mouth and chewed so slowly Melody wondered if she was ever going to bother to swallow. She eyed the sunglasses still caught in Juliana's hair and vaguely thought that it was not a sunglasses kind of day – the sky having been a thunderous shade of grey all week. Seconds passed until they became a minute, then two, the air between them becoming stretched and uncomfortable, and Melody began to wish she hadn't asked. But then Juliana finally spoke again.

'Shall we just say *sex* has been put on hold for the moment...' She stabbed her fork aimlessly at the remaining food on her plate while Melody was left totally confused.

'Why?' she breathed.

Suddenly, Juliana dropped her cutlery with such a clatter that people in the bistro turned their heads. 'Because my husband... is... he's a *fucking* dick! That's what he is!'

Melody gasped, not so much from what she'd said but because she'd said it *so* loudly. The heads were still turned, all eyes focussing on the pair of them until Juliana reached across the table and placed three fingers under Melody's chin to close her mouth. Then she addressed the prying eyes in the bistro and calmly announced, 'The show's over.'

Here it was, Melody realised. The reason for the urgent visit to Exmouth. She'd heard so much over the years, about their amazing house and how they were positively drowning in an abundance of Laura Ashley. She'd heard about the CD player, the coffee machine, the soda stream and the home computer, of the parties and the holidays and how Aunt Isobel had always said they were 'a match made in heaven'. Yet, clearly, something had gone very wrong.

'What's he done?' she asked carefully, aware that the prying eyes had now become prying ears. She leant conspiratorially closer, planting an elbow on the table in a way that Aunt Isobel would have said was not good table manners. Juliana swallowed and her expression looked pained as if, whatever her husband had done, it was a terrible thing. A flush coursed up her neck and it met the bloom of alcohol across her cheeks, making her look rather rumpled in a way that Melody had never seen before.

'Let's finish up here and go for a walk along the esplanade, I could do with a breath of air, couldn't you?' Pushing her knife and fork together, Juliana waggled her fingers in the air for the bill then hunted inside her bag. Polished nails picked carefully inside the soft leather of her purse while Melody hurriedly used her bread to mop at the remains of her delicious food before it was whisked away. She'd rather hoped there would have been a dessert.

'I was hoping this meal might have been more expensive,' Juliana declared, taking a credit card out of her purse and dropping it onto the table next to the bill. 'This is on Alastair.'

'You should spray it within an inch of its life like mine!' Juliana called to Melody over the sudden sea breeze which whipped up from the sea and pushed at them as they walked along the esplanade. She shoulder-bumped Melody. 'I'll do it for you later. Your make-up, too, if you like?' Melody didn't like. Juliana's hair barely moved for all the hairspray she had on it and to Melody it looked more like a meringue than a hairdo.

Juliana hadn't mentioned a further word about Alastair and for the duration of their walk had been chatting away as if they were just two girls taking a stroll without a care in the world. How different they were in many ways, Melody thought, and yet, how alike they were in others. Their worlds were falling apart but still they couldn't seem to reach out to each other as they might have done when they were children.

Melody looked out at the horizon, the wind teasing the loose bits of her own hair out of her plait. They swirled around her head and caught against her face, yet, *unlike* Juliana, she preferred it like that – it made her feel gloriously windswept. She breathed in deeply as if sucking her life source from the ozone. An elderly couple held hands in the seafront shelter beside her, a man walked past with a spaniel that looked like Oliver Cromwell, and on the yellow ribbon of sand in front of them, winding its way towards the red cliffs of Orcombe Point, a little girl carried a bucket of water up from the shore. Tipping it into a moat gulley of the sandcastle she'd built, the water swirled around a single sandy turret before she turned and ran back for more.

'Don't you just want to hug it?' Melody called over the sound of the wind.

'What?' Juliana's forehead furrowed into a neat little twist as she pulled her jacket across her body and shivered.

'This! All of it,' she cried.

'I'm suggesting I do your hair and make-up, which most girls would love, and you just want to hug the scenery. You're so random, cousin of mine, but that's what I love about you. It's what I've always loved about you.' Juliana laughed and the sound of it was kind, with a warmth that belonged to the old Juliana.

'Shall we help?' Melody pointed to the little girl struggling with her buckets of water and, without waiting for an answer, pulled off her horrible wedge shoes and hitched her skirt into her knickers, ready to hop over the wall.

'Mel!' Horrified, Juliana tried to tug at Melody's skirt but Melody slapped her hands away.

'Come on,' she laughed. She climbed onto the sea wall and looked down grinning.

'I can see your knickers,' Juliana hissed. 'We aren't children any more, we're in our thirties – we're grown-ups!' She picked up Melody's shoes and tugging on her wrist pulled her back down to the pavement. 'It's flipping freezing. Let's buy ourselves some nice bits for tonight then go home.'

Sadly, Melody rearranged her skirt until it swung down by her calves again and, holding her shoes, rather than putting them on, she began to walk home barefoot. 'You would have joined me, once,' she said.

Juliana laughed. 'Yes, but now I'm wearing Gucci.'

The fun in Melody's day slipped away so quickly she wondered whether it had happened at all.

'You've kept these?' Juliana hadn't even taken her coat off when they stepped inside Spindrift before she was holding a large bunch of keys she'd just spotted on a shelf in Milo's room. Melody squeezed her eyelids together and took her own coat off, placing it on the hook on the wall. She could feel herself tensing. *Juliana had promised to mind her own business. This was her house. Her safe place.* 'You found these ages ago. You can't possibly still need someone else's old keys?' Juliana held them by their Vauxhall Viva leather fob and a plastic troll with a tuft of lime-green hair dangled upside down from the key ring. Melody wondered if it was worth telling her that they belonged to a bright and sunny

Sunday in September and that they'd inspired one of her best stories for Milo. But she held back.

'I left them outside the front of Spindrift for *three whole weeks* after I'd found them, *and* I asked around to see if anyone had lost them. No one claimed them and in the end I brought them inside.' Melody didn't say that the keys had become a brilliant story for Milo all about a man who built a house with fifteen front doors. She didn't say that he would enter the door that reflected his mood. That when he felt cheerful he would go through the yellow door. And when he wanted tranquillity he would go through the blue door. If he needed energy he would go through the orange door and so on. She didn't say that ever since she'd made up this story she'd imagined that the front door of Spindrift could also reflect her own mood, turning various shades of colour depending on the day. She didn't say that recently she imagined her front door to be black.

Juliana was not impressed. 'I know I said I'd mind my own business, Mel, but I can't. It's too much. This –' she swept an arm towards Milo's room and the sitting room '– is all too much. Come on, let's start here. Right now!' She nipped into Flora's room and soon emerged wearing a pair of fur-trimmed house shoes and a dove-grey cashmere cardigan, still carrying the keys and the newspaper they'd been placed with as she went past. Before she took another step, however, Melody jumped forward and grabbed them out of her hands, holding them furiously to her beating heart.

Surprised by her reaction, Juliana looked worried. 'What's this all about?' she asked. 'I was only suggesting I help you and now you've gone all flared nostrils over it.'

'You're overstepping the mark, Jules,' Melody said, defensively. 'You can't throw them away... because they...' She stalled.

'They what?' Juliana waited for an answer, a cloud of worry on her face.

'They represent more than just a bunch of old keys.' Melody chewed on a fingernail. 'They have a story attached to them.'

Brown eyes stared hard at her. They said so much, those eyes. They spoke of so many things, so much more than the summers they'd spent together. They spoke of privilege and refinement, of experience and education and a complete and utter belief that her cousin had gone totally bonkers. 'A story about what?' she ventured.

'About doors...' Melody's voice petered out into nothing as the Brooke Shields eyebrows began to move this way and that, somewhere between sympathy and confusion.

Juliana's gaze said it all. It flitted between Melody and the bunch of keys clutched to her chest until eventually her words found their way out. 'Mel, you're not being serious, are you?'

But Melody was serious. And as a terrible silence fell upon them she imagined they were both teetering precariously either side of a chasm. Suddenly, dropping the keys to the floor, she reached out and hugged Juliana so hard it took them both by surprise.

# 6

A two-year-old Juliana stood in front of Melody wearing a dress made from soft material in a pattern of tiny pink and white squares. It had the most beautiful flowers embroidered on the bodice with puffed sleeves and delicate white lace around the smocking. Melody's envious eyes travelled from the white ribbons in her cousin's strawberry-blonde hair to the white ankle socks that topped a pair of the shiniest patent leather shoes she had ever seen. Melody herself was wearing a yellow cotton dress that she could still fit into from last year because her mother had taken it out a little and sewn a deep band of fancy lace daisies around the hemline. Flora had also sewn the same band of fancy lace daisies around the neckline, which Melody thought was just the best thing. It was now her favourite dress. She absentmindedly fingered the matching yellow ribbons which wound around her own long blonde hair and wished for the briefest of moments that she also had a pair of shiny patent leather shoes. She knew, though, that even if she asked her parents for a pair, she wouldn't keep them on long enough to justify the cost of them. Juliana, holding two large packages, stepped forward in her patent shoes and shyly leant her cheek against Melody's waist, her little face looking up at her.

'I think someone's pleased to see you,' Flora said, as Melody wrapped a protective arm around her cousin, feeling a surge of affection for the little person who had attached herself to her side.

'Give Melody and Milo their gifts, Juliana.' Aunt Isobel stood beside Juliana and nudged her daughter, prompting her to hand over the wrapped presents she was holding. Juliana passed Melody and Milo a package, each wrapped in soft, coloured tissue. A beautiful set of Enid Blyton stories for Melody and a picture book for Milo. Melody clutched them to herself with genuine pleasure because, even though she was only six, she already loved books.

'Melody will love her gift, Isobel,' Flora smiled. 'She's already showing promise of being a proper little bookworm. She's even started to read stories for Milo at bedtime and play act the characters for him when he's bored. Say thank you to your Aunt Isobel, Melody.'

'Thank you, Aunt Isobel,' Melody repeated obediently, helping Milo to sit on the floor to look at his own book. Juliana sat down next to him and Melody turned the pages for them, her eyes widening at how their little cousin could already speak with confidence about what she could see. 'Car. Flower. Big dog,' Juliana said, pointing to the brightly coloured pictures while Milo, a year older than Juliana, tried to copy her sounds, a huge smile on his face.

'We'll leave you to it,' Aunt Isobel said to the three of them, placing a perfunctory hand on each head before she went over to her sister where they held each other's hands in a silent show of affection. Melody could still feel the light imprint of her aunt's hand on her head and, although it was meant well, it didn't have the soft arms or tight squeeze of her own mother's greeting towards Juliana.

Aunt Isobel was not like Flora. Melody thought she had a hard shell, like a crab that scuttled out from beneath a rock only to disappear back again within the dark, weedy crevices. The air in Spindrift seemed to change whenever she was around as if everything about their visit came with greater expectations to please. Uncle Gordon, on the other hand, who was currently unloading the car, was not at all like Melody's own father, Daniel. Uncle Gordon's smile reached his eyes, almost his ears even, and he was the kind of man who made the air around them feel nicer somehow. He was like a cushion or a soft blanket that took the angles and the echoes away from a room, and she liked him.

'She's doing well,' Flora commented, nodding in the direction of Juliana. 'She's a bright little button.'

'Thank you,' Aunt Isobel replied, glancing back at her daughter with a look of adoration and pride. 'As is Melody.'

Aunt Isobel's brown eyes switched briefly from Juliana to Melody and Melody felt uncomfortable within the scrutiny of them. 'And Milo?' Aunt Isobel continued. 'Are you... I mean, is he...? I mean...'

'I know what you mean,' Flora replied briskly. 'He's just got a bit of catching-up to do. He's still in nappies but at least it means I've got all the changing paraphernalia here for Juliana – so that's good, isn't it?' She smiled brightly towards Juliana but this time Melody thought that it was her Aunt Isobel who looked uncomfortable.

'Oh, Juliana is out of nappies now – during the day at least. She will ask you if she needs to use the lavatory.' Melody felt her eyes widen again. Milo had still not managed to use the potty, let alone the *lavatory*. 'She really is the easiest little thing,' Aunt Isobel continued. 'But I worry that her staying with you for the whole six weeks is too long?' She asked a question but Melody saw that she didn't wait for an answer. 'I would have you and the children to stay with me but...'

Flora put a comforting hand on her sister's shoulder and patted it. 'And I would love to have you to stay with me but we've talked about this already, Isobel. It's going to be lovely that the three of them can play together and Melody is so excited. You go, use the time to catch up on business things.' Then she left the room and headed towards the kitchen. 'Tea? I've made a fruit loaf.'

Alone with her cousin, Melody found herself marvelling at her again. She was only two years old but already she could walk and talk and turn the pages of a book. Her hair, gathered into two little golden bunches, bounced from the side of her head when she moved and to Melody she was like the beautiful walking, talking doll that a holiday-maker had once brought to the bungalow next door. She was a wonderful, living doll. Melody sat down on the floor next to her brother and her cousin and hugged herself over how lucky she was. Juliana was going to be staying for the summer and she could hardly wait for it to start.

# 7

Melody picked the keys up from the floor and put them back on the shelf in Milo's room. The hug that she'd impulsively given Juliana caused a shift in the air, a stirring of things previously latent. She now regretted it. The secret Melody had been keeping from her cousin swelled between them like an overinflated party balloon ready to pop. She wanted desperately to let it do just that.

'What was that hug for?' Juliana's surprise was evident in the furrowed lines that shot all the way up into her hairline.

'Just because,' Melody answered. She shrugged her shoulders as if it was no big deal and hurriedly made herself busy in the kitchen opening one of the bottles of wine they'd brought back with them. Next she opened the crisps and nuts they'd also bought and put them into bowls. She very much wished she hadn't done the hugging thing. 'We've bought enough wine to drown a small village,' she said, picking up the bowls to take them outside.

'But the hug? You don't want to talk?' Juliana halted Melody in her path with a gentle hand on her cousin's arm.

'Do *you*?' Melody parried. 'Do you want to talk about Alastair?'

'No, I don't. Not right now,' Juliana answered breezily, removing her hand from Melody's arm and shimmying behind her into the narrow kitchen to open the cupboard where the wine glasses were kept.

'Me neither,' Melody said.

Juliana brought out two small glasses and wrinkled her nose at them. The wrinkle did not go unnoticed by Melody. 'These glasses are dusty, Mel. In fact the whole cupboard is dusty. Don't you drink wine any more?'

'Yes,' Melody replied dismissively.

'Not out of these you don't, you haven't touched them since I was here last. You could grow mushrooms in these.' Juliana filled the washing-up bowl with warm soapy water and set about washing them, drying them carefully with a clean towel while the leaky tap dripped steadily into the water. She held them up to the light and flicked the glass bowl with her fingernail, laughing as it gave off a *thunk*. 'They're definitely not crystal, darling.'

Melody laughed. 'I don't need crystal, *darling*. I use a mug, it's more practical. Coffee, tea, water... wine – who cares? It's just something to drink out of.' She walked out to the terrace, carrying the nibbles plus two blankets while Juliana followed with the bottle of wine and the clean and shiny glasses.

'That's awful. No one should drink good wine out of a mug, Mel,' she moaned.

'Perhaps I don't drink good wine,' Melody retorted. She placed the nibbles on the table and eased herself into one of the sun chairs, pulling the blanket over her knees and waiting quietly for Juliana to fill their glasses with Rioja. Even she could tell, on the first sip, that the oaky fruitiness of it was really very good indeed.

'Nice, hey?' Juliana watched Melody take another sip.

'Maybe,' Melody grinned, raising her glass towards Juliana's. 'A toast! To not talking about things we don't want to talk about. At least for tonight.'

'Agreed.' Juliana raised her glass, chinked it against Melody's, and took a mouthful of the very good wine.

The sun was hidden behind a mesh of grey clouds and a cluster of Mirror dinghies tacked their way back towards the sailing club, their red sails popping with colour against a cool sea. The wind blew an oyster shell wind chime hanging from the eaves and it tinkled in the air. They fell silent for a while, quietly contemplating the view, their gaze following the dinghies as they dipped and bobbed against white-crested waves.

'Another toast.' Juliana raised her now half-empty glass. 'To red sails and red wine!' She chinked it against Melody's whereupon they both finished the remains of their drinks in one. Juliana poured them another. 'You could do with bigger wine glasses, Mel. These are so small they're practically last century.'

'You could always try a mug,' Melody replied slyly.

'Never,' Juliana laughed. She cupped the small bowl of the glass in her palm to warm the wine a little and Melody, seeing this, was suddenly reminded of Flora. It hit her quite unexpectedly somewhere in the soft part of her core where grief tried to hide, ready to pounce. For several seconds she found it hard to breathe.

'Mum liked a small glass of red,' she said eventually. She looked wistfully into the depths of the dark liquid as if she might see her mother reflected in it. Flora didn't drink much, the occasional glass on a Saturday or a special occasion, but the memory of her holding one of these glasses brought her briefly to life.

'To Aunty Flora!' Juliana toasted.

'To Mum!' Melody lifted her glass towards the memory of her mother who she crafted in her imagination as surely as if she was standing right next to her. They smiled at each other, she and Flora, and they took a silent drink together.

'Do you ever think about your dad?' Juliana asked, her voice dipping as if uncertain that she should be treading such delicate ground.

'Not often,' Melody lied. She shrugged her shoulders and, leaving the line of red-sailed dinghies, laid her gaze to rest on the landscape of the horizon.

'Then why do you still keep his boots by the front door?'

Melody went quiet after Juliana's question. It was true, her father's boots had been by the front door for years but they had a story behind them, one too complex to share over a handful of nuts. The truth was that she still thought about him frequently, her heart full with anger, loss, love and sadness and all the racing emotions of a child whose father had been there one day and gone the next.

Tentative forgiveness had come to her when she'd found the photograph in her mother's belongings and she so wanted him to know that if he ever found his way back to her she had done just that. She had forgiven him. The halcyon years of her childhood, she now knew, had been far more complex than she had ever realised. The thought of Milo, being caught in the middle of it, made her heart ache so badly that it constantly threatened to spill tears upon her cheeks. She wondered again how love could be so comforting and yet so cruel.

'To Milo,' she said quietly.

Juliana raised her glass. 'To Milo. Dear, dear, wonderful, darling Milo who taught us what living was all about.'

'He did, didn't he?' Melody said, pushing away the harsh reality that, sadly, Daniel had run from all that Milo had to offer him, seeking life and love in other places when all along it was right there in front of him – in the crooked smile of his own son. She took a sip of her wine for her brother and scanned the darkening evening clouds for his face. It was there, shining in the iridescent lining between rain clouds and sunset.

# 8

'*She* could recite her alphabet by the age of three.' Daniel pointed a finger in Melody's direction as if accusing her of something bad. She realised another one of those *not very nice* moments was about to happen and she felt herself stiffen. She had been the one who'd caused it.

Melody liked it when everyone in her family was happy. When the air felt light and when everything about the day happened as it should happen. She liked it when she returned from school to play with Milo who was always waiting with the biggest of smiles. She liked it when her father came home from work at the dock, tired but pleased to see them all, sniffing the air to see what supper her mother was getting ready to put on the table. Today, however, she was faced with the kind of moment that made the room vibrate with a horrible kind of feeling. The kind of moment when her father would decide that Milo wasn't learning quickly enough or well enough. When he poked holes into the smoothness of the day and made Milo cry.

Today, Milo wanted a biscuit, yet, when Melody took him into the kitchen to get one, her father stepped in and placed his hand over the packet before she could get it.

'He needs to *ask* for it,' he instructed, picking the packet up and holding it in front of Milo's face. 'What do you want, Milo?' Milo, who was now sitting on the floor, held his hand up for a biscuit, his fingers spread out ready to take one from a packet that remained frustratingly out of his reach.

'Leave him be, Daniel.' Flora appeared at the doorway and sighed wearily. Melody hated it when, during these conversations, the ready upward curve to her mother's lips and the twinkle in her eye slipped away, replaced with a look as chilly as the sea on a grey day. It hardly ever happened but today was one of *those moments*. 'It's not a competition between them,' Flora said flatly. 'He'll get there in time.'

'He's not though, is he?' Daniel hissed at her. 'He's not *getting there in time*. He's not reaching his milestones when he should. Melody was doing so much more than he is at this age and now she's stopping him from advancing because she's doing everything for him – and so are you. By the time he goes to school he's going to be so far behind he'll look stupid in front of all the other children.'

The hard edge to his voice, annoyed and desperate, made Melody feel even more uncomfortable and she pressed herself against the kitchen cabinet in an effort to disappear. Flora, calmly placing her hand on his pointing finger, lowered it and pulled her face into a meaningful expression that Melody didn't really understand. One eyebrow raised slowly and her lips pressed together so tightly that Melody could hardly see the colour of them any more. She wondered if her mother was telling her father off because it wasn't polite to point. She didn't know what a *milestone* was either, but what she did know was that at six years old she was a very grown-up girl and that Milo was just a little boy.

Since he was tiny she could tell what he wanted, when he was thirsty or hungry, or when he was tired. She would help him when he wanted to play with a toy or support him when he tried to crawl and, eventually, when he tried to walk, she held his hand and was there for him when he fell. She understood his babble when it came, replacing the squeals and cries of a baby with adorable chatter, and now she could understand the half-formed words he attempted to say, catching the essence of them as surely as if they had fallen perfectly from his mouth. She couldn't work out why this made her father angry and why he didn't understand Milo.

'Ask for it, Milo,' her father insisted, more gently now. 'Say, I want a biscuit please.' Milo nodded eagerly at the word *biscuit* and stretched his hand out further. 'I... want... a... biscuit... please,' Daniel repeated his question, still holding the packet out of Milo's reach, crouching on his haunches, their faces much closer. Although he was smiling at Milo, it was the kind of smile that balanced on the edge of desperation and the air in the kitchen seemed to Melody to be vibrating. She wanted it to stop. Her father was using too many words for Milo. He was expecting too many back. Why didn't he just give Milo the biscuit he was trying so hard to ask for?

'... Kit,' Milo said, a sheen coming to his big eyes. 'Bic... kit.'

'I said, leave him be.' Flora scooped him into her arms, seeing that hot pink blooms had appeared on Milo's cheeks and that his starfish fingers had now closed into a fist which he'd brought to his mouth to suck at his thumb.

'He must be lazy, that's what it is, because Melody second-guesses everything for him.' Daniel glowered at Flora and then over at Melody. 'We're going to show ourselves up when

Isobel and Gordon get here with Juliana. That child will probably be able to recite Shakespeare next summer with all the fuss they make of her.' He put the packet of biscuits back on the work surface and stood up, pushing past Melody and Flora. 'When he asks for one, he can have one,' he called, putting his coat on and walking out of Spindrift.

Although the air was still vibrating, Flora jiggled Milo on her hip and winked at Melody to take a biscuit from the packet. 'You're not lazy and you *have* asked, haven't you, Milo?' She gently tugged at his wrist to remove his thumb from his mouth and Melody placed a biscuit into his hand. 'You just do things in your own way, don't you, our sweet boy.'

When the front door closed behind Daniel, Flora put warm cardigans on Melody and Milo and ushered them out of Spindrift. 'Some fresh air will do us all good,' she said, still carrying Milo on her hip as she made her way down the wooden ladder to the beach. Melody, her feet bare, feeling suddenly gloriously free of the heavy atmosphere her father had created, ran in circles around her mother, making Milo laugh each time she appeared in front of him. The wind whipped at her hair and it rose and fell in silken ropes against her back and as she leapt around she breathed in cool salty air that tasted of happiness. Grabbing Flora's apron she dragged her mother to the edge of the shore where they waited for each wave to wash over their bare feet, feeling the sand stirring beneath them, tickling their toes.

'Come on, Milo,' Melody cried as Flora lifted him from her hip and placed his bare feet on the sand. He squealed with delight and bobbed up and down as the next wave draped a length of seaweed around his ankle and rolled the empty shell of a crab into shore. When he suddenly fell down in the water, getting his shorts and the hem of his cardigan wet, he laughed so happily that Melody plonked down next to him, the skirt of her dress floating around her, lifting in the water and catching on the skin of her legs. Flora looked down at them both fully clothed, soaking wet, laughing and splashing in the sea, and then, shrugging her shoulders and laughing, too, she sat down in the water as well.

Delighted, Melody cried, 'Mumma and me are mermaids and you're a merman, Milo. We live in a golden cave under the sea and sleep in giant clam shells with pearls for our pillows.' She pressed her knees together and waggled her feet as if they were the fins of a tail and tried to show Milo how to do the same. She knew he wanted to make his skinny legs obey him in the same way that her legs obeyed her but they just wouldn't. And yet, as they all played in the cool September sea, their spirits now as high as the seagulls in the sky, she tried to believe he was getting stronger. That soon, she could teach him to run and swim so that she and her little brother would have the most marvellous adventures together.

1962, MAY

The door to her parents' bedroom was open a crack and, with one eye peeking into the room, Melody stood outside as quiet as a mouse. A letter had arrived. She knew that whatever was in the letter was causing a nasty stir because the air in Spindrift had become suddenly colder than the frost that settled on their windows in winter, glimmering a thousand icy stars on the glass. Her mother had tears streaming down her face and her father was agitated. Melody knew it must be about Milo because her parents had been expecting news from an appointment they'd recently taken him to. Even she could tell that her brother wasn't quite the same as other five-year-olds.

Flora had asked her to keep Milo occupied in the sitting room while they had a little talk but, instead, she tiptoed to the ajar bedroom door and peeped through the crack. She shouldn't be listening, she knew that, but her beating heart was doing somersaults and she simply *had* to know what had made her mother cry. Desperately praying that the picture books, biscuits and drink of juice she'd hurriedly given Milo would keep him occupied for a while, she quietly waited.

'Does it say why Milo can't speak yet?' Daniel demanded, pointing to the letter in Flora's hand.

Her voice was flat when she answered him, lacking all the normal positivity she always had when talking about Milo. 'He *can* speak, Daniel. He just doesn't say all the words together or in the right order yet.'

'Let me read it for myself.' Daniel tried to extricate the letter from Flora's clenched fist but in her distress she couldn't let it go.

'It says...' She sniffed back her tears. 'It says Milo is physically and mentally handicapped. And they say that he's...' Her breath came out in a thin squeak as if her throat was being squeezed. 'It says he's ineducable...' She wiped at her tears as Daniel, the colour slipping from his face, stared at her.

'*Ineducable?*'

Melody saw how her father grabbed again for the letter and the sight of his anger frightened her. He was banging one fist against the other in bitter torment as if trying to punch the letter itself for giving them bad news. Mumbled words she didn't really understand tripped from his mouth as he read it for himself. '*Congenital muscular dystrophy. Hypotonia. Ineducable.*' He looked up from the crumpled paper and his face was ravaged. 'Oh God. My son. My son was born... *backwards.*'

The words, issued from her father's mouth, sounded so agonised, as if torn from the very core of his being, and to Melody it felt as if Milo had suddenly become a terrible disappointment to him but she didn't understand why. *Backwards*, her father had said. What did that mean? Is that why, she wondered, there had been so much shouting in the bedroom the day Milo was born?

'If anything it will get worse,' Flora added quietly.

Daniel scanned the letter further. 'It says that we should consider putting him in that *place* at Starcross because there's nowhere here in Exmouth for children like him. Isn't that the *idiot asylum*, Flora?'

Melody heard a crack in his voice and, for the first time ever, she saw that he was crying. It was deep and wretched and awful. But as far as Melody was concerned, Milo hadn't changed overnight because of a stupid letter – he was just Milo, the most special thing to ever have happened to them.

Still peeking through the gap in the door she saw Daniel shake the letter in the air before angrily screwing it into a ball. 'Call himself a doctor? He's a *coward* for not telling us to our faces, that's what he is!' He threw the ball of paper hard against the wall and sat back down on the bed next to Flora as if all the energy had come out of him. The bed sighed beneath his weight and the springs let out a groan of sympathy. Her parents remained, side by side, for several minutes, silent within their own grief, while Melody struggled with a great fear that was stirring in her stomach. For a moment she thought she might be sick and her eyes filled with so many tears she had to put her hands over her mouth to stop herself making a sound.

It was then that Flora suddenly stood up, raised her chin and straightened her back as if fired by a new strength. She blew her nose into the hanky and cleared her throat, speaking with a sharp volume to her voice that Melody had never heard before. 'Right! Let's be clear about this,' she said. 'One, it isn't called the idiot asylum any more, which was a *despicable* term. It's a residential school for mentally defective children, although to my mind this term is no better. They are just children. Two, Milo isn't going there. Milo isn't going anywhere – regardless of whatever the place is called. If they won't let him go to a regular school then he's staying right here at home in Spindrift.' Her last sentence held a finality to it that made tears of relief fall from Melody's eyes and spill over in hot trickles.

Retrieving the letter from the floor, Flora smoothed the pages of it with the palm of her hand. She spoke with a steady calm as if the doctor who wrote it could hear what she had to say. 'I'll teach him myself. My child, *our* child, is *not* ineducable.'

Melody suddenly wanted to push the door open and rush into the bedroom shouting, *I'll teach him, too.* She wanted to tell them how she was already trying to teach Milo to write his own name, but she knew well enough not to make a sound.

'You need to accept this, Daniel,' Flora advised. 'You must accept our child for who he is.'

The bedsprings creaked and as her father stood up Melody took a step back from the door. 'And you think you can?' he asked quietly.

'Yes, I *can*,' Flora raised her chin again. 'Because *this*,' she tapped her fingers against the letter, 'might be saying that our boy has the kind of condition that means he will see the world through his lovely young eyes forever, and it might be saying that he has the kind of *congenital whatever it is* that means he may never grow old, but he is still our son! Our beautiful boy. We all love him, and we will all make sure he lives his very best life. Whatever that life may be and for however long or short it is.'

Melody wiped at her damp cheeks and quietly tiptoed back to the little boy who was still happily playing with his picture books. She wrapped an arm around his shoulders and kissed his cheek, whispering a solemn promise into his blond curls. *'Little brother, I promise you that I will make sure you live your very best life.'*

1963, JANUARY

'Story?' Milo held out a book for Melody and grinned at her with expectation. She'd read it to him for what felt like almost every day since he'd chosen it from the library but he never seemed to get bored of it. At nearly six years old now he liked nothing more than to chatter his way through each book Melody read to him, pointing at the pictures and doing his best to form the words. 'Yes!' he squealed, pushing the book back towards her when she came to the end.

'But we *know* what happens to the man and the dog and

all the animals in the zoo,' she replied, unfolding her legs and getting up from the floor to replace the book on the shelf.

'Yes!' Milo shouted, holding his hands out for Melody to help him get up from the floor. He stared up at his sister, his huge brown eyes appealing to the better side of her, pleading for her to change her mind. She was doing well at school and was almost top of her class when it came to most subjects. She was a good reader, which was just as well because Milo loved nothing more than hearing stories. She glanced at his little pile of books. His favourite one was there of course but as for the others they needed to go to the library again soon. Out of the seven they'd borrowed, she'd now read every one so many times she could repeat them by heart with her eyes shut.

The world outside, however, was white. Snow covered the beach and lay heavily on the roofs of the bungalows that surrounded it. The air was almost blue with the brightness of it and the sea had turned the colour of molten silver. A snowman built only days ago was already covered in another layer of snow and the milkman hadn't been able to get his float through the roads for days. They woke in the mornings with ice on the inside of the windows and with their breath clouding into the air. Just to get to the Pier Head Stores, Flora wore Daniel's rubber boots and dragged an excited Melody and Milo along the road on a homemade sledge made from the largest of their kitchen trays. The library was unfortunately too far for such a venture.

According to the wireless, they were in the throes of one of the harshest winters in history so Melody knew that the drifts that banked the outside walls of Spindrift weren't going to melt for a very long time. They were doomed to stay inside, bundled up in woollen clothes. The wood store, gathered from the beach all year round to fuel the fire, was running low again but a paraffin heater did its best to toast a patch of warmth into the area around it. Milo continued to plead. An elongated version of 'please' squeezing out from between his tiny white teeth until, finally, she sat back on the rug, crossed her legs again and pulled him down beside her. The smell of apple shampoo was in his hair and his slippers were on the wrong feet, she realised. She laughed kindly and switched them to the correct feet before kissing his head. He was adorable and she loved him more than anything but even love couldn't persuade her to read any of those books one more time. Taking a big breath, she fell silent for a moment and let the inner workings of her mind take over. She closed her eyes, allowing her imagination the freedom to fill with anything that might come its way. Pirates, islands and treasure began to formulate in her mind and, when the vision of a huge galleon made entirely out of shells appeared in front of her, almost real enough to touch, she knew she had the answer. She wasn't sure exactly how her story was going to go just yet but that, she decided, would be the fun of making something up. Why limit Milo to the characters in a book, when there were a thousand stories she could think of to make his small world a magical place?

'Once upon a time,' she began, reaching for his pirate's cutlass.

1963, MARCH

It was beginning to frustrate Milo that he frequently fell over and couldn't run in the same way as the other children. Flora knelt on the floor and, having wiped his eyes dry, she vigorously rubbed his legs and arms, a look of steely determination coming to her face. 'If Milo has to fight this disease, and indeed if we all have to fight it with him, we'd better get to know it on first name terms. We shall call it Long John Silver.'

Melody, who wanted to cry for Milo, smiled brightly at him and played along with the game and, as the very best of swashbuckling pirates himself, he was delighted. Long John was Milo's favourite pirate. Not as terrifying as Blackbeard or as ruthless as Zheng Yi Sao, but the work of brilliant fiction, complete with a colourful parrot and a big red beard. Melody told him a story that very day, dressing them in their father's white shirts tied at the waist with string and with eye patches made out of black paint and paper.

'We're going to make that dastardly blaggard walk the plank,' Melody said, poking a cushion with the end of a cutlass made from one of her mother's knitting needles. Milo yelled and threw his own cutlass at the cushion which bounced off and skittered along the floor. He didn't fully understand, Melody knew that, but right now it was all they could think of. She'd been told by Flora that Milo's physical condition might be stable for weeks at a time but that Long John would surely return. He would sneak up on Milo, maybe in the dead of night, forcing him to gradually surrender over time, rendering him weaker than ever before. Today, however, Milo was happily playing along with the game. They were ready for battle and Long John Silver, she was determined, was not going to win for a long time yet.

1963, APRIL

'I thought I was going to have the kind of son I could take for a pint of beer.' Melody's father was speaking in low tones and her mother sounded as if she was at the end of her tether again.

'You *have*,' Flora replied. She was being clipped and frosty with him, something that had started happening ever since the letter had arrived months ago. Her father had never been as easy-going as her mother but lately, as today, his tempers burst out of nowhere.

'I reckon it'll be me and Long John *bloody* Silver propping up the bar while Milo sits in a wheelchair in the corner. Long John Silver for *fuck's sake*!'

'Daniel!' Flora reprimanded. 'That's not called for. He likes Long John. It's a coping mechanism and it helps him to be less afraid, plus it helps Melody to be less afraid. In fact, it bloody well helps me, too. And the way he is doesn't mean he can't experience life to its fullest. He's still your son. He might never be able to do trigonometry but, let's face it, who can?'

Melody sniffed loudly then blew into a hanky and her insides felt all twisty again. She couldn't think what Milo had done wrong today. He'd spilt his drink all over the armchair and put his shorts on back to front but that was just him being Milo.

Only that morning her father had taken Milo fishing, his face full of triumph upon their return telling them all how well Milo had done. 'He can help reel in and nearly unhook the fish, can't you, Milo?' he'd said. Milo hadn't answered but had examined one of his fingers where a nasty gouge flamed red on his skin and Melody had guessed that *nearly* being able to unhook the fish meant that he'd struggled with this task. But then he'd held his fish aloft and grinned with pleasure.

'Three,' he'd said proudly, holding them towards Flora. 'One, four, three!'

They'd eaten the fish for lunch and, all the while, Melody had tried her best to enjoy it but her father had acted as if his clothes were too tight and as if his chair had become uncomfortable. Something about that particular day had changed the shape of things.

'What's happened since this morning?' Flora asked. 'You were fine when you came back from fishing. And now you're not. Why does this keep happening?' She wrung her hands on her apron and her voice held a plaintive note to it. Melody stood by the door frame, quietly, unnoticed, listening to what her father had to say.

'I keep thinking I can do this, Flora, but I don't actually think I can. I can't cope with the stares that people give him or the comments muttered under the breaths – about *my* son. He's six years old now. It *shows*.'

'Who cares what mindless people say, Daniel? The people that count don't do that, our friends, our neighbours, they all accept Milo. They love him for who he is. Don't you?' Flora's voice was tense and hard and Melody held her breath as a horrible silence followed her question. 'Don't you?' Flora repeated, demanding a reply.

'I do... I *want* to but...'

'But what?' Flora prompted him again, as another silence stretched between them.

'What is he ever going to do? With life? He can't go to school. He'll never get a job. He won't learn to drive a car or pilot a boat. He can't even count to three properly for *fuck's sake*!'

'Yet.'

Melody heard her mother reply with one simple word and in her nine-year-old way she was proud of her.

'He can't count to three properly... *yet*,' Flora repeated. 'I *knew* it. I knew that's what you were annoyed about but you must be able to see he can already do more than he could do six months ago. He can understand so much now. He knows lots of colours, can recognise some letters and numbers, and he *can* count, even if it's sometimes in the wrong order. Melody has also taught him how to do up his buttons and use a pencil.'

Melody swelled with pride at hearing this. Between them, she and her mother had played and encouraged, cajoled and bribed Milo into learning. Every day, he would wait for Melody to come home from school and bring him something from her day. She would hang up her coat and, while she still had her school uniform on, would teach him something that she'd learnt. It was pretence of course, the things she taught him she'd learnt long ago, but he loved how each day she would bring him a new word or a number or a picture to copy. He was beginning to learn. It broke her heart into pieces that he couldn't join her in putting on a school uniform and going to school like other children. How much her darling brother would have loved to do that.

'We don't know how far Milo can go, given the chance.' Flora spoke with passion and it echoed her own thoughts. 'He's certainly capable of learning a lot more than the doctor thought. *Ineducable*, my foot! And as for beer, who's to say he can't have a beer when he's eighteen? Not me, that's for sure.'

They both turned to see Melody standing there, their conversation dying quickly on their lips, leaving only silence and injured thoughts behind. Melody hugged her dressing gown tightly across her body and found that she was shivering, but she wasn't cold. Daniel's eyes looked sad and empty, glinting like the black rocks that appeared when the tide was very low. She recalled the triumphant look on Milo's face as he pointed to his three fish and wondered why his joy at life could not be enough for their father.

Two days later, Melody and Milo's father left Spindrift. He took with him his coat and all his clothes except a pair of rubber boots left neatly by the front door.

# 9

After making their toasts to Flora and Milo, Melody and Juliana sat on the terrace drinking wine for hours. They toasted everything. A seagull that landed on the balustrade and pooped on it, the candles they lit when it began to get dark, the space shuttle, the invention of the artificial heart, underwear past and present including the chastity belt, bloomers, and the glorious invention of the thong. They drank, ate and talked their way into the evening, both of them tactfully avoiding any further subject that might prove awkward. A glass was accidentally smashed and another knocked over, causing a river of red to seep through the blanket Juliana was wrapped in and onto the lemon of her shift dress.

Eventually, unexpectedly, the laughter started. It came in loud and regular bursts and was followed by a good deal of 'shhhushing' and giggling the likes of which they hadn't indulged in since they were teenagers. The wine, topped up from all that they had consumed at lunch, brought memories from their past summers rushing to the surface, bubbling with a host of tales that triggered even more tales after that. One or the other of them would recall something and then they would feel the need to toast that event, too.

'Remember when you fell off the rocks and cut your head open?' Juliana said.

'A toast to blood and stitches!' Melody cried. 'Remember when Milo gorged on ice-cream and vomited in Isobel's handbag?' she said.

'A toast to vomit!' Juliana cried. 'And remember the days when Big Joe Wiley and his dad would take us across to the beach at Dawlish in rowing boats? The campfires we lit when it got dark so we could toast crumpets in the flames.'

'A toast to Big Joe!' Melody cried, opening another bottle and pouring Juliana's glass almost to the rim.

'To the beach dude!' Juliana yelled, putting her fingers to her lips and wolf whistling so loudly Melody was extremely impressed.

'Shhhut up, he'll hear you,' Melody hissed, ramming the corner of the blanket into Juliana's mouth and pressing her hand against it. She turned towards Joe's bungalow where the lights were on to see that the curtains were still, thankfully, drawn.

'I don't care,' Juliana shouted, her voice muffled by the blanket and her make-up now slipping into messy streaks around her eyes. In the flickering candlelight she looked like a tired clown and, when Melody released the blanket, they both blew their laughter out in long raspberries forced between closed lips. And they didn't stop laughing for a long time.

Midnight brought with it a fourth bottle of wine, some sherry that had been in the cupboard forever, a moon veiled by thin cirrus clouds that trailed their wispy reflections into the sea and a neighbour who tiredly called out for them to *shut the fuck up*. Finally, dragging themselves from their cocoon of blankets, totally and utterly inebriated, Melody and Juliana crawled to their beds.

They woke to the hangover from hell. Shuffling around Spindrift, trying to muster some semblance of normality, drinking strong black coffee, downing paracetamol and offering each other intermittent groans.

The previous evening had escalated – or declined, they weren't sure which. As Melody attempted to clear the broken glass from the terrace outside, Juliana, wearing sunglasses and wincing at every noise, took the bowls inside, the remains of their nibbles soggy from overnight damp.

'I'll say you girls made a night of it.' Mrs Galespie called to them from the terrace of her bungalow, Spinnaker. A billowy kind of woman, with a Devon lilt, ruddy cheeks and a generous smile, she was wearing a light blue housecoat and puffing on a cigarette. When she wasn't wearing her housecoat, she was dressed in enormous shorts, a khaki bucket hat and a pair of purple jelly shoes.

'I think I'm dying,' Melody called back.

Mrs Galespie laughed, cackling her way through another drag of her cigarette. 'I bet you are. And you probably think you're never going to drink again, 'ey?'

'I'm not,' Melody answered. 'Not ever.'

'Not till the next time – I know.' Mrs Galespie flicked her ash into the ashtray she was holding and a sharp gust of wind blew it straight back out. She nodded knowingly. 'I was a young girl once. I can still remember the bits I can't remember.' She laughed and displayed the gaps in her teeth where she hadn't yet got around to putting her dentures in.

'You young things,' she clucked. 'Make the most of it, that's my advice.' She turned and made her way inside, squashing the stub of her cigarette into the ashtray as she went.

Nursing another cup of coffee and with the evidence of their debauchery cleared away, Melody and Juliana sat once more on the terrace hoping the sea breeze might blow the cobwebs away. Despite the fact that her temples thumped and there was a distinct sensation of sawdust in the back of her throat, Melody liked that she and Juliana had managed to drink their way into remembering just how much they loved each other. It gave her a warm glow and she wanted to hang on to the feeling of it for as long as possible.

'Why don't we go out again? Take the ferry to Starcross? Or we could walk up to Orcombe Point?' Melody scratched an itch in the crown of her hair and hoped that her suggestion might be met with some enthusiasm but it was clear from the pink cracked eyes that stared back at her that there was little enthusiasm for anything.

'I don't know if I can face a boat trip, Mel. All those rolling waves...' Juliana puffed out her cheeks as if she was going to be sick and just the thought of her throwing the contents of her stomach turned Melody's own stomach in the process. In truth, Melody wanted to go back to bed. She wanted to sleep off the morning until, at some point when the world felt normal again, she could do what she always did – she would go beachcombing.

'A bacon sandwich! That's what we need.' Juliana sat up in her chair. 'Nothing like a load of pig fat and salt to repair the damage of a night before.'

'Well, when you put it like that...' Melody grimaced.

'But the Pier Café's closed, which is annoying because it's

within crawling distance and I'm not sure I can drag myself any further. Where's the next one?' Juliana's voice was as feeble as her expression. Despite her wan pallor, though, Melody thought that, this morning, she looked beautiful. She didn't have any make-up on, her freckles were out and her pale lashes were back, framing her eyes with strawberry blonde.

'We'll go to the Harbour View,' Melody replied. 'You'll have to crawl a bit further along the esplanade but their breakfasts are good, too.'

When finally they were ready to tackle the day, Juliana emerged looking more like the Juliana of yesterday. Unfortunately her hair once more looked as if it had been blasted by the morning wind and suspended in the air – frozen in time. It was very big hair. Even bigger than yesterday and, despite her pounding head, Melody stifled the urge to laugh. Her own hair looked positively exhausted by comparison, tied into a loose ponytail with a green ribbon and hanging limply over one shoulder like a dying swan. In addition, Juliana was wearing a short pink dress, a lot of make-up, and a pair of American Tan tights that made her legs look as if they'd been on holiday without her. The pink cracked eyes were now sporting a halo of bloodshot red, causing Melody to entertain the notion that if there was a human equivalent of an electric shock Juliana was quite possibly it.

'Still no hall mirror?' Juliana held a deep pink lipstick in her hands and pointed to the wall where nothing but a single screw and a perfectly clean circle of paint indicated the spot where the mirror used to hang.

'I haven't got round to making the border for it still,' Melody answered. She really should have finished it by now, or at least found something else to cover the patch on the wall that highlighted her failings. It was still in a bag under the dining room table, half worked on, half abandoned.

'Anyway,' Juliana sighed, interrupting Melody's internal altercation. 'With or without a mirror, I look like shit!' She shot a look at Melody. 'All self-inflicted so it must be a sign of a good night.' Her lips were partially opened, her lipstick poised at the ready when she paused. Her eyes fixed on the cheesecloth maxi dress Melody was wearing. It lingered there, taking in the embroidered bodice of it, before sliding down to the bare feet that poked out from beneath the hem. Melody waited patiently, knowing that a comment must surely be about to come from the partially open lips. 'Um…' Juliana began hesitantly.

'Um, what?' Melody questioned, her fingers now fiddling with the beads around her neck.

'Um… Mel? Have you heard of the eighties? We've moved on from *peace man* to big and…'

'Brash?' Melody interjected.

'Bold,' Juliana corrected. 'Vibrant. Eclectic. Pouffy hair.' She pointed to her lacquer-coated head while her gaze came to rest on Melody's hair. Melody stopped fiddling with her beads and instead ran a protective hand over the silky softness of her own blonde hair. She knew she was almost a decade behind the current fashion and she really didn't want to care that she was. She'd embraced the seventies when the decade came, loving the flowers and the flares and the hippie vibes that perfectly reflected who she was in every way. She hated how easily that fabulous era had been left behind for a brand-new fashion – for sharp lines and colours capable of bringing on a migraine. She struggled with the idea that joggers had taken to running up and down the esplanade with their knickers on the outside of their leggings, and that children looked as if they were still wearing their pyjamas. This whole, crazy fashion was aggressive, capable of poking an eye out if you got too close, and she hated it. Melody, apart from the awful wedge shoes she'd stupidly bought for Juliana's arrival, would remain faithful to her first love, the fashion of her formative years. Her own wardrobe, when opened, was comforting, enfolding her with floaty fabrics made from soft cotton or pretty wool and she wasn't prepared to swap it for neon and Lycra.

'The eighties should have come with a warning,' Melody muttered. 'That pink with my hangover is making it worse. I think I'm going to have to dig out my sunglasses.' She held her hand over her eyes as if pretending to protect them from the glare and kept it there for so long they both had to laugh.

Juliana quickly applied her lipstick, popped it into her bag and then tugged gently at the cord that laced through Melody's neckline. 'I'm sorry. It was mean of me to pick on you.' She sucked on her bottom lip while ineffectually adjusting the criss-cross lacing of the cord on Melody's dress before patting the string of beads that she wore around her neck.

'Let's go with bohemian. Your style is... unique, unconventional, yes, definitely bohemian. Very Melody.'

Melody slipped on her suede coat with the sheepskin collar and cuffs while Juliana donned a beige mac with a turned-up collar and a belt that nipped her tightly in at her slim waist. It was a terrible June but Melody and Juliana, as different as chalk and cheese, were suitably prepared for the weather at least. The temperature was no warmer than yesterday and the clouds, hanging on to another cargo of rain, were bruised purple, ready to burst. Melody picked up the bright red umbrella that was propped against the corner by the door. It was Milo's. Daniel had bought it for Flora from Thomas Tucker's, the drapers on the Strand, but Milo had loved the colour so much she'd given it to him instead. It gave Melody pleasure to think that a little bit of all her family would join them for breakfast today.

'I said you should bring galoshes,' Melody called out to Juliana over the noise of the rain as they left the café, their bellies full of breakfast baps. It was coming down in sheets and Melody did her best to hold Milo's umbrella more over Juliana than herself. The tide had now come up so high that the waves were smashing against the sea wall, exploding into watery gems that sprayed over the path and up their legs. The American Tan tights were speckled to brown.

'This weather's ridiculous,' Juliana called back. 'It's June for crying out loud. I've never known it to be like this in all the summers I've been coming here. I thought this place was all ice-cream and sunburn.'

Melody pushed Milo's umbrella into the wind for fear of it turning inside out. The kiosks on the esplanade selling ice-cream and fishing nets were open but, apart from the merest straggle of people caught short by the rain, the esplanade was empty. By the time they shut the door to Spindrift behind them they were drenched. They spread their outerwear on a clothes horse to dry by the old paraffin heater and half an hour later they were cosily talking over the top of the rain that was hammering against the roof. Through the windows the sea was a muddle of iron grey and dark green, and the tide had covered the entire beach to the point that it was now halfway up the wooden ladder to Spindrift. The waves crashed repeatedly into the concrete footing of the bungalows, throwing spray over the terraces, and Juliana was beginning to find it alarming.

'Blimey, Mel, the waves are going to crash against the glass doors soon.'

'Probably,' Melody said confidently. 'Don't you remember what it's like when there's a spring tide along with a storm? It's exhilarating. It's fabulous!'

'Fabulous,' Juliana said uncertainly.

'I remember when we had two floods in one year. Milo and I were only little. I thought it was really exciting but then I was only a child. I think it did a lot of damage but at least people's boats came in handy. Some went shopping in their canoes!' She smiled at the memory but Juliana was frowning.

'I don't want to have to go out for our next meal in a canoe, Mel. Aren't you worried that this little shanty can't stand up to the weather much longer? Only the other day I read in the paper that something called global warming is changing the world's climate. Everything will get more extreme. By the look of this...' she indicated towards the sea that was now little more than a foot below the line of the terrace '... it's already started.'

Melody nodded, only too aware that climate change had become front-page news. The idea of the oceans and the seasons changing their rhythm worried her as much as regeneration and modernisation. A large wave rose towards the terrace gate and slapped down on the concrete by the double doors.

'I'd rather Spindrift were swept out to sea than...' Stopping abruptly, Melody bit her lip. She wasn't ready to tell Juliana what was really going to happen to Spindrift. That the demolition of Shelly felt worse than nature's wrath.

'Than what?' Juliana asked.

'Nothing.' Melody waved a dismissive hand in her direction just as another wave hit the terrace. A trickle of water began to find its way under the ledge of the doors.

'Don't you ever want to live in a real house?' Juliana pressed. 'The kind that copes with all the seasons – stays warm and doesn't flood? The kind that doesn't smell of damp and isn't stuck in the Victorian era?'

The way she was talking reminded Melody of how Aunt Isobel would talk about their way of life in Shelly. It hurt her terribly to think that Juliana was beginning to feel the same way.

# 10

'Juliana will be here soon, Milo.' Melody squeezed herself with excitement and, taking Milo's hands, jumped up and down as he laughed and did his best to join in with his weakening limbs and unsteady gait.

'Soon,' he echoed.

'Yes, Saturday,' Melody answered. 'Four more days, four more nights.' She held four fingers up so that Milo could see them and he called back excitedly.

'Summer. Four more. Juliana!'

Summer for Melody and Milo was on its way again. Another year of coastal seasons coming and going in their own glorious way had passed. Autumn had brought a fresher, busier breeze with it, and as its days had blossomed and faded more quickly they simply showcased the beauty of twilight across the water all the sooner. Winter had cast glittering droplets of ice on the sand with plumes of cold breath that mingled with the steam of hot milky drinks, and spring, when at last it came, blended soft lilacs and yellows into the palette of grey sea. Now summer, Melody's favourite time of the year, lazily warm and bursting with promise, was heralded once more by the arrival of Juliana.

Juliana and her mother, the unfathomable Aunt Isobel, were visually glorious things. They always arrived in a whirl of shimmering air making everything more colourful but somehow more complicated at the same time. Uncle Gordon, who always escorted them, followed behind in his quiet, unassuming manner. They never stayed long at Spindrift. They simply brought Juliana, consumed tea and homemade cake, then spirited themselves away again. Away, Melody supposed, to lead their business-driven lives. Juliana would remain, accompanied by an abundance of new clothes, several books and an excited air of expectation for all Shelly could offer a child through the holiday season.

The summer of 1965 was no different from any other summer other than it was the year Melody turned eleven. She'd grown teenage tall, her cheekbones emerging, high and freckled, with her hair now trimmed so that it flicked outwards on her shoulders. It was also the year that she became aware of some of the subtleties that seemed to surround Juliana's visits. She wasn't sure how her aunt and uncle managed it, and no one had ever discussed it, but she realised there was, and probably always had been, a certain *something* that demanded the frenzied tidying of Spindrift before their arrival. Copious washing billowed from the line, the best china was unpacked and washed, and soft pink toilet paper materialised again in the lavatory.

Uncle Gordon was the one who apparently made things happen in Juliana's family. Before Daniel had left them, he would refer to her uncle and aunt in disparaging tones. Uncle Gordon's purpose in life, he would say, was to do too much, earn too much money, fund a ridiculously flamboyant lifestyle and pander to Aunt Isobel as if she were a delicate orchid.

On this particular visit, Melody decided that her father might have been right. Uncle Gordon drove the car, carried the bags, took off coats, pulled out chairs and opened doors while Aunt Isobel held Flora's hand and smiled indulgently. Melody adored her Uncle Gordon but had never quite taken to her aunt, or maybe it was that her aunt had never quite taken to her. Either way, it was a fact that her Aunt Isobel was about as different from her sister, Flora, as it was possible to get.

Her aunt wished to be addressed as Aunt Isobel. Never shortened to Izzy, never rounded to Aunty. As far as Melody was concerned, it was a mouthful of a name. Melody's mother, on the other hand, liked for Juliana, or indeed any child who came to be in her presence, to call her Aunty Flora. She believed it was friendlier for children to say, and she was right. It was a soft and squishy sounding name and Florentine, or the shortened Flora, was Latin for flower, which Melody liked. Flora was a perfectly lovely name for the extraordinarily lovely woman her mother was.

This year, same as every other year, the now seven-year-old Juliana arrived positively jiggling around with excitement ready to rip off her city clothes and put on her swimming costume. 'Calm down, Juliana, and pay your respects to your Aunty Flora,' Aunt Isobel reprimanded. 'You have all summer to behave like a wild thing.' Melody saw that Juliana did as she was asked. She assumed a demeanour of polite calm and stopped her fidgeting – only the discreet waggling of her fingers behind her back gave away her impatience. And she continued to stand, doll-like, while Melody leant against the fence in silent resignation of all the necessary respects that had to be paid. Juliana's pleated skirt and white-collared blouse were, she thought, bound to be from a proper shop like Ladybird or British Home Stores because she looked as if she'd stepped out of a magazine. Whereas Melody was clothed in a new red tunic dress adorned with huge floral pockets, fashioned by her mother especially for the occasion out of an old blouse and a pair of second-hand curtains given to them by a neighbour.

It was during this moment that Melody found herself comparing the differences in their respective mothers. Sisters in every way except age and outlook. At a glance, striking similarities in genetic make-up couldn't fail to be detected – deep brown eyes, fair hair, heart-shaped faces – but everything else about the two of them, Melody realised, was different. Aunt Isobel, younger by several years, seemed to glide effortlessly through life as if on wheels, gathering privilege by the armfuls as she went, while her mother, Flora, attacked life with enthusiastic gusto as if she owed it to do so.

'You go on, Juliana. All of you – go!' Flora smiled cheerfully and waved her hands, ushering them away. 'Have fun. Take cake.' They didn't need telling twice. The doll-like child that was Juliana turned into the wild thing that Aunt Isobel had dreaded, her hair flying in the wind as she whooped and yelled, grabbing at a currant cake before dashing into Spindrift to get changed. Melody took Milo's hand, each taking a currant cake, joining her with the whooping and yelling. Ten minutes later they were back with a clatter of buckets, spades and crab lines, wearing their swimming costumes. The knitted costumes had long gone and now Melody and Milo sported matching costumes of orange towelling.

Only vaguely aware that Aunt Isobel had to duck to avoid being hit by a yellow bucket, Melody took a running leap straight off the terrace and down the five-foot drop onto the beach. Juliana, wearing a gingham ruffle costume with halterneck tie, did the same, yelling 'YABADABADOO' as she went. Then, they both helped Milo to join them, who landed with more of an ungainly flop on the sand. It wasn't long before the three of them were gouging the soft bodies of limpets from shells that Melody had prised off the rocks with an old kitchen knife. Now, a handful of empty domed shells lay scattered beside them, their innards ready to pierce with the hooks of their crabbing lines, and the incoming tide was almost perfect. The adults, Melody could hear, had begun the customary tea party refreshments, drinking tea from the best china teacups, poured from the spout of the best china teapot. The holidays had begun.

It wasn't long, though, before Melody's ears pricked over what she heard when Aunt Isobel's voice drifted through the fence and down to the beach. 'These Shelly bungalows are beginning to get noticeably shabby. I expect it's due to being constantly hit by the coastal weather… and the fact that they were built last century.' Melody felt indignant. As her aunt's lowdown on her home continued, a nasty worm grew inside her until her stomach felt all angry with it. 'And Spindrift feels as if it's getting smaller every time we visit,' Aunt Isobel continued. The worm inside Melody grew, irritating her insides and crawling up her throat. Spindrift, she thought, may have been small as homes went but as far as she was concerned it was huge in terms of everything else.

Could Aunt Isobel not see that Spindrift embraced the expanse of sea and kissed the sandy shoreline that edged the land all the way to the red Jurassic cliffs of Orcombe Point? Could she not see the huge canopy of ever-changing sky above it, or taste the air that rushed towards it on the waves? Melody felt her heart beat a little faster when no defending answer came from Flora.

'I don't know why you won't consider moving to the house in Cheltenham, Flora?' her aunt went on. 'Our tenants are due to move out soon and you know Gordon and I won't charge you rent, will we Gordon? You would have space for your own art studio there and you could rent Spindrift out to holiday-makers like other owners do.' Melody's heart skipped a beat and the worm wriggled violently. *Say something*, she urged her mother silently. She'd always known that Aunt Isobel preferred a different kind of life, polished floors, gleaming ornaments, sofas that were too perfectly plumped to actually sit on. But what had all that to do with them? Her mother, frustratingly, didn't immediately leap to the defence of Spindrift but Uncle Gordon quietly answered through his mouthful of cake.

'No rent whatsoever. You could live a little easier. Be closer... to us.'

'You could be part of the *real* world again,' Aunt Isobel added.

'You could be part of *our* world again,' Uncle Gordon echoed. They were on a roll, Melody thought. She could hear it gathering strength like one of the really big waves that swelled behind the smaller waves on a choppy day. It was the kind of wave you could see in the distance and knew it was coming. And then it did, crashing harder against the sand than all the others, pushing surf and seaweed and shingle up the shore with such a rush it caught your feet in its net of glistening bubbles.

'There's nothing to keep you here in Shelly,' Aunt Isobel

continued. 'No Daniel because the no good so-and-so went and buggered off leaving you here dealing with Milo on your own.'

'I don't *deal* with Milo,' Flora calmly asserted.

'All right, then he left because *he* couldn't deal with Milo. And now you have to take in darning and ironing just to pay the bills. And honestly, Flora, I've really no idea why you still keep his boots by the front door.'

Flora chose to ignore the comment about how she earned her money and answered as if the reason she kept Daniel's boots should be obvious. 'Because, with a thick pair of socks, I can wear them and make use of them in the bad weather. He did at least leave Spindrift for me and the children.'

Melody felt a hot flash tickle the hairline at the nape of her neck while the worm swelled to the point of bursting out of her. It was true, her father wasn't coming back, but the fact that his boots were still by the front door comforted her. They made her feel as if a part of him was with them still. She missed him. She missed the good days when they'd been a united family, laughing at something funny or swimming in the sea together. She missed the joy on Milo's face when their father swooped him onto his shoulders or pretended to lose at a board game.

She didn't, however, miss the fact that, for months, Milo had repeatedly asked when his daddy was coming back and she didn't like the fact that her mother always had to work so hard. But how they coped with all of that, and where they lived while they coped with it, was none of Aunt Isobel's business.

Melody realised there was something about the way they all lived at Shelly that was upsetting Aunt Isobel. She was speaking with secretive underlying notes that couldn't be explained by the limited understanding of an eleven-year-old girl. The limpet dangled, sticky and shapeless, from Melody's orange crab line as she held her breath, catching her finger on the barb of the hook as she strained to hear more. Aunt Isobel lowered her voice and leant towards Flora. 'Please let us help you, Florentine. You're being so stubborn and yet we could ease your financial burden if you'd only let us.'

But Melody saw her mother shake her head. 'We don't need money. Spindrift is paid for and the children never go without.' Flora waved her hands towards the sea and smiled at the view at almost the same time as her sister threw her hands up in despair.

'But Milo is eight now,' Aunt Isobel pressed. 'We all know that he... well he...'

'He's happy?' Flora interjected.

'Well, yes, he's happy... of course he's happy, but is that enough? He was already, shall we say, having... *difficulties*, and now with his physical situation... well, he's getting worse, isn't he? He's going to need a wheelchair one day, and this place is simply not adequate, Florentine.' Melody crept up the wooden ladder leading to the bungalow and peeped over the top, watching Aunt Isobel stir two lumps of sugar into her tea as if she'd simply passed comment on the weather. 'Despite everything, I think Daniel was right. I think perhaps Milo should go to a place where he'll get proper support. You agree, don't you, Gordon?'

Uncle Gordon took a sip of his tea and, peering over his cup, nodded silently while Aunt Isobel carried on. 'There's a special home now for children like him near where we live. It has the best facilities. And Melody could...' Melody waited in silent panic, her ears straining to hear about what *she* could do '... and Melody could go to a good school, have access to more things, be free to live as a teenager – she could be unburdened by having to... well, having to care. You think so, too, don't you, Gordon?' Again, Uncle Gordon nodded quietly, surreptitiously glancing at Flora.

Furious, Melody jumped back down onto the sand and urgently ordered Juliana to take Milo over to where the incoming tide had reached the best crabbing rocks. Willing to do anything her older cousin asked, Juliana readily took Milo's hand. But when he stumbled he pulled her down with him onto the soft sand and they flailed around together, helpless with laughter. Melody wanted to giggle, too, but her fury at Aunt Isobel was more pressing.

She raced back up the wooden ladder, her breath catching in angry rasps. 'Milo is my brother! I don't *have* to *care* for him. And we're not going anywhere and nor is he. Your houses are huge... too huge... but if you ask me your world is small... and it's *not* better than ours.' She ran out of suitable words to fight with and, as her voice trailed away, she was left with three shocked adult faces, a heart that pumped with indignation and legs that trembled beneath her.

'Melody!' her mother scolded, picking up the best china teapot to top up the best china teacups. Angry tears stung Melody's eyes and she glowered at her mother who didn't bat an eyelid but, instead, calmly poured the last of the tea. Melody decided she hated that teapot and the stupid china cups. Their real teapot was chipped and wore a blue crocheted jacket and it did the job of brewing the tea-leaves just fine. Their mugs could be clasped in both hands. And why were buns or cakes always bulging from brand-new paper cases and huge bowls of strawberries glistening with sugar whenever they visited? Flora smiled brightly at Aunt Isobel and Uncle Gordon as she placed the teapot back down. Then, catching Melody's eye, and with five simple words, she soothed her daughter's fears as surely as if stroking them with a warm hand.

'Spindrift is all we need,' she said softly.

## 1965, AUGUST

As the summer wore on, the best day of the holidays arrived. There was an excitement in the air that morning. Melody, Milo and Juliana could hardly wait. The annual event to take several of the children of Shelly over the water to Dawlish was going to happen that very day. It was August and there was a perfect tide for launching, perfect weather for swimming and two rowing boats ready for the off. There would be a campfire to bake a supper of potatoes wrapped in silver foil and there would be marshmallows and crumpets pierced on sticks plus plenty of squash to drink.

Flora had packed towels and dry clothes and a sun hat for each of them that they were never going to keep on their heads. A bucket was at the ready to bring back shells and other glorious beach treasures and Milo asked repeatedly if it was time to go yet. At eight and a half he was taller than Juliana and catching up with Melody, his hair, light in colour and wildly curly, still brushed his shoulders in length.

Big Joe Wiley, fifteen years old and already six foot three, helped his father Tom Wiley drag their two rowing boats to the edge of the shore. A girl of about fourteen with short black hair, a holiday-maker to Shelly, helped Joe get the smaller children into the boat and Melody could tell they were sweet on each other. Another family of holiday-makers sunbathed nearby on the sand, watching everything that was going on while their teenage son threw stones at the seagulls. Melody didn't like him and was glad he wasn't joining them on their trip because she felt like throwing a stone at *him*.

'How come you're letting the salad go?' the boy shouted as the children climbed into the boats.

'*Salad?*' Big Joe Wiley stopped what he was doing and shielded his eyes from the sun to follow the direction the boy was pointing in.

'That kid with not a lot going on.' The boy pointed directly at Milo and laughed cruelly but Melody and all the other children didn't laugh with him.

'I rather like salad,' Big Joe replied calmly, turning his back on the boy. Holding out two strong hands, he helped Milo take his seat in his rowing boat, *Wild Rose*. As Milo bumped down on his bottom and squealed with laughter, the boy on the beach pointed at the side of his own skull and pulled a silly face. Melody instantly wanted to climb back out of the boat to punch him. She wanted to tell the boy that her lovely, kind, funny, beautiful brother was better than he could ever be but Big Joe placed a restraining hand on her shoulder. And Flora, who was waiting on the beach to wave them all off, called out to her, running a silencing finger over her lips and tracing the outline of a smile across them. Melody knew the sign. She was being reminded again that unpleasant people should keep their unpleasantness to themselves and that if they didn't she shouldn't allow them to spoil the day. Moodily, she traced her own finger across her lips and pulled them into a smile. It was for her mother's sake, and also for Milo's, but never for the boy on the beach.

She continued to dutifully smile at her mother until the sound of stones against the hull of the boat was followed by the gentle movement of water beneath them. Then, when Flora turned to make her way back towards Spindrift, the smile dropped away from Melody's face. She pressed the thumb of her finger against her nose and, with her tongue out, waggled her fingers at the boy. He replied by sticking two fingers up at her just before his father cuffed him hard around the head. Melody giggled and settled herself in her seat squeezing Milo's hand as Juliana, on the other side of him, squeezed his other hand.

It was wonderful, as always. A day of new things to explore. New games to be invented. A brightly coloured dragonfly was found, a host of shells were collected, hide-and-seek was played in the tall beach grasses and someone brought with them a kite that wouldn't take off no matter how hard they ran with it. In addition, Milo won the competition for the best sandcastle and Big Joe Wiley did a handstand for longer than they could all chant a playground song.

A sailor went to sea sea sea

To see what he could see see see

All that he could see see see

Was the bottom of the deep blue sea sea sea

Finally, when their noses and cheeks had turned pink from the sun, they played in the sea until the last heat of the sun slipped away and a campfire was lit. The girl with the short black hair sat next to Big Joe and, while the fire burnt in the evening light, they held each other's hands. Melody thought that one day she would like to have a boyfriend like Joe.

When at last the food was baked almost black by the fire then eaten as if it was the best-tasting thing any of them had ever tried, the songs began. Milo couldn't sing. But that didn't mean he didn't try. Unsure of the words but seemingly confident of the tune, Milo joined in, getting louder and louder and more and more tuneless until they all had to sing ridiculously loudly just to keep the song going in a way that was recognisable. On the last note, everyone laughed until their bellies hurt and by the very last song both Melody and Juliana had to clap their hands over Milo's mouth to hush him.

'That racket could probably be heard back at Shelly,' Big Joe laughed, helping a tired but happy Milo onto his feet as the day came to a close and the children made their way back towards the boats.

Seated in *Wild Rose* once more, Melody watched Big Joe rhythmically pulling the oars. She'd known him all her life. A boy with such a gentle nature who was never too busy to help the younger children build sandcastles or play games on the beach. The last veil of evening sunlight fell across his face as he concentrated on taking them all home across a sea that had become an oil painting of colour. Navy blue with tinges of gold and ribbons of purple peaked and dipped all around them. Joe had given them each a torch to help light their path for other boats to see as he dipped the oars into the water, lifted again and paused briefly before dipping back in. Splash, pull, pause, splash, pull, pause.

Melody could just make out the sitting room light shining out from Spindrift and she pointed at it for Milo who had become sleepy under the rhythmical movement of *Wild Rose*. He nodded, blinking heavily and smiling his crooked smile as Juliana yawned.

'I can see Spindrift, too,' she said. 'I can see home.'

Summer, Spindrift and Shelly, for the three of them, was the most special place in all the world and they hugged that thought to themselves as the light slipped from the sky with every child holding their torch to light the way. We're like floating moonbeams, Melody thought as the boats made their way through the torchlit water. She yawned deeply as the bungalows of Shelly grew clearer, the rocks becoming more distinctive, the dock and the curve of the bay, closer with each dip and pull of the oars. Milo caught Melody's yawn, and Juliana after him, and as each child smothered tiredness with their hands to their mouths, quiet now from their adventures, the lights of home were there to greet them.

# 11

'You used to love it here once. You used to call it home.'
Melody slumped back in her armchair as Juliana stood
to look out of the windows through the curtain of driving
rain. It was as if she could see something different from the
view that had been there all their lives. As if she had forgotten
that they had grown up collecting limpets and winkles from
rocks, digging for lugworms in the sand or hunting for
mermaid's purses caught up in the seaweed. Forgotten that
they had shared dreams with each other and swum in storms
together.

'Time moves on, Mel,' Juliana sighed, as if Melody didn't
already know that. Of course she knew that time moved on –
July was almost upon her and June was simply slipping away
in the blink of an eye. 'Of course I used to love it here. It's
the seaside. I was a *child*. Aunty Flora was just the best aunty
anyone could possibly want. I still love it, but surely even you
can see that all these bungalows are getting old. The whole of
Shelly is getting old – it's dying.'

*Dying*. Melody echoed the word sadly inside her mind. 'It's
being murdered,' she said quietly.

Juliana sighed again, an exasperated whoosh of air that

continued even as she spoke. 'It's hardly being *murdered* for crying out loud. You do overdramatise things, Mel. These little houses were never built for living in permanently, you know that. They were supposed to be holiday homes, glorified beach huts. It's nothing but a shanty town now and you really can't live here forever. You don't have central heating and you freeze your tits off in winter, you know you do.'

It was true, Melody did get very cold in winter but she'd got very cold in winter her whole life. She was used to it. Apart from 1963, when it was so cold they had to wear woollen hats and socks in bed, they had managed. She smiled at the memory, recalling how, that year, Flora had to bring the paraffin heater into the bedrooms just so that she and Milo could get out of bed in the mornings. How ice would form on the inside of the windows in thick layers and snow had banked up against the sides of Spindrift, cascading inside when they opened the door.

It was the year Melody discovered what it might have felt like to be Milo. What it felt like to be mainly confined to the house, restricted by something you couldn't control. But, because of that, it was also the year she'd begun her stories for him. The year she realised how, through those stories, she could make her little brother's world so much bigger and more exciting than the one he had.

'What on earth are you smiling about?' Juliana asked.

Melody pictured the old cutlass that Daniel had made Milo all those years ago and which was still in his bedroom propped against his wardrobe. She remembered making up her first story about a pirate, and a galleon made entirely out of sea shells, which she'd told while their warm breath clouded in the cold air. 'I'm smiling about the Big Freeze,' she said.

'And that was a good thing?'

Juliana's puzzled face caused a smile to play on Melody's lips. 'Yes,' she said. 'Yes, it was a *very* good thing.'

'You're a weird one, Mel.' Juliana laughed as she gave Melody the kind of smile that said she liked something but couldn't fathom out why.

'Is it weird to hold on to memories?' Melody asked her. She wasn't really asking, of course, because she didn't think it was weird in the slightest. To her, it felt as if life were a mosaic and each memory was a piece of it – to forget anything would be to lose a piece of life.

'Is that what *this* is all about then?' Juliana turned full circle in the room, scanning everything she could see. 'About holding on to memories?'

Melody nodded silently. Her memories were everywhere. They were in the flotsam and jetsam she collected from the beach. In the treasures she found for Milo and the stories that she told for him and the newspapers they rested upon. They were in his bedroom when she sat in his wheelchair and in his handprints which were still visible from having once dipped them in white gloss paint and pressed them against the outside wall of Spindrift. Two sets of perfect white handprints had outlived the sounds of their father shouting at him for doing it.

The memory of Flora was everywhere. She was in her paintings that decorated the walls and in her knitting patterns in the magazine rack. The smell of her perfume, Lily of the Valley, had not faded from her handkerchief or from the collar of her blouse even after twelve years. A mother's hug was still inside her yellow towelling dressing gown. When Melody slipped it on and pressed the cuffs to her cheek she could feel her embrace once more.

'It's been long enough, Mel.' Juliana sat down opposite her and her voice was gentle. 'Their coats are still on the hooks in the hall. They don't need them any more. *You* don't need them as memories any more, those memories will be in your mind... forever.'

'Their belongings are staying. Their coats, like everything else, are part of the furnishing. If I take them away it would be like moving a painting or taking down a curtain. It would leave a space. I don't *want* a space.' Melody pushed her words through her tightening throat. She still had another whole year to keep everything exactly as it was. Flora and Milo might not need their things any more but she did.

'I don't want to put life, theirs or mine or anyone's, into bags and take it all away from here. I *can't* let them do that to us.' Her fear over her fragile future was showing and a tidal wave of awfulness was about to drown her if she didn't escape from it. 'I'll make us a hot drink.' Cursing herself, she stood up but as she tried to make her way to the kitchen Juliana caught her sharply by the wrist.

'Woah! You just went down a whole different path, Mel. *Who* is going to do *what*? What is it that you're not telling me?'

Melody looked down at the familiar features of Juliana's face and wished there was no make-up on it, that the carefully applied foundation and coloured mascara didn't mask it. She sighed resignedly. Juliana obviously had her own problems, too, so perhaps it was only fair that they both came clean with each other. 'How long are you staying?' she asked.

Juliana was looking increasingly perplexed. 'What's that got to do with whatever it is that you can't let happen?'

'Because I'm pretty sure we've *both* got a lot we need to talk about.' Melody spoke quietly and her fingers found Juliana's until they were holding hands – a bridge across the broken structure of each other's lives. 'I'll make us that drink, shall I? I get the feeling we're going to need a *lot* of coffee.'

'And I've got a feeling that we're going to need a *lot* of wine,' Juliana called. 'And as you've only got little wine glasses, we may have to use your mugs after all.'

Melody filled the kettle and waited for it to boil, listening to the familiar sound of thousands of bubbles collapsing and bursting inside it. Rain slashed against the window pane and ran in rivulets down the glass while the tap dripped steadily onto the scratched stainless steel of her sink. She put granulated coffee into two mugs, thinking that Juliana probably drank her coffee out of tiny little cups like the French. She could have used her mother's china tea set for Juliana, she supposed, but she'd never been keen on it because the memories attached to it were so complicated. They spoke of the fancy show that Isobel and Gordon's visits had instigated. Her old mugs came from Walton's department store and they always reminded her that they were purchased on the same day that her father had bought her a very exciting gift. Her very own transistor radio which could fit in her pocket and came with an earpiece.

Taking a bottle of milk from the fridge she poured a little into the mugs. She wasn't sure what sort of conversation she would end up having with Juliana – perhaps a gruelling unravelling of the structure of their lives. Yet, as the kettle boiled and a cloud of steam rose into the air around it, she became aware that, even though life had taken them both on different paths, in their hour of need, it was each other they could turn to for support. The realisation of that began to grow inside her like a little brown seed which promised a flower.

Rain continued in a deafening rally on the roof of Spindrift, flinging itself against the windows as Melody handed Juliana her steaming mug of coffee. 'Here,' she said, sitting down in the armchair opposite and tucking her legs comfortably underneath herself. Such was the anticipation that had bloomed between them in the last few minutes, a silence grew and it was clear that neither was keen to begin.

'You start, Jules.' Melody studied a tiny chip on the rim of her mug, seeing, with disappointment, how a thin grey line ran down the length of the glaze.

'Me?' Juliana flushed a little, looking around the room as if searching for something in a hurry to delay. 'I feel as if we should put me aside for the moment and start with you.'

'No, *you* start,' Melody repeated firmly. 'The investigation into my quirks and failings can wait. Your situation sounds as if it's a trifle more urgent than mine. You're running from something and you've landed here.'

Juliana examined her nails, peering into her coffee where her thoughts were floating on the surface of it. 'You're right, I have *landed* on you rather than just paying you a visit and I realise that's selfish after it's been so long. I should have been more upfront with you and I'm sorry.'

'Apology accepted.' Melody dipped her head as a gentle

acknowledgement. She was dying to find out more about what had happened with Alastair and, judging by Juliana's face, it was something big.

'I'm buying time by being here,' Juliana began.

'For what?' Melody blew across the surface of her drink before talking a scalding sip. Rain suddenly came down even harder with a noise like pebbles beating against the roof and they both looked upwards as if they could see the sound of it.

'Time to work out what I want from life. What I want for myself... my marriage.' Juliana sighed. She looked directly at Melody, her brown eyes giving away a terrible kind of despair, making Melody feel sorry for her. Perfection was a high place to fall from and Juliana had obviously hit the ground hard.

'With the dick?' Melody queried, knowing she was asking the kind of question that suggested she already knew the answer.

'Yes, the dick.' Juliana took a sip of her coffee and grimaced slightly at the taste. 'My *husband* has been having an affair.'

She said it almost as if she were announcing something innocuous such as 'I must remember to put radishes on my grocery list,' but her face told a different story. Melody gasped, her jaw dropping so low she was in danger of her mandibles detaching. *What an utter pig*, she thought, imagining that if Alastair walked into the room right now she'd possibly punch the living daylights out of him. She didn't know quite what she'd been expecting Alastair to have done but in truth an *affair* wasn't it. Juliana was everything. She was intelligent, articulate, fashionable... *glorious*. Melody hadn't ever held Alastair in high regard but, even for him, this was low.

Two red patches started to bloom on Juliana's cheeks and

she was working her jaw as if she'd unleashed a beast of anger and was chewing on it.

'Who's he having an affair with?' Melody asked, wondering immediately afterwards why she'd bothered to voice such a question. She hardly knew any of the people they did. She ran her memory through the crowd that had been at their wedding, searching her mind for any contenders. It had been an enormous, flamboyant affair, a veritable ostentation of fascinators that had put her off ever having such a wedding herself. Had some woman who'd attended their special day been green with envy at Juliana's catch? Or had Alastair taken advantage of his position with a member of staff from his office?

'It's my best friend!' Juliana blurted.

'Tell me you don't mean Sonia. Sonia who you've known forever?' Melody squealed.

'Yes, Sonia who I've known forever,' Juliana replied flatly.

'Oh, that's shit.'

'Yes,' agreed Juliana. 'It's a massive double dose of hot shit.'

'And you're absolutely sure?' Melody pressed.

'Mmmm, fairly sure,' Juliana replied thoughtfully. She stared at nothing in particular for a minute as if pondering something. 'I could be wrong... but unless Sonia had lost something valuable in her knickers and Alastair was helping her look for it... with his *face*, I'd say I'm correct. I came home unexpectedly early from a shopping trip bringing fresh pastries from the bakers for Alastair only to find that he was already having his lunch!'

Melody gasped again, but this time the gasp, inflating her chest fit to burst, threatened to come back out again on a flow of inappropriate laughter. She had to clap her hand over her mouth to smother it.

'They were in my house, Mel. In my living room on my *cream* sofa.'

'The *cream* sofa,' Melody repeated, her words muffled by her hand which was still firmly over her mouth.

'Yes, the cream sofa… and what's more… it's *new*,' Juliana cried then. The word 'new' coming out in such a long agonised wail that it caused Melody to leap off her chair and rush to her side. The laughter, instantly replaced with a terrible anger towards Alastair and Sonia, prompted her to thrust both arms around Juliana, hugging her tightly to her chest.

'Oh, Jules,' she mollified, a torrent of responses rushing through her mind, each punctuated with the worst swear words she could possibly muster. But as Juliana sagged in her arms, laying a weeping head upon her shoulder, she decided to hold back on the swearing. There was no need to add crudity to a situation that was already crude. She really didn't know what to say and instead came out with a simple, and rather pathetic, 'Why?'

'Why, what?' Juliana sniffed. 'Why would they do that on my cream sofa?'

Melody smiled mirthlessly into her hair. 'Why, when he had it all, would he possibly want more?'

'I don't *know*,' Juliana wailed, a loud, fresh burst of sadness which leaked a messy patch of make-up onto Melody's dress. 'And with my best *friend*, too.'

'She's obviously not your best friend and by the sound of it she never was. Friends don't do that to each other, do they?'

'*No*,' Juliana wailed again.

'No, exactly. So, as for buying time regarding a decision

over your marriage, it sounds as if your husband *and* your best friend have already made that decision for you, don't you think?' There was no reply. Only the sound of the rain and the occasional gurgle in Juliana's nose to be heard. 'Don't you think?' Melody pressed.

Juliana sat up slowly, pulling away, searching Melody's eyes as if for an answer, or perhaps for strength. Her mouth flapped with words that couldn't make their way out and two smears of wet mascara ran across her cheeks. She anxiously pushed her fingers through her hair but her nails caught in all the hairspray. With the confession out in the open, Juliana was now a complete and utter mess. Melody studied the apparition in front of her, remembering how Juliana used to arrive for the summer ready to shake off the regimentation of a British boarding school, so desperate to free herself from the confines of her privileged upbringing. She'd always been the kind of girl who would arrive in her best clothes yet fling them off as soon as she was able in order to climb the rocks or dance barefoot in the sand. Melody felt bad for the sad, sniffing, snotting vision in front of her and didn't quite know where to start to make her feel better. This situation was going to take some delicate handling and something pretty special, she decided.

Juliana pressed her palms to her eyes, attempting to wipe away her tears, sounding more mournful by the minute. 'That's why I wanted to buy time by coming here. I don't know what to think any more. Mummy would be horrified if I left him, even though it wasn't my fault. She thrives on the idea that I've "made it" in life and that I'm married to a wealthy banker. She'll think that it was me who messed it all up somehow. I can hear her now, "What will the Presswell-Barratts think or the members of the Croquet Association?" You don't understand, Mel, my life is *not* the sort of life you walk away from.'

Melody thought she could understand. She could absolutely hear her Aunt Isobel talking. Juliana was right, she would expect her to get on with her marriage, to think of England and simply keep her personal problems behind closed doors. The photograph and the information she'd found was enough evidence to know that Isobel was the kind of person who would do anything to ensure a secret was kept. Despite all that, for Melody, it was not enough to ruin a life over. 'If it were me I'd want to file for divorce.'

'It's not that easy,' Juliana groaned. 'I'm not sure I've got the strength to go it alone.'

'In my opinion you're stronger than you think, Jules.' Melody levered herself up from the sofa and nipped into the bathroom, returning with a bottle of face cleanser and a glass jar of cotton-wool balls. She handed them to Juliana. 'For your face,' she said, giving her a wooden hand mirror. 'It's covered in streaks of mascara.'

'Oh my word!' Juliana inspected her reflection in the mirror and hurriedly moistened a cotton-wool ball with cleanser. Five cotton-wool balls later, along with plenty of wiping and dabbing, her face was clear of make-up but covered in blotches.

Feeling sorry for her, Melody had an idea. 'Come on, you.' She put the cleanser and cotton wool aside and pulled Juliana to her feet. Going to the doors that led out to the terrace, she opened them and secured them to the sides by two iron hooks screwed to the exterior wall. Rain still lashed down in torrents and splashed onto the concrete outside and the wind blew some of it inside Spindrift, spraying the floor with dark droplets.

'What are you doing?' Juliana shivered as Melody dragged her towards the grey downpour. The sea, thankfully calmer than it was but still high against the footings upon which the bungalows stood, appeared to be almost boiling with the force of dancing rain on its surface.

'It's more what are *we going* to do,' Melody answered mischievously. Then, she hitched up her dress and made a knot in the fabric of it. 'Come on, we're going swimming in the rain.' She grinned broadly at a horrified Juliana who stepped back as the rain splashed into Spindrift against her legs.

'You've still got your clothes on. Are you batty?' she complained.

'Yes, I have and yes, I probably am!' Melody's hair was already plastered to her head and her dress so wet it clung to her skin, but she beckoned for Juliana to join her.

'You're joking,' Juliana cried, folding her arms around her body. 'We'll get swept out to sea.'

Melody simply laughed out loud. 'It's a rising tide so it will bring us in rather than take us out, it's quite safe. It isn't a rough sea, just a high one. *Come on*, it's almost as if it's come to collect us,' she urged. Then she spun around on her toes, unlatched the gate and, with the high water almost covering the top step of the wooden ladder, she jumped in. Seconds later she was breaking the surface again with a yell of delight.

'Is it cold?' Juliana called out to her, her expression still one of horror but with a flicker of the old Juliana within it.

Melody ducked her head under again and swam to the ladder, looking up at Juliana and grinning with all the appeal she could muster. 'Of course it's cold. It's the English flippin' Channel. It's hardly a spa bath, but that's what makes it totally fantastic.' A couple of the neighbours came to their windows, laughing and waving, and Mrs Galespie opened her door and called out, 'You're off your bleedin' nut!'

Guardedly, but much to Melody's delight, Juliana slipped off her house shoes and peeled off her tights, unclipped a delicate gold watch and placed it on the windowsill. Melody, still by the ladder, smiled fit to burst, the swell of the waves bobbing her up and down. Finally, Juliana took cautious steps across the terrace, where the rain instantly sprinkled her carefully styled hair with a thousand watery beads.

'I can't believe I'm doing this,' she said, dipping a foot in the water and instantly withdrawing it and grimacing. 'I tell you that my husband is having an affair and your solution is to force me into the ocean fully dressed!'

Melody laughed out loud again and swam away from the ladder, making space for Juliana to get in. 'I have my reasons,' she called, her voice almost lost by the sound of the rain.

'And they would be?' Juliana shivered.

'To rediscover *you*,' Melody shouted. 'We're finding Juliana, that's what we're doing.'

# 12

'You're lucky.' Juliana sat cross-legged on the bed in front of Melody who sat cross-legged on the bed opposite her. They still had their pyjamas on with a plate of hot buttered crumpets for breakfast on the blanket between them.

'Milo's still asleep, girls, so keep the noise down, all right?' Flora placed two of her brand-new mugs filled with hot chocolate, each with a fancy geometric design, on the bedside table then kissed them both good morning. Juliana, Melody noticed, watched Flora leave the room with a kind of envious awe, her cheeks positively shining as the door closed behind her. As soon as they were alone again she turned to Melody.

'Your mum is amazing. She brings you breakfast in *bed*. Mummy would never, *ever* let me do that. I'm not even allowed to take a drink to bed unless it's water.' Juliana rolled her eyes and adopted a silly voice. 'Mummy says things like, *you might spill it on the bed linen*, or *it's not good for your teeth, darling*.' She took a huge bite out of her crumpet, grinning with hot butter on her lips and spilling down her chin. Melody did the same and spoke through her mouthful.

'My mum says that treats should be something you don't do all the time. That's what makes them treats.' She swallowed the soft, warm buttery crumpet then washed it down with a mouthful of hot chocolate. It travelled down her throat and landed on top of the place inside her where gladness lived. Flora was *her* mum and she *was* amazing. At the same time she felt sorry for Juliana that Aunt Isobel wasn't so forgiving. 'Does your mum ever let you have treats?' she asked, her mind already racing with all the boundaries her own mother pushed. Once, Flora had called the school to tell them Melody was sick just so that they could go into town to eat banana splits in the Golden Egg for Milo's birthday. Those banana splits had tasted like the sweetest nectar in the whole wide world.

'Yes,' Juliana answered. 'I'm allowed sweets on a Saturday and ice-cream on a Sunday. I'm also allowed to stay up late when my parents have evening soirées.'

'What's a soirée?' Melody said, wondering if her own mother had soirées that she'd never told her about.

'It's a fancy evening party where everyone dresses up in lovely clothes and they drink out of our best glasses. Sometimes I wear my best dress and play the piano for everyone.'

'Sounds riveting,' Melody said, thinking quite the opposite. Her mother had definitely never had one of those soirée things. She stifled a yawn.

'It's fun. Sometimes Sonia stays for a sleepover. She's my very *best* friend… other than you, of course,' she added hastily. 'You're like my other best friend even though you're older than me and my cousin. We're *more* than just cousins, though, aren't we?' Juliana reached a hand out for Melody who took it, nodding solemnly. She didn't have another best friend, she had Milo and she had Juliana, but yes, they were more than just family – they were everything.

'I creep down and raid the fridge at night once everyone has gone home,' Juliana confessed, giving a mischievous smile as if this was a daring feat. 'There's always something yummy left over. Vol-au-vents or cheese and pineapple on sticks. And sometimes, on other days when Mummy's out doing something with one of her societies, Pops and I make cake. He lets me have the leftover mixture from the bowl. He's not like other dads. Even though he works in an office and wears a suit and carries a briefcase, he's really good at baking.'

This time it was Melody's turn to feel a stab of envy. She imagined Juliana and Uncle Gordon in their big kitchen baking cakes together while her own father had done a *moonlight flit*, as her mother called it, or *buggered off*, as Aunt Isobel called it. Over the years it hadn't gone unnoticed by Melody that when Juliana talked about Uncle Gordon her voice became soft and her words breathed out on a drift of positivity. Aunt Isobel wasn't a bad person but she wasn't like Uncle Gordon. Uncle Gordon went with the flow and swayed with the breeze, he laughed easily and ruffled Melody's hair, he pulled out sweets from his pockets when no one was looking and he'd wink at them. When they all took the sweets from his hand, he'd put his finger to his lips with a shush. Melody loved him. Her own father, although she had loved him in a way that hurt too much to think about, had not been as easy-going as Uncle Gordon. She'd grown to accept her father's absence but from time to time she'd sit quietly by his rubber boots, still in the hallway by the door, and pray that he'd come back. With sadness she pushed him to the back of her mind and brought herself back to Juliana.

'Sonia and I are going to the same school when we're

eleven. It's a boarding school. But we'll come home in the holidays so I'm still coming to stay with you in the summer.'

'How… *Malory Towers*,' gushed Melody. 'Do you think you'll have midnight feasts and play lacrosse?' She felt a thrill of excitement at the idea of Juliana's new school. She enjoyed her own school and couldn't bear the thought of leaving Flora or Milo for boarding school but that didn't stop her devouring every book that had ever been written about it.

'Maybe,' Juliana answered. 'But Sonia's sister already goes there. She says they have to eat horrible food and they're forced to trudge around in the cold and the mud to win sports trophies. She says everything is set to an agenda and that they're not allowed to leave the boundary or climb the trees. I don't suppose I'll be running barefoot through the grass like you can in the sand. That's why you're *so* lucky.' She took Melody's other hand and, still sitting cross-legged facing each other, they looked deep into each other's eyes. 'I sometimes try to imagine that I live here. That I can have bed picnics or jump down onto the beach whenever I want. That I can go barefoot and be free like you are.'

Melody fought for the right reaction. Clearly her cousin, who arrived every summer dressed to the nines, having mastered a new talent, be it music or maths or poetry recitals, wanted a simpler life than the one she had. She wanted the life that Melody had.

'I've had an idea,' Melody said brightly. 'Every summer, let's pretend that you live here in Shelly and that Spindrift is your home. And while you're here we'll make sure that we just do whatever it is that we want to do. We'll raid the fridge whenever we want to and run barefoot in the sand every day like wild things and we'll fling ourselves into the sea with all our clothes on.' At that, they squeezed each other's hands tightly before shoving the rest of their crumpets into their mouths. Then they climbed off the beds, jumped down onto the sand and ran straight into the sea, still in their pyjamas.

# 13

Melody trod water with her face tipped up towards the sky, letting the driving rain splash on her cheeks and eyelashes. 'Swim with me, Jules,' she called again. 'Remember how we used to do this when we were young? In sunshine or in storms, we said. We could get all metaphorical about it or you could just take a leap.'

Juliana took a leap. All of a sudden she ran, her long legs striding out into the air, shouting as she used to do when she was a child, 'YABADABADOO!' She broke the surface of the water, yelling her head off. 'Ohhh, fuck me, Mel, it's *freezing*.'

'It's only water,' laughed Melody. 'Remember when you used not to care about such things.'

Juliana was treading water and shouting above the noise of the rain on the sea. 'I'm a grown woman. I don't make sandcastles or go crabbing either. I'm a deckchair, cocktail and good book kind of girl these days. Not a freeze my bits off in the English Channel wearing Valentino kind of girl.'

'You are today,' Melody laughed. 'And didn't you say Alastair bought you that outfit?' Melody looked down at Juliana where the bright colour of her dress was visible below the surface of a grey sea.

'Yes. He said I look sexy in pink,' she replied. Then she laughed. 'I don't look sexy now.'

Melody laughed, too, but the reference to Alastair made her cringe. She thought Juliana looked more beautiful than she ever had before, her previously big hair now hanging down her back in strawberry-blonde tendrils. Melody pushed her feet out in front of her until she was lying flat in the water and Juliana copied her.

'Oh look! My dress has gone completely see-through,' Juliana laughed. They both looked down at her floating body, where her matching bra and pants were visible to the world through the sheer wet fabric of her dress. 'Oh, who cares?' she laughed.

'Yes, who cares?' laughed Melody. They were lying on a floating, watery bed, blanketed by a tumbling sky like the floating treasures that washed up on the shore. They were a gathering. A story. A memory in themselves. She imagined writing a story about it and yet, because of the secret she still kept, this time she didn't know what the ending should be.

They floated there rocked by the waves, the rain splashing on their faces until Melody didn't know whether to smile or cry with the sweetness of it. She reached for Juliana's hand. 'It's wonderful, isn't it?' she called.

'Do you know what?' Juliana replied, hooking her fingers into Melody's hand. 'It is! It really is.'

When at last they climbed up the wooden ladder, cold, shivering and totally invigorated, Melody remembered the bygone years when Flora would greet them in from the sea with warm dry towels in her arms. Only this time it wasn't Flora who was there to greet them – it was Big Joe Wiley.

'I saw you two out there and thought you might appreciate

sustenance,' he called over the noise of the rain, his face a sheen of wet with droplets cascading down his hair and over his thin waterproof jacket.

He'd let himself in around the side of Spindrift and now stood on the terrace holding a wicker box. 'Hot sausage rolls and a flask of warm apple cider?' He kicked his deck shoes off and stepped inside and they followed him in, leaving a trail of wet splashes on the floor.

Dried and dressed and warm again, Melody and Juliana sat opposite him, side by side on the sofa, their tousled hair hanging around their shoulders. Three mugs of warm cider filled the room with the scent of cinnamon and apples while they all ate the sausage rolls, flakes of puff pastry clinging to their lips.

'These are delicious,' Melody said, as the taste of salty pork with sage and onion filled her mouth.

'I made them,' replied Joe coolly. 'I nearly joined you when I saw you both flinging yourselves into the sea in the middle of a rainstorm.' Big Joe, relaxed in his chair, looking, as he always did, tanned and strong and totally at ease with himself. 'Except I decided it might be a good idea to bring warm sustenance instead.' He glanced at Juliana and raised an eyebrow. 'Yabadabadoo?'

Juliana grinned. 'For old times' sake. I used to shout that as a child,' she replied.

'And did you also shout, "Fuck me it's freezing" when you were a child?' he laughed.

'Maybe not, but it *was* freezing.' She pretended to shiver and took a sip of her warm apple cider.

'You should have joined us, Joe.' Melody tried to sound

casual about it but inside she was privately wishing that he had.

'Maybe Sunday,' he said. 'Will you be here until then, Juliana?'

'Well…' Juliana looked at Melody, appealing for inspiration over the right thing to say. 'I think I might be here for a little while,' she replied. 'I've got some things to sort out. This and that, you know. Bits and bobs.' The corners of her mouth twitched and Melody was fearful that Juliana might burst into tears again. To give way in front of an audience, even if it was Big Joe, would be the last thing she'd want. She leant into Juliana's side in a silent show of support.

'She's working on a project so she's come to sunny Exmouth to plan it.'

'What sort of project?' Joe asked.

'Um, it's…' Juliana looked again to Melody for answers.

'It's for her business – interior design,' Melody shot in. 'Her client wants a coastal theme in her house and Juliana is here searching for inspiration.'

Joe nodded, with casual interest. 'Then you may not have to search that far because Melody here has got a creative eye, you know.'

As he said it Melody blushed, while Juliana, confused, made a brief but damning survey of Spindrift. 'She *has*?'

'She has!' Joe insisted. 'Mark my words. I've noticed her combing the beach with her basket and I've seen what she collects… and what she does with it.' He looked at Melody then, with such intensity that she thought he could see right inside her. He'd noticed her, she thought happily. 'And I hate to be the bearer of bad news but sunny Exmouth might not be that sunny for a while. The rain will ease off in the night and tomorrow should be hot – possibly the next day, too, but by Sunday it's supposed to be teeming again.'

'Great.' Juliana rolled her eyes with disappointment and peered outside at the weather which was still a grey, misty blur over the sea. 'I've packed for sunshine by the coast. I've brought a selection of bikinis and a Vivienne Westwood sun hat which I need to get some use out of. By next summer the fashion will probably have changed and I'll want to sun myself on the terrace in something current.'

'Next year?' A frown appeared on Joe's face. 'By next year everything will have…'

'Thank you, Joe!' Melody abruptly stood up and took Joe's empty plate and half-finished mug of cider from him. 'The sausage rolls were delicious, as was the apple cider, but Juliana and I need to dry our hair.' She put the lid back on his flask, took the container that had held the sausage rolls, placed them back in his bag and handed him his waterproof jacket. A bewildered Joe, in no doubt that he had just been given his marching orders, bid Juliana goodnight and followed Melody to the front door. 'I still haven't told her what's happening to Shelly,' Melody whispered, placing a silencing finger to her lips.

'Why?' Joe whispered back.

'Because I'm going to tell her tomorrow, that's why. We've agreed to talk. And until now I haven't been ready to face the whole conversation with her about where I'll go and what I'll do. I know she and her parents will probably try to insist I go to Gloucestershire to be near them.'

'Oh,' he breathed softly. 'And you don't want that, I suppose?'

'No,' she whispered.

As he looked down at her so tenderly she felt sad, as if she were an old soft toy whose stitching had come undone. Then, he leant towards her and, for the first time since she'd known him, he kissed her goodbye, brushing her cheek with his lips and lingering just long enough for the scent of cider on his warm breath to blend with the scent of salty skin and drying rain. Raising a hand to her cheek, where his stubble still prickled and his lips had landed, soft as the wings of a bird, she didn't know how to react.

'We all have to leave, Melody,' he said softly. 'You don't need to cope with everything on your own.'

'I... I'm used to coping on my own,' she stuttered.

The look he gave her wasn't easy to read. It was fleeting and without any light to his eyes and he dipped his head by way of a parting gesture, closing the door behind him. Melody stayed rooted to the spot, unsure of what had just happened and still holding her cheek, until Juliana called out.

'What are you doing lurking in the hallway, Mel?'

Melody came back into the sitting room and stood by the doors to the terrace. A lamp in Joe's bungalow came on throwing a glow of orange through his curtains and she could see his silhouette moving inside. She touched her cheek again and kicked herself over the missed opportunity, hardly daring to hope that maybe he liked her too.

'You're a bit red, are you OK?' Juliana asked.

Melody turned away to hide her emotions just as a chink in the clouds threw a ribbon of light upon the iron-grey sea. The tide had started to retreat and soon an abundance of seaweed, always brought in by the swell of such a sea as this, would be lying in swathes of green along the beach.

'We're going to have an invasion of seaweed,' Melody said by way of an answer. 'We'll be out there first thing tomorrow clearing it, me and Joe and some of the others who have got boats.'

'That's nice,' Juliana said disinterestedly.

She'd curled up on the sofa taking the space that Melody had left and was leaning, swollen-eyed against the cushions. Despite their uplifting swim, the evidence of Juliana's upset was clear and Melody did her best to push her own feelings aside. 'Do you fancy doing anything?' she asked kindly. 'A game, some television?

Juliana shook her head. 'Absolutely nothing. I've only just got warm and I'm drained. Admitting that my life isn't all it's cracked up to be has taken the stuffing right out of me so I think I'll just read my book, if you don't mind.'

Melody nodded, tearing her gaze away from Joe Wiley's bungalow. She was happy to read, she was always happy to read, and so, curling up on the other chair, she opened her book where her homemade bookmark, bound with striped thread and the lace of an old handkerchief, held the page for her. Barely two lines in, though, she looked across at Juliana, taking in the sight of her pinched cheeks and bedraggled hair and felt worried.

'Are you OK, Jules? It's big – you know, all that awful stuff about Alastair. You're going to need time to get over it and I want you to know that if you stay here you've got all the time in the world.' As soon as her generous words were out of her mouth she realised they weren't exactly true. Of course she couldn't give Juliana all the time in the world – there was so very little time left.

Tears sprang immediately to Juliana's eyes and Melody

felt even worse for triggering them again. 'I *do* need some time, Mel, you're right. I feel so bruised by everything and I can't seem to stop crying.' The tears spilt even more. 'I cried all the way down here from Cheltenham and then had to pull over at the esplanade to reapply my make-up before I got to you. And, now that I've told you, I don't even know if I feel better for sharing it or worse for admitting it to myself.' She hiccoughed with sadness and placed a hand over her mouth. 'I'll be all right. I'll bounce back, I always do.'

Melody nodded sympathetically and returned to her book. But again, no more than two lines in, she found herself looking out of the window. It had been two days since her last chance to go beachcombing and now, with the aftermath of the spring tide, the need was calling to her again, like a mermaid's song luring her in. She would go in the morning before the seaweed clear-up, she decided.

She lowered her book. 'I'm going to go for a walk along the beach at first light. Do you fancy coming? I could wake you with a nice cup of tea and we could watch the sunrise. It will be nice.'

Juliana looked surprised. 'What time is first light?'

'About five a.m.,' Melody answered. To her mind, the idea of getting up before everyone else and being the first to tread the smooth, sea-washed sand was a thrill. It was the best thing she could offer to soothe Juliana's troubled mind. They'd done it as children in the summer holidays before Milo woke, slipping on their shorts and tee-shirts and jumping down onto the cool sand to hunt for shells or beadlet anemones stuck like red blobs of jam to the rocks.

But Juliana pulled a face and smothered a yawn. 'Thank

you but I shall be in bed doing what sensible people do at that unearthly hour. I shall be sleeping.'

Melody nodded. It was sad that Juliana wouldn't experience the calming wonder that was an early morning by the sea but, if she was honest with herself, picking her way through the treasures of the sea was something she preferred to do alone.

They both fell silent reading their books, the soothing sound of rain against the roof of Spindrift. This time, it was Juliana who put her book down. 'What did Joe mean when he started to say that by next year everything will have... will have what?' She sat up a little against her cushion and waited, intrigued, for Melody to elaborate.

Melody shrugged and hid behind her book.

'Well?' Juliana pressed.

'Well... I'll tell you tomorrow – when it's my turn to talk.'

'OK, that's fair,' Juliana agreed. She read a few lines of her book then lowered it again. Despite her swollen eyes and red nose, she smiled mischievously. 'The beach dude isn't that bad, is he? And he can cook! I guess there's more to him than first meets the eye. Plus, I'm pretty positive he likes you.'

# 14

'I saved a sea turtle today, Milo.'

Melody placed a tangle of green fishing net on Milo's lap. 'This could have found its way to the Indian Ocean and either been mistaken for food by a leatherback or it might have become all caught up in it.'

She wiped at a film of sweat on her brow and tucked a lock of limp hair behind her ears. It was the hottest summer for as long as anyone could remember and the sea was calling her to swim. They were sitting together, she and Milo, stifled by the heat, their old parasol barely offering protection from the intensity of the sun.

Melody lowered her voice so that Flora, who was inside painting a canvas, couldn't hear. 'Milo, I've got a great idea how to use this netting to make a new surround for our old hall mirror. Mum will love it.' She fingered the green fibre and pictured how it would look entwined with some sea-bleached rope she had found a few days ago. She had enough now to fashion a beautiful frame of knots and coils all around the mirror and to give it a whole new lease of life.

Milo agreed, trying to nod his head. His hair was sticking

to his sweaty face and Melody picked up a magazine and used it to fan them both, wafts of warm air brushing their skin. Putting the magazine down, she reached into her basket then taking Milo's hand she turned it over, dropping a ragged strip of yellow and red cloth into his palm.

'I found this wedged in the rocks over by the pier.' She smoothed it out with her fingers so that a pattern of coloured stripes could be seen. 'How we missed this on all our adventures over the years I'll never know. It's been there for nearly four hundred years, torn from the clothes of a Barbary pirate when he attacked our shores in the dark of night. Imagine, Milo, the turbans and the swords and the chaos!'

Milo curled his hand around the cloth and widened his eyes. 'Barbary pirate,' he slurred.

'Barbary pirate,' Melody confirmed, picking up the magazine again and fanning them both as best she could. 'Remember? I got you a book about Barbary pirates from the library.' Milo, of course, had always loved pirates and still did but the games they'd played as children were long gone. At nineteen, Milo no longer floated in a galleon made from the inflated inner tubes of a lorry tyre on the sea. He would no longer beach his imaginary ship on the shore and shout 'SHIVER ME TIMBERS' at the top of his voice or pretend that shells were treasure or that juice drunk from the neck of old glass bottles was rum.

Holding a drink up to Milo's mouth, Melody took the cloth from his hand. She 'Yo, ho, ho'd at him and they grinned at each other before he sucked thirstily from the straw, a dribble of liquid escaping and running down his chin. She wiped it away with a towel. 'I shall sew strips of this Barbary cloth with a piece of this handkerchief to make a bookmark.'

She showed him a white cotton square, edged in lace, that she'd found and, running the pad of her index finger over the initials DSM, she wondered who had so delicately embroidered them out of the thread of blue silk. Little blue forget-me-nots were also embroidered next to the initials, each with tiny yellow and green centres.

'This handkerchief tells quite a different kind of story. A beautiful story…' she began, hoping that the person to whom it had once belonged now lived forever in someone's heart, never to be forgotten. 'It's a lovers' handkerchief, Milo,' she began. 'Forget-me-nots are a symbol of true love.'

Milo interrupted her with anguished sounds. He was looking wistfully at the sea where people were cooling themselves from the heatwave. His words dragged from his throat now, catching in his jaw as he worked on them. She saw how the sweat sheened on his face and clung to his damp hair in the heat. Long John was, at last, winning his fight, taking her brother's voice as surely as he was taking his body. The days when she and Flora could help him get in and out of the water were in the past.

'I can't get you there, Milo. I'm so sorry.' She bit her lip with regret and reached for his hand, squeezing it tightly. The agony over her inability to do this for him ripped holes in her heart. Even if she could get him down the wooden ladder to the beach, the task of getting him in and out of the water was too much. Milo, to her great sadness, carried on staring at the water and she felt the intensity of his frustration, deep within the core of her own self. How trapped he was by his chair and his stupid disease, and how stoically he dealt with it. It made her want to cry. But crying only ever happened alone and behind closed doors. She would muffle her grief into her pillow or smother it with the palms of her hands, emerging only with her chin raised, her back straight and her smile wide. This was what Flora had taught her. If Milo had to face it, then so could they.

Having an idea, though, she leapt from her chair and disappeared around the side of Spindrift, appearing, after some banging and clattering, with two coloured buckets they'd used as children to make sandcastles.

'Look!' she exclaimed. 'I'm going to bring the sea to you.' Then she tossed the buckets down onto the sand and climbed down the wooden ladder after them, grinning mischievously at him as she went. A few minutes later she was pouring cool sea water over her brother's arms and legs and he was grinning with delight as the water splashed over his wasted limbs. It trickled along his skin, dripping and pooling on the concrete beneath his feet. Misshapen sounds were coming from his throat and out of his mouth in an unmistakable request for 'more'.

'Glorious weather, isn't it?' Big Joe Wiley had just finished pulling *Wild Rose* ashore and was walking past with his catch of fresh mackerel. Barefoot and shirtless, he wore a pair of shorts and a beaded necklace and his hair hung in pale tendrils down his back. Melody, who was halfway down the ladder again to retrieve more water, turned to see him looking up at her. Seven fish hung by their tails from string, shimmering iridescent blue in the sunlight, bright against the tanned skin of his hands.

'It's a mighty fine heatwave if you're able to get to the sea,' she called back to him. 'Otherwise it's a complete nightmare.'

'You want to go in?' He addressed Milo directly, jerking his head in the direction of the water.

Milo forced out another sound. A definite affirmative. 'We can't get him there, Joe – why would you ask such a thing?' Melody scowled at him with dismay and her heart broke again at the look of hope on Milo's face. Big Joe knew Milo's physical dexterity wouldn't allow him to enjoy such pleasures any more. But Big Joe seemed not to care.

'Hang on, mate.' He ignored Melody's question and sprinted towards his bungalow. 'I'll just put my catch in ice and I'll be back.' They hung on, long enough for Big Joe to reach the end of the beach, hop up the wooden ladder leading to his bungalow, Pebbles, re-emerge and jump down onto the sand and sprint back. Within a couple of minutes he was standing on the terrace of Spindrift. 'May I?' he asked, indicating that he wanted to help Milo out of his chair. Both Milo and Melody looked at each other with hesitation but nodded silently and, within a short moment, Big Joe had Milo propped in his strong arms, helping him into a sitting position at the top of the wooden ladder.

'He's wearing his clothes.' Joe looked at Melody as he pointed that out, but then immediately addressed Milo again. 'But you don't care, do you mate? It's only shorts and a tee-shirt.' A lazy smile spread across Joe's face and Melody smiled back. It didn't matter in the slightest. It only mattered that her brother, after months of staring at the water, was finally going swimming again. With her help, Joe manoeuvred him down the ladder then, lifting him up in one swoop, waded into the sea with him. Milo's face and the delight that shone from it as his body, in the cool water, became weightless and free would make Melody love Big Joe Wiley for the rest of her life.

## 15

The rain, as Joe had predicted, finally stopped in the night and now the air was quiet again, all bar the rhythm of the waves. In the early hours of the morning, while Juliana slept, Melody slipped out of Spindrift wearing a thin cardigan over a cotton dress, her hair scooped into a tie-dyed bandanna, her basket on her arm. She climbed down the ladder onto the beach, the touch of Big Joe Wiley's kiss upon her cheek. She needed a moment to herself again, to walk the shore and to feel the breeze upon her face. She needed to ground herself then to sit in Milo's room and allow her thoughts to unravel and her mind to escape through the stories she'd tell him.

The seaweed, washed in by the high tide, was thicker than even she thought it would be. Piles of it carpeting the sand all the way up to the footings where the bungalows stood, the redolence of it pleasingly filling the air. The promised warmth was already showing itself in a lemony sun that peeked over the top of its blanket of night, shining a halo of light blue across the early sky.

Treading a path amid the seaweed, Melody lifted clumps of it in the hope of finding something interesting. She was rewarded. A fashion doll with a missing arm was caught in the green fronds and it dangled upside down by its feet, its waspish waist exposed between a pink crop top and a pair of silver trousers.

'*Gloria*,' Melody said matter of factly as she picked away the slimy green weed and popped her in the basket. By the time the sun was giving a confident heat to the air, painting the whole sky with a pretty kingfisher blue, Melody had cleared the beach of several plastic bottles and gathered items for at least three good stories to tell Milo.

With Juliana still in bed, she made herself comfortable once again in Milo's old wheelchair, apologising to him for her recent absence. 'I've had a lot going on, Milo,' she said quietly, hushing her voice. 'As you know, Jules is here.' She placed her gatherings on his bed and decided that the more *sensitive* details of Juliana's recent drama were best left unaired. Stroking the tangled mess of the doll's hair she allowed the first threads of a story to come to mind.

'Meet Gloria,' she began. 'She swam across the English Channel with only one arm and is in training for the women's freestyle Paralympics in October. Hers is a story about strength of character. About a woman who will never let anything in life hold her back.' She pressed the pad of her finger into the empty shoulder socket of the doll and was just working out how to elaborate on the empowerment of people with disabilities when she heard Juliana emerge from her bedroom.

'You're up!' Melody met her at the doorway and thought how tired and drawn she looked.

'I'm up,' Juliana replied. 'Joe said it was going to be warm today and I don't want to miss any of the sunshine.'

'How do you feel about joining in with the beach clean-up,

then?' Melody asked. But Juliana frowned, rubbing the sleep from her eyes, one side of her hair more matted than the other and a crease along her cheek where the pillow had been.

'I'm not sure it's my thing.' Juliana yawned as they went into the kitchen. She took a box of cornflakes from a cupboard and hugged it to her chest while Melody poured enough milk in two coffees to turn the brown liquid an unappealing shade of grey.

'You can come with me – in *Serendipity*. You used to love going out in my boat,' Melody pressed. 'You might find it fun.'

'Green slime is not my idea of fun,' Juliana said.

Disappointed, Melody took the cereal box out of Juliana's arms and poured it into a bowl, adding milk, sugar and a spoon and handing her back the full bowl. 'You're clearly no longer a morning person,' she murmured, nudging Juliana outside. The community were beginning to wake from their sleep, emerging onto their terraces to get the most out of the temporary change in weather. They greeted each other with the liberation of a summer's day while two children played on the mountains of seaweed and another waded and kicked through the boulders of sea foam.

When Juliana sat down to eat, Melody thought she looked pensive. She ate half-heartedly, wiping a stray cornflake from the corner of her mouth and licking the sugar off her lips. 'While you're out... I might use your telephone, if I may? I need to make a call.' She scooped another spoonful of cereal into her mouth and chewed thoughtfully while watching three more children who'd appeared and were now wading in the sea looking for fish below the clear surface.

Melody's suspicion was instantly aroused. 'You can,

of course you can, but... you're going to ring *him*, aren't you?' Juliana didn't flinch. She screwed her eyes against the brightness of the morning sun and kept her profile to Melody. She continued watching the children. 'You are, aren't you?' Melody pressed.

'Yes,' Juliana answered simply.

'But why? He... he did a terrible thing.' Melody could hardly believe what she was hearing. Was Juliana really running back to Alastair so soon?

'I know exactly what he did. I was there,' Juliana defended. 'But I've thought about it overnight. Even after everything I told you yesterday I realise that, despite what he did, I should try to work it out with him.' She put her bowl down on the table, still avoiding Melody's gaze as she spoke. 'Now that I've got it off my chest and slept on it I think maybe it was just a blip. I feel I should give him a second chance.'

'Does this blip *deserve* a second chance?' Melody asked, so aghast that the frown she was pulling hurt her face. If something similar had happened to her, no *friend* would *ever* get a second chance.

'He said at the time that he hadn't meant for the... *indiscretion...* to happen with Sonia. He said it was a "one thing led to another" situation and he begged me not to run off. He wanted me to stay at home to talk things through – but I wouldn't listen to him.'

To Melody, nothing she was hearing was helping Alastair's case. 'Did he really say, *"one thing led to another"*?' She had to stop herself laughing that this was his only defence.

'What if he's right, Mel? What if it was Sonia who came on to him? What if Sonia's jealous of everything I've got that she hasn't?'

'What have you got that Sonia hasn't?' Melody was incredulous. 'What could possibly be of more worth to anyone than the loyalty of a lifelong friendship?' She peered discreetly out of the doors, noticing that people involved with the beach clean-up were beginning to congregate outside. She was anxious to join them. Big Joe was on the terrace of his bungalow, finishing the dregs of a tea or coffee or whatever it was, and he caught her eye, raising his mug in salute. Melody waved her hand, a cautious, embarrassed acknowledgement, remembering the moment his lips brushed her cheek and kicking herself again for not grabbing the moment.

'Sonia could be jealous of my new car...' Juliana said, breaking into her thoughts.

Melody turned away from the window. 'That'll do it,' she said, rolling her eyes.

'And we've got a brand-new orangery.'

Melody whistled through her teeth. 'Wow, a new car and an *orangery*.' She sighed loudly. 'You've got a husband who can't be trusted, Jules – that's what you've got! Do you really think Alastair innocently tripped and fell into Sonia's lap and that she deviously leapt at the opportunity by pinning him there by his ears?' It was out before Melody could stop it and she winced at the reaction it caused. 'Sorry, Jules. That was unnecessary.' She placed an apologetic hand on Juliana's shoulder who, unsurprisingly, turned away.

Melody had overstepped the mark and she knew it. She went over to the wooden ladder. 'I'll give you some space. Forget I said that and use my telephone, if that's what you want.' She started to go down the ladder to the beach but hesitated for a moment. 'Promise me something, Jules?' She waited but there was no response except for a quiet sniff as

Juliana wiped at her eyes. 'Promise me that you won't go back to him just because you're scared to be without him. Alastair is not the better part of you. *You* are the better part of you.'

Then, she jumped the last few steps onto the sand and made her way to begin the beach clean-up.

Juliana was sunbathing on the terrace when they all got back but still she didn't join them. Not when they pulled their boats to shore, and not when they stripped off their clothes down to their swimming costumes to fall into the cool water with sweet relief. Melody didn't ask her if she'd spoken to Alastair when at last she climbed back up the ladder to Spindrift, and Juliana didn't enlighten her. Instead, their previous conversation thankfully brushed aside, they talked about nothing while Melody squeezed the water from her hair then plonked herself in the chair next to Juliana to dry off in the sun.

'I was thinking,' Juliana said when at last Melody was comfortable. 'I've told you what is going on in my life and now I think it's your turn.' Melody took a deep breath and in a quiet voice she began. 'I'm going to lose Spindrift.'

Juliana snapped her head round to face Melody and almost shrieked. '*What?* What do you mean you're going to *lose* Spindrift?'

'It's going to be bulldozed. Spindrift and all the other bungalows – the whole of Shelly flattened. They're calling it *regeneration*. My home. All our homes. They're to be torn down one by one until there's nothing left but dust. I've been evicted. We all have.'

Juliana sat bolt upright causing her sunglasses to slide

down her nose. Announcements such as this clearly needed her full physical attention. 'Jeez, Mel! That's awful. I don't understand. I thought you owned Spindrift?'

Melody sighed glumly. 'Yes, I do, but all these bungalows in Shelly were built on plots of land that have leases. Some leases have already expired and by next year most of the remaining ones will have expired, too. Mine runs out on the thirtieth of September next year so I've only got until then.'

'My God! I thought you were going to talk about the things that are in Spindrift, not Spindrift itself. I can't believe you've kept this to yourself all this time! Do Mummy and Pops know about this?' Juliana exhaled with such incredulity that Melody could feel the breath of it on her skin.

'No,' she said quietly. 'To tell you before now would have made it real and I couldn't face all the conversations about it. I still can't, if I'm honest, but the days and months are now rolling by so quickly that I don't have a choice.' Melody squinted over at her, a hand shielding her eyes from being blinded by the sun, a prickle of tears stinging her eyes. She blinked them back before they could betray her. 'Many people have already had to find other places to live. Next year it's my turn.'

'The whole of Shelly,' Juliana echoed sadly, whistling between her teeth.

'Eradicated,' Melody confirmed. 'Soon it will be all brand-new apartments and brand-new houses.' She pictured all the little bungalows disappearing and huge buildings replacing them, rising out of the ground and towering towards the sky, blocking out the sun. It hurt to say it. It really hurt.

'And what of the beach? Will it still be here?' Juliana looked out from Spindrift and down to the stretch of sand below. Children were playing there, two canoes, three rowing boats and one sailboat were beached and a fringe of Mirror dinghies were sailing by, their red or white sails inflated with sea breeze.

'I don't know but I expect they'll need some big old foundations to build a block of apartments here. My beach… our beach will probably still be here but not quite as we know it today.' Despite herself, a single tear escaped and dispersed into her hair. She brushed casually at it in the hope it had gone unnoticed, telling herself off for letting it go. She *wouldn't* cry.

'But… where will you *go*?' Juliana asked. She was still sitting upright and she still had a look of horror on her face.

'I don't know,' Melody answered honestly. That answer alone caused fear to fizz inside her. She had options, but those options crowded her, frightening her so much that she had to stop thinking about them. The idea of not being able to open her doors to her view of the sea whenever she wanted, or to simply jump down onto the sand and be at one with the coast, made her feel as if she couldn't breathe. She wouldn't be able to greet her neighbours each day or catch up with the people she loved who returned to Shelly year after year for their holidays. She wouldn't be able to swim when the fancy took her or greet the outgoing tide with her basket in order to gather stories for Milo. And she would no longer be near Joe.

All that she knew would be crushed and distorted. The children they'd been, the teenagers they'd become, Flora, with her beautiful smile, baking cakes in the kitchen or sitting on the terrace with a good book. It would all be buried by the regeneration of Shelly. New people would come and they would sit on their brand-new balconies, layers of them one above the other, and they would look upon her view of the water with the boats spilling from the new marina and their hearts would be brimming with satisfaction at all that they had. They wouldn't know or understand what she and others like her had lost in order for them to have their shiny, modern lives.

Panic washed over her again at the enormity of what she was facing. It was out. She'd spoken about it and now it was real. A child on the beach laughed at something and other children joined in. Several seagulls caw-cawed as they wheeled in the sky and a single seagull called to them from a nearby roof. Juliana reclined in her chair again but her voice was flat when she spoke. 'I know how much you love this place, Mel. I honestly don't know what to say other than, I'm so sorry.'

'Don't say anything,' Melody answered. She didn't want a sticking plaster to put on her woes. No words could mend or change anything. 'It's enough that I've shared it with you, Jules.' Juliana reached across, silently taking her hand, and they stayed like that, holding on to each other, while waves fell upon the shore with the music of the sea, sizzling with foam and leaving patterns in the sand.

'I've told Alastair I'll go back on Monday, after I've spent the weekend with you.' Juliana stepped out onto the terrace with cold drinks, giving Melody an apologetic glance as she placed their glasses on the ground. 'You were right. That's what the phone call was about this morning when you went off seaweeding. I needed to speak to him – but now that I have, I need to go and see him.' Melody's jaw dropped open, unsure that she'd heard correctly. Juliana was already talking about flinging herself back into the arms of that infidel after leaving him sweating for only mere hours. She was hardly punishing him for the crime he'd committed, in fact she was rewarding him. 'I know he's done an awful thing, Mel, but he sounded so desperate on the phone this morning... so *sorry* about it. I told you he was sorry, didn't I? I tried to hate him, really I did, but I can't.' Juliana's face was red from the sun and she realised one arm was more burnt than the other. She laughed a little, an incongruous sound considering the moment. 'Look at me! I need to bake my other side before I go home looking like a barber shop pole.'

Melody didn't laugh. She wanted to leap up and shake Juliana. 'He's *cheated* on you, Jules. What part of that hasn't sunk in? If he can behave like that with your best friend in your own house what makes you think he won't do it again with the woman next door?'

'Because the woman next door is eighty-two!' Juliana spread her towel on the terrace and lay face down on it. She pulled her hair away from her neck and carefully positioned her arms so that they'd get an even tan. Melody scoffed.

'And that will stop him?'

'You're being horrible now, Mel. Alastair said it was a one-off. A mistake. And I believe him.'

Melody scoffed again. 'He's *really* sorry you found out more like.' She couldn't help herself, she wanted to be sympathetic – after all, their time together had been about sharing confidences – but while her own situation was out of her control, Juliana's was different. She had the power to rise above hers and take the lead.

'Anyway,' Juliana continued. 'Alastair knows we have a lot to talk through and he's asked me not to tell my parents or anyone other than you until I've given him a chance to explain himself.'

Melody gave a sharp laugh. 'Of *course* he doesn't want you to tell anyone, Jules. He's got his reputation to think of. Billy big balls at the bank. Captain of the rugby team. He's almost a celebrity in your neck of the woods by all accounts so of course he doesn't want the shame of people finding out that he's been *up close and personal* with someone else's wife!'

Juliana groaned. 'Oh blimey, Mel! Please stop. I wish I'd never told you anything. But you're right about one thing, when you said yesterday that you thought I was running away from something, I was. Now I need to go back, so let me.'

They fell into uncomfortable silence then, each wrapped in their own thoughts. The sun beat down on them and, although Juliana seemed content to roast herself, Melody fidgeted, hot and impatient for the tide to come in a little further so that she could go for a swim. Before long, though, Juliana nudged Melody's foot with her own foot. 'I know you're not happy with me, but I feel caught between you and Alastair. I have to sort this out, Mel, but I also feel bad about leaving you here after everything you've told me. That's why I told him I was staying for a couple of days.'

'I've got to work anyway, I'll be fine,' Melody sighed.

'If you ever need to, you know… when the time comes, you *must* come and stay with me and Alastair while you work things out. You could have the annexe. It's got a kitchenette and an en-suite and it's really quite lovely. Only…'

'Only what?' Melody waited for the conditions attached to the offer, not that she could be lured by a kitchenette or an en-suite or even a palace if it was far away from the coast.

'Only your *stuff*, Mel. You have too much stuff. And I've

been thinking.' Juliana opened her eyes and looked at Melody from the corner of them. 'I believe there's a silver lining here. The end of your lease is the perfect opportunity to get rid of the... *overspill*. Having to leave Spindrift might actually be a good thing. You could have a therapeutic cleanse and start a different kind of life.'

Quietly, Melody stood up. She wiped the sweat from her face and pulled her cotton dress on. A deep hurt was squeezing every inch of her. In the same way she had with Alastair, Juliana was again easily brushing away the terrible thing that was going to happen to Shelly. A *therapeutic cleanse* of everything she had ever loved. It was not that simple. 'You think it would be better if my life were all tidied up and filed away in a little modern box somewhere?' She was smarting and it showed. She quietly hung her towel over the fence to air in the sun.

'Oh gosh, I don't think that at all.' Juliana reached a reddening arm out to touch Melody's leg.

'I'm going to the shop,' Melody said quietly. 'I need to buy milk and pick up the newspaper.' She managed to make her voice sound casual but she had to get away from Juliana before her hurt showed.

'Are you OK?' Juliana queried.

'I'm fine,' Melody answered coolly. 'I just need to get some bits, that's all.'

'Do you want me to come with you?' Juliana tried to crane her neck round to her but Melody was already walking away.

'No,' she called simply.

It was for the best, she realised now, if perhaps Juliana didn't stay long after all. Stepping inside Spindrift she made her way past all her belongings. Flora's knitting and easel were there, her father's rubber boots and Milo's red umbrella, along with the scent of salt and sea that clung to the walls and the furnishings. Everything about her home embraced her with love. How could she ever imagine a different kind of home? A different kind of life? She couldn't. She couldn't imagine a different kind of anything.

Walking back from the Pier Head Stores, she waited while a cargo ship, pregnant with barrels of salted sprats, left the dock. The bridge swung open yawning the ship into the sea while Melody watched, fascinated as she always was by how something so huge could perform such balletic moves only inches from the pier wall. Joe and other dockers, busy with their tasks, paused to call out to her, to bid her good day, and she hailed them back. She loved the working dock and everything about it. There was an industry here, a pride in all that was going on. Fishing boats bobbed against their moorings, nets and orange buoys were in higgledy piles. Grain stores pointed skywards next to a boat-building yard and sheds that edged the wharf. Children licked at ice-creams, mesmerised by the size of the ship manoeuvring through the narrow gap, while the drivers of two cars patiently waited either side for the bridge to swing shut again. Later, the workers would be in The Beach pub, washing away the dust and toil of the day with a cold pint of beer and a belly full of contentment, and Melody wished she could join them. When Juliana went home she would make sure it was one of the first things she did.

Melody hung on to her bag of groceries, storing the image of everything she could see in her mind like a cine film. A terrible rumour was going around that the dock was to suffer the same fate as many other small working docks in England. People were saying it would probably be converted into a yuppy marina and livelihoods would be lost. She was heartbroken at the thought that in the future, the whole of the Shelly area would be completely different.

When the iron bridge swung shut again, children ran across it, stopping to peep through the iron portholes on its steel sides, and Melody walked past them, remembering how when she and Milo were very young they would do just the same.

Entering Spindrift, she slipped quietly into Milo's room so as not to disturb Juliana and, placing her groceries on the floor, she indulged in a few moments to read her daily newspaper. 'Oh, gosh, Milo, listen to this,' she read to him. 'As from next month, pubs are going to be allowed to stay open all day long. No more shutting at three o'clock in the afternoon just as the workers who've come in on the fishing boats want a drink. That will be great, won't it?'

'What will be great?'

Melody jumped as Juliana appeared in the doorway looking even redder than before and fanning her face with both hands. She peered into Milo's room as if to see who else was in there.

'I was talking to myself,' Melody flushed. 'Pubs are going to stay open all day as from next month. I think it's great.' She quickly placed the folded newspaper on the shelf next to Gloria and grabbed her bag of groceries.

'I guess so,' Juliana answered noncommittally. She followed Melody out, plonking herself down on the sofa in the sitting room where she stretched her limbs out against the coolness of the fabric. 'Phew, it's so hot out there. Not a rain cloud in sight,' she panted, picking up her book and fanning herself.

'You're burnt,' Melody observed as she made her way into the kitchen. 'Do you want anything while I'm here?' she called. 'I'm having bread and clotted cream.' She unwrapped the paper from the large white loaf she'd just bought and proceeded to cut a fat slice from the rectangular crust. Juliana called back from where she sat wilting on the sofa.

'Have you got anything else? Anything nice?'

'This *is* nice,' Melody called out, calmly spooning two heaps of thick white clotted cream onto the soft bread. Then, without cutting it into smaller pieces, she took a huge bite. Rolling her eyes with absolute bliss as the sweetness of the cream, combined with the soft texture of the bread, filled her mouth, she carried the tempting slice in her hand to show it to Juliana. '*This* is delicious,' she said. She swallowed her mouthful, licked the cream from her lips and took another bite, wondering why Juliana was screwing up her eyes and recoiling at the idea.

'You're all right, thank you,' she said, crinkling her nose.

'You don't know what you're missing,' Melody murmured.

'Anyway, I've been thinking,' Juliana announced. 'I'm only here for a couple more days but we could make the most of my time. I'd like to help you get ready for your move. We could get some bin bags and make some real headway and, before you know where you are, we can have Spindrift looking shipshape. Together, we can make a positive start for when you have to begin the process of moving out.'

Melody froze, her slice of bread and cream turning sour in her mouth. *Here we go again*, she thought to herself. Juliana wanted to rush through the contents of a lifetime just so that things appeared neat and tidy.

'I'm offering my help here, Mel.' Juliana looked hurt. 'I think, perhaps, you're overwhelmed,' she added.

Melody still didn't move, the half-eaten slice gripped in her hand. She remembered Joe's words, whispered in her ear last night. She'd been brave. She'd admitted to Juliana that she was losing her home and, if she were honest with herself, it had made her feel better. They'd bonded again, shared their confidences together, and that had been a good thing but there was still more to tell her. Melody had been so nearly ready to talk about the photograph and to face all the repercussions that would unfold but, now, Juliana wanted to throw half of Spindrift away then rush back to Alastair. 'You should go now, Jules,' she said. 'Go back to Alastair and sort things out. Don't wait until Monday.' Her voice came out stretched and controlled.

'But why?' Juliana queried. 'I know you said you've got to work now but I want to spend a bit more time with you. I thought we could put some music on, get sorting, have a giggle.' She scraped herself off the sofa and collected the doll with the missing arm from Milo's room. 'This, for example. Why have you got this?' She picked Gloria up by her hair and studied her quizzically. Melody tried to snatch the doll out of her hands but Juliana held it out of her reach.

'She's part of a story,' Melody began nervously. 'A good story about a...' She paused.

'A what?' Juliana pressed.

'A powerful woman whose disability doesn't stop her achieving whatever she wants.'

'A *powerful woman*?' Juliana's confusion grew to such an extent that Melody couldn't deal with it any longer.

'Go please, Juliana. Go *now*. I don't need music and giggles and I don't need any help.' Melody went into Flora's bedroom. She laid Juliana's huge suitcase on the bed and opened it. Next, she took Juliana's mac from the hook in the hall and placed that next to the suitcase. 'I can't do this with you, Jules,' she said, doing her best to stay controlled. To be restrained. But, catching sight of Flora's dressing gown still hanging on the back of her door, she suddenly felt so terribly alone. The reality of coping with everything on her own and never seeing Flora and Milo again punched her in the solar plexus.

# 16

It was all so horribly raw. Unexpectedly, and with no time to prepare themselves, Melody and Milo lost the person who'd taught them how to live and love and grow into their very best selves.

Flora had been in the middle of putting the finishing touches on a painting of a starfish and seagulls when she'd collapsed. It seemed so unfair that, at only forty-two, someone with such a big heart could be suddenly let down by it so early in life.

When Melody's anger finally abated, it was replaced with a feeling of terrible emptiness, as if she was floating, loose and untethered, somewhere above reality. She wanted to go with it and to float entirely away but Milo needed her. She knew he needed her more than he'd ever needed her before and for him, and him alone, she had found her way back.

Despite Isobel's constant nagging over the years for them to up sticks and live in Cheltenham, Flora had always been quietly steadfast about remaining in Exmouth. Upon her death, Melody discovered that Flora had gone so far as to have this written into her will. Paragraph 4 had stated that she wished for a simple service, a small bouquet of flowers and for her daughter, Melody, to arrange her funeral. Torn apart with the pain of loss, Melody found herself in the position of ensuring that her mother's end of life wishes were honoured.

Aunt Isobel and Uncle Gordon took a few days to arrive after Flora's death, having abruptly halted a business trip to fly back from Dubai. Upon their eventual arrival, Aunt Isobel spent a solid, tearful hour persuading Melody to reconsider the arrangements and allow Flora's body to be taken back to Cheltenham.

At only twenty-two, Melody now felt so much older than her years. 'Mum wanted to be buried in Exmouth, Aunt Isobel, I have to honour her wishes.'

'I know she put that in her will, Melody,' Aunt Isobel argued, 'but such a request in life, even in a will, holds no legal weight in death. Plus, it was drawn up when Daniel was still around and he probably had some persuasion in it. As he is no longer on the scene, I'd like Florentine to be taken home, laid to rest in her birth town surrounded by all the people who wish to pay their last respects.'

Uncle Gordon, awkwardly shuffling his feet and twiddling his hands in the background, did his best to chip in. 'Your grandparents on your mother's side are in the cemetery, Melody. They have a beautiful family plot.'

'Exactly, Gordon.' Aunt Isobel dabbed at her watery red eyes. 'Florentine has family and friends who want to be there for her. *I* want to be there for her.'

Melody, fired by the sure knowledge that, even from the other side, her mother was quietly insisting she remain in her little corner of beautiful by the sea, found the courage to stand up to her Aunt Isobel. 'With all due respect, Aunt Isobel, all the people who want to be there for my mother should have, perhaps, considered visiting her while she was alive. No, these are Mum's wishes and it's my place to honour them. I *will* honour them.' She stared her aunt directly in the eye, challenging her to say differently, until Aunt Isobel drew in a deep breath ready to do battle again.

'Let me bring her home, Melody,' she begged. 'And you and Milo, of course, must come to live with me and Uncle Gordon. You're too young to deal with all this on your own, darling.'

Aunt Isobel, to Melody's recollection, had never called her darling and it sounded strangely soft coming from her, like the fluffy wind-borne seeds of a garden thistle. At that moment, Uncle Gordon, in an entirely out of character way, stepped forward. He took his wife's arm and pressed a gentle but silencing finger against her lips.

'Enough now, Isobel,' he said. 'We will accept a graceful retreat and allow Melody to do what Flora has asked.' Removing his finger, he bent down until he was looking into her eyes, as if sending a silent message to her. Her aunt looked so fragile and vulnerable but then, quite suddenly, she did something she'd never done before. She reached out with both arms and enfolded Melody within them, holding on to her with a desolate fierceness.

On a blustery day in Exmouth, the community of Shelly came together to support Melody and Milo in sending Flora on her final journey. Among others, the Franklins, Enid Johnson, Old Tess and Old Albert along with Tom and Joe Wiley were there. Mrs Galespie, wearing a pair of shoes that looked decidedly difficult to walk in, ran a soft hand down Melody's arm and kissed Milo on the cheek with a loud smacking sound. Then, popping open the top buttons of her black overcoat, she covertly revealed to Melody that she was wearing a lime-green dress underneath. 'I 'ave a rule for funerals,' she said with her voice lowered and gentle. 'Wear black to be appropriate but something bright to celebrate. Your mum's life is something to celebrate, my lovely.' Mrs Galespie lightly touched Melody's hand before stepping discreetly aside as Juliana, Isobel and Gordon approached. The dress was a terrible colour and it reflected a luminous shade against her chins but Melody was touched by her gesture.

Aunt Isobel wept noisily into a hanky, the black netting hanging from the brim of her very wide hat, hiding her face from view. At the door to the church, Uncle Gordon tapped Melody with awkward affection on the shoulder. 'Anytime you need us,' he said quietly.

Melody knew that he was trying again, in his own gentle way, to offer his support, and his kindness constricted her throat and moistened her eyes. She smiled as best as she could, reached for Milo's wheelchair and repeated her mother's mantra, 'Thank you, Uncle Gordon, but Spindrift is all we need.' Uncle Gordon looked as if he wanted to say more, as if words were caught in his throat that he couldn't release into the open, but, instead, he tapped her shoulder again and nodded silently.

Juliana, now eighteen and with a tear-streaked face, slipped into the pew at the front of the church next to Melody. She reached out and took Melody's trembling hand in hers and Melody, in turn, sat next to Milo in his wheelchair, holding his hand. As the three of them weaved their fingers tightly in and out of each other's, it was the only thing that prevented Melody from splintering into a million little pieces. She didn't cry at the funeral, or let her agony go in the way she needed. Instead, she held it in for Milo's sake, the bravest of smiles on her face while her head and her heart and her throat throbbed with the agony of it.

And so it was that Flora was buried in the grounds of an old stone church in Exmouth, surrounded by her closest of people, a posy of sunflowers and the sound of seagulls calling her song.

## 1976, OCTOBER

Melody peeled the foil from an enamel dish and put it in the oven to warm. She hadn't made the food herself and she wasn't sure who had, she only knew that it could be any one of her neighbours who'd rallied around ever since Flora had died.

A never ending supply of fruit puddings, homemade casseroles, pastries and tarts had arrived at Spindrift with her friends leaving their offerings on the terrace, the doorstep or even letting themselves in and putting things in the kitchen. Invitations for her and Milo to dine or simply have a cup of tea in other bungalows had been frequent and Melody felt overwhelmed by their generosity.

Gordon and Isobel had also tried repeatedly to make her reconsider living with them in Cheltenham. She had politely declined. Everyone had been so helpful and she was grateful for that, but she was unable to find a way through her grief for anyone other than Milo.

'It's cottage pie, Milo.' She sniffed the aroma of their supper and smiled sadly at him. He'd found everything over the recent weeks so hard, becoming quiet and withdrawn, unable to articulate his emotions. He'd seemed lost in his own mind, frequently looking up towards heaven to see if he could see his mother, and no amount of stories about underwater worlds or ghost ships could help to bring him back.

The sun was sinking in the sky and the wind was blowing a hooley outside when Melody made him a cup of sweet, milky tea and sat him where he could look at the view outside. Milo had no idea about the photograph and the things she'd found in Flora's possessions. His grief was simpler than that. It was uncomplicated and unconcealed.

They sat together watching clouds changing shapes, lit by the evening light and quilting the sky and the sea with colour. Melody contemplated how lilacs and silvers became purples and yellows, and how the edges of the clouds bloomed pink or orange with the altering light. It was at that moment that another story began to unfold in her mind. She touched Milo's hand.

'Milo? Have you ever heard of a Sky Catcher?'

Milo shook his head silently and continued to search the heavens for his mother.

'The Sky Catcher is very special, Milo. His job is to mix amazing colours and paint them in the sky to make it beautiful for us. See, how it changes all the time?' She pointed to the horizon over the Haldon Hills. 'The sky is bruising with spruce and berry blue over there and yet, out to sea...' she pointed to a gap in the clouds '... sunbeams are falling into the water in shades of sunflower yellow and marigold orange. But the sky is *so* big that, do you know what?' Milo shook his head again, his gaze now fixed on the fingers of bright light that shone from above. 'Because Mum was an artist, the Sky Catcher has asked her to help him.'

Milo's mouth dropped open in wonder and Melody smiled at him through a veil of unshed tears. 'Our mum, Milo, is now a Sky Catcher, too.'

Milo continued to stare out of the window while Melody rubbed his feet to bring back the circulation, tucked a second blanket around his lap and wiped at the glisten of saliva that ran from the corner of his mouth. And now, with their dinner almost ready to serve, the sun was greeting the moon in a lambent glow of taupe and dolphin grey.

Melody took Milo's hand and followed the line of his gaze. 'What can you see?' she asked him gently. She was so used to seeing a melancholy in his eyes but this time he smiled at her with such radiance that she kissed him for it.

He turned back to the window and, still beaming, said a single word. 'Mum.'

# 17

Juliana stood with her mouth agape, her eyes moving between Melody and the suitcase on the bed. 'I... I don't know what I've done,' she whimpered.

'You haven't done anything,' Melody said measuredly. 'I just know that we will deal with my belongings differently, that's all. You need to go back and do whatever you need to do with Alastair and I need to sort out my own life.'

'Can I at least change out of my swimsuit?' Juliana asked, attempting a feeble joke. Melody, however, couldn't take her eyes off Flora's dressing gown hanging on the back of the door. She imagined that her mother was there, in the room, wearing it. *You should be here, Mum*, she said silently. *I wasn't ready. Milo wasn't ready. I can't do this alone.* She thought for a moment she might pass out in her effort not to cry in front of Juliana and so, grabbing the gown, stumbled out of the room saying, 'Do what you like,' as she flew into Milo's bedroom. Sitting in his wheelchair, she scooted it towards the bed and, clutching the dressing gown, she laid her head on the pillow next to the shell of the giant sea snail. 'I miss you. I miss you both too much,' she whispered.

She lay against Milo's pillow for some time, listening to

the sounds of Juliana showering, drying her hair and moving around Flora's bedroom until, eventually, the door to Milo's room creaked open. 'I've packed my things,' she said quietly. 'I'll be going, then.' She was dressed in a blue jumpsuit with a white belt, the make-up was back on and the hair was big again, she balanced on white heels, smelt of expensive perfume and her lips were shiny with gloss. Melody noticed that Juliana's neck had stayed white where the sun hadn't reached and for some reason it made her want to change her mind. She wanted to rush over and hug her. Instead, keeping a tight grip on her emotion, she simply followed her out towards the front door.

'Mel, I'm worried about you,' Juliana said carefully, pausing for a moment at the threshold of the door. 'You hold on to too many things. I don't know why you do but it's a kind of overzealous collecting habit or something. It's not healthy and I think you might have a problem.'

This was new, Melody thought. Did Juliana really think such a thing... that she had a problem? Calling it stuff was one thing but *problem* was a big word to use. It was a word so big it brought with it a whole host of insinuations. Who was Juliana to flit by and comment on her life, when all she was doing was loving? Loving Milo and Flora, and Spindrift and Shelly. Melody had thought that Juliana of all people would have understood because she had known them and loved them, too.

She opened the door, lifted Juliana's suitcase over the threshold onto the path outside, hugged her quickly and turned around, shutting the door behind her. Leaning against it, she listened to the sound of Juliana's stunned silence until, eventually, there was the tap-tapping of heels along the path, the shutting of the boot of the shiny red car, the engine turning over and, at last, the roar of it down the road. Still clutching the dressing gown, Melody ran back into Milo's bedroom and sobbed until her throat hurt.

Once Melody had managed to pull herself together, she washed her face in cold water, slipped on her shoes, walked to The Beach pub and downed two pints of beer from the tankard she kept stored behind the bar. She was back with her own people, the dock workers she knew and loved so well, sitting at the bar shrouded by smoke trailing from their cigarettes and mushrooming into the air around her. Someone was playing the piano again and a few people were singing along and spirits were high. She tapped her foot in time to the music and, picking at a bowl of nuts on the counter, thought she might finish the bread and clotted cream for her supper when she got home.

'Your cousin has gone back, then? She didn't finish her project?' Big Joe Wiley appeared carrying his tankard of beer and pulled a bar stool up to the counter beside her. He dipped his huge fingers into the same bowl of nuts she was eating from and dropped several into his mouth. As he sat down, a piece of her heart fluttered in the air between them and she hoped he couldn't see it.

'Juliana had something she needed to sort out at home.' Melody replied as casually as she could muster and took another handful of nuts, their fingers touching as they dipped into the bowl at the same time. She flushed pink at the touch of him.

'When will she be back?' he asked.

Melody thought about how best to answer as a horrible niggle of regret stirred in her belly. She stalled for time, waving to the barman for another drink, hating the feel of the new one-pound coin in her hand rather than the soft crumple of an old pound note. Why does *everything* have to change, she thought.

'Would you like a drink? My round?' Joe's tankard was almost empty so she took another coin from her pocket. He knew better than to offer to pay for her so he nodded, downing the last of his beer and handing the barman his empty tankard. 'I don't know when she'll be back,' Melody answered regretfully. She took her change and dropped the pennies into the collection tub for the lifeboat. 'To tell you the truth,' she ventured, 'we sort of fell out.'

'Sort of...?' Joe probed.

'Well, definitely then. She doesn't understand me.' Melody stared into her beer.

'And are you easy to understand?' he asked.

When Melody looked up she saw he was sporting the lazy grin she knew so well and she found herself trying not to smile at it. She also noticed the glisten of stubble on his chin and how his pale lashes curled upwards. '*I* understand me,' she smiled wryly. 'That's all that matters.'

'Is it?' Joe fell serious then. 'Is it enough that only you understands you?'

As Melody didn't know where he was going with this question, she took three long mouthfuls of beer before she answered. 'I only have me, Joe,' she said quietly. There was a pause while he stared into her eyes and, this time, unable to tear her gaze away, she thought she might drown in them. She felt as if he was trying to read her and, although she liked to think that she was a strong, independent woman, she felt strangely vulnerable because of it.

'Maybe Juliana doesn't understand you because you don't let people in?' He spoke as if asking a question, testing her or teasing her, she wasn't sure which, but it grazed her with its accusation. 'We all have a lot to face,' he said. 'We are all losing our homes, and if the dock closes, which is looking increasingly likely, we'll lose our jobs, too. The whole of Shelly needs all the love and support it can get so you are not alone, Melody.' He looked around the pub to reinforce what he was saying. The workers and the locals were chatting together, laughing and mingling in their familiarity, like family, bonded by time and circumstance.

She was not alone in this nightmare, that was true, but once the community of Shelly were all scattered to the wind, it would be as if they had never been there at all. She would be on her own then.

'Where will you live, Joe... when you have to leave Pebbles?' She braved the question but dropped her gaze into her beer, scared that his eyes could pierce a hole inside her again. So fearful was she of his answer, of a time when he would no longer greet her in the mornings or share his catch of fish or flasks of homemade cider with her.

'I might buy my own boat and live on it,' he answered. 'I don't know where yet but I certainly couldn't afford any fancy marina fees.' He shrugged nonchalantly and smiled. 'Something will come along. It always does.'

Melody couldn't imagine what could possibly come along that would give either of them a place to live that matched what they already had. 'What would you do for work?' she asked.

Big Joe Wiley took a deep breath and Melody guessed he was about to say something he was not entirely comfortable about her hearing. 'I would probably work on the development.'

As with the bread and clotted cream from her conversation with Juliana that morning, Melody's beer turned sour in her mouth. Big Joe Wiley was entertaining the idea of working on the very thing they were all dreading. The demolition... the *devastation* of Shelly. He could end up playing a part in erasing their homes and building the apartments that would replace them. She put her glass on the counter and fixed her gaze upon him, no longer afraid that the windows of her soul might give her away.

'Don't you think you'll feel like a traitor if you do that?' she asked.

'No, Melody,' he answered steadily. 'I adapt. It's different. And I *would* need a job and I'd rather stay here than leave to find work in Exeter... or worse, even further away. With or without our blessing, Shelly as we know it *is* going.' He placed a warm hand on her arm and she looked down at it. His hand felt reassuring and she wanted to take it in hers and hold it to her cheek. As he continued speaking, tears threatened behind her eyes and she blinked them back before they betrayed her weakness. 'We've all known that the leases weren't going to be renewed. Half the population of Exmouth feel that this whole area is little more than a shanty town, you *know* that. Little wooden houses that are past their prime, half the properties already empty and a dock that's struggling to cope with the newer, bigger cargo ships. We have to accept that the world is changing. We can't stop progress.'

Melody waited until he'd finished talking, then, moving her arm away from his hand, she downed the rest of her drink in one before calmly walking out of the pub. Joe called after her but he made no attempt to stop her and she made no attempt to turn back to hear what he wanted to say. She knew, in her heart, that he was right but she could hardly bear the idea that he, of all people, would have a hand in tearing down her home. It would surely break her in two.

Walking away from The Beach pub, she turned left towards Exmouth beach instead of right towards Shelly where she made her way slowly along the esplanade, the sound of the piano and the raucous singing of a sea shanty fading behind her. The evening light was failing and a navy sky was gathering to the east. The sun was sinking below the skyline, leaving an orange stain in the sky over Dawlish and the Haldon Hills behind and the wooden beams of the pier's structure formed a skeletal silhouette against the orange reflection on the water. She made her way past The Grove pub, The Deer Leap, the Cavendish and Imperial hotels, the flower beds and the clock tower. She waved to the elderly people who had not yet left for home, sitting in the beachfront shelters looking out at an evening sea, dreaming of the tea dances of their youth or what they might cook for their supper. Pausing for a while by the old red and yellow swing-boats, she remembered how she and Milo had loved them, along with the helter-skelter that stood nearby. And when, at last, she reached the cliffs of Orcombe Point, she slipped off her sandals to paddle in the sea, admiring how the darkening sky was turning the ancient red rock an imposing shade of burnt umber.

Looking back along the esplanade, the string of lights that roped their way along the front were now lit and boats twinkled their way across the sea as they headed back towards the dock. The sand moved under the soles of her feet as she stepped her way along the waterline where tiny pebbles rolled across her toes and bubbles of foam popped around her ankles. Big Joe's words echoed loudly inside her head. *We have to accept that change is coming and we can't stop it.* Regeneration was going to rip the heart right out of Shelly and gorge on the carcass but she simply couldn't bear it.

With her feet still damp, she carried her shoes and took the road into town, stopping at every estate agent she passed and casting her eye over the adverts in the windows. There were several properties to rent or buy. Flats and bedsits that looked out onto other flats and bedsits, or little terraced houses that soldiered along narrow streets opposite other terraced houses – all without a sea view. It wasn't time to move yet but these properties, she knew, would suffocate her, squeezing her within their narrow walls until she couldn't breathe. Her heart started to beat too fast and the panic she'd tried for so long to quell threatened to overtake her again. Many of her neighbours had nothing and would have to move far away, pensioners who could never afford the rent of other properties would be sucked into care homes never to come out. Until now, she'd never needed more than her part-time wages and she'd never asked much from life other than to breathe the ozone-rich air and look out at the sea. A voice inside her head now nagged at her of the money tucked away in a private account but, cross with herself for being tempted, she immediately dismissed the thought of it.

She brushed the sand off her feet and slipped her shoes back on, leaving the estate agents behind her. For now, she still had all that she needed and would continue, for as long as possible, to squeeze the very last drops out of life as she knew it.

\*

Melody closed the front door to Spindrift behind her and turned on the lights. Then, she kicked off her shoes and opened the double doors to the terrace. The curtains were drawn in Joe Wiley's bungalow but a soft glow from his lamps shone through the thin fabric. She imagined that he was in there reading a book or mending his fishing net, perhaps with a late supper or a mug of warm milk.

She'd been sitting outside for a long time, quietly contemplating everything, when the doors to Joe's bungalow opened and he slipped out. He jumped down onto the sand and made his way down to the sea. He didn't notice her sitting on her terrace but instead stood on the beach looking out at the watery darkness, waves lapping at his bare feet. She continued to watch him as he made his way over to *Wild Rose* and lay in her looking up at the stars. *The beach dude who sleeps in his rowing boat, sometimes.* And tonight, it would seem, was one of those times.

He stretched his long body out, arms behind his head, his feet crossed at the ankles in recumbent pose, and she wondered, as she often did, what he was thinking. She wondered if he, too, was mulling over the events of the day and whether their conversation had affected him as much as it had affected her. He had been in her life forever. Her neighbour and her friend. Someone to look up to while she was growing up, a solid, unassuming kind of guy who'd learnt well from his father, Tom Wiley.

When Tom moved away, Joe had remained in Pebbles and Melody had been so pleased. Like her, the coastal life was ingrained in his very being. He could be found fishing for mackerel on *Wild Rose* or at work at the dock unloading shipments. She'd always loved the casual way he had about him and how kind he was to the children of Shelly. How readily he would organise races or play sand bowls and cricket or teach them how to go sea fishing.

Milo had adored him. After that first time, when he'd realised Milo could no longer swim and had carried him from the terrace to the sea, Joe would frequently appear to take Milo's weak frame into his big arms, taking him to the water whenever the weather was warm and the tide was right. Melody would join them, swimming around and between them, ducking below the surface and bursting back up to make Milo laugh.

She knew, as she watched him now, that, whatever his plans for the future, nestled in her heart and flowing through her veins, there was still love.

Soon, everything would change and Melody could hardly bear the agony of it.

She eased herself out of her chair and closed the doors to Spindrift softly behind her, leaving Big Joe to the night. But as she stood in the middle of her sitting room a heaviness and feeling of despair settled again upon her shoulders. Another day had come to a close, another day had brought her closer to the day she had to move away and, with it, she was so very alone.

She had a dream that night that was so vivid she woke with it clear in her mind, warm and lovely, and the kind she wanted to slide back into. Flora had come to her in the night, holding a batch of homemade cupcakes set out on the same floral fibreglass tray that had been in the kitchen for twenty-five years. Then, Milo had appeared, striding into Spindrift, his limbs strong, his body tanned, the curls of his blond hair brushing his shoulders, glistening with water from a swim in the sea.

Her brother had been straight and tall in her dream. He'd brimmed with energy and confidence, his limbs strong. The sight of him had made her feel happy and she'd watched him take a cupcake from the tray, holding it as if it were an apple and biting hungrily into it.

'Take it, Melody,' he'd said, and she heard his voice, saying her name as clearly as if he were standing next to her, deep and rich and glorious to hear. He took the tray from Flora and extended it towards her, the scent of baking strong in her senses. 'They are an act of love.' Then he took another bite and grinned at her while Flora stood next to him smiling in the way that Melody knew so well. She repeated the words in her sleep, *an act of love*, something that Flora always used to say when she presented her homemade cakes. The cupcakes, as always, were delicious and full of little black currants that burst with sweetness in her mouth. She could taste her mother's baking even as she slept and it was just as she'd remembered it.

She woke with the taste of sweetness on her lips and the belief that if she'd only held out her arms in her dream she could have touched her mother and her brother, as real and solid as they had been in life.

Sitting on the edge of her bed, Melody hoped to see glimpses of Flora and Milo out of the corners of her eyes but the harsh reality was that she couldn't. Already they were fading into the periphery of her mind. 'Are you happy in your other world?' she said out loud. But, as she listened to the sound of her own voice calling into the emptiness of the room, she knew she would never hear the answer to her question. She slid her feet into her slippers and padded into the sitting room to let the early morning air breeze through the doors of Spindrift. Looking out to sea, she contemplated the day ahead while trying to shake off the terrible sense of loneliness that had been with her all night. Big Joe's boat was empty now, no doubt he was getting ready for work, but a line of footprints left in the damp, dewy sand told the tale that he'd been for an early morning swim.

She studied the line of footprints leading from Joe's boat to the shoreline thinking, again, about how he used to carry Milo to the water for a swim. Two people, one single line of footprints. Milo had come to her in her dream. His limbs had been strong, his hair glistening wet from the sea. 'Did you swim with Big Joe today, Milo?' she asked. She spoke out loud again, listening for an answer that she would never hear but, even so, she wanted to believe that Milo, although his own footprints weren't visible, was now free to walk beside Big Joe and swim with him in the waters of Shelly.

# 18

Melody hugged her coat tightly around her and set off along the shore with her basket to find something that would inspire another story for her brother. An early morning mist was hanging over the sea with promises of a warm day to follow and Milo was still asleep. The happy little boy who'd grown into a teenager and finally to a young man, now spent his remaining days in bed, his breathing laboured, his skin the colour of wax. His bedding hid a rubber mattress-cover and Melody had to spoon his food into his mouth in tiny, manageable amounts. The only thing his wheelchair was good for these days was as somewhere for her to sit by his bed while she fed him, chatted to him about the day and took him on adventures with her stories.

So far that morning, despite searching along the sand flats where the tracks of gulls and wader birds had sewn lines across the sand, she'd found very little to inspire her. Meandering past the wiggly casts of lugworms and stepping over banks of cockleshells, her sandalled feet had slapped against shallow water and crunched among pebbles. But, apart from an empty crisp packet which she'd put in a rubbish bin by the sea wall, only two cuttlebones had made their way into her basket. It wasn't until she was much further along that she found it. Half buried in the sand among clumps of weed left by the outgoing tide was an earring. She washed it clean in a pool of water then held it in the palm of her hand to study it. She could tell it wasn't valuable in terms of money but, already, the large, shiny, cultured pearl had a brilliant story behind it. A painting in one of Milo's favourite books came to mind and, aware he would be awake soon, she hurried home to him, a fabulously daring tale of a famous explorer already bursting to be told.

'Milo, look at what I found today! Can you guess what it is?' Melody dropped the pearl into his palm then moved his hand to where he could see it. She'd washed him and fed him and, now that he was propped into a better position against his pillows, she sat down on his wheelchair next to him. Widening her eyes to play out her excitement she placed her elbows on his bed, cupping her chin in her hands. Milo looked at her, his dry lips catching on his crooked teeth as he rolled his eyes between hers and the earring in his palm. She moistened his mouth with a wet sponge as he looked at the item in her hand.

'I'll tell you, shall I?' Melody could tell that he couldn't think what the item was and enjoyed the anticipation. She showed him his well-thumbed book of seafaring heroes and opened it to a double-page spread, jabbing her finger at an old painting of Sir Walter Raleigh. He was wearing his finest clothes and a large pearl earring.

She picked the earring out of Milo's hand and dangled it in the air between the two of them. 'Do you remember that

I told you he once sailed out of the dock here?' She paused while Milo nodded, waiting patiently for her to continue. 'This, Milo,' she said, jubilantly, 'is one of his earrings!'

The large pearl jiggled from its silver fitting and Milo, his eyes now fixed on the shimmer of it, made a gurgle of delight in his throat. Melody held a glass to his mouth, allowing him to sip at water through a straw and wiped at his dribble with a small towel. 'The tale of how he came to lose his earring is a really good one,' she said, resting comfortably into his wheelchair as she took his hand in hers.

An hour later, before her story had finished, Melody was riding in an ambulance with him, blue light flashing and siren blaring. For his whole life, Milo had been leaving her in stages, his body playing the cruellest of tricks on him and, as she clutched his precious sea snail shell in her hand, she begged him to stay with her. For two whole days he had.

Now, on his third night in hospital, his breathing was shallow and rapid, interspersed by increasingly alarming bouts of silence. Melody placed Milo's shell to his ear.

'Listen, darling boy,' she whispered. 'Inside the shell – can you hear the sea?'

Milo opened his eyes again and the corners of his mouth curled into a smile.

Melody then held the shell to her own ear and smiled widely as if, inside the shell, there were an abundance of wonderful things. 'Inside is the rise and fall and crashing of the waves,' she told him. 'And, if we listen *extra* carefully, Milo, we can hear the call of a seabird.'

She put the shell back against his ear and paused for a

moment, allowing him to join her with her story. 'This seabird is beautiful and *very* special,' she continued. 'Its feathers are of pure white and its wings are so big they could carry you over the ocean.'

Melody wiped at her nose and took a breath. 'And, somewhere, far away in the middle of the ocean where the water is blue and warm, there is an island edged with white sand and full of palm trees so tall they touch the clouds.'

She cupped Milo's hand and his fingers moved within her palm. 'This island, Milo, is a *magic* place. It makes people strong again and it's full of adventures to be had. Nobody on this island has to lie on a bed or sit in a chair, here you can run across the sand and swim in the sea or climb the trees to eat sweet coconuts.'

She kissed him on the cheek and he stared directly at her with eyes that were dull and had red veins crackling through the whites of them and she missed the mischievous shine that, until now, had always been there. Milo forced two sounds from his throat and she knew what they meant. 'I know you're tired,' she answered gently. And as Milo's breathing became rapid again he forced three more sounds from his throat.

'I love you, too, darling boy,' she whispered. She squeezed his hand and leant closer to him, pressing the shell to his ear, doing her best to make her words sound as if she were smiling through them. 'If you would like, Milo,' she said. 'The white seabird will carry you on his wings to the magical island. I can't come with you this time but it's OK if you want to go. You can let go of my hand and climb upon his back.'

Melody continued to speak to Milo with a smile in her voice even after the nurses had rushed to his bedside and his hand had slipped away from hers. She continued to speak to him and hold his shell to his ear until she knew, for certain, he was on his way, on his final adventure, flying over the ocean on the wings of a bird.

And then, finally, and with a heart that felt broken beyond repair, she wept.

For the two years since Flora had gone, Melody had been both mother and sister to Milo, filling his days with the most exciting of stories.

No longer able to take him out in *Serendipity* she wheeled him to the dock to watch the cranes or the cargo ships, or to see the three-masted schooner that had once moored there. She'd whizzed him along the esplanade until the puff came out of them both, stopping at the bright red and yellow swing-boats or the boating lake. They'd lapped at ice-creams by the lifeboat hut or eaten chips in the Pier Café.

The little community of Shelly had come together for her, helping to support Milo in his decline, or sitting with him when she had to work. And, in the early hours of the morning, while he slept, she would walk the shore for beach treasures so that, even as his body let him down, his mind could go on adventures.

And now he was gone.

The unfairness of losing Flora and then Milo so close to each other caused a black hole to open up beneath her and she was at risk of falling into it. At risk of flailing around in the dark without purpose and losing herself. And so, Melody chose survival. Each and every day she combed the shore and gathered treasures and stories and talked to Flora and Milo as if they were listening still.

# PART 2

# 19

## Exmouth, Devon

On Christmas Day, Melody woke to ice on the inside of her bedroom window and with her breath making misty clouds in the air. The temperature had dropped, so much so that Melody had taken to wearing in bed a woollen hat and bed socks that Flora had knitted, plus Milo's old brushed-cotton pyjamas, yet she was still freezing.

She could hardly believe that her last Christmas at Shelly had already arrived and that it had been months since she'd last seen Juliana. Summer had become autumn and autumn had become winter and life had continued – except it had been life without Juliana.

Pulling the covers off she quickly slipped on her swimming costume and covered her coldness with her mother's yellow towelling dressing gown. The sitting room, when she entered it, was sweet with the scent of pine and cinnamon and the sight of the little Christmas tree over by the window gladdened her heart. She and Joe had never discussed the evening at The Beach pub when she'd walked out because he'd been talking about working on the development. She'd swallowed her pain as she always did and buried her head in the sand. But three nights ago, she'd opened the door wearing Milo's pyjamas and with her hair wet from a shower to see Joe holding a tree and grinning at her. The tree had been potted in a bright red container complete with pine cones and sticks of cinnamon.

'Oh, a tree,' she breathed in surprise. 'I haven't had a Christmas tree since... since Milo...'

'I know,' Joe replied, carrying the tree past her and plonking it down in the best space he could find in the sitting room. Then, he'd pushed a small, gift-wrapped present into the branches of it. 'For Christmas morning,' he'd said. 'No peeking.'

'But we don't *do* gifts,' Melody had replied, crestfallen that she'd had nothing to give in return.

'We don't,' Joe agreed. 'But it's the thought that counts as they say. Oh, and I'm inviting everyone to Pebbles for drinks Christmas evening, Mrs Galespie, Enid Johnson, you know, the usual gang. Please say you can be there.'

'I can be there,' Melody answered softly.

'Good,' Joe said, equally as softly. 'Because this Christmas is special. It's our last one together.'

Now, shivering, she lit a fire so that driftwood, gleaned every summer from the beach and estuary edges, soon crackled and popped in her fireplace, thawing the tip of her nose. Then, pulling her curtains open and breathing on the glass to melt a patch in the frost, she peered out at the world. The sky and the sea meshed into grey but there was a lovely ice-blue tinge to the air and a single spray of yellow sunlight fell into the water below. Someone had placed a tinsel star on a pole outside their bungalow and it glittered in the breeze. 'Our last Christmas,' she whispered to herself.

Just then, Mrs Galespie appeared, ready for the traditional Christmas Day swim, dressed head to toe in a wetsuit and a

Santa hat. Jiggling from the cold, Melody opened her doors and jumped down onto the sand to join her. By the time she reached the shore edge, Mrs Galespie was already floating around as relaxed as if she were in a bath and Old Tess had appeared with a blanket around her shoulders to watch. Old Albert eased himself carefully down their steps and waded ankle-deep in the freezing water, his trousers hitched up to the knee, while Joe went running past him and straight into the ice-cold sea, yelling 'Happy Christmas' to everyone.

'Last one to the orange buoy and back is a sissy,' Melody called as she ploughed through the water only to be caught up and overtaken by Joe on the turn at the buoy.

'I guess you're the sissy,' he laughed as, breathless, they grabbed their gowns and wrapped themselves within them.

'I let you win, Joe Wiley,' she said through chattering teeth. 'It's your Christmas present.'

'We don't do presents,' he laughed. Then, he called to everyone as he ran up the steps to his bungalow, 'See you all at mine this afternoon.'

Later, warm and dry, with Christmas carols from the radio filling Spindrift, Melody hummed along, occasionally bursting into song as she busied herself making breakfast. She ate it beside her little Christmas tree where the present from Joe was still unopened. Next to it was a selection of cards from friends and neighbours. The biggest card, gold and tartan with a greeting in black calligraphy, was from Gordon and Isobel. Sitting by the phone and holding the curly cord she dialled their number. 'Happy Christmas,' she said when Isobel answered.

'Oh, darling, and happy Christmas to you, too,' Isobel breathed down the phone. 'Are you OK? Are you alone or with some of your neighbours? You are always invited here for Christmas with us, you know.'

Melody knew. Ever since Flora had died, Gordon and Isobel had invited her and Milo for Christmas. Without fail, even though she was now on her own, she had never accepted.

'Would you like to speak to Juliana? She's here.' There was a rustling sound and the echo of footsteps before Isobel could be heard calling to Juliana. 'Come here, darling, speak to Melody, she's on the phone.'

'Hi.' The sound of Juliana's voice brought a sadness to Melody and she wished the telephone line wasn't so impersonal, so lonely. It only served to highlight the awkwardness between them.

'Happy Christmas, Jules,' Melody said timidly.

'Happy Christmas, Mel,' Juliana replied.

Their call had lasted little more than a couple of minutes and by the time Melody put the receiver back in the cradle she was deflated. They had sent each other a card for Christmas but, apart from that, it felt as if they were broken. As if maybe they could never be repaired. She wondered what it would have been like if she'd taken Isobel and Gordon up on their offer. She tried to imagine what it would be like to sit around a tree that almost hit the ceiling, or to eat at a table with twelve seats, to have both a roaring fire *and* central heating and family to spend the day with again.

This Christmas though, she and her neighbours had been invited to Joe's bungalow for the evening and she was looking forward to it. And as the radio played a perfectly haunting rendition of 'Silent Night' she opened his gift. A little wooden box he'd made by hand opened to reveal tiny scissors, a selection of needles and pins, twists of coloured embroidery threads, a reel of tape, some marker chalk and a silver thimble. It was delightful. Laying it all out on the sofa beside her she studied each item in turn. There was so much thought and care in this gift, with every item hand-picked to fit in the box.

Joe had walked into town to buy all these things, choosing everything just for her, and it touched her soul. She loved it. In fact, she loved it so much that she decided to use everything that came with her gift to sew a Christmas tree ornament for him as a thank you. Using the remnants of an old blouse and the felt from a child's toy that she had among her gatherings, she made a coloured bird the size of the palm of her hand. In the space of just two hours, its body was adorned with patterned stitching and looped flowers, and with coloured wings that were pinned to its side with tiny green buttons from her blouse. A cord to hang it by was fashioned from the cuff of the sleeve.

Having showered and dressed in a pair of flares and a warm woollen jumper, she filled a bag with homemade biscuits and marzipan treats, plus the little bird, and put them beside her boots ready to take with her when she went. Then, as the tangerine clock ticked its way to 3 p.m. she sat down with a mug of tea to watch the Queen's speech. It was another Christmas tradition insisted on by Flora for as long as she could remember and one that she would not break.

This year among the tragedies and triumphs the Queen talked about how it was four hundred years since Sir Walter Raleigh's encounter with the Spanish Armada. Melody found herself looking out of the window as if she might see the ghost ships of the Armada sailing past. She also wondered if Milo minded that the pearl earring she'd found all that time ago hadn't really belonged to Sir Walter Raleigh at all.

At the end of the Queen's speech, she stood up and pressed her empty mug solemnly against her heart and said, 'Thank you, Your Majesty,' before setting her brand-new video player to record *Back to the Future* and making her way to Big Joe's.

Joe, to her horror, was so delighted with the little bird she had made that he passed it around all his visitors.

Brian Franklin, who was wearing a three-piece suit and a tie patterned with frogs, turned it over in his hands. 'The embroidery is exquisite, isn't it, Stella?'

His wife was also dressed smartly for the occasion, appearing to be adorned in the entire contents of her jewellery box. 'It is indeed exquisite, Brian,' she approved, passing it to Old Tess for her inspection.

'I can't see the embroidery because my cataracts are too bad, but the colours are beautiful.' She peered at it through her National Health glasses, bringing it so close to her face that Melody thought she was going to eat it.

'It's bootiful. Really bootiful.' Mrs Galespie took hold of the little bird and grasped it by the cord where it dangled for everyone to admire again while Melody turned as crimson as the poinsettia Enid Johnson had bought for Joe.

'Thank you, Melody,' Joe said, putting it back on the tree. But Mrs Galespie wasn't satisfied with that.

'Is that it?' she cried. 'Go *on* Joe, give the girl a Christmas shmoozle for goodness sake.'

'What in heaven's name is a shmoozle?' Brian Franklin asked.

'You know, a bit of a kiss and all that. Got any mistletoe, Joe?'

'I've got some holly.' Joe held a piece of holly above his head and, with a twinkle in his eye he leant towards her. Melody would have loved nothing more than to kiss Joe passionately under the mistletoe or even the holly but she knew he was only playing with her. She pressed her lips briefly against his but stepped away to the sound of Mrs Galespie sighing.

'Oh, for 'eaven's sake, you two make me completely betwaddled. Are you ever going to see sense?' She gave one sharp nod of her head which made her cheeks wobble. 'You're a pair of gurt noodles. If you can't see what's under your bloody noses then gawd 'elp you.'

A week later, having enjoyed themselves so much at Christmas, they were all back in Pebbles raising a glass of port for the old year and the lives they had lived thus far. For the whole of New Year's Eve they laughed and they cried together, retelling tales of as much of the passing years as they could remember. Then, when the day, and ultimately the year, drew to a close, they each took turns to talk about 1988, what it had meant to them and where they were going from here. The Franklins had gained two more grandchildren, lost a dog and bought a small house in Kent. Enid Johnson, at seventy-two, had gained a newfound love for aerobics and was planning on finding husband number three. Mrs Galespie was staying. She'd inherited one of the brick houses a stone's throw away in Camperdown Terrace, a road to be untouched by the development and only yards from the estuary side of Shelly. Old Tess and Old Albert, however, had no choice as to their fate.

'We've had a good year. We've had a good life,' Old Albert

said. His hair was thin, creating a wispy halo of white around his head, and his rheumy eyes watered with age. 'But now we're to be despatched.' Both he and Old Tess said the word *despatched* in unison, making Melody's heart break for them. They'd lived in their bungalow for as long as she could remember but, with very little money and no family to speak of, they were now at the mercy of the authorities.

'We're going to some sort of facility on the outskirts of Exeter,' Old Albert said.

'It might as well be a million miles away,' Old Tess added.

Melody could see in their eyes that their light was already dimming and wondered what it would do to them to have to go.

When it was her turn she wasn't sure exactly what to say. 'Well,' she began thoughtfully. 'I'm now working in The Beach pub because they're open all day now and the hours and the tips are better than I could get at the shop. And... well... that's just about it!' She grinned at them all, hoping to get away with that, but seven sets of eyes stared back.

'Is that it?' Mrs Galespie was disappointed. 'Is that all we're getting?'

'I guess so,' Melody said, unable to think of much else to add.

'And what about other plans such as where you're going to live when the bulldozers come?'

Melody shrugged.

'What about going to stay with that cousin of yours? Juliewotzit or something? The one you made a complete tit of yourself with when you both got drunk back in the summer. The one whose hairdo can't make up its mind.'

'Juliana, you mean?' Melody laughed.

'That's the one.' Mrs Galespie gave a sharp nod of her head. 'Lovely girl.'

Melody's laughter turned into a sigh. All sets of eyes continued to remain fixed on her until she felt as if she were being peeled. She shrugged her shoulders and her answer cracked in her throat. 'I'm not going to live with Juliana, Mrs Galespie, but I don't have any plans made yet for where I am going to live.'

'Oh, that's not good,' Old Tess said.

'No, that's not good at all,' Old Albert said.

'Could you buy one of the fancy new apartments? Put your name down on one maybe?' Stella Franklin asked.

Again, Melody wasn't sure what to say. Even earning more money at the pub, her wages could never pay for such a place even if she wanted it, they must know that. 'I… I don't think so. I… I can't face it yet,' she stuttered.

'My turn!' Joe tapped his glass with the ladle from the mulled wine pan and Melody saw that he gave her a fleeting wink. 'You've all had your say and now you can hear mine.' He topped up everyone's glasses, fishing out a cinnamon stick that plopped into his own glass. '1988 was the year that I did what I do every year. I fished and I swam, I worked and I went to the pub. But, as for where I'm going to live, like Melody here, I don't know either. I may go and live somewhere else.'

'Like one of the apartments?' Mrs Galespie interjected.

'No, not like one of the apartments,' he replied, giving Melody a quick glance and catching her eye. 'I may go to…' he hesitated '… I may go to work somewhere *entirely* different.'

'Like Margate?' asked Brian Franklin.

'Like Rotterdam.'

Melody thought her heart had stopped because it took

her a moment to find any breath. '*Rotterdam?*' she echoed. Her voice, when it came, sounded thick with dismay and she kicked herself for letting it show.

'Rotterdam,' Joe repeated. 'It's a huge port and I'll be able to find work easily. Of course...' He caught her eye again. 'This is only if the rumour is true and the docks close. Or...' he continued to hold her gaze, 'if I don't get any other work here.'

A crease furrowed in his brow and the laughter lines at the corners of his eyes had disappeared. Melody looked away. This was her fault. The conversation she'd had with him in the pub had come back to haunt her. 'You had... er... talked about working on the development,' she ventured delicately.

'Not if it breaks hearts,' he replied. Melody thought he'd been about to say something else when Mrs Galespie interrupted.

'I feel like you two are 'aving a private bloody conversation 'ere? Whose 'earts would you be breaking, as if I didn't know?'

'I think it's Melody's,' Old Tess said.

'I think they're sweet on each other,' Old Albert added.

'Nooo, nothing like that, Albert!' Melody gasped, almost spilling her drink. Even though she caught the glass before it fell, a drop of red wine splashed the cheesecloth of her top and bloomed there.

'Well, you should be. You're perfect for each other.' Mrs Galespie grinned and lit up a cigarette, blowing the smoke away and over her shoulder before flicking the match expertly into Joe's fire. 'What do you say, Joe?'

'*Hush*, Mrs Galespie,' Melody hissed. Joe, she noticed, was fidgeting uncomfortably and she felt for him. As if they were trying to pin the wings of a beautiful bird and put it in a cage.

This man belonged to himself, not to her, not to anyone, and she, along with Mrs Galespie, needed to let him go. 'We don't like each other in that way.' She laughed a little too loudly, then tipped her glass to her lips and drained the contents of it. A fat segment of orange flowed into her mouth and, while they all stared at her, she ate it, including the rind.

'Phew!' Joe said, mock wiping his sweating brow. 'After all, I've known you since you were all spots and bruised knees, Melody. When you wore knitted swimming costumes and were always carting round a bucket full of crabs.'

Melody did her best to keep laughing. 'You make me sound irresistible,' she said.

At exactly midnight they all stood and raised their glasses to Shelly. They didn't, as would be normal, cheer at midnight for the coming of the new year but, instead, they celebrated the old year with an inharmonious rendition of 'Auld Lang Syne'. As the twelfth bell at midnight sounded they all linked arms and held hands in a circle as one and began to sing. Melody could basically hold a note, as could Enid Johnson, but all the others were utterly tuneless but, thanks to more mulled wine and a couple of brandies, nobody cared.

As their voices died down, they heard a shaky voice filling the room. Old Albert, standing with the pride of an old soldier, continued a tuneless but traditional version of the entire ballad. Not only that but he sang it complete with a Scottish accent which, as it happened, Old Albert didn't possess, having nearly as strong a Devon accent as Mrs Galespie. The rest of the room listened, their mouths hanging open with wonder. When he reached the last verse, Old Albert took a break for a moment. 'I went to university in Scotland,' he said. Then, and with everyone joining in, he resumed singing for the last verse.

For auld lang syne, my dear

For auld lang syne

We'll tak a cup o' kindness yet

For auld lang syne

At the end of the night, they embraced and, instead of wishing each other happy new year, they simply wished each other happiness. Joe hugged Old Tess and Old Albert until they were almost off their feet and when he reached his arms out for Melody, she could smell Pears soap on his skin. The last time they'd been this close his lips had lingered on her cheek, but this time he simply squashed a friendly cheek against hers and wrapped his arms around her shoulders.

She was released from the embrace almost as soon as it had begun.

## 1989, AUGUST

Christmas had soon become bleak January, which became an ice-cold February leading to a very rainy March. Finally the weather warmed again, bringing with it a summer sky of cobalt blue and a bright sun that scattered diamonds on the sea. And just as the moon kept rising and the sun kept setting and the sea rolled in and out with the tide, Joe had carried on being just Big Joe Wiley, the beach dude who worked, fished, swam in the sea, and slept in his boat *sometimes*.

So it was when Melody saw him jump down from Pebbles and stride purposefully across the sand towards Spindrift that she knew he had something to tell her.

'I'm moving out,' he'd said. He'd climbed up the first three steps of her wooden ladder and paused there, his chest bare, his hair scooped back with a bandanna. 'I'm going to live in my friend's cabin cruiser moored in the dock.' Melody returned his smile, but she was pretty sure it didn't reach her eyes. He looked over in the direction of his rowing boat pulled onto the sand near Pebbles and grinned his lazy grin. '*Wild Rose* can stay on the beach for now.'

Melody followed his gaze towards *Wild Rose* and with great sadness knew that soon she would no longer find him sleeping there. She would no longer swim with him in the sea or wake to find his footsteps in the sand.


Joe moved out swiftly and without fuss, taking his clothes and fishing gear and little else, having given away the few bits of furniture he possessed. Through her kitchen window she'd watched him walk past Spindrift, wearing a rucksack on his back and pulling his belongings strapped to the boat trailer he used for *Wild Rose*.

Three weeks later she found herself following an estate agent around the top-floor conversion of an old Victorian terraced house buried in the centre of town.

'This property is basically unfurnished but comes with some very attractive period features,' the estate agent said, pulling aside a beaded curtain for them to enter a room where a panelled wall created a small sitting room out of a once much larger room. 'Every room has radiators and double glazing.'

'And in here is an electric fire,' Melody said, wondering if he was aware that it was hardly a period feature.

'Yes. It's positioned in front of what was once a bedroom fireplace. Behind it you can see the mantel and hearth but this is less effort and more time-efficient, look here.' The estate agent exuberantly flicked a switch and instantly the room was filled with the orange glow of plastic coals. 'It gives the room ambiance,' he said, saying the word *ambiance* as if he had a mouthful of marbles. 'It's very nice, isn't it?'

'No,' replied Melody.

The man was dressed as if ready for a disco with a light grey suit and a shiny pink tie and he was already annoying her. 'You'll note that the property benefits from the extensive view due to it being top-floor accommodation.' She walked to the window of the room and looked out at the road below which was edged by an office block, a car park and a fast food restaurant. A mini supermarket on the corner spilt with empty delivery boxes and a dog tied outside to a rail barked for its owner. If she strained to see past the rooftops of the town and between two particularly large chimney pots of a hotel, she could just spot the tiniest strip of sea.

'You said in the particulars that it had a sea view.' She looked him in the eye and he looked her in the eye in return, his comb-over beginning to hang free at the side of his head.

'It has,' he said. Then, he straightened the pink shiny tie that had meandered to the side of his collar. 'It's a *very* popular location, madam. This flat will be snapped up in no time.'

Melody eyed a cobweb that trailed from the lampshade and could smell the dust burning on the filaments of the electric fire permeating the room. She asked him to turn it off before she passed out.

In the bathroom the floorboards creaked under their feet and she tried to imagine herself washing in an avocado-coloured bath in a bathroom that didn't have a window. 'So, bath with very useful overhead shower and privacy screen.' The agent tugged at a plastic curtain where a sad shower head hung from a bracket on the wall. 'Toilet, sink and so on and so forth,' he said, pointing to each item as if Melody should be somehow impressed that a bathroom contained a toilet and sink. 'And this,' he said, with a fanfare, 'is the *fully* equipped kitchen.' She followed him into the kitchen where an oven with an overhead grill rusted patiently in the corner and a big window framed the brick sidewall of the house next door. 'It has a rather lovely partial view,' he said, stepping aside for her to take a look. The house next door did indeed have a lovely garden bursting with greenery and colour and she could just about see it if she craned far enough around to almost break her neck. 'There is a very useful waste bin fitted into the cupboard under the sink and your general household waste can be placed in one of the modern wheelie bins in the yard outside. And here,' he continued, extra enthusiastically, 'is a particularly exciting feature of the property – *a buffet à déjeuner!*'

The agent beamed at her, pulling a leatherette bar stool out from one end of the counter top and Melody stared at the little breakfast bar. She imagined eating her clotted cream and white bread there and wondered how she might feel staring at the fading yellow paint on the wall directly in front of it. She was used to a tiny kitchen so the size of it was fine but the reality was that she'd stopped cooking herself sensible meals the day Milo had died. The *buffet à déjeuner* was hardly a selling feature for her, regardless of how many languages it was said in.

In the bedroom, she watched how the stray lock of the agent's comb-over released itself completely and flipped over his head as he stood in the middle of the room. 'It's not a big room but it's perfectly big enough for a double bed. Cosy enough for two... if ever you should need it.' He winked, then laughed at his own idea of funny, so much so that Melody could see two gold fillings in his back teeth. She turned away and sighed wearily. Whatever size the room was, she would no longer be able to walk next door into Milo's room. No longer be able to imagine the place where she used to sit in his wheelchair, hold his hand and kiss him goodnight. She would no longer be able to stand in her mother's room where her clothes still hung and her slippers still were. And she would no longer be able to pad her way across the sitting room to fling open the double doors that led to the sea.

'So, what do you think?' the agent asked, running a hand over his head to fix his hair back into place across the shiny top of his head. 'Like I said, we have more viewings booked and it will be snapped up very quickly. I think this property is perfect for a young lady like yourself.' He smiled greasily at her again and something inside Melody withered. He knew nothing about her. The dismay, the utter terrifying despair of leaving her house by the sea to live on the top floor of an old Victorian house in a narrow street in town crawled inside Melody and died.

'I'll take it,' she said.

\*

The flat, now secured and signed for and deposit paid, waited for her in the shadows of her future, a stranger without a personality. Melody walked home from the flat, over the dock bridge and towards Spindrift with a feeling of betrayal in her heart.

*Shelly was dying*, Juliana had once said. And it was. Shelly was taking its very last breaths. Some stalwart residents had refused to budge, staying firmly in their bungalows with the holes of devastation all around them. Their homes were caked in building dust, the demolition closer, the crashing of rubble louder as the days had tumbled on. And there, where metal and steel coiled upwards from the carcasses of their homes, were the red faces of poppies dancing in the detritus.

Three days later, she stood in the middle of Spindrift, the doors open to the sea breeze, an abundance of so many things to work out what to do with that her heart was doing cartwheels with her stomach. The very items that had given her comfort over the years were now holding her back, tethering her to Spindrift by so many strings she wasn't sure she would ever be able to snip herself free, and it made her feel quite ill. It was impossible to know what to pack. Some things were easy, of course, knick-knacks, clothes, books, her bed, a bedside lamp and a standard lamp, sofa and chair, table, rug, radio and television. But everything else... how on earth was she to choose? She wanted to take all of Milo's belongings with her, all of Flora's. And she wanted to take all her gatherings and beach treasures, too.

'Don't you ever lock your doors?'

Juliana appeared, standing by the kitchen door, and Melody screamed as if plugged into the mains. Losing her balance and falling backwards into an overstuffed plastic bag, it popped under the weight of her and split down one side as she landed on it, spilling a tangle of fishing rope and shells onto the floor. Unable to move with shock, she took in the vision in front of her.

Juliana looked different somehow. Softer, and her eyes were lighter as if she'd relieved them of her unhappy baggage in the months since her last visit. She wore wide-legged trousers with a little cropped jacket and her hair was loose, cut into a flattering messy layer around her shoulders. Melody wondered if Juliana could hear her heart thumping in her chest, or detect the adrenalin rushing fiercely through her veins. 'We don't ever lock our doors round here,' she squeaked. 'Remember? We've never had to lock them.' It felt silly that after such a long time apart, they should be having this conversation with Juliana standing in the doorway while she was still spreadeagled in an ungainly position on a plastic bag.

'Aren't you pleased to see me?' Juliana asked, squashing a smile.

'Yes,' Melody squeaked again.

'Then, could you tell your face that?' Juliana smiled with bashful relief.

Just then, the crash of a building being demolished nearby cracked through the air causing Melody to wince and cover her eyes. When she peeked them open again Juliana was standing in front of her holding out her hands. A tentative smile between the tears revealed a dimple on her right cheek, a reflection of the dimple that Melody had on her own cheek, her smile, a shy gesture of reunion. Melody's heart bled with a gladness that caused her to grasp at the offered hands, peeling herself off the bag and flinging herself up into the embrace as if her life depended on it.

'Oh, Jules. I am so, so, so glad you're here. Thank you,' she sobbed into Juliana's shoulder.

They stayed like that for a very long time, their hugs squeezing tighter for every crash and bang going on around them, Juliana's heart mirroring the rhythm of her own heart through the thin fabric of their summer clothes. And when, finally, they both moved it was only to lower themselves onto the sofa in the kind of fragile silence that shouted a thousand apologies. It wasn't until a sharp evening breeze billowed the curtains into the room, brushing a corner of one of them against Melody's hair, that Juliana spoke.

'I was a clumsy, bossy dunderhead last year, Mel. I was too proud to come back and apologise to you and that was wrong of me. Can you ever forgive me?' She shivered with the dropping temperature and Melody pulled a blanket over their shoulders, wrapping them together like a parcel.

'Forgiven, of course, a million times over,' she said, leaning into Juliana's side, stroking her hand in hers. 'And I was stupid and stubborn for kicking you out and then not telephoning you when all along you were right, I *was* overwhelmed by all my stuff. And now...' Her voice cracked and she paused for fear of crying again, forcing her tears back with so much effort they threatened to spout through the top of her head like a whistling kettle. She stared at a spot on the carpet until her throat relaxed enough to allow words to come out. 'I'm so... I'm *so terribly* overwhelmed I'm drowning in it. I just can't do it on my own.' She brushed angrily at rogue tears and breathed shakily. 'If I was a snail it wouldn't be a problem.'

This sounded much funnier than it had inside her head and it made Juliana giggle. She squeezed Melody's hand and Melody squeezed back. 'You're not a snail, more of a hermit crab, and it's time to move on.'

'But I can't be a hermit crab,' Melody moaned. 'They move into a bigger house as they grow but I'm doing the opposite. The flat I'm going to be renting is half the size of Spindrift and because I was cross with you it doesn't even have a spare room for you to stay.' Tears threatened again and she felt sick with the effort of keeping them back. Her mouth filled with so much saliva it squelched when she swallowed. Recalling the tiny strip of sea that was just visible over all the roofs if she looked out from the sitting room window gave her a feeling of suffocating gloom that took her breath away and she could hardly bear it. She heard Juliana clear her throat as if what she was about to say might be taken the wrong way.

'Is it… you know, is it money, Mel? Forgive me for asking but I could help if it is?'

Melody pondered this question and wondered if now was the time to tell Juliana about her money. The thousands of pounds she had tucked away in a building society account she'd never touched – and never wanted to. She imagined coming right out with it and watching the expression on Juliana's face change from one of pity to one of disbelief. She imagined it, but she didn't do it.

'I have enough money, thank you,' she said. She watched Juliana nod her head, cautiously accepting her answer as if she didn't really believe it.

'If you say so,' Juliana replied.

'Big Joe's bungalow is empty now,' Melody deflected. 'His lease on Pebbles has run out. For now, he's sleeping in a boat moored in the dock.' She thought of him sleeping on the water, every night after his shift in the dock, cooking his supper in the galley kitchen.

'Do you ever see him?' Juliana asked.

Melody pretended to think when, in fact, she had thought of little else except Joe since he left. 'I serve him his beer in the pub at the end of the day and we catch up then,' she said casually. 'He won't be bringing us flasks of warm cider, though, or any more hot sausage rolls. That galley kitchen in the boat is only just about big enough to boil an egg!'

Oblivious to Melody's internal dialogue, Juliana nudged her. 'Why you and him haven't ever *got it on* beats me. You're roughly the same age and he's positively gorgeous.'

Melody blushed furiously and the conversation that had happened with all the neighbours at Christmas echoed in her head. 'I've *told* you he's not interested in me.' She sighed as she said that. She hadn't meant to sigh, it just came out, but Juliana, thankfully, appeared not to notice.

'Mmm, I'm not so sure, Mel. I saw the way he looked at you. That was not the look of a loner. It was the look of someone who's found their soulmate.'

'Spots and bruised knees, that's what Joe said about me, Jules. That he's known me since I had spots and bruised knees.' She shook her head. 'He sees me as the kid that I used to be, a friend at best. You're making up your own stories.' She wished Juliana would stop going on about it and, needing to escape from the subject of Joe Wiley, she shook the blanket off her shoulders and got up from the sofa. 'Can I get you anything? You've just driven all the way from Cheltenham and you must be parched.'

Juliana followed her and, finding the bag she'd brought with her, delved into it and pulled out a bottle. 'How about this? I've brought wine... obviously, it's what I do.' She grinned. 'I've also brought music. CDs. Lots of them – and a CD player. I know you've got cassettes and records but we're going to need all the help we can get if I'm going to help you properly this time.' She took a step towards Melody and hesitated there for the smallest of moments before pulling her into another hug and talking into her hair. 'I've left *him* for good,' she murmured. 'He was a total twat and I'd become a supercilious witch. You could see it but I couldn't and you were right when you tried to tell me that *I* was the best part of me. *This...* is the new me. Or, strictly speaking, this is the old me.'

She stepped back for a second, showing Melody her whole, smiling self. It was, indeed, the old her. The Juliana before Alastair. Juliana pulled her once more into her arms. 'I have a gorgeous little house now, away from him and all his desperate social climbing. Mummy and Pops were none too happy to start with but they've accepted it now and I love my new life. You *must* come to stay when we've got you settled. For now, I'll stay for as long as you need me or want me, and I'll do whatever you ask – even if it's just to sit and look fabulous while you do all the work... *if* that's what you want. No orders. No being horribly bossy. Just me, your favourite cousin.'

Melody breathed in Juliana's perfume, feeling her strawberry-blonde hair upon her cheek. Her Juliana. The Juliana she loved was back. And so, without rehearsal, like a rush of water flowing up from her feet, through her body and slipping out of her mouth, came the thing she'd wanted to tell for so many difficult years. Just a handful of words but ones which were about to have the biggest impact out of anything she'd ever said in her whole life.

# 20

Melody's twenty-fifth birthday had been uneventful other than a few cards from friends, a crab and two mackerel from Big Joe, plus a phone call where Uncle Gordon, Aunt Isobel and Juliana passed the phone between them to wish her many happy returns. It was, however, another phone call that she received two days later, and a subsequent visit arranged, that floored her. She was unsure as to the purpose of the visit but, tired of all the unanswered questions that had assaulted her ever since Flora had died, she resolved to tackle things head on. After all, she'd sat in silence dealing with it alone for too long.

Now, one week after her birthday, she waited as calmly as she could and did her best to push back her nerves. She had dug out the blue folder containing the photograph, the yellowing envelope and the twist of hair and fought, once more, with all the jags and jangles that spilt from it, wounding her with their truth. They made her think about Daniel on the day that Milo had been born. How he'd flung open the doors to Spindrift shouting to the world that he had a son, and, in a rare display of emotion, had suddenly scooped her up, swinging her round in his jubilance. How, a year later, when Juliana had been born, Daniel had started to compare her progress with Milo's, becoming increasingly frustrated by it. How disappointed he'd seemed when he realised Milo wouldn't be the son he'd dreamt of having. Both she and Milo, she understood now, had, in their own different ways, been difficult for Daniel.

Despite everything, she felt sorry for him. 'It's OK,' she said to the photo. 'I understand now.'

A northerly wind was singing its way around Spindrift, rattling the rubbish bin against her fence, and, due to the dullness of a heavy cloud, she'd put the lamps on to soften the room, placing a brightly coloured blanket on each chair. She wasn't sure why, but she'd done her best to make her home as comfortable as she could for the visit. When she heard a car pulling to a stop outside Spindrift, she put the things back in the folder and, with her heart in her mouth, opened the front door.

'Uncle Gordon,' she said.

'Melody,' he smiled.

'Come in.' She swept a hand towards the sitting room and he walked in. The little china tea set was unpacked for the occasion and on the delicate plates was a shop-bought Battenburg cake plus egg and cress sandwiches cut into triangles and organised as appealingly as egg sandwiches can be. It was all set out on her mother's floral tray. 'Tea?' she asked politely.

'Please,' he nodded, allowing her to pour his tea, just as she knew how he liked it, a drop of milk and one sugar. As she handed him his tea she saw that he was surveying Spindrift, casting his eye across all the gatherings that were growing.

'Tell me why you're here?' she said.

Gordon cleared his throat and tearing his gaze away from an overstuffed bag of flotsam and jetsam he fidgeted a little in his chair. She noticed that his breath was coming in short, anxious puffs and she waited patiently to hear what he had to say. 'As you know, your Aunt Isobel and I have been worried about you since Flora's passing. We are aware that, because of... shall we say *circumstance*, you didn't attend university and as such it might be a little... *tricky* for you to find suitable employment worthy of your intelligence – to sustain your upkeep moving forward, so to speak.'

Melody kept silent.

'We know,' he continued, 'that you are fiercely independent and we admire that in you, Melody, very much indeed. But we believe that it is only right to help you financially. To that end, I have something for you.' Gordon reached into his inside pocket and withdrew some papers. 'A building society account has been set up for you... it is yours to do with what you will.'

Melody smarted and the hair on the back of her neck prickled. She opened the papers for the building society account and printed on the page in front of her was a sum of money the likes of which she could hardly even imagine. How she managed to stop herself leaping out of her chair and yelling *HOLY MOLY* at him, she really wasn't sure – but she did. Calmly, she folded the papers again and handed them back.

'It is quite a substantial sum,' Gordon stated unnecessarily.

Melody took a measured breath. 'And Aunt Isobel, my *godmother*, she isn't with you today. Does she know about this... substantial sum?'

'I was hoping to keep this between the two of us. Isobel...

she doesn't need the stresses of such matters at present.' He cleared his throat as if he felt uncomfortable.

'Secrets. So many secrets,' Melody muttered, the contents of the blue folder screaming at her. 'And why should it be such a stress for Aunt Isobel?' she asked.

'It's complicated,' he replied, flushing even more.

Melody gave nothing away of her internal turmoil other than a deliberate veil of mirthless laughter that trailed out on her breath. Slowly and deliberately she opened the blue folder to reveal its contents. 'I thought you might have come to discuss something else...' She picked up the photo and held it out for him to see. Flora and Daniel smiling for the camera, young and in love. 'See this photo? It has a date on it...' She turned it round to reveal the date penned on the back, watching as a look of awful understanding came to his face. 'I have other things, too,' she continued, taking out of the folder the twist of hair tied with a red ribbon and the yellowing envelope.

Eyes that once twinkled began to dull with fear, or apology, or even regret. Perhaps, Melody thought, all three. Whatever it was, it writhed, barely contained, behind the flecked hazel of them. 'How long have you known?' he whispered. This question stabbed at Melody. The man in front of her had played his part in the secret so well for the whole of her life, yet now here he was, husked and exposed.

'Don't worry, Flora took it to the grave with her. She'd hidden the evidence of it but when she died I found these things inside an old book. It wasn't hard to put two and two together.'

Gordon had a look of overwhelming fear on his greying face and Melody realised he wasn't asking, he was begging.

He gave the smallest of sighs and a shimmer of tears fell from his eyes.

'What must you think of us?' he said quietly.

Melody shrugged. It wasn't the kind of shrug that might say she didn't care what she thought of them, but more the kind that said she cared too much.

# 21

Melody stood back and faced Juliana. 'You know we're *not* cousins, don't you?' she said.

As the opportunity to make this declaration had taken Melody by surprise, caught out by it, she screwed up her eyes over the total stupidity of how she'd just said it. This exact moment had played itself out in her mind so many times and never once had she rehearsed it as a question. Of course Juliana didn't know they weren't cousins, otherwise the world might have been a totally different place for both of them from the onset. A wonky kind of smile appeared on Juliana's face and she tilted her head with such a look of complete and utter confusion that Melody felt bad for delivering the news in this way.

'What do you mean we're *not* cousins? Of course we're cousins. You and Milo, you're the only cousins I've got.' She stepped backwards, scrutinising Melody's face for a sign of a joke or a clue as to why she'd said something so *outlandish*, but there was more to come. Pacing the room at a furious speed, a caged animal looking for a way out, Melody pushed each careful word out of her mouth.

'We...' she sighed '... we... are *sisters*.' She halted for a second to cast a pained glance at Juliana before continuing with her pacing. In and out of the bags and boxes she went, searching for the best way to impart the knowledge she'd kept to herself for so long, now almost incapable of saying it sensibly. 'Milo was your cousin, but also *my* cousin. Milo was *not* my brother.'

She struggled admitting this out loud – just as she'd always known she would. She was a traitor to Milo and wanted to scoop the words back inside as if they'd never been said. But they were out. They'd birthed themselves from her gullet, tearing at her throat, sour in her mouth – and the guilt that came with them was unbearable. So much guilt. Not because Gordon had begged her not to tell, but for beautiful Milo who was always standing in the shadows of her mind, now denounced as her brother, pushed aside for a sister.

'What?' The sound, like the thin wail of an injured animal, came through the fixed lips of Juliana's wonky smile, issued in the kind of pitch that suggested Melody had gone a little mad. Juliana grabbed at her, holding on to her arms and forcing her to be still. 'Stop! Stop pacing about. You're not making any sense.' Melody tried to shake her off but the grip was too tight, perfectly varnished nails biting into the skin of her arm. 'Breathe, Mel. In and out, like this.' She sucked air in through her nose and out through her mouth until Melody was able to do the same, calmly in, calmly out. 'Now,' she said, still gripping her arms. 'Tell me what the *fuck* you're talking about.'

Melody's answer was caught on her teeth, frozen on her lips and inside her head was a muddle of emotions. She had a sister. A beautiful sister with strawberry-blonde hair and eyes the colour of her own, and she knew, that despite all the years of remaining true to Milo, she needed her. She needed and loved her so much. The barriers she'd built up around herself were tumbling down and now that the truth was coming out she could hardly wait to let her sister in.

Juliana didn't move and as the seconds passed the skin of her face seemed to become almost translucent. 'I'm so sorry, Jules,' Melody said. 'But I've been carrying this around with me for such a long time. I can't do it on my own any more. They tried to keep it from us but I found out.'

'But I... I don't understand. What are you saying? This is horrible and you're... lying. You must be.' Juliana's grip on Melody relaxed and her hand dropped to her side as if the weight of it was too much. Then, as if she were melting, she sank her body into the sofa and her brown eyes, exactly the same depth of brown as Melody's, sheened with tears. 'Are you trying to tell me that my father and your mother... That *he*... with *Aunty Flora*...' Her face twisted into an ugly knot and red blooms appeared on her cheeks, stark against the sickly yellow of her pallor.

Melody sank into the sofa next to Juliana and allowed her own tears to fall.

'No, Jules,' she replied. 'That's *not* what I'm trying to tell you.'

# 22

Gordon hadn't touched the cake or sandwiches Melody had put out for him and his tea had grown cold in the cup. He held the photograph in his hand turning it to see the date on the back. Daniel was dressed in a blazer and shirt while Flora wore a cotton dress nipped tightly in at the waist with a belt.

'April 1954,' Melody clarified. 'Only a few weeks before I was born. Incredibly slim for eight months pregnant, don't you think?'

It was as if time waltzed around them in the gap that followed. Time, which in its silence screamed of lies. She waited for him to gather his thoughts, filling his lungs and exhaling again as if he were standing on the wings of a stage for the greatest performance of his life. His cheeks were pulled into hollows that hadn't been there before, and she saw that he was fighting for words, a nervous tongue running over dry lips. When, finally, Gordon was able to talk, his words floated into the room on a breath of sadness.

'We were so young, Isobel and I – she was only sixteen and I was only seventeen, but we were very much in love.' He tried to smile at this but the memory of it caused his breath to snag in his throat. 'Isobel didn't even realise she was pregnant with you until it started to show and when we did realise... oh, we were both so frightened.' He glanced at Melody and his pain was etched in lines across his face, darkening his eyes with so many things left undone and unsaid. Melody, in turn, waited expressionless for his story to unravel – a seemingly tragic love story that would lead to the tale of her own abandonment.

'So you gave me away.'

Gordon shook his head. 'We didn't want to give you away but we had little choice. Isobel's parents were so strict. It was another era back then, a time when their unmarried daughter being in the family way was unthinkable. Overnight, we became a social disgrace and our love for each other... well, that didn't come into it, I'm afraid.' He put his head in his hands and rubbed at his hair until, finally, when he looked up, his hair was at angles, his agony clear for Melody to see. He looked so unlike the well-groomed Uncle Gordon she'd always known that a wave of pity almost made her lose control and she had to battle against an impulsive need to hug him.

'Go on,' she said, coolly.

'Isobel's parents, your grandparents, simply wouldn't listen to me when I told them that, if they allowed us to get married, I would work every hour possible in order to provide for Isobel and for our baby. They wouldn't listen, though, because like them, society had other ideas. A child born too soon after marriage would still cause a scandal to fall upon their family and they simply wouldn't consider it. Instead, Isobel was to be sent away, to disappear until it was all over and then return to her studies.'

Melody only vaguely remembered her grandparents. Two

austere individuals on the periphery of her memory, grey images in grey photographs. She'd given them little thought until now. They didn't sound very nice and she was glad she hadn't known them. Her thoughts grew so huge they filled her head like bubbles, swelling and jostling for answers. 'But Flora was their daughter, too. Why was it all right for her to raise me instead?' Melody crinkled her mouth at Gordon, confused. 'To take a baby from one sister but give it to the other is a scandal in itself, isn't it?'

'Flora and Daniel were older and they were married. They hadn't been married long, but it was long enough… if you get my meaning and, at that point, they didn't have a child. Isobel was sent to stay in Exmouth with Flora and Daniel under the pretence that she was recovering from an illness. She was to return when it was all over. Flora rarely visited your grandparents due to being in disgrace for marrying beneath herself – Daniel, a dock labourer, was hardly the right match for a well-brought-up girl like Flora, in their opinion.'

'But he was good enough to save the family name… *in their opinion*.' A flash of anger burst from Melody and she wished she could give them a piece of her mind. So many people had suffered because of them and their pandering to society's values. For a reason she couldn't rationalise, she grabbed a piece of Battenburg cake and took an enormous, angry bite. It crumbled into dry lumps in her mouth which she swallowed down with cold tea, her hands shaking so much she nearly spilt the liquid before the cup reached her mouth. She swallowed and it made an irritating gurgling sound in her throat.

Gordon studied the palms of his hands. 'Isobel leapt at the

idea of Flora raising you, rather than lose you forever. Daniel had little say in the matter and Flora was a strong woman.'

'She was,' Melody agreed. She thought about the two sisters and the bond they'd forged and tried to put herself in Isobel's position. How had Isobel felt when she had to go home, childless, her arms empty? Unbidden tears blurred her vision as she imagined herself as a tiny baby caught up in the tangle of it all. 'All the times Isobel visited, she barely gave me more than a pat on the head. She was always so distant with me and I couldn't understand why you never stayed long when you brought Juliana. Not ever. You came every year only just long enough for tea and cake and to leave Juliana's suitcase. I always thought we weren't good enough for you.'

Gordon sagged before her eyes as if the awfulness of everything had grown in density and, now that it was out in the open, was crushing him. A lifetime of questions slotted into place as she saw how he wrung his hands, twisting his fingers into knots, his carefully manicured nails cleaned and buffed to an opulent shine. He smelt of aftershave and Harris tweed and a life far removed from the one she'd lived and the scent of him filled her with a longing. Longing for a father that she hated herself for admitting.

'Try to find it in your heart to forgive us, Melody. To forgive Isobel for seeming so distant as you say. She was never the same after she had to give you away and to mentally shut off from you was the only way she could cope. Let me tell you that it broke both of us but Isobel cried so much when she handed you over, and she cried all the way home to Cheltenham, then she cried for weeks and weeks after that. I'm not entirely sure she's ever stopped. She couldn't hug you or soften towards you when she visited because to do so would have broken down the barriers she'd worked so hard to build. She's a *good* woman, Melody, but she would never go back on her agreement with her sister. The minute we handed you over, you were no longer our daughter. You were Flora's – and that's the way it had to be. A sister's bond, they called it.'

'A *sister's bond*,' Melody whispered.

Gordon sipped delicately at his stone-cold tea as if it were piping hot and she thought briefly about making a fresh pot if only she could bring herself to move. She was glued, though, to the spot she sat in. 'Flora insisted that she be allowed to bring you up in her own way. She was never the kind of girl to seek the higher things in life and her way was to raise you with her values – a simple life by the sea.'

Melody smiled to herself. She remembered the quiet hugs the sisters would give each other each summer. How Aunt Isobel had repeatedly invited them to move back to Cheltenham. How Flora had replied, *Spindrift is all we need*. How quietly steadfast she had been to raise her children where they could be free of the constraints of middle-class society and the values that forced mothers to give up their babies for propriety. The same values that had tortured Isobel with loss and pain and guilt for all those years.

Through the windows, she could see the ferry from Starcross making its way back to Exmouth and how the clouds reflected in the sea and the waves bubbled with white crests. And she was so glad that Isobel had brought her here to Flora.

'When Juliana came along I think Isobel saw her as an opportunity to make amends for losing you.' Gordon's voice broke into her thoughts. 'She showered her with everything a child could possibly want. Beautiful clothes… the best education.' He gave a sad shrug. 'But, of course, making up for lost things in this way isn't how it works when it comes to our loved ones, is it?'

Melody shrugged back. She felt sorry for Juliana. Juliana – the protégée who had to shine too brightly. Enough for a mother's guilt. Enough for the baby who was given away. Enough for a sister she didn't know she had. 'So, which one of you decided that Juliana should visit me every summer?' she asked.

'They agreed it between themselves,' he replied. 'Flora and Isobel loved each other dearly and neither sister could bear the idea that you two couldn't experience at least some of the same – that even if you never knew the truth about each other, you would, at least, know love.'

They had known love, Melody mused, recalling midnight feasts, adventures on the water and games on the beach. But their love for each other, sadly, was not as sisters, it was as cousins sharing their summers together, a relationship built on fleeting sun-kissed days. The reality was that Juliana, now at university, had always lived a very different life from Melody's own. She went to parties, stayed with friends in the holidays, and had a boyfriend called Alastair who wore her on his arm like an expensive gold watch.

She picked up the twist of hair and studied it. Strawberry-blonde hair intertwined with her own blonde hair was tied with a thin red ribbon and she pressed it to her lips. 'Our hair,' she whispered. 'Flora must have snipped some from each of us one summer and wound us together.' She picked up the yellowing envelope, remembering how, when Juliana was born, the letter had arrived at Spindrift. She'd been doing a puzzle of a circus and Milo had been asleep in his pram when Flora had read the letter quietly to herself before announcing that Aunt Isobel and Uncle Gordon had a new baby. Melody now opened the envelope and read it for Gordon.

March 1958

My dear sister, Florentine,

I am writing to let you know that Gordon and I are now the proud parents of a little girl we have named Juliana. She came into the world in the early hours of this morning with the fiercest of screams and the softest curls of damp, golden hair. We can honestly say that our hearts are fit to burst with joy.

This is the last time we will talk of matters past because we know what we have lost and you have gained, my dear Flora, but I hope that, with your help, mine and Gordon's two daughters may, in some way, come to know and love each other.

With our undying love and gratitude,
always and forever, your sister,
Isobel.

Melody finished the letter, wondering why Flora had never destroyed these things. Why she'd felt the need to keep that letter or make a twist out of their hair. Surely she knew that this evidence would, one day, out the secret? Had her mother left clues, unable to break the bond with her own sister but, equally, unable to let Melody and Juliana suffer forever because of it?

'Isobel wrote in that letter that it would be the last time that *matters past* should be mentioned. I believe that we should keep this between ourselves and not tell Isobel or Juliana that you know.' Gordon ran a nervous hand around his collar. 'To revisit it will only open old wounds for Isobel.'

A polite smile trembled on Melody's lips belying how she felt about this request. She suspected that the wounds for Isobel were not old at all, but as fresh as if her baby had been plucked from her arms only minutes ago. She had been railroaded into giving up her child and now that child was being railroaded into keeping quiet about it. The stupid, old-fashioned attitudes that Isobel had been forced to contend with had such far-reaching effects and now they were all caught up in it.

Gordon tried again to give her the details of the account he'd set up for her, but when she refused he exhaled with frustration through his nose. 'Isobel and Flora may have had an agreement but you were my baby, too, Melody. As a father, I needed to protect both of you. To ensure that you wouldn't be divided by opportunity as well as our mistakes. Juliana has and will be financially supported until she reaches the age of twenty-five and you, my dear, are now that age. This money was the only way I could think of to make up for everything. Every penny that's been spent on Juliana I have matched for you – in this account. I've endeavoured to calculate the equivalent that has been spent on her birthdays, Christmas, our trips abroad, her school fees – all of it. She's at university now and I've also reflected the expense of that in this account as well.'

Melody chewed on the inside of her cheek. She felt sorry for him thinking that money was the answer. Putting a price on all that she'd missed out on made it sound as if he thought her own life had been less rich than it had been. 'Thank you, Uncle Gordon. But I have money.' She pulled a cheerless smile, hoping to hide the fact that her job would barely pay enough to save for a new home if the time arrived. 'In fact, I have a shift soon so I have to get ready for it.' She was lying, of course. Her shift wasn't until tomorrow but their conversation here was done. Standing up, she placed their cups on the tray and took it into the kitchen. She needed to get away from the eyes that belonged to the man who wasn't really her uncle.

Gordon, understanding that he was being dismissed, followed her to the kitchen doorway with the papers for the account and implored her one last time. 'I had... *I have*... two daughters. One who had every advantage in life and the other who was running barefoot and likely to be wearing something made from curtains. And Daniel left you all in the lurch. What a weak, selfish man he turned out to be.'

Melody flinched. She remembered the dresses made from curtains and how she'd stood on a stool so that Flora could place pins along the hem. How, when the dresses were at last finished, they'd both swirled around the room singing songs from *The Sound of Music* with Milo clapping as they danced. She gently pushed Gordon aside and made her way towards the front door.

Gordon, knowing he was losing the battle, balled a fist and smacked it into the open palm of his other hand imploring her to listen to reason.

'Uncle Gordon,' Melody began, raising her chin in defiance.

'I get the feeling that you're apologising for my life. Don't do that. Don't ever do that. Apologise for your own mistakes or for society's mistakes – but don't apologise for *my* life. Everyone did their best and their best was good enough for me.'

'Even Daniel?'

'Even Daniel,' she replied. 'He could have refused to take me on but he didn't because he loved my mother enough to bring up someone else's child in an era which wasn't very understanding. And he did his best, I know he did, despite you and your family coming here every summer to remind him of his failings – Spindrift ageing with each winter that passed, or a wife who knitted, sewed and darned to keep us all clothed. And Juliana and I, we hit all our milestones, reading and writing well in advance of our ages while Milo, dear, sweet Milo, Daniel's *own* flesh and blood, seeming, in his eyes, unable to compete with us. It may have been hard for Isobel but it was also hard for Daniel.'

'Then, I'm a clumsy fool, Melody,' Gordon apologised, hanging his head and looking hopelessly apologetic.

She glanced briefly up at him, unable to linger on eyes so anguished they hurt her heart. Opening the front door she moved aside to allow him to leave. Stepping over the threshold, Gordon halted, imploring her to see reason. 'Life changes as surely as the seasons, Melody, and you never know what the future holds. I'll be here waiting to help you if you ever need me. And the money? Even if you dispose of the details of your account, it will still be there, accruing interest, waiting should you ever need it.'

Melody swallowed, her agony rising to her throat. The money, this meeting, the need to continue keeping the secret – it was all so clandestine. She gripped the edge of the door and stood half behind it.

'I loved you from the moment I saw you.' Gordon walked backwards away from her still begging. 'Leaving you, a tiny scrap of a thing, was the hardest thing Isobel and I ever had to do. Juliana couldn't make up for you, she just highlighted everything about you that we'd missed out on.'

'Goodbye, Gordon,' Melody said, clicking the door shut. Then, when after an age of time passed, she heard the engine of his car roar into life as he drove away, she slithered down the door and there, on the floor beside Daniel's old rubber boots, she cried as if her heart would break.

# 23

Side by side on the sofa, Melody braced herself to tell Juliana everything.

'I'm your *whole* sister, Jules... not a half-sister.' She waited to allow the information to sink completely in, studying the knot on Juliana's brow as it became tighter, trying to process what she'd just heard. Melody left her for a brief moment, rushing into Flora's bedroom to return with the blue folder and taking out the photograph of Daniel and Flora. She held it up for Juliana to see. 'Look, April 1954, written on it plain as day.'

'So what of it?' Juliana peered at the photograph. 'I don't know what you're trying to *say*.'

'I'm trying to say that this photo,' Melody jabbed at it, 'is dated *April* 1954 and I was born in *May* 1954.' She pointed to Flora's image, to where her dress was nipped in tightly with a belt revealing a tiny waist. She waited again for the penny to drop, quietly amazed that someone with a university degree could take so long to do the maths. 'My mother is not pregnant.'

This time she waited only a matter of seconds before

Juliana's hand moved slowly to her mouth covering it with quivering fingers, the whites of her eyes showing her understanding. 'Oh my God... you're adopted!'

Melody took a steady, patient breath realising that this was going to be harder than she thought. 'Jules, I said I was your *whole* sister. My mother, Flora, was not pregnant in 1954... but *your* mother was.'

'*Mummy!*' Juliana exclaimed. 'What has *Mummy* got to do with anything?'

Melody took yet another patient breath and tried again. 'I am Isobel's baby!'

'But in 1954 Mummy was only *sixteen*...' Juliana shot Melody a disbelieving look.

'Exactly,' Melody replied. 'Because of the harsh, old-fashioned attitudes of the day, our grandparents forced her to give me away.'

Juliana's fingers pressed hard against her mouth in an effort to force her shock inside and she released them only long enough to speak. 'So who...? Was it my dad?'

Melody nodded and sank down onto the rug in front of the sofa, placing her hands on Juliana's knees. 'Yes, she was with Gordon. I didn't know the whole story myself until my twenty-fifth birthday. I discovered that Flora wasn't my birth mother when I found the photograph and letter and that Milo wasn't my true brother but I didn't understand all the details until I met with your dad... our dad... *Gordon*. It was just after my twenty-fifth birthday when I confronted him.'

'And what did he say?' Juliana had gone the colour of wax and Melody could feel her knees trembling against her.

'He told me not to tell you... or Isobel.' Melody knew it was harsh of her to phrase it like that, as if no other conversation had taken place on that day. In fact, she still remembered all the details of it. Every word. Every heartbreaking tear.

'But... they stayed together. They got married and had me.'

'That's what makes it even sadder,' Melody sighed. 'When they were old enough they got married and then, a year after that, you came along. Everything done by the letter and with the full seal of approval from the grandparents and society.'

'And by then, I guess, they could hardly ask to have you back.' Juliana's voice came out in a dry rasp as if the news had sucked all the moisture clean out of her. 'They have never breathed a single word to me.' She scratched her head and her mouth turned down at the corners. 'I don't quite know what to make of this. I feel... well, I feel deceived by my own parents.' She looked at Melody and her eyes were imploring her to help make sense of it all.

'Gordon says that Isobel never dealt with the reality of it all. I think she really suffered, Jules, that's why he begged me to keep the secret. He's been trying to protect her, so, for her sake, I did.' A sob issued from her throat and she hiccoughed it back in. 'But it isn't fair on either of us, is it?'

'We're sisters,' Juliana whispered. She raised a hand and stroked Melody's hair. 'All these years...' Her voice petered out and her chin started to wobble. 'We've led such different lives,' she sniffed. 'I've had so much – all the experiences money can buy. I've spent years telling you about how many parties, restaurants, *countries* even that I've boozed my way through on champagne and cocktails and yet...'

'And yet, what?' Melody asked, already knowing what she was alluding to. Gordon had suggested the very same thing.

'And yet... *you* haven't...'

'Oh, but I've had *everything*,' she cried. 'I've had all of this.' She threw her arm out in the direction of the double doors where all she loved was out there. 'I don't regret anything... apart from you.' She wiped at her face. 'When I found out the truth, I wanted so much to share it with you and for such a long time I battled with whether to tell you or not. I wanted to talk to Isobel, too, but Gordon said no.'

'Pops should never have asked you to do that,' Juliana said. 'It was wrong of him in so many ways. It's not fair on you, it's not fair on me now and it's certainly not fair on Mummy. It must have torn you into shreds keeping this to yourself.'

Melody sat back on her heels and pulled strands of her hair away from her damp face and wondered if Juliana would be able to understand what it had really cost her to keep such a secret. She took a sad breath. 'What really tore me to shreds was the guilt.'

Juliana looked surprised. 'Guilt?'

Melody sagged as she realised Juliana didn't understand the depths of it all. She'd just gained a sister but, for Melody, it was not that simple. 'I felt guilty for knowing that I had a whole other family when I already had my own family. I couldn't cope with the idea of being a traitor to them. Embracing the idea of another family and you as my real sister so soon after they died would have come with complications that I couldn't deal with at the time. It was all too much for me and I fell down such a hole that I thought I'd never come out of it.'

Unexpectedly, revisiting the awful moment she'd discovered the truth, Melody started to shake. She could feel it unleashing inside her, stampeding through her whole body, leaving no part of her intact. Flora dying so suddenly, so cruelly snatched away, had been too much to bear. She'd been wading through the mud of grief, heavy with loss, yet all the while having to put on a smiling mask for Milo. And then she'd found the photograph. For so long she'd stared at it, trying to process what it meant. Trying to come to terms with the fact that the beautiful lady who now lay in her grave was not her birth mother. Trying to come to terms with the fact that there was another mother, another father, a *sister*.

Alone, she'd continued to care for Milo, to wash his wasting body, to feed him and bring him stories and adventures from the beach. She loved him to the very core of her being and, all the while, had done her best to push the truth back inside where it couldn't hurt either of them. It had been such a hard, lonely, awful time.

Juliana wrapped two strong arms around her, holding her together. She could feel the warmth of Juliana's breath against her skin and, as on the day of Flora's funeral, just the touch of her prevented Melody from splintering into a million little pieces. They stayed like that, silent, enfolded within each other, the tendrils of their hair entwined much like the twist of their hair that had been tied with a red ribbon all those years ago.

And when, at last, Melody stopped trembling, Juliana still did not let her go. 'Tell me about your conversation with Pops,' Juliana whispered into her hair. 'I want to understand why they had to give you to Aunty Flora and why he doesn't want you to tell Mummy. I want to understand so that you never have to feel alone again. Let's put our pyjamas on and bloody well tuck into that wine I brought while you tell me everything.'

And so it was that two sisters, one in a rose-print silk robe and the other in an old yellow towelling dressing gown talked into the night, their fingers locked as one. By the time they hugged each other goodnight, having talked for so long that their eyelids were swollen, their noses red with blowing, dawn was painting a verdigris sky and the early fishing boats were heading out to sea.

After only a few hours' sleep, however, they woke mid-morning to hear someone knocking so urgently on the front door of Spindrift, and so loudly that it sounded as if nothing short of a calamity had happened. Rubbing sleep dust from her eyes and still wearing her nightclothes, Melody ran out of the bedroom and ploughed straight into Mrs Galespie who, being unable to wait, had let herself in and was already standing breathless in the hallway. 'We,' she announced, planting her hands on her ample hips, 'we, are going to 'ave a party!'

'Right now?' Juliana appeared yawning and knotting the belt of her silk robe.

'Next Saturday. Beach games, barbecue, the lot! We, as in the last members of our community and anyone who wants to join, are going to give Shelly the ruddy good send-off it deserves.' Mrs Galespie pursed her lips, gave a single, sharp nod of her head then, as quickly as she'd arrived, she left. Given no chance to answer, Melody and Juliana stood dumbfounded in the faint waft of stale cigarette smoke left in her trail, until they heard a distant shout coming from the path outside. 'AND BRING A SAUSAGE!'

# 24

In the summer of 1981, Melody found herself following every newspaper article and television programme on the subject of the wedding of Prince Charles and Lady Diana Spencer. It was with even further excitement that she accepted Joe Wiley's invitation to join him for an evening barbecue with his father and various members of his extended family to celebrate the event.

'What shall I bring?' she asked, thrilled to be included on such a special day.

'Anything,' Joe answered casually.

'Anything?' Melody queried. 'Bread rolls? Sausages? An entire suckling pig?'

'Whatever you like. I'm supplying the bread rolls but other than that we're all bringing something to share. It's going to be a pot-luck kind of feast so if you end up bringing a cabbage, that's what we'll have.'

Melody didn't buy a cabbage but instead bought a case of beer, plus a very generous fifty Cumberland sausages from the best butcher in town. She had thought about baking some cakes because that's what Flora would have done but the royal wedding was to be televised for much of the day and she would be glued to it. She also reasoned that with all the bread rolls filling everyone up, people were bound to be more inventive than she was, probably bringing bowls of bright salad or punnets of strawberries. Sausages, she believed, never failed to go down well at a barbecue.

On the day of Joe's barbecue, Melody spent hours in front of her television mesmerised by the length of the train on Lady Diana's dress and how it flowed behind her like a glorious waterfall of taffeta and lace. Melody immersed herself in the wonder of it all, the beautiful carriages, the gleaming uniforms of the Horse Guards, the procession and ceremony, the huge crowds all cheering for the princess and the fairy tale. The beach was noticeably quiet that day with most of her neighbours and holiday-makers likely doing the same as her, all swooning over the wonder of a royal marriage that was bringing an entire country together.

When, finally, the wedding was over, Melody sighed happily, cleared away the debris of tea and biscuits, nuts and crisps she'd nibbled on all day, and got ready for the barbecue. Still lost in the romance of the royal wedding she chose her clothes carefully. A long calico skirt, a linen vest top, a selection of handmade leather and bead bracelets with a jade-green polished stone necklace. Her feet were bare, her hair was loose and she'd dabbed her mother's favourite perfume behind each ear. It was perfect for such an evening.

Joe's family, who had finished watching the wedding, were spilling out into his terrace and onto the beach by the time she made her way down her own wooden ladder and across the sand. Joe was piling coals into an old but huge barbecue he'd situated on the beach and he grinned warmly when he saw her. 'Melody,' he said, as she approached, and her heart, as always, missed a beat. She imagined for a fanciful second that she was a princess and he, her prince, saying her name as if he was caressing the sound of it in his mouth. She knew she could listen to him saying it forever. 'You look nice,' he said, smiling at her, causing a crimson blush to travel up her neck and across her cheeks. Unsure of how to respond to such a compliment she simply held up the two bags she was carrying.

'Beer and sausages,' she said. For some reason, Joe took the bags and started laughing and Melody's bubble of fanciful imagination immediately popped.

'What's so funny about beer and sausages?' she asked.

'Nothing's funny about beer,' he answered. 'But...' He lifted a cloth from a picnic table near the barbecue to reveal the biggest mountain of fat pink sausages that Melody had ever seen. He grinned. 'Everyone had the same idea. I'm spectacularly over-sausaged.'

Mrs Galespie happened to walk past just at that moment and elbowed him in the ribs. 'Ooh, spectacularly over-sausaged, 'ey?' she cackled, giving Melody a theatrical wink.

'Oh!' she mumbled, smothering a laugh, as Joe flexed his muscles and posed like a Greek god before he threw his head back and laughed.

'We're going to have a sausage fest,' Joe's grandma called out, giggling into a glass of shandy, which made Mrs Galespie cackle even louder.

Joe, his eyes crinkling with a huge grin, grabbed Melody's hand and pulled her away, calling over his shoulder, 'Don't you start on the sausage jokes as well, Grandma. I'm going to get Melody a drink but it sounds like you've had enough shandy.' He didn't hold her hand for long, releasing it from his grip as he walked her around his family introducing her to anyone she hadn't already met.

Melody spent the evening mingling with Joe's family, enjoying the conversation and laughter that went on all around her. A border collie dog ran tirelessly up and down the beach fetching a ball while a handful of youngsters took two red-sailed Mirror dinghies out on the water to catch the last of the evening tide. It was a perfect day – even if by the end of it people were vowing never to eat another sausage for the rest of their entire lives.

When darkness came and the night air glowed with the flames of a campfire, Joe went to find his guitar and, sitting at the water's edge, played for everyone until the early hours of the morning. I love you, Joe, Melody thought silently, as she yawned and slipped quietly away from the party, the cooling sand beneath her feet.

## 25

Putting the kettle on and setting out two mugs, Juliana, still bleary-eyed from sleep, began to laugh at Mrs Galespie's invasion of their morning. 'Bring a sausage? I've had more refined invitations to parties to be fair.'

Remembering the sausage incident at Joe's barbecue, Melody shuddered. 'I think I'll take a cake.' She took a jar of marmalade and a pat of yellow butter from the fridge and, glancing at the tangerine clock, felt her stomach rumble. Unwrapping a fresh loaf of white bread from its paper covering she cut two thick slices and put them under the flame of the grill pan. 'I'm supposed to be working next Saturday but I'll swap my shift because there's no way I'm going to miss out on this party. And will you come, Jules? Say you'll still be here?'

Juliana paused in mid-scoop of the instant coffee and dropped the spoon back into the jar. She took both of Melody's hands in her own. 'I've got at least two weeks so I can be here right up until you move into your new flat and beyond if you need me. I've made arrangements. I have a new business manager, Keith, and he'll be holding the fort while I'm away – plus, you'll never guess what I've got. Wait for it...' She rushed into the bedroom and came back grinning from ear to ear clutching a black leather case. 'Look at this. I've got a *mobile* telephone! I can be contacted anywhere with it.' She handed Melody the case and, still grinning, watched her open it. Inside was a wedge-shaped cell phone with number buttons and a thick black antenna. 'It's brilliant, isn't it, Mel? And I'm going to get one for my car as well. *I* shall be contactable at *all* times.' She sighed happily as if being contactable at *all* times was a good thing and Melody, although fascinated by the mobile telephone, inwardly recoiled at the idea. 'I've told Keith only to ring me if it's really important because I'll be busy helping my…' Juliana stopped in mid-track and suddenly laughed with glee. 'I told them I would be busy helping my cousin but I won't be, will I? – I'll be busy helping my *sister*.' She suddenly swung her sister round the tiny kitchen which took Melody so much by surprise she dropped the mobile phone and it landed on her foot like a brick.

'Shit!' Juliana bent down to pick up her new gadget, inspecting it closely for damage.

'Don't mind me – your sister with the broken toes,' Melody groaned, checking her toes for signs of bruising just as a terrible smell of burning came from the grill pan. Putting the phone on the counter top, Juliana yanked out the grill pan while Melody, forgetting her toes, rushed to open the window and fanned the smoke with a tea towel. 'I'm not wasting this toast,' she said as she scraped off the charred bits with a knife, sending flakes of black in a fine layer across the stainless steel of the sink. Then, she covered the damage with a thick layer of butter and marmalade and took it outside, pretending to limp all the way.

They ate their breakfast, studying the new mobile phone

which sat on the little table between them as if it were an objet d'art worthy of their full admiration. 'Are your toes all right?' Juliana glanced down to where Melody wiggled her toes to show that they had survived. 'I'm so sorry, I didn't realise it had landed on you and it isn't the lightest of things, admittedly. It is one of the most useful, though, and I believe it's a thing that's going to really take off. Soon, everyone will have one.'

Melody thought to herself that, whatever happened, she most definitely wouldn't have one. 'Surely no one would have a moment's peace?' she complained, and just as she said it the phone sprang to life with such a shrillness that it went right through her head and made her jump out of her skin. Juliana reached for it as calmly as she could bring herself to and answered it with an air of delighted importance as if she didn't already know who was ringing her. 'Juliana speaking, how may I help you?'

For the next ten minutes, Melody felt distinctly awkward in her own home, eavesdropping on a conversation with Keith about colour swatches and paint options and the best shape of lampshade.

'Keith is great,' Juliana sighed when at last she turned the phone off and placed it back on the table. 'He is *so* competent.'

'Clearly,' Melody answered, stifling her wish to ask why, then, did Keith feel the need to telephone his boss on her holiday.

Juliana stood up and, with a certain amount of businesslike authority, collected their cups and plates, scraped a blob of butter, loose crumbs and a half-eaten crust into the kitchen bin, washed up quickly and dried her hands on a towel. Melody followed her and stood leaning against the door frame. She recognised the assertiveness and her heart quickened. 'You and I have put the world to rights, haven't we, Mel? We've talked our hearts out, slept on it, made a sacrificial offering to the gods of burnt toast and now today is a brand-new day... what's left of it. How about...' she laid a gentle hand on Melody's arm '... we *start*?'

To Melody's relief, the two of them started in the kitchen. 'It's the easiest,' Juliana advised, ushering Melody along with a pile of old newspapers. 'You don't have to get rid of anything, just wrap it carefully in the newspaper and pop it in a box. Keep out only what we're going to need for the next few days.'

Two plates, two mugs, two sets of cutlery and two wine glasses, some food, the kettle, a saucepan, a frying pan and a spatula were kept for use but everything else from the cupboards and the shelves was cleared out, wrapped up and packed, including the tangerine clock and a rock and shell ornament that had been on the windowsill next to the washing-up liquid for over twenty-five years.

Without really knowing why, afterwards, Melody cleaned the entire kitchen. She scrubbed the cupboard shelves, wiped the windowsill, soaked the oven trays and mopped the floor. It was all going to be crushed into nothing but she couldn't help herself. Spindrift would not meet her fate without looking her absolute best.

# 26

When Gordon and Isobel arranged to visit Melody for her twenty-eighth birthday, she thought she was going to be sick with the build-up of anticipation. They had all, of course, had some contact since her conversation with Gordon, but that contact had been few and far between. Melody struggled to act as though nothing had changed and, as a result, she had done her best to avoid them. Now, however, due to their insistence, they were on their way.

As was Flora's tradition, Melody prepared the tray with the china tea set and a plate of homemade butterfly cakes stuffed with apricot jam and fluffy butter icing. It was the third batch she'd made that day, having mucked up the previous two and given the evidence of them to the seagulls. She wanted Flora to be proud that she was doing her best for Isobel.

When her guests finally arrived, Melody was a bundle of nerves. She greeted them stiffly, hardly knowing where to put her eyes and, finding herself looking at Isobel, she would snatch her gaze away as soon as Isobel caught her eye. She nearly toppled the milk jug when pouring their tea and then spilt drops of it onto the butterfly cakes, watching with dismay how dull patches of damp bloomed in the dusting of white icing.

Melody was confused by her feelings. Isobel, with years of rehearsal behind her, appeared the same as she had always been. Her smile was wide behind a slick of red lipstick and her legs stayed neatly crossed at the ankles, her pinkie finger crooked to perfection as she sipped at her unsweetened tea. Yet Isobel was her birth mother and Melody was her child and perhaps they were not so dissimilar after all. They were both playing a charade and they were both very good at it. It was the first time Melody realised that Isobel, with her cool, flawless demeanour, was simply still a sixteen-year-old girl wearing a heavy suit of adult armour.

'What are you doing with yourself these days?' Isobel asked as she placed her teacup back in its saucer.

'Oh, I'm very busy,' Melody answered brightly. 'I'm still working at the Pier Head Stores so that keeps me out of mischief.' She wondered if she could spot a flicker of disappointment ripple across Isobel's expression knowing that her little job hardly compared to Juliana's first-class degree or her germinating design business.

'And is there a young man on the scene?' Isobel asked. She looked hopeful, Melody thought.

'There isn't a man on the scene.' She flushed a little. 'I'm fine, Aunt Isobel, Uncle Gordon,' she said carefully, pronouncing their full titles for their benefit rather than her own. 'I don't need any romance in my life at the moment but if I change my mind and decide to get married, you'll be the first to be invited. You could walk me down the aisle, Uncle Gordon.' She grinned at them immediately realising that this throwaway comment had been grasped at as if it were a precious thing. Isobel's red lips formed a brief 'O' of delight and the tips of her fingers, barely noticeable had Melody not been looking, nudged Gordon's leg. Gordon coughed with pleasure and Isobel hid the threat of any telling emotion by sipping fervently at her tea. 'That would be lovely, wouldn't it, Gordon,' she said.

'Very lovely indeed,' Gordon smiled, catching Melody's eye and holding it.

When the visit was over, Melody walked them both to the door, wondering, as she performed the standard, ritualistic embracing, if for all the years of their visits, Isobel and Gordon experienced the same turmoil she now felt inside – a fragile, desperate kind of love which burnt so fiercely in the mere seconds of a hug goodbye.

# 27

'Do you ever see much of Mummy and Pops now?' Juliana asked.

The kitchen was, at last, finished, having taken them a lot longer than they thought to pack up. They were now sitting, exhausted, on the terrace eating fish and chips out of the wrapper and drinking cold Coke straight from the can.

'Not a lot,' Melody replied.

'Spoken to them at all?' she probed.

'Not much.' Melody could hear that her answer was transparent, sounding as if she were denying herself a tantalising slice of a summer berries pavlova after a meal. How often she had sat by her phone, playing with the coils of the line, imagining how it would be if she rang them, a deep need to hear the sound of their voices again. 'The thing is...' She stopped in mid-sentence, unsure as to whether to go on but, now that she and Juliana were sharing everything, she decided to tell her the final piece of the story. 'You know I said Gordon came to give me money on my twenty-fifth birthday?'

'Yes,' Juliana replied slowly, as if she could tell something bigger than a few pounds in a card was about to be revealed.

'Well it was more than a few pounds in a card. A lot more. A huge amount that he said matched everything that had been spent on you in your lifetime, holidays, university, birthdays. He wanted me to take it.'

'You took it, right?' Juliana froze, just at the point of putting a forkful of crispy batter into her mouth.

'No,' Melody answered as if it should be obvious that she wouldn't want to take a life-transforming amount of money and was a little surprised when Juliana coughed so violently a crumb of batter shot out and landed on Melody's plate.

'You didn't take it?' she cried.

'No.' Melody shook her head again, removing the crumb and dropping it on the ground beside her.

'Then could I be so bold as to ask something?' Juliana sipped at her Coke to quell her choking cough.

'Go ahead,' Melody replied.

'Why the *fuck* not?' She leant forwards pressing her hands into her knees in disbelief, her eyebrows almost disappearing into her hairline.

'Because I told you, I don't need money.' Melody looked her steadily in the eye.

'You don't need money... even when it's handed to you on a platter,' Juliana said, a hint of sarcasm in her voice.

'I'm *Flora*'s daughter,' Melody responded. 'She'd turned her back on the trappings of money and a privileged upbringing, so I will too.' She pushed two chips into her mouth and busily dipped two more in tomato sauce, aware that Juliana was still staring at her.

'Honestly, Mel, I don't know how much Pops tried to give you but I can hazard a guess that it's the difference between renting a pokey flat in town and buying somewhere by the sea that most people could only dream of.' She slumped back in her chair, almost causing her fish and chips to slide off her lap. 'It is, isn't it?' she pressed. 'And if I know my Aunty Flora, there is no *way* she'd want you to fester away in that pokey little flat when you could have something better.'

'You should be an estate agent,' Melody said.

Juliana frowned at her. 'Why? Where did that come from?'

'Because you described my flat as charming when I told you about it.'

Juliana speared a chip and pointed it at Melody. 'That was before I knew you didn't have to live there.'

'I may not *have* to live in that flat, but I'm going to because I don't want guilt money. I also don't want to talk about it any more.' She fell silent for so long after this that Juliana took the hint. Several seagulls had joined them, lining the wall, their beady eyes on every move Juliana made, and she turned her attention to them instead.

'How come these things aren't ogling you?' she asked amid a rumpus of wings and cackles of delight when she harpooned another chip onto her fork. Melody smiled knowingly, relieved by the change in subject and eating her food unhindered.

'Because I stare them down. I read somewhere that eye contact intimidates them so I've been doing it for years. I'm sure I told you before but you didn't believe me.' As she spoke, a bolshy gull swooped past and took the next chip straight off the end of Melody's fork and the irony of it made Juliana laugh so much that she impulsively threw her own chip into the air to see what would happen. A gull caught it mid-flight.

'So much for staring them down, Mel,' she cried. 'Anyway, does it matter if we share our meals with the gulls now? If you're going to move into that flat of yours you need to enjoy all of this while you can.' This time she placed a chip on the wooden edging of the fence, encouraging another feathered frenzy to follow. Melody imagined that within only a matter of days she would be eating her supper at the *buffet à déjeuner*, sharing her food with only herself and the faded yellow paint on the kitchen wall. Losing her appetite she threw the remainder of her chips into the air for the gulls to catch.

'If you could be any living thing you wanted to be, what would you choose?' she asked.

Juliana smiled and thought about it for a minute. 'I'd like to be a cat. I would lie around on cosy chairs and sunny windowsills being pampered and spoilt yet independent at the same time. Basically the feline equivalent of the human me.' She gave a sharp nod of contentment, happy with her choice.

'I'd be a seagull,' Melody answered wistfully, watching the gulls, with their bellies now full, cartwheel in the sky above the bungalows. 'I never understand why people think they're little more than rats with wings. To me, they represent everything that I love about the coast. Have you heard of the book *Jonathan Livingston Seagull*?'

'No,' Juliana replied.

'It's about a seagull called Jonathan who wants to know all there is about flying faster and higher. He doesn't want to blend into the crowd or conform to their rules or join their squabbles for food and so eventually the other gulls banish him from their community. After that, Jonathan spends his days doing what he loves most – flying higher and higher, learning more and more about flight. Anyway, to cut a long, brilliant story short, on his journey of learning he meets some enlightened gulls who teach him all about freedom, the value of love and of being your true self. You should read it.'

Having listened quietly to this story, Juliana rested a meaningful hand on Melody's shoulder. 'I will read it but perhaps, Mel, you should read it again and listen to the teachings of Jonathan Seagull – ditch the idea of a flat in the middle of town and take the advantage I've had in life and use the money to buy a place by the sea where your heart is and where your soul can take wings. That would be true to yourself, wouldn't it?'

Melody mulled this idea over. Was Juliana right? Was she stopping her soul from flying? Having to move away from the water's edge was so real, so imminent, that she had to question herself as to whether she could survive the pain of it. She'd battled for so long with what she thought she should do, or what Flora would want her to do, that she wasn't even sure herself now.

'I think I'm going to have an early night,' she said, yawning to prove her tiredness. 'Tomorrow we'll tackle the sitting room but for now I've got a headache and I'd like to go to bed. Goodnight, Jules.'

Juliana called after her, her voice soft with understanding. 'Goodnight, Mel. Sitting room it is. It's *your* choice.'

As Melody closed the door to her bedroom behind her, she knew that, for her, the sitting room was the *only* choice. She would preserve Flora and Milo's rooms until the bitter end. Remaining in her bedroom until she heard Juliana go to bed, she put her swimming costume on and silently crept back through Spindrift, opened the double doors and slipped outside, climbing down the wooden ladder to the beach. Alone, in the dark, she swam in the inky water looking up at the sky above her, wondering if the glow from the streetlamps by the flat in town would prevent her from seeing the depth of this starlit sky. She tried to imagine how it might feel to live, instead, in one of the apartments when they were built. How she might enjoy drinking her coffee or glass of wine on a balcony that overlooked the same horizon she had overlooked her whole life. Turning over and floating on her back she allowed the sea to rock her gently, the moon dropping silver into the waves around her.

# 28

The ground was white with frost beneath Melody's feet and the frozen grass crunched with each step she took as she picked her way past the headstones of other people's loved ones. Each was engraved with a name and a date and sometimes an epitaph that succinctly encapsulated all that the visitor to the grave might need to know. *Gone but not forgotten*, or *We miss you*, or sometimes something romantic such as *Never stop singing*.

She spread a thick woollen blanket on the ground and sat cross-legged in front of Flora and Milo. She pulled the plastic sunflowers out from the flower holder and cleaned each one with the cloth she always brought with her for this very purpose. Then, pouring a coffee from her flask and opening cheese sandwiches from their greaseproof paper wrapping, she ate.

After eating her sandwiches, she opened the lid of Flora's old cake tin to reveal a batch of chocolate muffins. Thanks to Flora's talent in the kitchen, cake had always been very much a family affair. Flora believed that spending time choosing, mixing and baking for someone was an act of love. The smell of baking would fill Spindrift every time there'd been a celebration, a birthday, guests, Christmas.

'An act of love,' Melody said out loud, placing a muffin on Flora's grave. 'Happy birthday, Mum.'

Flora's headstone, *Forever in our hearts, souls and minds*, was Isobel's idea as she'd insisted at the time that she had *some* input to her sister's resting place. Melody read it, as she always did, but still she hated it. To her mind these words didn't encapsulate the essence of Flora at all. They wouldn't be able to tell a passing stranger how sweet and loving was the person who lay there, or how strong and kind she'd been, how she never judged a book by its cover. These words didn't express how, when it had come to Milo, and people could only see his disability, Flora had been his advocate, a woman before her time, only ever seeing his capabilities.

Milo's grave had a far simpler stone. Before anyone in the family could have their say about what epitaph they thought he should have, Melody had arranged for it to simply have his name, his dates and the carving of a bird in flight. She placed a muffin near the carving, talking as if Milo were sitting right next to her. 'It's chocolate. Your favourite.'

It had been five years since he'd gone. Five years without the need for stoic pretence or to shut doors in order to hide her tears of pity from him. Five years of not having to find the straight back, chin up and big smile that Flora had instilled in her to offer for the benefit of others. Spindrift and Shelly beach hadn't minded when she'd sobbed out loud when he'd died or called her agonies into the sleepless night sky. Five years for Melody alone with her grief.

It wasn't true what Isobel had said all those years ago when she was just eleven years old. She'd never *had* to care for Milo, not even when Flora had died. Not even when her back ached from moving him, or her sleep was disturbed by him calling out in the night. He'd simply been part of who she was. And when, at the age of twenty-one, Milo's body, flooded with pneumonia, had finally stopped working and set his soul free, Melody had lived for all three of them.

# 29

1989, SEPTEMBER

Despite her long, moonlit swim, Melody was so restless in bed that night that she became tangled in her sheets, unable to settle her mind. She realised she must have slept at some point, though, because Milo and Flora came to her in her dreams once more.

Like before, they were smiling brightly and bringing her baked treats – this time cupcakes frosted with bright yellow icing. Milo, tall and strong again in her dream, was holding the tray out for Melody to take one. 'An act of love,' Milo insisted, stepping closer with the tray of cakes. She dutifully took one, biting into it, the taste of lemon icing filling her mouth, the sweetness of it causing her to wake instantly. Flora and Milo, neither real nor ghost, had gone.

The dim light of a new day eased through a gap in her curtains, casting a blue veil where they'd been standing and, despite the early hour, she got up, pulled on a pair of shorts, a vest top, grabbed her basket and, leaving her sandals behind, went for a barefoot walk along the beach. A heavy early mist clouded the view where the haunting shapes of moored boats rose out through the gauze of it and lazy waves lapped a gentle rhythm as she made her way along the water's edge. But however hard she tried that morning, and however far she walked, nothing felt the same.

It was not until the flaxen hue of a morning sun dispersed the mist with the beginnings of summer warmth that she returned home to Spindrift. Her basket today heavy with nothing but all her wishes that life didn't have to change.

'I had a dream last night,' she told Juliana later. 'Flora and Milo brought me cake. What do you think it means?'

'I think it means you went to bed with low blood sugar.' Juliana looked over the top of her coffee with one eyebrow raised.

'Very funny.' Melody squashed a smile and stared into her own coffee. She thought hard. 'It's strange, though, isn't it? It's not the first time I've dreamt about them and they always bring me cake. They could at least say something meaningful.'

'Does Flora speak in your dreams, then?' Juliana asked.

Melody shook her head. 'No, but Milo does. He just says, *an act of love*, which is something Flora always used to say when she baked cakes for people. But I don't know why I keep dreaming it. It doesn't make sense.'

'Milo?' Juliana looked surprised.

'Yes, Milo. He looks and sounds...' Melody struggled to find the right word. 'He looks and sounds *complete*. Like he spent his whole life fighting Long John Silver but in the end it wasn't Long John who won the battle for his soul, it was Milo himself. That sounds silly, doesn't it?'

Juliana vehemently shook her head. 'Gosh no, Mel. That

sounds *lovely*. And perhaps dreaming about cake *does* mean something. Perhaps it means they want to tell you that good things are coming your way.'

Melody cast her gaze around Spindrift and shrugged again. 'I don't call having to leave my family home a good thing. It's a nightmare in its own right.' She chewed on a nail and despairingly assessed all the work ahead of them.

'Well, that's a matter of perspective,' Juliana said. 'You have the ability to change your nightmare. Don't forget the teachings of Jeremy the seagull…'

'Jonathan Seagull,' Melody corrected.

'Yes, him. Perhaps Flora and Milo and even a goddamn bird are all telling you to take Pops' flippin' money!'

Juliana took out a Bananarama CD and popped it into her player. Then, she turned up the volume and opened up a plastic bag. 'We can do this thing!' she said, dancing to the music.

'We can,' Melody agreed. 'I'll start by filling that bag with things for charity.'

Juliana waved the bag like a banner of celebration, the sound of its plastic crackling joyfully in the air. 'Great choice,' she beamed. 'I'll hold the bag open and as you find anything you don't want to keep that someone else can benefit from, you just pop it right in here.'

Melody picked up a vase and pictured someone else benefitting from it. Someone in another house, in another place, arranging flowers in it, setting it on a table by their window. Daniel had bought the vase for Flora's birthday years ago and she and Milo had filled it with homemade tissue-paper flowers on pipe cleaner stems. Her mother had hugged the vase to her chest, in the same way Melody was doing now. She silently put it back down again and moved on to find something else. Her hand hovered over two candlesticks painted with little blue and yellow flowers.

'These are too pretty. They'd look nice in my new flat,' she murmured. 'And this definitely isn't going anywhere.' She placed a protective hand on the transistor radio that Daniel had bought her in his moment of rare generosity when she was a child. 'Or these,' she pointed to the shelves where a collection of *National Geographic* magazines were stacked.

'Something, Mel... *anything*,' Juliana groaned. 'What about this?' Melody turned to see that she'd opened a cupboard and was pointing to the old wooden Noah's Ark set that she and Milo used to play with. 'A child would love this. A child would love all of these.' Juliana opened the cupboard door next to it and revealed that it was packed full of old toys and games.

'Oh, not Noah's Ark.' Melody's face fell and she sank to her knees to refamiliarise with her childhood toy. Lifting the top off the ark she took out the animals, lining them up in their pairs as she had done with Milo. She'd used the set to teach him the names of all the animals and how to pair them together. They'd played for hours, sometimes on the beach, pretending that the incoming tide was the floods that Noah had predicted. One time, a giraffe and the two turkeys had been lapped up by a vigorous incoming wave and she'd had to wade in to retrieve them. She remembered how impossible it had been to teach him to pronounce the word *hippopotamus* without them both laughing.

'It's a lovely set and still in good condition,' she murmured, studying the pieces closely. 'Maybe one day I'll have a child of my own, or I could give it to you, Jules, if you have children.'

Melody could see that Juliana was doing her best to keep a lid on her frustration and was grateful to her for not getting annoyed. 'We don't even know if we'll have children,' Juliana levelled. 'There's no point keeping things for *just in case* when a child can enjoy them now. Come on, let's put the ark in the charity bag.'

Melody collected an empty box and placed the ark inside it. 'This box is for the things I'm taking with me,' she said firmly. She crouched down and took out Milo's collection of Dinky cars, the old Viewfinder complete with picture wheels and the wooden puzzle of the circus. She put them all in the box next to the ark. 'You can have these,' she said, reluctantly giving Juliana a bag of Jack Straws. 'And this.' She put an old and battered boxed game triumphantly in the bag.

'Generous,' Juliana muttered.

'And these.' Melody pointed to more battered boxed games, a rusting biscuit tin of toy figures and an old sagging bear. Once they were all inside the bag, however, she felt uncomfortable, almost as if her possessions were calling to her through the black plastic. When Juliana wasn't looking, she dug the bear back out and tucked it away in the box of things to keep. Three hours of hard work and general frustration later, they had loaded Juliana's car with two miserable charity bags and had stopped for a much needed coffee break.

'I can see it, you know,' Juliana said casually between sips of her drink.

'See what?' Melody asked.

'A paw. A brown paw, waving to me from the corner of the

box behind Noah's Ark.' They both squashed a smile as they looked over at the box.

'Rumbled,' Melody said.

'Rumbled indeed,' replied Juliana.

It wasn't until Juliana found a large quantity of empty plastic bottles, though, stacked inside a sackcloth in the corner of the room that she began to lose her cool. 'Surely these are rubbish? Why would you even keep them in your house?'

'They distress me,' Melody said evenly. 'It's become all the rage for everyone to drink water from plastic bottles and yet no one is thinking what a curse they're going to be in the future. Models are even carrying them up and down the catwalk like they're a must-have fashion accessory and yet, while the world thinks this is a fantastic idea, the used bottles are blowing out of rubbish bins, into the sea and along our beaches. They're going to destroy our planet one day.'

Juliana placed a weary hand of despair on her forehead and pressed it into her face. 'Then throw them away in your bin and let the council take them away.'

'And you think that's going to solve anything?' Melody argued. 'We've got a crisis on our hands – they're calling it the landfill crisis of the eighties – and I'm not prepared to be one of the people who adds to it.' She slumped down on the sofa and gave a loud expulsion of air to which Juliana followed suit, collapsing beside her.

'This is pointless, Mel! You can't solve the world's problems by yourself.'

'But I can do my bit!' Melody snapped.

'Not like this,' Juliana snapped back. 'Tomorrow, I'm putting those bottles in my car and taking them to the dump.'

Crossly, she suddenly levered herself back off the chair and went outside. 'Perfect timing,' she called as the track 'She Drives Me Crazy' by Fine Young Cannibals blasted out of the CD player.

As she stared at the weary profile of her sister, Melody knew she was the cause of it. Juliana had promised so faithfully that, this time, she would be there to help, come what may, and yet Melody was the one putting too many roadblocks in her way. It wasn't fair of her and it wasn't going to get the job done. Quietly, and bravely, she slipped off the sofa and emptied a cupboard all by herself. Old school books, a set of beach bowls, a game of tiddlywinks and a ragdoll went to the charity pile. Dried-up paint, felt pens without lids on, some Plasticine and an ancient chemistry set went to the pile for the dump. An hour later she'd cleared the cupboard and several drawers and, feeling better about everything, brought Juliana, who was still out on the terrace, a mug of tea, some biscuits and a silent apology. She pulled a downward smile as she handed over the steaming mug. 'I'll try harder, Jules, really I will.'

Just then, Mrs Galespie appeared on her own terrace looking completely worn out, a clutter of boxes everywhere, and her son carting her belongings backwards and forwards from her bungalow to his car. She gave them a half-hearted wave and they gave a half-hearted wave back. 'See you at the party on Saturday,' Melody called.

'You will that,' Mrs Galespie called back, raising her cigarette to her lips and sucking the life out of it. 'Joe Wiley's going.' She gave a broad wink. 'Tell 'er, Julie.'

'Juliana,' corrected Juliana.

'Tell her, Julia, she's young and lovely and she shouldn't be all on her own like she is and nor should Joe Wiley. Both of these 'ere gorgeous young things dilly-dallying around each other for years on end, I could bang their 'eads together.' Mrs Galespie breathed out a plume of smoke and sucked another lungful back in.

'Are you bringing a fella?' Juliana called to Mrs Galespie, grinning at Melody from behind her mug.

'Me?' Mrs Galespie cackled. 'Even my dear departed husband would agree that I've passed my sell-by date. No, dear, I'm so old and my face is so craggy I could grow cress out of it on a wet day. Anyway...' She pointed the remaining stub of her cigarette in the direction of Spindrift. ''Ow you getting on with the move?'

'Not too bad,' Melody lied.

'And 'ow you feel about it now it's 'ere?' Mrs Galespie brought the stub up to her lips and squinted through the smoke.

'I'm OK,' Melody replied.

Mrs Galespie gave a loud 'HA!' and stubbed her cigarette out before stopping to pick up a large box. 'Yeah, you, me and Pinocchio.' She disappeared back inside until all Melody could hear were the sounds of her and her son, Colin, shifting furniture and shouting instructions to each other.

'Shall we give it another go, *Julie*?' Melody grinned.

'Let's,' Juliana grinned back. 'But call me Julie one more time and you're on your own.' She immediately went to tackle a huge bag that was pushed against the wall and had been very much in the way for a long time. 'How about this?' she asked, opening the bag before Melody could answer. Inside, it was stuffed with lots of old crab lines and bits of fishing nets of all shapes and sizes and Melody's face fell.

'Don't throw that one away, please, it's for projects,' Melody begged.

'Projects.' Juliana groaned and sat back on her heels, lowering her head as if trying to gather strength. But when Melody handed her the mirror that had once been hanging in the hall, showing the delicate work of her unfinished surround, Juliana's expression totally changed.

'I have ideas,' Melody began. 'Instead of throwing away some of the things that wash up on the shore, I want to reuse them – give them a new life. Only...' She felt the heat of shame creeping into her face. '... I haven't got very far.' She waited, her cheeks hot as Juliana, appearing deep in thought, turned the mirror over and over in her hands.

'Flippin' Nora, Mel,' she exclaimed, 'it's *beautiful*! And there it was just shoved in a pile with everything else. Why on earth haven't you finished it?'

Melody shrugged as if she didn't have a clue why she hadn't finished it but, in fact, she knew exactly why. She'd been making it when Flora died and never picked it up again. 'I... I guess I lost motivation,' she said quietly.

'Well, let's find that motivation, you clot.' Juliana held up the mirror and kissed it as if it was the women's Wimbledon trophy. 'You could sell this kind of thing. Have you made anything else?' She delved further into the bag and before Melody could answer pulled out a wad of fishing net. Caught up in it was a seahorse made from green knotted crab line plus a wall hanging threaded into a wind catcher and decorated with tiny shells and seabird feathers. 'You have got to be *joking* me!' Juliana shrilled with delight, her eyes like saucers.

'These are *fantastic*, and I'm pretty sure I can sell this kind of thing for you. I've *got* to tell Keith – we could put them in our brochure.' She immediately went to find her mobile phone and was enthusiastically opening the leather casing for it when Melody stopped her. She wasn't ready for this.

'One thing at a time,' she said, taking the mobile phone carefully away from her and returning it to its case.

In the end, it was Juliana herself who set aside the bags and boxes containing anything that could possibly be turned into artwork – the nets and discarded crab lines, sea glass, pottery pieces, pretty shells and driftwood. In one of the bags she found a small piece of flat wood where Melody had glued sun-bleached hessian onto it and decorated it with a curved piece of glass from a little cobalt-blue bottle. She'd stitched green silk thread into the sackcloth and sewn fragments of coloured shells and pottery to the ends. The result was an exquisite picture of a vase of flowers.

'You're unbelievable, Mel. You've been hiding yourself under a bushel all these years,' Juliana exclaimed.

Melody shrugged and couldn't help hearing the echoes of Joe telling her the very same thing. And when Juliana found yet another picture – a little row of seagulls on a wire made from thread and tiny bits of crushed mother of pearl – she went into action as if going to war. 'Right!' Juliana said decisively. 'None of this is going. We keep any flotsam and jetsam that could be described as arty or crafty and tomorrow we concentrate on the other stuff.'

The next day started well, with a breakfast of warm rolls from the oven, eaten outside on the terrace, the promise of yet another glorious day filled with sunshine and blue skies ahead of them. Even Juliana, who could not be described as a morning person, was awake promptly, dressed and ready to tackle the task ahead.

It was unfortunate then, that Juliana started by focussing on Milo's room.

She sat on the end of Milo's bed while Melody sat in his wheelchair. 'The art and craft stuff makes sense to me,' Juliana began, 'but I just can't get my head around all these bits of newspaper and random *things*. So *many* things.' She got off the bed and went over to the shelf. 'Broken sunglasses, an old glove – it's all endless.' Then she picked Gloria up by the feet. 'And you've *still* got this.' It wasn't a question, or even an unkind dig, but more of a depressed acknowledgement of fact that Melody had kept hold of such a thing. She screwed up the accompanying newspaper and dropped it into a bag, causing Melody to stiffen and her insides to twist in a knot. But it was when she dropped Gloria into the bag as well that something triggered inside her, snapping and giving way under the weight of it all.

A dark, awful panic exploded and rushed to the surface, giving her a terrible feeling of being out of control. It brought with it all the grief that Melody had found ways to smother. And if she'd thought that she'd already cried all the tears she could ever cry over the people in her life who she'd loved and lost, she was very, very wrong. Daniel leaving them without a word, Flora dying so suddenly, Milo dying so slowly and now the loss of her beloved Spindrift.

She had no idea how long she cried for that day, how long her body was wracked with the pain of it all, or how long Juliana had spent holding her hand, brushing the hair away from her damp face. She had no idea what the terrible sound was that came from deep within her own self – the agony of all that she'd carried for so long. Grief that had not abated with time at all but had festered, waiting for an opportunity to spring from the confines of her body. She had no idea how much toilet paper she went through to wipe her cheeks and blow her nose before twisting it into damp pulps, or for how long she slept when finally she was spent. She only knew that it had happened and that afterwards she felt as dull and flimsy as a wilting plant.

When Juliana brought her one of the little wine glasses filled with water, apologising for the fact that they'd packed all the larger glasses, Melody saw that all colour had leached from her face and that a worry line had made a furrow of imperfection between her two perfect brows. 'I'd like you to come and live with me – just until you get yourself sorted.' Juliana took a seat next to her and stroked her hand.

Melody sipped at the cool liquid, not caring if it was in a glass or a mug or even a bucket, but words failed her regarding Juliana's offer. Juliana, her sister, wanted her to go and live with her in the little cottage in the countryside that she'd described as being a haven. A little cottage that looked out on trees and fields, hedgerows and country lanes and where an owl visited the tree at the end of her garden, calling its melancholy hoot into the night. It sounded like a lovely home; soft furnishings, ambient lighting plus a little bistro table in a leafy garden where they could share their hopes and dreams under the shade of a garden parasol. That kind of offer deserved an animated reply, a gushing of appreciation for its generosity, but Melody couldn't regulate her thoughts. She sat quietly, enjoying the deliciousness of the idea of not having to live alone any more. They would have fun, she thought, getting to know each other properly for the first time in their lives, forging a close bond that would last them a lifetime.

'What do you say?' Juliana pulled her mouth into a mischievous curve which threaded splays of kindness from the corner of her eyes.

Melody put the glass of water down and cupped her sister's hand. She had to leave Spindrift, that much was certain. She had to leave the echoes of Daniel, Flora and Milo within its old walls and begin a new life – that was also certain. She loved her sister for offering a lifeline that meant she would never have to be alone again – but she also knew for certain that she wouldn't take it.

It took Melody the rest of the day to feel more in control of herself. She had told Juliana, thank you for the offer but, although it was terribly tempting to stay with her, and the countryside was a beautiful place to live, it was the coastal breeze that called her name. Juliana, she could tell, was disappointed but not surprised.

'Just rest,' she said, putting the fourth mug of coffee of the day into Melody's hands as she sat outside in a sun chair.

'Then stop bringing me coffee because I'll be bouncing off the roof soon,' Melody replied. She took the mug and tried to laugh but the sound of it slipped away before it had begun. Juliana eased herself into the sun chair next to her and grasped her own coffee. 'I want to understand everything,

Mel. I so want to help you but to do that I need to understand you and why you hold on to so many things.'

Melody wasn't sure if it was the caffeine that made her talk, or Juliana's gentle concern, or perhaps because she was so terribly tired of keeping it all to herself but, whatever it was, she took a deep breath.

'When I was about nine years old,' she began, 'Spindrift was banked by huge drifts of snow and we couldn't get to the library for books or play outside so I made up a story for Milo. He adored it.' Melody fixed her gaze on a white-crested line in the sea and could almost see her long-ago galleon made out of shells. 'I frequently made up stories for him from then on. But it wasn't until Flora died and Milo's condition was so much worse that I started beachcombing every day to find things for him. I'd bring my gatherings back and sit with him weaving tales about all the treasures I'd found.'

'Like the bunch of keys that had a story about doors?' Juliana queried. 'And the broken sunglasses and the single glove?'

Melody nodded. 'Yes. Everything in Milo's room has a magical or mystical tale behind it, or one of triumph or maybe love. The sunglasses enabled anyone who looked through them to see into the past and the future. Milo really loved that one. The person who wore the glove could tell what people were thinking. He was so isolated, Jules. He would look out of the window or sit on the terrace spending endless hours watching the world go by without him.' She swallowed a lump in her throat as the agony of her memories crowded round her. 'I knew I couldn't give him his life back, Jules, but I could bring the beach and the adventures to him, and everything I found, I put in his bedroom for him to look at.'

'Gosh, the stories sound lovely, Mel. But you carried on beachcombing and telling him stories even after he died,' Juliana ventured.

'I couldn't stop,' Melody confessed. A tear dropped from the rim of one of her eyes and Juliana gently wiped it away. 'Life had taken so much from him that I had to... *still* have to, believe that death hasn't stolen his soul as well. And that Flora is still here, too... *somewhere*.'

Juliana sipped her coffee thoughtfully. 'I think...' she began carefully. 'I think you keep hold of everything, clothes, possessions, beach treasures, *everything*, because the emotion of losing everyone in your life, even Daniel, was too much for you. It's as if you think that letting go of anything will make your memories fade away.' She looked into Melody's eyes for the truth. 'Am I right?'

Melody nodded slowly. She had never heard it put into words before but she realised that was exactly what she'd been doing. And she'd started doing the same thing with the newspapers, storing every precious day since she'd received her eviction notice.

'Now I'm losing Spindrift as well,' she whispered.

'Now you're losing Spindrift,' Juliana echoed mournfully. 'I understand now, Mel, and I only wish I could help you. If only we could shrink all your treasures so that you can take them with you.' She pushed her sunglasses into her hair and suddenly turned to Melody, her eyes widening as if she'd thought of something. 'Will you be OK if I leave you for a while? I've had an absolute brainwave.'

★

Later, as the evening sun painted a yellow hue to the air, and the waves crashed and rolled along the sand, Melody was still on the terrace, only this time with the large mug of wine that Juliana had poured her. A mysterious bag was now on the terrace beside her and Juliana was breezing around with a very satisfied smile on her face. She wagged a finger at Melody. 'No looking, I'll explain after we've eaten.'

Two meals of dressed crab, salad, new potatoes and crusty bread came out on trays just as the sun set fire to the evening sky, silhouetting a trio of seagulls in flight. Juliana spread brown crab meat onto a chunk of bread and topped it with sweet white crab meat and a sprinkle of pepper. She bit into it and closed her eyes in bliss. 'I don't think I'd ever get bored of seafood if I lived by the sea.'

'I don't,' Melody replied, piling crab onto her own bread and eyeing the mysterious bag. 'Come on, Jules, I've waited long enough, what did you buy?' she begged.

'I told you. It's my brainwave.' Juliana smiled a secret smile. 'Eat first and gather your strength because everything you need to survive leaving Spindrift is in that bag. And when you open it we need to get busy because, even though I say it myself, this idea is a bloody good one but we don't have much time.'


When Melody opened the bag, the first glimmer of hope that Juliana might be right about her idea being a bloody good one uncoiled itself in her belly and began to glow.

'*This...*' Juliana could hardly restrain herself. '*This* is how you can take all your memories with you.'

From inside the bag, Melody retrieved a brand-new Polaroid camera. '*Wow*, you got me a camera?' she said, turning the box around in her hands while Juliana excitedly flapped her hands, desperate to explain.

'It's one of the instant ones! You just point it at whatever you want to take a picture of and, hey presto! Out comes a photo. You can take a photo of the doll, the glove, or Gloria or whatever you want to keep a memory of and attach the photo to the newspaper headlines. One whole memory but in a fraction of the size.'

Melody tried to sound positive and she loved the camera, she really did, but she really wasn't sure how Juliana's idea could possibly work. 'But I've got an awful lot of things I want to keep a memory of,' she said carefully. 'That's an awful lot of film.'

'Then it's a good job I bought you an awful lot of film!' Juliana went inside and took out another bag from behind the sofa and presented it to Melody. Inside were enough boxes of film to keep even the most enthusiastic photographer going for a very long time.

Melody peered at the contents of the bag hardly able to believe how much was in there and puffed out her cheeks. 'Blimey! This must have cost you a *fortune*!'

Juliana grinned and, looking very pleased with herself, she pointed to a large box in the corner of the room.

'More?' Melody gasped, crouching down beside the box.

'It's a house warming present for your flat – a home computer!' Juliana exclaimed. 'It's got a word processing function which means you can write to your heart's content and who knows, one day, I might be able to boast that my sister writes books. Because you, my lovely Mel, are a storyteller.'

She handed Melody one of the boxes of film plus the new camera and kissed her on the forehead. 'You probably need to make a start,' she said.

She left Melody speechless, staring at the home computer and clutching the camera to her chest as if it were a newborn baby. Here, in the form of these wonderful gifts, Juliana had given her a lifeline.

Spindrift was cleared in three days.

She was no longer a home but an old Victorian seaside dwelling with curling linoleum floors and empty walls. Other bungalows had been abandoned, still with bits and pieces that weren't worth taking: faded pictures hanging on the wall, a discarded kettle, a pile of junk mail, a vase with dusty plastic flowers, a split bucket or broken washing line. But Spindrift stayed proud, scrubbed to within an inch of her life, still with the sun chairs on the terrace, as if they would always wait for Melody and Juliana to sit on them.

A frenzy of photograph taking, paper clipping, furious sorting, lots of music, bouts of uncontrollable laughing and a whole lot of crying, plus many trips to the charity shop or the dump ensued after the opening of Juliana's gift. Melody kept Flora's yellow towelling dressing gown, her knitting bag and her old bicycle, Daniel's rubber boots, a favourite jumper of Milo's and his wheelchair. She also kept the pebble shaped like a phoenix egg, Sir Walter Raleigh's earring and the shell of the giant sea snail. Everything else was cleared. Milo's and Flora's clothes had been hugged and put in a bag for charity. The rubber mattress on Milo's bed had been folded neatly and disposed of and his and Flora's beds were to be taken away, along with the commode, in a few days' time.

And now, on the eve of the party, with every task finished, they climbed into *Serendipity* with a picnic hamper and a bottle of champagne. They didn't row far, just out far enough to tie *Serendipity* to a buoy where they could sit and admire the view of Shelly.

'You did it!' Juliana raised her champagne towards Melody, who raised hers in return. The bowls of the little glasses she'd had forever gave a dull *ding* as they clinked together.

'*We* did it,' Melody clarified. She tried not to think about how bare it all was. The gaping mouth of the brick fireplace, the peeling gloss paint of the curtainless window frames, the steady note of the kitchen tap dripping against the stainless steel of the sink. Instead, she tried to focus on how, over the last few days when they'd needed a break from it all, they'd walked to the Pier Head Stores together for ice-creams or they'd changed into their costumes to run into the sea, drying off on their towels in the sun. How lunch had been eaten perched on the rocks by the pier looking down into the water for fish and anemones. And their evenings had been spent out on the terrace feasting on prawns, cockles or crab.

'I'm going to miss Spindrift,' Juliana sighed. 'I'm going to miss all of this. Even though we've been busy we've had fun, haven't we? These few days have helped me remember how much I love it. The freedom we had just to be children.

The endless summer days when we played as if there was no tomorrow.'

Melody smiled and sipped at the cool bubbles in her glass. Juliana was back.

*Serendipity* swayed in the water and their feet, hooked over the gunwale, dipped in and out of the waves that rolled against her hull. From where they were moored they could see everything. They could see how the pier jutted out at the mouth of the dock edging her own beach with its crescent of bungalows and Spindrift in the middle. They could see how the land curled around to the west where the rest of Shelly beach, the sailing club and the estuary began, and how it snaked up towards Lympstone and Topsham, dotted with a multitude of moored boats. And they could see the empty windows and the dust that rose from demolition work being carried out on the road behind Spindrift.

'It was beautiful, wasn't it?' Melody sighed.

'It sure was,' Juliana agreed.

'Do you get the feeling...' Melody looked across at Spindrift and halted mid-sentence, feeling suddenly very silly about what she was about to say.

'Do I get the feeling that they're still there?' Juliana asked. 'That Aunty Flora and Milo haven't left just because we cleared out their things?'

'Yes,' Melody whispered. She squinted towards the empty windows of her home as if she might see them still inside, looking out to sea. 'Do you think they'll stay?'

'Yes,' Juliana answered simply. 'Their souls are here. That's why I believe they didn't mind you untethering them from their belongings. They don't need them any more.' She wrapped an arm around Melody where they lay in *Serendipity* and rested it on the mantle of her shoulders. 'Do you really think that Aunty Flora, that beautiful, kind lady, would mind if you started a new life?'

Melody leant her head on Juliana's shoulder and pictured Flora and Milo walking out onto the terrace and waving at her. 'No,' she answered. 'I think they would want me to start a new life with my sister by my side.'

The day of the party arrived, greeted by a warm, dry forecast with spells of intermittent sun. Melody and Juliana nipped into town to buy food and drink for the event and were browsing the aisles of a supermarket when Melody suddenly halted in her step, a French baguette in her hand.

'I'm going to take Gordon's money and buy one of the fancy new apartments.' She felt strange as she announced this, hearing herself declare it out loud, as if she were suddenly liberated by the freedom of saying it.

'And you made this decision when?' Juliana's eyebrows shot into her hairline and she was smiling a smile so big she could hardly talk through it.

'Just now,' Melody answered. 'Somewhere between the crisps and the cheese.'

'Bloody Nora... way to GO, Mel!' Juliana yelled so loudly that a shop assistant, a family of four and an old man with hearing aids all turned around in surprise. 'She's come to her senses at last,' she told them all, punching her fist into the air. 'This is just the best news and I'm pretty sure that Aunty Flora would be delighted about this. I'm so pleased for you. The new apartments are going to be big and bright and almost on top of the water – the next best thing to having Spindrift.'

Then she grabbed Melody's arm, a sly and mischievous grin sliding across her face. 'You could even ask Big Joe Wiley if he wants to rent a room from you...'

Melody, as always, felt her heart rate increase at the sound of his name and, bombarded by Juliana's puppy dog enthusiasm, turned away towards the tills. She thought, for a fanciful moment, as she unloaded her shopping basket onto the conveyor belt, how it would be if Joe really did trade living in the boat at the dock for a room in a new apartment with her but she knew almost before she'd begun that it would never happen. 'I think he prefers to live alone,' she said. 'He's an eternal bachelor.'

'Peter Pan more like,' Juliana answered. 'He hardly looks a day older than when he first took us out on the boats over to the beach at Dawlish. Nor do you come to that, Mel. Your hair is still as blonde as it's always been and there isn't a wrinkle in sight.' Melody wasn't sure that she didn't look every bit of her thirty-five years but quite liked Juliana saying it. She paid for their food and carried the bags while Juliana lugged two bottles of wine and a crate of beer to the boot of her car. 'I must say, all these years that I've been coming here I never quite appreciated what a *good*-looking guy he is. You two have been neighbours your whole life so why have you never hooked up with each other?'

'I don't think I'm his type.' Melody shrugged and hoped it looked as if she didn't care. She thought about the girls she'd seen him with in the past and how they never seemed to last long.

'But you've had a dalliance with each other *somewhere* along the line?' Juliana peered quizzically at her and Melody felt her face flame. She wordlessly shook her head.

'But you *have* had a dalliance?' Juliana asked. Melody burnt under her sister's scrutiny and held her gaze. 'With someone... *anyone*,' Juliana pressed.

It was a bold question and one Melody didn't know how to respond to. Juliana was not only a married woman but a woman of the world, according to all the stories she'd relayed about her university and party years. 'It depends on what you call a dalliance,' she answered cagily, an uncomfortable memory of that first kiss with the boy called Clive who'd sucked at her lips like a dying fish gasping for air.

'You know what I mean,' Juliana insisted. 'Come on, we're sisters now, we can share this kind of stuff.'

'Do you mean...' Melody hesitated. Confessing that, despite her age, she was inexperienced in that department was hardly something to chit-chat about in the car park of a supermarket. It made her feel extremely uncomfortable. 'Do you mean *doing the do*,' she said, under her breath.

Juliana's face broke into creases and she snorted through her nose with delight. '*Doing the do?* You're thirty-five for heaven's sake, Mel. I mean *sex*!' She laughed out loud. 'Good old-fashioned, tear-off-your-clothes-and-go-at-it-like-rabbits kind of sex.'

They climbed into Juliana's car and Melody opened the window to let the air in and her shame out. 'I'm fine without all that business,' she clipped.

'But there's a world of exploration and abandonment out there, Mel. Sex, love, rock 'n' roll and all that. You've got a lot of time to make up for. How will you know you've found Mr Right if you've never tested out the Mr Wrongs?' Juliana turned the key in the ignition and drove out of the car park, briefly checking her appearance in the rear view mirror.

'Maybe I don't need Mr Right,' Melody said. 'Maybe I only need Melody.'

Juliana scoffed loudly and negotiated a mini roundabout at speed. 'Tell that to Big Joe Wiley.'

The day that followed was a bitter-sweet kind of day.

Several people came to say goodbye to Shelly as they'd always known it.

Sadly, Old Tess and Old Albert couldn't make the journey and they were sorely missed, but the Franklins were there, as was Enid Johnson, and several other ex-residents, sitting on blankets or chairs they'd brought with them from their new homes. Children were playing on the beach or swimming in the sea, the sound of their laughter catching on the breeze and mingling with the scent of food grilling on the hot coals of a barbecue. A group of students sat on the sand or in *Serendipity* and *Wild Rose*, smoking cigarettes and drinking from cans while Mrs Galespie walked around with a drink in one hand and a cigarette in the other.

'I'm glad you're here with me for this,' Melody said to Juliana as they sat on the rocks together, their feet dangling in the water.

'I'm glad, too,' Juliana replied, leaning in to Melody's side. 'It's the end of something big but it's also the beginning of something new and I know you're going to be OK.'

Melody looked towards the bungalows and noticed that her oyster shell wind chime was still hanging from the eaves of Spindrift offering musical notes of the sea as the shells tapped against each other. She loved that, for today at least, it was still there. Spindrift, scorched by the sun and battered by the tides, would not win her battle against time but she would stand proud to the bitter end. 'I'm sure I will, Jules,' she sighed.

It was a meaningful moment, only marginally ruined by Mrs Galespie wading into the water and yanking Juliana off her rock. 'Come on you two, dance with me,' she yelled, kicking her legs into the air and splashing water everywhere. She was wearing a very large pair of green shorts that had once belonged to her husband and they came almost to her knees, framing her very round calves. Her blouse was slightly askew, as was her hair, but the thing about Mrs Galespie was that she could really dance. Fortunately, the years of extracurricular lessons Juliana had endured at school had included ballroom dance and so, flinging herself into the moment, she took a delighted Mrs Galespie in her arms and together they waltzed their way across the shallow waters of the shore while Melody watched and laughed.

'Shall *we* dance?'

Joe was standing beside her holding his hand out, just as a timely burst of sun came out from behind the clouds shrouding him in light and making him look like a divine apparition. She squinted up at him and immediately panicked. 'I don't know how to dance,' she said, looking back at Mrs Galespie and Juliana who were twirling around in the waves. She wished, for the first time in her life, that she'd had lessons, too.

'Everyone can dance,' Joe said, leaning towards her to take her reluctant hand. He pulled her off the rock, more steadily than Mrs Galespie had with Juliana, until she was standing in the water beside him. The students were singing a ballad and Joe moved her slowly around in the water as if they were singing just for the two of them. A lock of his pale hair fell against her shoulder and he hummed the tune softly in her ear until she thought she was in danger of doing an old-fashioned swoon with the loveliness of it.

That was until, for the second time, Mrs Galespie ruined the moment. In her inebriated state, despite Juliana's best efforts at steering her away, she collided into Melody and Joe and, losing her footing, fell sidewards into the water with an almighty splash. She emerged with her hair plastered to her face and her bucket hat floating in the water, laughing her head off fit to burst. Joe stooped to help her up but she pulled him in with her and as he landed face down in the water she cackled so loudly she almost choked on an incoming wave.

Before they knew what had happened, the children, the students, Enid Johnson and two excited dogs all ran to join in. Melody and Juliana, Joe and Mrs Galespie found themselves in the biggest water fight they had ever had in their lives. The students started piggy-back fights while children tossed buckets of water and strands of seaweed over everyone. Mrs Galespie threw Juliana over her shoulder as if she were light as a feather and waded up to her waist with her before unceremoniously flinging her in. Laughing, Melody caught Joe's eye. He smiled innocently at her before suddenly scooping her up in his arms before she could escape and throwing her several feet into the water near Juliana.

It was a mad moment filled with laughter, yelling and dogs barking. It only finished when Brian Franklin, wearing a baseball cap, neon-orange sunglasses and a novelty apron with 'Mr Goodlookin' is Cookin'' on it, shouted to everyone that the food on the barbecue was ready. Soon, the water was empty and the beach was full of people grabbing at burgers, hotdogs and chicken drumsticks before running off to play team games on the beach.

At last, when the embers of the barbecue and the campfire had dimmed, and the sun was sinking low in the sky, Mrs Galespie brought out a basket of flowers. 'Come 'ere my lovelies,' she called to the children. 'The tide has turned now so take a flower each.' The children did as she asked, forming a line along the shore where a band of smooth damp sand was already visible in the ebbing tide. As each child threw their flower into the sea, petalled heads of different colours bobbed and swirled while the tide played with them, lifting their colours over the waves and taking them slowly out to sea. Each person there watched them float away, silently imagining that their love for the higgledy-piggledy community of Shelly would be absorbed by the heart of the ocean, never to be forgotten.

As the last flower became a small, coloured speck on the water, a lone student began to sing a solo, a beautiful, haunting ballad, during which someone lay down on the sand, closing their eyes and crossing their arms over their chest. Gradually, one by one, everyone followed, each lying down and crossing their arms, too. As the solo came to an end, there was not a sound to be heard other than the gentle crashing of waves as each person, lost in their own thoughts, lay on the beach like tombstones in the graveyard of Shelly.

There was a lot of crying, swapping of addresses and promises to keep in touch when Melody turned suddenly to find Big Joe standing right beside her. She blushed at how close he was and was about to step back when he placed a hand on the small of her back and lowered his face towards hers. She thought he might kiss her cheek again as he had the night she'd swum with Juliana but, this time, his lips found hers and they were soft and warm and there was the taste of sweetness on his tongue. He slid his hand along her back until his fingers were in her hair, cupping the back of her head and pressing her gently towards him. Never in her life had Melody been kissed in such a way and it was so beautiful that she imagined she was blossoming like a late summer flower.

'He kissed you last night, didn't he?' Juliana waited, her eyes wide with anticipation, but no answer was forthcoming. 'He did, didn't he?'

Melody smiled to herself and kept silent, the moment far too sweet to put into words.

'Are you seeing him again? Tell me you arranged something, Mel?'

Melody shook her head and hoped that Joe might come knocking at Spindrift before she had to leave but Juliana had a glint in her eye that Melody knew only too well. 'We've got a whole hour before Man with a Van gets here to take your stuff to the flat so go to the Pier Head Stores and get some orange juice or something. You have to walk past the dock... Well, I'm going even if you're not,' Juliana grinned. 'You always end up missing the opportunity so, should I see a certain person, I might just stop to pass the time of day. You said he had a friend staying with him so with any luck he's a hunk, too.' She walked straight out of Spindrift, her chin in the air and a wide smile on her face, shutting the door behind her.

Two minutes later, Melody came running up behind her, her sandals slap-slapping on the ground. 'Don't you dare say anything I'm going to regret,' she hissed, grabbing hold of Juliana's arm and trying not to laugh as Juliana dragged her along. Something inside Melody was singing with hope. Finally, she could dare to believe that tomorrow may be a whole new adventure after all.

When they did round the corner, however, their laughter died in their throats and Melody froze.

'Oh,' she said almost in a whisper, a prickle of tears springing to her eyes.

'Oh, indeed,' Juliana said.

On the deck of the boat that Joe was living in, was a girl. She was wearing a bikini top and a pair of denim almost-shorts. They were *so* short, Melody thought, that she may as well not have been wearing them at all. The girl's hair was in a high ponytail and she was painting her toenails and Joe was lying on the deck laughing at something she'd said.

'He didn't say his friend was a girl,' Melody squeaked. 'She looks like she's spent the night. There's a girl's dress and underwear hanging on the line.'

'Well… yes, quite possibly,' Juliana muttered.

Melody turned on her heels and tried to head back towards Spindrift but Juliana grabbed her. With both hands on Melody's arm she forcefully, but as casually as she could, ushered her towards the dock bridge. 'Stay cool, Mel,' she urged from the corner of her mouth. 'Keep walking, keep chatting. That girl could be anyone. Just wave if they see us. For all we know she could be his niece.'

'He hasn't got a niece. I've met his entire family over the years and there is no niece,' Melody hissed. She broke free of Juliana's grip and hurried ahead, not looking in the slightest bit *cool*, her face aflame with embarrassment. She slipped back to Spindrift the long way round with Juliana almost having to jog to keep up as she kept out of sight of Joe, making her way behind the timber yard, dock buildings and grain silos and into Shelly Road from the other end.

'I'm so sorry, Mel. Are you OK?' Juliana peered carefully at her when they were back in Spindrift, the sounds of their footsteps echoing off the walls of the almost empty bungalow.

Melody shrugged. 'He does his own thing and obviously doesn't want to be pinned down. It was the alcohol talking. It was nothing.' It hurt to hear herself saying that it was nothing out loud when only minutes before she'd dared to think that there may be something. She wished she didn't feel as if she had razor blades tearing at her insides. 'Nearly time to go,' she said, cheerlessly checking her watch.

Going outside and taking the oyster shell wind chime from its hook, Melody glanced briefly over at the empty windows of Pebbles and balled her fists. She so wanted not to care. Placing the wind chime with her belongings, she brushed past Juliana and went back out through the front door. 'I'm going to say goodbye to Mrs Galespie if she hasn't already gone.'

At Spinnaker, Mrs Galespie and her son, Colin, were just loading the very last of her belongings into his car. 'I've come to say goodbye,' Melody said.

'Don't get too close, my lovely,' Mrs Galespie cackled. 'My breath this morning could kill a goat.' Then, noticing Melody's sad face, her laughter immediately died to pity. She opened her big arms wide enough to tuck Melody inside. 'Oh, come 'ere, my lovely,' she cried, circling Melody and squeezing her so tightly against her ample chest it made her cough. 'I'm not going far, only round the corner so you come and visit me any time you like, you 'ear?'

'I hear,' Melody replied, her words lost inside the billowy squeeze.

'It won't be all bad, my lovely, if you don't let it be,' Mrs Galespie crooned kindly into her ear. 'There's always silver linings in these 'ere Devon clouds. You just gotta look for 'em.'

'But everything has changed,' Melody moaned, a sob threatening to leave her throat and bury itself in the fleshy part of Mrs Galespie's arm.

'It 'as that,' Mrs Galespie confirmed. 'But oftentimes there's something else for us, just round the corner. Something better maybe. Don't you forget that, my lovely.' She kissed Melody on the top of the head and made a clucking sound into her hair. 'But all that we 'ad – our little community, our open doors, our simple, beautiful lives 'ere – will forever be inside us. In our 'earts and right in 'ere.' She tapped Melody gently on the head. 'We will never forget it, will we?'

Melody sighed, her face squashed against Mrs Galespie's wheezy old chest, breathing in the scent of cigarettes and kindness. 'No, Mrs Galespie, we will never forget.' She loved this lady and suddenly, wrapped in her big arms like a child in its mother's embrace, the sob escaped her throat and caused her chest to heave. 'But Joe, he's... he's...' Her words croaked and died on her lips.

'What, my lovely?' Mrs Galespie asked.

It was then that Juliana came running down the road shouting that Man with a Van, which turned out to be two men with a van, had arrived. 'They need you at Spindrift,' Juliana called. She waited while Melody unravelled herself from the embrace calling, 'Good luck in your new home, Mrs Galespie.'

'Thank you, my lovely,' she replied. She patted Melody on the shoulder and smiled down at her. 'I'm always 'ere. Now you go on, my lovely. Chin up, straight back, big smile, like your mother always taught you. Remember?'

Melody sniffed a bubble up her nose and straightened her back. 'I'll try.'

# PART 3

# 30

## Exmouth, Devon

Melody and Juliana sat on two boxes in the new flat, their chins in their hands, contemplating where to start. They'd bought a bunch of bright flowers to set in Flora's old vase which was now on the windowsill in the sitting room and on the kitchen windowsill was the rock and shell ornament that had been in the kitchen at Spindrift.

'This place is bigger than I remembered,' Juliana commented, looking up at the high ceiling above her. 'I'd say it's definitely more charming than pokey. The windows are big, plus the picture rails and ceiling rose look very attractive. I bet there's a gorgeous Victorian fireplace behind that electric thing.' She moved to look out of the window. 'You can actually see the sea from here.'

'With a telescope,' Melody replied, going over to join her.

'Don't be picky. It's not right outside your back door, obviously, but it's still there, over the rooftops, glinting in the sun. People pay good money for this sort of view. It could take a while for the Shelly development to be built and for you to get your hands on the keys to a new apartment so let's make this place homely while you wait.'

Melody studied the horizon where she could just see a huge cargo ship heading out to sea, bound for Europe. She felt as if she was in a tower compared to Spindrift and tried to push away the feeling of being trapped in it. Standing next to her looking through the window, Juliana leant into Melody's side. 'How are you?' she asked. 'You know, about Joe and everything?' Melody continued to look out of the window, wordlessly searching the view outside for answers she didn't have. 'You should find out for definite, you know,' Juliana continued. 'Don't damn him without a trial.'

Melody laid her gaze on a rooftop where a chimney rose from the side of it, a crack in the pointing. A pigeon was perched on the television aerial bolted to its side but all she could see behind her eyelids was the girl's underwear hanging on the line of Joe's boat. She wanted to change the subject. 'I've been thinking, Jules. Tonight we'll christen the flat with takeaway and beer and then, in the morning, I'm going to let you go.'

Juliana snapped her head round in surprise. 'I thought we'd got past your need to push me away, Mel. You don't have to *let me go*, I'm happy to stay. I've got Keith and my mobile phone and I'm here for you.'

Melody smiled gratefully at her and loved her all over again. 'You've already spent ages with me and without you I would not be in the strong frame of mind that I am. But look at all this.' She swept a hand around her flat, indicating the boxes and bags the removal man had left in various rooms. 'I don't have to get rid of anything this time, I just need to make decisions about where I'd like it all to go. You can't make those decisions for me. Plus, and this is a big plus, both of us squashed up in that double bed for any length of time? I don't think so, do you?'

Juliana and Melody glanced in the direction of the bedroom where Melody's old and slightly saggy double mattress awaited on her old iron bedstead. It was the kind of fatigued mattress that devoured its occupants, causing them to roll in to the middle. 'It's been perfectly all right for me on my own,' Melody said, beginning to regret the fact that she hadn't spent more money renting a flat with two bedrooms instead of one. 'You go. Really. I've got to start somewhere and I'm better off doing this bit on my own.'

Juliana nodded uncertainly. 'You can come to stay with me in my cottage, you know?'

'I know,' Melody smiled. 'But I belong here. And anyway I'm due at work tomorrow night.'

'If you're sure,' Juliana said.

'I'm sure. I'll visit your lovely cottage when I'm settled. Especially as I take it we wouldn't have to share a saggy old double bed at yours?'

Juliana shook her head. 'I have two super-kingsize beds and two en-suites, a conservatory plus a hot tub in the garden and more than enough space not to crowd each other out. You'll be more than comfortable and more than welcome.'

'It sounds terrible,' Melody joked. 'I'd love to come – but not before I've turned this place into a palace of its own.'


In the morning, Melody woke up with Juliana blowing puffs of breath into her face with something between a sigh and a snore. She felt a dart of pain catch her in the pit of her stomach and it took her a few seconds to recognise it as loss. She wasn't in Spindrift and she could no longer fling the double doors open to the beach or drink her coffee on the terrace. She was in her new flat, pressed against Juliana in the sagging bed on the iron bedstead that squeaked and creaked with every move they made. The light in the room was grey as it pushed its way through net curtains and, as Melody lay there, she realised they'd left the window shut. The air was stale and each corner of the room was darkened with an abundance of removal boxes and bags. She got up, rolling towards the edge of the bed which caused Juliana to roll with her.

'Oh my God! This bed,' Juliana grumbled, opening her eyes and blinking as Melody pulled the net curtains aside. She propped herself up on Melody's pillows and the bed creaked again as she stretched noisily. 'If you're planning on bringing someone back to this flat, you'll have to get a new bed. This thing is enough to put off even the most rampant of suitors.'

Melody thumped and yanked at the window until it opened, silently thinking that there was only one person she would like to bring back to her flat but he was with another girl. Fresh air which smelt of the sea, even from such a distance, drifted into the room and leaning her head out of the window she surveyed her new world. 'I've still got seagulls,' she said, watching a gull on a nearby roof take off and land on another roof. 'And I've got pigeons,' she added, spying two courting pigeons on the guttering just below her windowsill nodding their heads at each other. 'I can also see into people's gardens and into their homes, too.'

'That's why God invented net curtains,' Juliana yawned.

Melody dropped the net curtain and went into the kitchen. She put the kettle on and spooned coffee into the mugs before opening the little fridge under the counter, not dissimilar to her own in Spindrift. She shook the milk bottle to disperse the cream on the top then peeled off the silver aluminium foil lid to pour some into the cups. Her every movement to start the day was the same as she'd performed every morning for years in Spindrift, only this time she hadn't been certain which cupboard she'd put the mugs in or where the coffee was. Juliana had tidied the cutlery away and now her knives, forks and spoons were in a different order from how she had them at home.

'It will be better when you get all your own knick-knacks in place,' Juliana said, appearing in the doorway behind her, wearing her silk robe and a rueful smile. 'I'll visit again soon and I'll bring swatches of fabric and a mood board and everything you could possibly need to make it perfect until you get one of those brand-new places. I'll be in my element.'

Melody didn't know what a mood board was but Juliana's enthusiasm helped her to feel brighter. She was also coming to grips with her decision to buy a new apartment. Hopefully one with a real view of the sea again.

'I could organise some beautiful Austrian blinds or curtains for you while you're here,' Juliana continued. 'With a matching cushion or two. We'll put glorious paintings on the wall, flowers in vases, things like that. Honestly, Mel, I think it will look lovely by the time you've finished with it.'

'Not pokey?' Melody offered a rueful smile back.

'Victorian charm,' Juliana said confidently.

*

Melody waved Juliana goodbye after several hugs, lots of kisses and a hundred promises to speak to each other regularly on the phone. 'If you got yourself a mobile phone we could speak whenever we want to.' Juliana tapped her bag where her mobile phone was inside its leather case and she looked hopeful. 'You could at least join the twentieth century and buy yourself a cordless phone so you could move around instead of being tethered by the length of your telephone cord.'

'My own phone works perfectly well, thank you, Jules.' Melody gave a wry laugh. 'Plus, I'd *never* be able to escape you if I had a cordless or a mobile. You'd probably be expecting me to chat to you even if I was on the toilet!'

'I absolutely would,' Juliana grinned.

'And I absolutely wouldn't,' Melody said, leaning in to kiss Juliana one last time through the open window of her car. 'Go! Ring me when you get home to let me know you got there safe and sound… and leave a message on my answer phone if I'm not in!'

'Then look at your flippin' answer phone once in a while,' Juliana shouted as she drove off, the sound of her laughter disappearing with the roar of her car engine.

As Melody turned away, her smile slipped from her face as, alone again, she made her way up the old Victorian steps to her flat.

Melody spent the rest of the day unwrapping her belongings and trying not to dwell on where they had been in Spindrift but on finding a brand-new place for them. The little wooden box with the needles and thread in it, the gift from Joe, she put on top of a huge sideboard in the living room that had come with the flat.

'Get creative,' Juliana had ordered as she placed all the bags with fishing nets, shells and sea glass next to the sideboard. 'This unit is big enough to organise everything, your scissors, paints, a drawer for the nets, another for the shells, et cetera. You'll have everything to hand to make things and I'm confident that whatever you make will be fantastic.'

Now, as Melody finished putting the last of her bits into the sideboard, she began to feel a tentative flutter of excitement about it. It was all neat and tidy and her first proper craft zone and it felt good. It felt *really* good. She put the half-finished hall mirror on the table and decided that it would be the first of her creative tasks. You've been waiting a long time, little mirror, she thought to herself.

When the phone rang, for a moment she couldn't remember where Juliana had plugged it in but, following the sound of it, found it in the entrance hall by the kitchen door. 'Hello, Jules,' she said into the receiver.

'How did you know it was me?' Juliana said.

'Because you're the only one who rings me.' The sound of running water was coming down the receiver competing with Juliana's voice. 'What's that noise? Tell me you're not in the toilet having a wee?'

'That's for me to know and you to wonder,' she laughed. The running water stopped at Juliana's end but next came the chinking of china. 'Actually I've just arrived back home and I'm making a cup of tea one-handed while I talk to you.'

'And ringing me couldn't wait until you'd made the cup of tea and were sitting down?' Melody frowned a smile into the receiver and tried to imagine Juliana struggling with such a simple task instead of being patient.

'It doesn't have to wait until I'm sitting down, does it?' Juliana said brightly. 'Because I'm not tied to the telephone like you are. My home phone is cordless. I bet you're standing in the hall staring at the wallpaper, aren't you?'

'No. I'm sitting on the floor staring at the wallpaper.' She traced her finger around a delicate design of roses on the wallpaper and thought that the hall mirror would look nice against the pattern of it.

'See!' Juliana's voice chirped down the phone as if her point had been proven. 'You're sitting on the floor whereas I'm taking my cup of tea outside now to sit in my comfortable chair in the garden.'

Melody smiled to herself. She didn't care if she was tethered by the telephone call and couldn't move around her flat, she was happy just chatting to her sister again. 'I've been busy since you left. I've already sorted the craft things,' she said proudly. 'And I'm working tonight but tomorrow I'm going to set up and work out how to use my new home computer.'

Juliana's voice came down the receiver, serious and gentle now. 'And are you going to speak with Joe?'

Melody didn't answer. Her bottom was starting to go numb. She shifted her position on the floor and made a grunting sound as she moved. 'You're uncomfortable, aren't you?' Juliana asked.

'I'm perfectly comfortable,' Melody answered, standing up and stretching her cramped legs. 'I just need to...'

'Move about?' Juliana laughed.

'Maybe.'

'I'll phone you again tomorrow then, but, for fuck's sake, put a stool or a chair in the hallway or you'll get varicose veins before you know it. Oh, and speak with Joe!'

After the call, Melody immediately realised she'd found the perfect home for Milo's wheelchair. She wheeled it into the hallway next to the telephone and placed one of her own cushions on it. Then, on the wall next to the chair, she hung the picture Flora had painted of her and Milo as children playing in the sand with Juliana. And, gradually, as the day wore on, finding other places to put her belongings around the flat began to make sense.

Her armchair was by the window to catch the best of the evening light and the electric fire was moved to the edge of the room to reveal the Victorian fireplace. She cleaned and blackened the grate and hearth then filled it with an arrangement of dried blue sea holly. The sea holly had been in one of the piles in Spindrift's sitting room and she marvelled at how well preserved it was, a memory of a day out with Milo at the nature reserve hunting for tiny bees that nest in the sand. Her oyster shell wind chime now hung from the bedroom curtain pole and it tinkled with the music of a coastal breeze when her window was open. Her new home was beginning to come to life. It was cosy and cheery and by the time she went off for her shift at The Beach she was confident that she'd come back to something resembling home.

Joe Wiley wasn't in the pub when she got there and, although he wasn't in there every night, on this particular night it tied Melody in knots. Juliana was insisting she give him a fair trial and she knew, in her heart, that she must. She knew she was jealous but understanding that didn't make her feel any better. In fact, it made her feel a whole lot worse. They had no partnership other than a drunken kiss and it was unfair of her to feel this way. They were simply friends.

When, two hours later, Joe walked into the pub and the girl on the boat was with him, Melody instantly flushed beetroot red. Unlike the Joe she knew, who kicked his working boots off before he stepped over the threshold of the public bar, this Joe was showered and cleanly dressed and looked so lovely it hurt. The girl looked half his age, with legs that were way too long to be decent while Melody, who was wearing cotton dungarees and a pair of deck shoes, barely reached Joe's shoulder.

'A beer and a Babycham please, Melody.' Joe placed a casual elbow on the bar but Melody refused to meet his gaze. She trembled as she poured the drinks and furiously pierced a cocktail cherry with a little stick before dropping it into a wide bowled glass. Placing the Babycham down on the counter she took Joe's money and, before he could say anything else, she hurried to the other end of the bar to serve another customer.

With their drinks, Joe and the girl went into the lounge bar of the pub, the side with the carpet normally used by captains, officers and pilots. They sat at a table near the window and Melody couldn't help overhearing how the girl laughed a lot, drawing in each breath of hilarity and blowing it out again through perfect white teeth. She thought that the girl must be witty in a way she'd never been blessed with and could see now, plain as day, why she and Joe had only ever shared a drunken kiss and never a proper *dalliance*.

For the rest of her shift she was all of a muddle over it. She gave three people the wrong mixers with their spirits, two pints of beer were poured so badly the foam head was worthy of a Dutch measure and she short-changed the harbour master.

By the time she returned back to the flat she was so distracted by her thoughts that the sight of Daniel's rubber boots winded her. How incongruous they looked by this new front door. These boots that had been by the unlocked door of Spindrift over twenty-five years. She had hoped that their familiarity would greet her whenever she came back to her new home but here, they simply looked irrelevant. Milo's wheelchair, too, parked at the end of the hall by the telephone also seemed sadly out of place. Despite her placing a bright cushion on the seat of it and the painting on the wall next to it, it was now shrouded by night-time shadows. These things that she had depended on for so long looked lonely where they were.

She went to bed in her new room, tormented by her thoughts until, at last, she slept, back with the ghosts of Flora and Milo where the moon dropped silver into the sea and the waves crashed and rolled against the shore.

The next morning, Melody rang work and told them she needed some time off.

'Are you going anywhere nice?' asked the landlord.

Melody thought about telling the truth. That she needed some time to grow a thick enough skin to do her job properly and to cope with the raucous banter in the pub or deal with seeing Joe Wiley drinking with another girl. Instead, she stared at the painting on the hall wall beside her, where Flora had so perfectly captured three little children playing in the sand without a care in the world. 'I'm snowed under with things to do in my new home,' she replied.

'Take as long as you need,' the landlord said. 'There's a couple of students that always want extra work.'

She replaced the receiver and tried to forget Joe. She spent her time learning how to use her new home computer and beginning the bitter-sweet task of going through all the Polaroid photographs. Her resolve, however, fell apart when she came across the photo of the tiny dried seahorse found on the same day that she realised Milo could no longer hold such a delicate thing. His fingers too loose and weak to perform such a task.

When Juliana rang, she was ready for her, sitting in Milo's wheelchair but still holding the photograph in her hand. 'How are Gordon and Isobel?' she asked as brightly as she could.

'They're fine,' Juliana answered. 'I'm finding it difficult, though. Every time I see Mummy and Pops I can't help thinking of the truth behind our family. I don't know if I feel angry or sad. I keep studying them and wondering if they think about it all the time like I am or whether they've really been able to bury the past.'

Melody looked up at the painting on the wall and shook her head. 'I don't think they've buried the past. I just think they've learnt to live with it.'

'I guess,' Juliana replied vaguely. 'But to be honest, I don't think it's really possible to forget such a festering hurt when you and I must remind them of the truth of it every single time they see us. Especially Pops. He's keeping two secrets now. Do you think we should talk to him? Tell him that I know?' Juliana breathed heavily into the receiver of her phone and

Melody could feel her pain. Now, she too was burdened by the old-fashioned attitudes of a bygone era.

'I don't know,' Melody answered.

'Me neither. And what about Joe, have you seen or spoken to him yet?'

Melody bristled. 'No, because he was with that girl from the boat. He bought her Babycham and she laughs a lot. They drank in the lounge bar.'

'Oh,' Juliana breathed her disappointment into the receiver. 'The *posh* bar.'

'The posh bar,' Melody repeated.

They both knew the relevance of the lounge side of The Beach. It was still very much a dock and shipyard environment but it was definitely more refined than the public bar side. It was the side you might go to if you wanted to impress.

'And have you done anything about the new apartment?' Juliana pressed.

'Not yet.'

'But people want the sea view, Mel. The good ones get snapped up in no time and if you don't act soon you're going to miss that opportunity as well. What's the delay?'

Melody, sitting on Milo's wheelchair in the narrow hall, fiddled with the cord of her telephone, unable to confess to not wanting to accidentally see Joe on her travels. 'I'll go tomorrow,' she promised.

'You do that. And report back!' Juliana commanded. 'I want to know all the details. Oh, and get a brochure.'

And so it was, on a cloudy Thursday morning, wearing one of her favourite dresses, a necklace of green beads, her leather sandals and with her blonde hair piled into a bun, that Melody made her way to the sales office for the new Shelly development. In her cloth handbag were the details of the bank account, a hanky, her purse, and little else. She'd never been one to carry a powder compact or lipstick or the paraphernalia that glamorous people like Juliana did or the girl Joe was with.

When she arrived at the sales office, however, the lights were off and the door was locked so, with a feeling of disappointment that she hadn't expected, she walked around the building to see if anyone was about but the building was deserted. There she was, finally with the courage to change her life, and there wasn't a soul to speak to. She checked her watch for the time, unsure as to why she did that. It was already mid-morning and the working world was wide awake.

Unable to stop herself she made her way towards Spindrift, heading around the back of the dock instead of using the dock swing bridge where she risked bumping into Joe. The air smelt of wood, boat engine fuel and fish and as she walked behind the grain silos she could see that Joe's boat was free from any evidence of a girl's washing hanging out to dry. This morning only two tee-shirts and a pair of Joe's shorts swung in the breeze.

Making her way along Shelly Road she could taste the dust in the air from the demolition work. She wasn't sure why she was doing this to herself but she just couldn't stop putting one foot in front of the other, tormenting herself with all of it. Shelly had been made up of over a hundred bungalows all in all, and now some had been flattened already, some had broken windows, some still incongruously had potted plants growing in their front yards, others were overcome with weeds growing between rubble. A gate swung on a single post and a broken washing line dangled against a fallen chimney. Spindrift and Pebbles and the others in her little crescent were still awaiting their fate. As she neared Spindrift, though, something felt out of place but she couldn't put her finger on it.

It wasn't until she pushed the front door open to Spindrift and smelt the combination of cleaning fluid and salt water that she began to work out what was missing. It lay heavily upon her in a blanket of guilt. Undoing the latch on the double doors she opened them, filling Spindrift with sea breeze. 'There you are, old girl,' she said stepping out onto the terrace. Her sun chairs were still there, but nothing else. There was an emptiness that ran far deeper than the worn-out décor or the fact that she no longer lived there. Something fundamental.

Melody stood with her back to the sea, looking in towards Spindrift, past the sitting room and down the long hallway where the doors to the bedrooms, the bathroom and the little kitchen hung open on either side. She scrutinised the floor and how the lino, cleaned and mopped, curled with age at the edges. She ran her hand over the peeling paintwork of the frame to the double doors and felt the gap where the weather-beaten wood was coming away at the corners. 'I'm so sorry, old girl,' she said, walking inside and turning back to look out of the doors and across the sea. 'After all you have given us, I've been letting you die alone.' She bowed her head, feeling emptier than the home she was standing in. It's as if I've left a beloved grandmother to slip away without a hand to hold, she thought.

An hour later, Melody walked back into Spindrift and silently returned Daniel's rubber boots to their place by the front door and hung Flora's yellow towelling dressing gown on the hook in her bedroom.

Making her way out to the terrace, she refixed the oyster shell wind chime back outside where it could continue to play its tune to the end. And finally, trying to keep her heart from breaking, she placed Milo's wheelchair, not in his bedroom, but by the double doors looking out to sea. 'This is yours,' she whispered, placing the shell of a giant sea snail on his seat.

Walking into the tiny front garden of Mrs Galespie's new house in Camperdown Terrace, she wiped her face of any residue tears. 'Mrs Galespie? Are you in?' she called, peering in through the open door.

A booming shout came from the back of the house causing Melody to smile at the familiarity of its volume. 'Is that you, Melody dear? Come in, come in! I'm in the kitchen at the back. You can make your own way through 'cause I'm up to my pits in cake mix.' Melody walked in and made her way down the length of the hallway towards the back of the house. It was longer than Spinnaker had been and the ceilings were high like the ones in her flat and, as she entered the spacious kitchen where Mrs Galespie was elbow-deep in dried fruit, the smell of brandy hit her.

'Oh, now don't you look smart. 'Andbag and everything. Don't mind me,' Mrs Galespie prattled on. 'I'm making my Christmas cake. I always make it early to allow everything to mature in time for the big day. I insist you come 'ere for Christmas. No excuses. Promise?'

'I promise,' Melody smiled gratefully.

'And that fella of yours, Joe, is also invited.' She took a sip of the brandy and offered Melody one but she declined. 'The brandy's the best part,' she laughed. 'Once I 've made the cake I 'ave to feed it every now and then with more brandy. One measure for the cake, one measure for me. That's 'ow it's always been and always will.' She smacked her lips and replaced the cap on the bottle.

'He's not my fella,' Melody corrected.

'Whatever you say,' Mrs Galespie answered. She washed her hands in the big old butler sink then put the kettle on. 'Nice cup of tea?'

'Yes, please,' Melody answered. She looked out of the open kitchen door and saw that the house had a narrow garden that led to a little jetty at the bottom. 'You're lucky,' she said taking in the view of the water. The house was situated where the land of Shelly curled round to face up the estuary rather than out to sea and the back of Mrs Galespie's garden led down to a small creek.

'It 'as a bit of beach, too, when the tide's out,' Mrs Galespie said, smiling happily. 'Plus, I can moor my little boat right outside my back gate now. Always a silver lining and all that. It's quite lovely round this little corner.' She handed her a cup of tea in a spotted pattern cup and saucer and led the way through the open back door. 'Come on, let's drink it outside and I can show you my new view.'

They sat at an old wooden garden table and in silence admired all that they could see. The tide was out and the water, reflected by the sky, was almost cyan blue and completely still. It snaked like glass towards Lympstone where rowing boats and sailboats listed in its shallow waters, weed clinging to their mooring lines.

'The reason I'm dressed nicely today, Mrs Galespie,' Melody ventured, trying to suppress a smile, 'is that I'm going to buy one of the new apartments.' She kept her gaze focussed on the beautiful view and sipped at her tea. Her smile still suppressed, she waited for Mrs Galespie to shout for joy as Juliana had done, or at the very least to greet her announcement with approval. But none came. Glancing at Mrs Galespie to see why such a declaration should be met with silence, Melody could see that her wide smile had completely melted away. Her plump lips now hung open in a questioning way.

'What do you mean?' Mrs Galespie asked, a gathering of wrinkles appearing on her already wrinkled brow.

'I mean,' said Melody, taking a homemade biscuit from the plate that Mrs Galespie had provided, 'I decided to look for the silver lining in our Devon clouds that you talked about and I'm going for it. If change is going to happen, I might as well embrace it rather than fight it. When the sales office opens, I'm going to secure an apartment near the water. You and I will be neighbours again – just in a different way.' Melody crunched on her biscuit and beamed through the crumbs. But Mrs Galespie shook her head vigorously until the skin under her chin wobbled.

'You 'aven't 'eard?' she asked.

'Heard what?' Melody answered.

'That the bank 'ave just pulled out on the deal. The development can't go ahead because the building company no longer 'ave the money. That's why some of the bungalows are still standing, like yours. It's the property crash, I'm afraid. I'm sorry, my lovely, but you're not going to be able to buy one of them fancy new apartments because they aren't 'appening.'

Calmly, Melody placed her half-eaten biscuit back on the plate. She felt sick. She thought that if she moved too quickly she might actually throw up. 'They've forced us all out of our homes for *nothing*?' she cried.

'Well now, it's not that simple,' Mrs Galespie clarified. 'Most leases 'ad run out anyway and it's no longer our land to 'ave. The Dock Company owns it.'

Melody could hear Mrs Galespie talking but her words were no longer going in. 'I'm sorry, my lovely, but you'll 'ave to find something else to buy or wait until they sell the land again and 'owever long that'll be, I really don't know.'

Melody gulped and felt as if she were underwater. The ground was spinning beneath where she sat. Seeing the carcass of Spindrift just now had really brought it home to her how very old the bungalows were. She hated the term *shanty* but a hundred years of being beaten by all the elements the sea and the rough coastal weather could throw at them, even Melody knew they had done their time.

'Our bungalows, that life – it's in the past. Perhaps wait until one of these brick 'ouses round 'ere come up for sale, 'ey?' She took two biscuits and dunked them in her tea, offering Melody the plate but Melody pushed her chair from under her and kissed Mrs Galespie on the cheek.

'Thank you, but I need to go,' she said.

As she excused herself and stumbled out of Mrs Galespie's house, Melody ached, not just for herself, but for all the people who had been affected by the need for *regeneration*.

★

It had taken her a long, angry day and a long, sleepless night before she could calm down enough to tell Juliana what had happened. The red light on her answer phone was flashing again and she knew before she pressed 'play' who it was.

'I know something's wrong, Mel, so if you don't ring me back soon I'm coming down there. That's a promise!'

Melody smiled at the tone of Juliana's message. How far they'd come in just a short space of time. Not so long ago they could go for months without much communication at all and now barely twenty-four hours could go by without one or the other of them ringing each other.

Now, sitting on the hallway floor on the cushion that she'd had for Milo's wheelchair, she dialled Juliana's number.

'Oh, Mel, this is a bit of a bummer,' Juliana said, when Melody told her about the land at Shelly.

'To say the least,' Melody replied heavily.

'What do you think you'll do?'

Melody leant against the wall and rested her bare feet on the skirting board in front of her. 'I don't know,' she replied. 'Stay here? Wait for the land to sell again…'

'Come and live with me?' Juliana interjected.

'You know how I feel about the coast,' Melody said softly. 'I couldn't move away from the water any more than you could up sticks and move down here.'

'I know,' Juliana replied. 'But a girl can always try.'

'And I love you for trying,' Melody said.

'At least come and visit me then. Have a little holiday,' Juliana pleaded.

Melody shifted on the cushion and thought about Milo's wheelchair now back in Spindrift looking out to sea. A deep sadness was inside her and she knew it was the kind of sadness that would probably stay with her forever. But she had a sister, and her sister was waiting with a big heart and open arms.

'I'd love to,' she replied.

The next morning, Melody was in her kitchen thinking about her trip to Cheltenham, having fed the pigeons who were eating greedily outside her window.

Picking up the old rock and shell ornament from her windowsill she cupped it in her hands remembering the day they'd made it for Flora. Periwinkles, cockles, conical shells and little whorled shells were clumped into an ungainly order upon a slice of grey rock. It looked terrible to her adult eye but as she held it she began to realise that there, in her hands, was the answer to the question she'd been asking for years. So many sleepless nights had been spent listening to the universe, hoping for answers from Flora as to whether to tell the secret or not. Answers that she couldn't hear and yet, all along, had been calling to her from this funny little ornament.

'This gift is more precious to me than anything you could have bought with a year's worth of pocket money,' Flora had said as she and Juliana along with Milo had presented it to her with pride. 'I love it, and I love you all for making it for me.' Then she had hugged them each in turn and popped it on the windowsill where she could look at it every day.

A rock, some glue, and a muddle of little shells was the

answer. Flora had loved her whole family fiercely and would never have wanted any of them to live with guilt and pain. Flora, she now believed, was telling her that it was time that Isobel was saved.

# 31

# Cheltenham, Gloucestershire

1989, NOVEMBER

Juliana beeped the horn of her car twice when Melody stepped out of the railway station in Cheltenham.

Melody had spent most of the morning sitting by the window in a train watching the countryside go by while she drank coffee from a flask and ate cheese sandwiches out of tin foil. The view, she decided, was pleasing to the eye. Trees were bursting into vibrant shades of late autumn gold and their red and russet leaves were dappling the ground beneath them. Acres of fields and hedgerows went past, peppered with houses, villages or whole towns all so different from her little corner of Devon. For the entire journey she didn't open her book, choosing instead to marvel at a leafy world without a sea view.

'Hey, you,' Juliana cried, opening her arms and hugging Melody tightly. 'Where are all your cases?' She looked behind Melody as if she were hiding something and Melody laughed. 'This,' she said, holding up a single holdall, 'is all I need.'

'If you say so but I could barely get my toiletries in that bag.' Juliana opened the boot of her car and Melody unceremoniously dumped the bag inside. 'New clothes?' Juliana pointed to Melody's coat as they climbed into the car.

She was wearing a green faux-fur winter jacket and chunky boots.

'Old clothes. I just haven't had an excuse to wear them for ages.' She was still very much bohemian compared to the preppy look that Juliana was going for lately but she was confident in her appearance and was looking forward to staying in the country cottage out of the shadow of Alastair.

'I've got lots of things planned for your stay,' Juliana said excitedly.

'And we won't talk about demolitions or Joe or anything like that while I'm here,' Melody replied.

'Whatever you say,' Juliana shrugged.

They drove through the Regency architecture of Cheltenham with its glorious buildings and iron picket fences until they reached a vast green world. Although it was far from the coast, Melody quietly delighted in driving past the prettiest of houses, farm shops and pubs all built out of warm yellow Cotswold stone, until they reached the twisting undulating country lanes that led to Juliana's cottage.

'It's absolutely gorgeous, Jules,' Melody gasped, as they pulled into the driveway of a beautifully renovated cottage edged by an ancient dry-stone wall that ran the length of the garden.

'It is, isn't it?' Juliana agreed. 'I am very happy here and I don't miss the grandiose life I had with Alastair one bit. I'm not like my friends, Mel. Babies will have to wait. For now, I'm independent and I've got a man working for *me* so what more could a modern woman want?'

She opened the boot and lifted Melody's bag out for her, carrying it into the house through a small oak door. Brushing their feet on a coir mat, they stepped onto a black slate floor before slipping their shoes off to place them in a cream-painted rack. All the woodwork in the cottage was painted cream with walls of a pale, fresh shade of green. Large, restful paintings hung on almost every wall. It was cosy yet bright and the kitchen opened up into a wall of windows that looked out over a lawn. 'There's the tree where the owl sits hooting into the night,' Juliana said, pointing at a huge oak situated at the bottom of the garden near a wooden gate.

The two bedrooms were big with soft cream carpets and the en-suites were modern and shiny. The kitchen had a green Aga throwing out heat and an enormous white marble island situated in the centre of an oak floor. The garden had a hot tub and there was a beautiful table and chairs situated under a leafy pergola. By the time Melody finished the tour, although she didn't want to compare the cottage to Spindrift, she couldn't help it. She thought of Juliana washing up or making supper in the tiny kitchen of Spindrift where the tap dripped and the paint peeled. She thought of her showering in the bathroom where the sealant was coming away and a plastic shower curtain had hung from a pole above the bath. And how she'd sat on the terrace having to drink wine out of mugs on sun chairs that were so old their fixings had rusted.

She giggled. The sound of it was unexpected but once it was out she giggled even more. 'It's a bit different from Spindrift,' she said, running a hand along the smooth oak counter surface of the kitchen that stretched in a huge L-shape around the edge of the room. 'You must have felt as if you were camping.'

'Only all the time,' Juliana laughed.

'The toilet wouldn't always flush, the seagulls pooped on your beach towel and I forced you to fling yourself into the English Channel fully clothed!'

'Oh, I'll get you back,' Juliana said, pretending to be serious. 'I'll make you sit in the hot tub with a glass of red wine until you positively can't stand it any more. Then I'll wrap you in a fluffy white robe and subject you to the underfloor heating while I torture you with coq au vin.'

'It sounds awful,' Melody answered with a straight face. 'When do we start?'

An hour and a half later they were still in the hot tub. Their hair was wet and their cheeks were glowing and the wine was delicious. They listened to several tracks of music and talked for ages about frivolous things before the conversation took a different turn.

'Jules? I've been thinking,' Melody began. 'I really think that we should tell Isobel we know the truth. I believe now that Flora would say the same.'

'I think I agree, Mel. I feel that Mummy changed after Aunty Flora died,' Juliana ventured. 'I now keep noticing things that I never noticed before the truth was spilt. It's such a strain on all of us.'

Melody nodded thoughtfully, moving position until the bubbles from the jet ran soothingly along the soles of her feet. She'd long since noticed that Isobel had been more tactile on the rare occasions that they'd met. More willing to hug, more *needy* of it almost. 'Maybe she feels freer, free to love me.' Saying this out loud made her feel guilty for avoiding Isobel. 'Whenever I'm around her now, I *feel* her pain.'

'Me, too.' Juliana leant her head against the edge of the hot tub and looked at the sky as if all the answers might be up there. 'I feel as if I can see it in her eyes that part of her is missing.'

'I've replayed all the moments over the years that we've

been in each other's company,' Melody added. 'They keep going around and around in my head because now I know how difficult it must have been for her. I don't really understand why Gordon insists that nothing is said when maybe it would be the best thing for all of us. It's time,' she nodded determinedly, 'that we released her from her prison walls.'

They arrived at Gordon and Isobel's house two days later after Juliana suggested they all dined together and made an evening of it.

Their house was of Regency architecture and situated in the centre of Cheltenham. White render, black iron fencing. To Melody, it felt imposing and unfriendly but the expression on Isobel's face when she opened the door told her that they had been right. It was time to release her from her prison walls.

Isobel took both Juliana's hand and Melody's in her own. 'How lovely to have you both here for dinner. Isn't it lovely, Gordon?' Gordon nodded and smiled at them both but Melody thought the worry lines around his eyes made him look tired.

Entering the house they went into a drawing room where their white baby grand piano was situated next to Georgian doors that opened onto their perfectly sculptured garden. 'Gordon, darling, would you make us all a nice drink? Take a seat girls.' Isobel ushered Gordon into the kitchen while they made themselves comfortable on the enormous feather-filled sofas. Melody thought she may never be able to find her way out of them they were so big and so incredibly soft. An ornate clock ticked on the mantel above a large marble fireplace and several photographs adorned the shelves either side of it. She could see that among them were her own photographs. There was a family photo of Flora, Milo and herself but next to that were three of Melody. A baby photograph, a junior school photograph and a senior school photograph showing that the likeness between herself and Juliana was more apparent than she'd realised.

Gordon brought in a tray of sherries and set it down on the coffee table. 'Now, girls,' Isobel began, smiling at each of them in turn, 'To what do we owe this lovely honour?'

Melody nibbled at the soft skin around her thumb in between giving furtive glances to Juliana and tucking stray locks of hair behind her ears. Fidgeting was the only thing she could do to survive watching the delicate scaffolding her birth mother had built around herself being taken down in front of them all.

'Pops,' Juliana began. 'Melody and I believe that it's time Mummy knew.'

It was two, long, difficult hours that followed in which Melody and Juliana listened to the entire path of love, loss, pain, guilt and regret that Isobel had trodden since that day in May 1954 when she had left Exmouth with empty arms.

All of them cried the kind of silent cry that was too heavy with pain to make a sound and, when finally there was nothing left to say, Isobel walked wordlessly into another room and returned with something in her hands. She took a seat on the sofa between Melody and Juliana and there, in her palm, was a twist of hair – white blonde and strawberry blonde woven together and held with a red ribbon. 'One for Flora, one for me,' she said. She ran the pad of her finger over it and gave a sad, wistful smile. 'We snipped your hair when you were just little girls. One summer so long ago.' She looked up at Melody and her eyes, which once Melody had thought were cold, now brimmed with agony. 'I have kept this under my pillow every single day since then. I wasn't allowed to keep you, Melody, but no one could stop me loving you.'

Isobel crumpled as if the pain was too much to bear and, in fear that she was going to fall to the ground, Melody and Juliana leapt up and held her in their arms. Gordon, too, rushed over and put protective, strong arms around them all and, for the first time in his life, held his precious family together.

# 32

## Exmouth, Devon

It was December before Melody went back to work but when Big Joe Wiley came into the pub she didn't know what to do with herself. She still wasn't ready to face him.

'Hi, Melody, where have you been? I was beginning to think you were avoiding me.' He frowned a little when he spoke to her as if confused by something. 'Pint of the usual please and one for yourself, if you'd like one.'

She could still hardly bring herself to look him in the eye. The memory of their kiss was so clear in her mind and how she'd responded so readily to him, only for him to pick up with another girl. And a glamorous one at that. Melody's hair was long and untamed, her deck shoes had a hole in the side but she was wearing a pretty dress, even if it was from the last decade.

'Go on, you're due for a break,' the landlord called over as Joe jiggled a couple of pound coins in his hand, waiting for her answer. 'Get yourself a pint, lass.'

'*Actually*, I would like a Babycham please, Joe,' Melody replied.

He looked surprised at this and she thought she saw a vague curl to the corner of his mouth but without comment she took his tankard down from the shelf behind her. Pulling the pump carefully, she filled it with his beer before getting herself a wide-bowled glass on a tall stem and opening a little green bottle of Babycham. She pierced a glossy red cocktail cherry with a stick and popped it into the glass and slid gracefully onto a stool beside him. Flicking her loose hair over her shoulder, she sipped at her drink as delicately as she could.

She'd never had Babycham before and suddenly knew why. It was sweet and sickly and frankly awful. Playing with the cocktail stick, she swirled the cherry around in the glass and wondered whether she would get away with downing it in one.

'You don't like it, do you?' Joe was grinning at her, and her heart sank. As much as Melody wanted to be that person who could sip from a dainty glass and look fabulous doing it, she just wasn't.

'It's...' she began. 'Well, it's...'

'It's vile?' Joe laughed and gently took the glass from her. He placed it on the counter, nodding to one of the other staff behind the bar. 'A pint of the usual for our Melody please. She'd temporarily lost her senses but now we have her back.'

The amber liquid, cool, hoppy and vibrant, slipped gratefully down and Melody sighed as she rested her tankard on the bar. 'Better?' Joe grinned.

'Better,' she answered. Then, finding the courage from somewhere deep within, she took a breath. 'The... er, girl isn't with you today?'

'The girl?' Joe frowned.

Melody eyed him steadily. 'She drinks Babycham, has long legs... laughs like a chicken.'

'Oh, you mean Lucy!' he replied.

Melody replayed the name inside her head. *Lucy*. It was a pretty name and one that went well with Joe's name. Joe and Lucy, she thought. Lucy and Joe.

'She's Mark's niece. She came for a couple of weeks to spend part of her holiday here.'

'Mark?' Melody frowned.

'The guy who owns the boat I stay in. Lucy is his niece. I was going to introduce you to her but you disappeared.'

'Oh,' Melody breathed. 'I thought... maybe you and her...'

Joe laughed out loud, tipping his head so far back that his hair trailed almost to the waistband of his jeans. 'You're joking!' he cried. 'She's half my age. Plus,' he giggled into his tankard, 'she really does laugh like a chicken.'

Melody spent Christmas morning on her sofa with a breakfast of smoked salmon and bagels speaking on the phone to Juliana, Isobel and Gordon. 'I love it,' she said, thanking Juliana for the gift of a cordless telephone that she'd opened first thing.

'Really?' Juliana asked. 'I was a bit worried about giving it to you. You've always been so determined to stick with your old phone.'

'Yes, well that was before I saw sense. I was wondering when to admit defeat myself having spent the last few months sitting in the hallway pretending I was happy to be tethered there by an old, and slightly grubby, telephone cord. And I'm going to love my driving lessons and rain check for a car.' Melody had never learnt to drive, not seeing the need to spend much time beyond the boundaries of Exmouth, but here, in

Isobel and Gordon's Christmas present, was the opportunity to do just that. 'Thank you so much, parents!' She pinked a little with pleasure as the word *parents* left her lips.

'You could drive to us for Christmas next year,' they called out together through the loudspeaker. 'We would all love that.'

Melody tried to imagine herself driving along the motorway, beeping her new car horn twice when she reached their house, and smiled happily to herself. They were all building bridges at long last and their future was filled with hope and love.

'Say you will, darling,' Isobel begged. 'I know you promised yourself to Mrs Galespie this year but it would be the best Christmas present in the world, wouldn't it Gordon?'

'It would,' he answered. 'It really would.'

'I will. There'll be no holding me back next year,' Melody promised.

She replaced the receiver, still with the memory of warm, tight hugs that they had all given her on the day she left Cheltenham, and went to get ready for Christmas lunch at Mrs Galespie's.

Ice sheets had formed like crazy paving on the surface of puddles, frost clung to garden railings and Christmas trees were sparkling in almost every window as Melody made her way into Camperdown Terrace. She spotted Joe at the opposite end coming towards her, carrying a card, a bottle of wine and a gift.

'What have you got her?' he asked, nodding in the direction of the parcel in her mittened hand. She looked down at the misshapen gift, wrapped in tissue, shrugging as if it were nothing special. In fact, Mrs Galespie's gift was handmade and had taken her the best part of four days' work to complete.

'A bag,' she replied. 'You?'

'A sack.' He held up a sack tied with nautical rope. 'Actually it's an anchor. I found it at a garage sale full of old sailing bits and bobs and I thought she might like it to put in her garden. It would look good propped against a wall or used as a coastal hook for a hanging basket or something.'

'It's a great idea.' She was envious of Mrs Galespie and her garden and the fact that it led down to the water, perfectly situated for views of the sunset over the water every evening. She'd give anything to be back by the sea again yet despite her regular visits to the estate agents she'd, so far, been unlucky finding anything. 'It was kind of Mrs Galespie to invite us round today.'

'It will be a different kind of day from last Christmas. No Enid Johnson, no Franklins or Old Tess or Old Albert...' Joe smiled sadly. 'I'm afraid I've just heard some bad news. Old Tess sadly died last month and apparently Old Albert isn't coping with it. He won't be far behind her.'

Melody pressed a mittened hand to her mouth, her stomach turning with the shock of what she was hearing. 'No! Not Old Tess, really? And Old Albert left behind like that. If only they'd been allowed to live out their lives in Shelly where they knew everyone and everyone looked out for them. I can't bear to think of them like that, it's too sad. Their bungalow is still there, still with junk post piling up on the front door mat.'

'This Christmas is the start of a new era for everyone,' Joe added. He said it quietly as if he had something else on his mind, more than just Old Tess and Old Albert, but as they arrived at Mrs Galespie's the door was flung open.

'Come in, my lovelies. Shake the cold off you and 'ang yer coats 'ere.' Mrs Galespie pulled them both into the warm as if they were long-lost family and indicated a row of hooks on the wall. 'Colin and 'is wife, Jennifer, are 'ere, but apart from that it's just us chickens this year.' She ushered them past the front room where a fire burnt in the grate and a Christmas tree stood on a table in the front window. A string of coloured lights woven through the branches flashed on and off and a very old-looking doll in a white dress was perched precariously on the top. 'Keep going, my lovelies,' she ordered, prodding them down the hallway until they reached the back of the house.

Colin and Jennifer were washing up pots and pans when they entered the kitchen and, as Christmas hugs and kisses were exchanged, Melody inhaled the scent of roast turkey, cloves, oranges and sweetmeats. It reminded her of home. Flora would cook enough Christmas fare to keep the family going for several days and, by the amount of dishes filled with steaming vegetables, it looked as if Mrs Galespie was of the same way of thinking. A pile of roast potatoes sat crispy and glistening on a metal tray on the old range cooker.

'We're just waiting on the parsnips because I put them in a bit late. Three more minutes and they'll be done,' Mrs Galespie said, taking the bottles from them and placing them on the work surface. 'Oh, you shouldn't 'ave done,' she cried, when Joe and Melody presented her with their gifts.

'I won't then,' Joe joked, taking back his gift and pressing it protectively to his chest.

'Oh, go on then,' Mrs Galespie laughed. She yanked it off him but immediately groaned at the weight of it. 'Blimey!

Weighs a tonne, what's in 'ere? By the shape of it, it feels like an anchor.'

'That's because it's an anchor,' Joe laughed. 'I thought you could use it in your garden.'

'I love it already,' Mrs Galespie blushed. 'I've got the perfect garden 'ere for my plants to grow around all my boating regalia. Fenders and ropes and the odd lobster pot, but this will be my first anchor and 'ere I am with nothing to give anyone except a warm 'ouse, a tot of the good stuff, and a full belly.'

'And great company,' Melody added handing over her own gift. 'It's perfect and we're grateful to be invited, aren't we Joe?'

'Speak for yourself, I'm only here to get fed.' Joe winked at her then lifted the lid off a terrine and popped a chunk of buttered carrot into his mouth. Mrs Galespie slapped his hand.

'Give over!' she chastised him, squashing a smile between pursed lips. 'Colin! Get them parsnips out of the oven and you and Jennifer can carry it all in. Then, Joe Wiley, you can fill yourself until you burst your banks.' While the others got busy, Mrs Galespie undid the raffia ribbon that bound the tissue on Melody's gift.

'Oh, my word it's bootiful.' She beamed with pleasure, pulling the bag Melody had made out from the tissue. It was fashioned out of an old pair of blue denim jeans and she'd used one of the back pockets for detail. The denim was edged in yellow blanket stitch with a pretty daisy embroidered onto the pocket and the whole bag was decorated with woven and knotted lengths of yellow fishing net with handles made from the same net plaited into tight circles. She'd made an identical one for Juliana which she'd given to her before she left Cheltenham.

'It's fabulous and I love it even more than the anchor.' Mrs Galespie winked at Joe then planted a wet kiss on Melody's cheek. Shoving the tray loaded with roast potatoes into Joe's hands, she pointed him in the direction of the table where Colin and Jennifer were. 'Seeings as you're 'ere you can be useful,' she ordered.

Christmas dinner was spent eating more than they needed and drinking more than they should. The dining room was decorated simply, with sprigs of holly around the fireplace, oranges pricked with cloves and a pyramidal arch of candles on the mantel. The table and the sideboard were laden with bowls of food, sweet treats and whole nuts. Beside every plate was a Christmas cracker which they pulled as soon as they sat down. 'Link arms and we'll do it proper,' Mrs Galespie ordered. 'And watch Jennifer, she's fiercely competitive.'

'I don't know what you mean,' Jennifer laughed, but two minutes later she was sitting triumphantly with two paper crowns, two prizes and two jokes. She unravelled one of the slips of paper and read the small print. 'What was the snowman doing in the vegetable patch?' she asked.

'Having a frozen pea?' Joe asked.

'It's snowbody's business?' Colin asked.

'Nooo,' Jennifer laughed. 'He was picking his nose!'

They all groaned except for Mrs Galespie who was, at that moment, with a look of comical distaste, spearing a parsnip with her fork.

The rest of the jokes were told with their paper hats balanced on their heads and playing with the plastic toys from each cracker. Melody found a little green jumping frog in hers which she pressed and it landed in the gravy boat, while Joe had a pink kazoo which he played until Jennifer snatched it off him. Mrs Galespie smoked between each course, then coughed so much that when she laughed she had to cross her legs, begging everyone to 'Stop being so bloody funny.' Lastly she brought in the Christmas pudding, complete with the blue flame of lit brandy, giving a healthy dollop to everyone whether they had room for it or not. And when Jennifer found a silver fifty-pence piece in her pudding they all cheered.

'I always put a big coin in the pud,' Mrs Galespie explained, 'because when I was young I swallowed a little silver sixpence and 'ad to spend two days searching for it... if you get what I mean.' To her immense hilarity, they got what she meant.

When, at last, they were given permission to stop eating in order to retire to the front room, they flopped onto the sofas in front of the television to listen to the Queen's speech. She talked about the greenhouse effect and the pollution of rivers and seas and how the earth shimmers green and blue in the sunlight. When the speech was over Melody fell asleep dreaming of a shimmering world and all the things she could do to turn pollution into works of art.

She awoke to the dulcet tones of Mrs Galespie's snoring in her armchair and couldn't help but smile over the fact that, despite everything they'd eaten that day, Mrs Galespie had a pile of empty sweet wrappers on her lap and a smudge of chocolate on her chin. She became aware that, while Colin and Jennifer were asleep on the small sofa, she and Joe, who had been sitting at opposite ends of the longer sofa, had, at some time in their sleep, both curled themselves into the cushions until the soles of their feet were touching. They both had warm socks on but, beneath the thick wool, she could feel the arch of his foot snugly against hers. It might have been a different kind of Christmas from all the other Christmases she'd ever had but, while Mrs Galespie rasped with all the racket of a small thunderstorm and the Christmas tree flashed colours into the darkening room, Big Joe Wiley slept beside her.

'Something before you go, dearies?' Mrs Galespie was loading plates with more food for them to eat before they left. Joe was washing up, Melody was drying up, and Colin and Jennifer were putting things away, and as Mrs Galespie took a variety of cheeses out of the fridge, each of them blew out their cheeks and their stomachs as if they couldn't possibly eat another thing. 'I've got 'omemade mince pies and clotted cream, too,' she beamed at them.

Dutifully filing back to the table in the back room, Melody and the others took their seats. Joe, Colin and Mrs Galespie managed to fill their plates as if they hadn't eaten since the day before while Jennifer and Melody eyed each other carefully, both hesitantly wondering how little they could get away with eating without upsetting their host. Melody put a single mince pie on her plate and braced herself, deciding, after just one delicious bite, that she did, after all, have more room in her stomach than she'd thought. 'These mince pies are scrummy,' she said, wiping the crumbs from her lips. They were light and sugary and full of delicious sweetmeat that had the same whack of brandy of Mrs Galespie's Christmas cake. Melody finished the mince pie, complete with a dollop of clotted cream, and, although terribly full, thought she could just have room to cram in some cheese and pâté. But just as she was slicing a ripe Brie, Mrs Galespie reached out and pressed her hand against Joe's arm.

'Colin just told me the news, Joe. I'm so sorry. I guess we all knew it was coming but to do it so sneakily and so close to Christmas is just awful.' She tutted and shook her head from side to side causing the soft part under her neck to wobble.

'I wasn't going to bring it up right now, Mrs Galespie,' Joe said quietly.

She clucked and waved a dismissive hand at him. 'Well that's very noble of you, Joe, but we're all 'ere for you.'

'Thank you, Mrs Galespie.' He glanced across at Melody who gave him a quizzical frown. 'Not everyone knows yet,' he added, looking solemnly into her eyes.

'Knows what?' Melody put down her cheese, her heart beginning to thump. Clearly something big had happened that had affected Joe and, whatever it was, she was about to find out.

'The dock's closing,' Colin jumped in. 'You've just been given your papers, haven't you Joe. *Disgraceful* short notice.'

'That's awful,' Melody answered lamely as Joe said nothing and Colin carried on.

'My own job is safe because I'm a sailmaker but we all knew it was a possibility for the dock. And now they reckon they've found a crack in the dock basin there's no arguing with it. They close on New Year's Eve! Great timing, hey?'

'*New Year's Eve?*' Melody gasped. She suddenly felt sick and everything she'd eaten that day shifted in her gut. 'What does this mean?'

'It means all the dock workers and many people round 'ere lose their jobs – their livelihoods,' Mrs Galespie answered while Joe sat quietly, nodding wordlessly at their comments.

Melody knew he was the only one in the group who depended on the dock for a living but she understood enough to know that in one way or another they would all be affected.

'The Beach pub,' she whispered. 'All the dockers drink there after work.'

'Not now they won't. That pub's going to be like a morgue,' Mrs Galespie tutted. She lit a cigarette and sucked angrily on it, blowing a plume of smoke out on a long sigh. 'Sorry, my lovely, I thought you would 'ave known.' She shot Joe a look of surprise and exhaled the next lungful of smoke in a thin plume towards the ceiling. 'Don't you two talk any more?'

Joe looked at Melody again and she struggled to read what was going on behind his eyes. Equally, she gave nothing of her own emotions away. 'We both lead busy lives,' he said and Melody nodded as if in agreement.

'So where...' Melody thought for an awful moment that her voice might give her emotion away. She sipped quickly at her port to keep the tears at bay. 'So where will you work now?' She remembered the conversation from last Christmas when Joe had told Brian Franklin that he would consider Rotterdam rather than break hearts. She held her breath and waited.

Still looking steadily into her eyes, Joe, without hesitation, replied with what she was dreading. 'Rotterdam,' he said.

It was fortunate for Melody that, just at that moment, Mrs Galespie reacted so loudly everyone turned their attention towards her instead. '*Abroad!*' she boomed. 'I thought you were joking about going to the Netherlands. But there's still fishing work to be 'ad in Exmouth. Or what about boat trips for tourists or something? Rotterdam indeed.'

Joe offered an expression that Melody couldn't read. 'It's

a *very* big and *very* busy port, Mrs Galespie. I have a relative over there and I already know I can get work more easily than I can here.'

Melody did her best to compose her features into feigned nonchalance. 'When do you go?' she asked, hating the squeak that came out with the question. She cleared her throat and picked up her nearly empty port glass and gulped down the last of it.

''Ere, my lovely.' Mrs Galespie held Melody's gaze in a private moment of solidarity and winked sympathetically, filling the glass back up almost to the brim. 'Get this down your neck.'

'I only have to clean the boat and prepare her to be left for winter and then I'm free to go.' Joe was still looking at Melody. Still with that way of his that always made her feel as if he could see right inside her – the cool light of his eyes, shining like an ice-blue gem around the black of his pupils. She looked away.

'That's not long,' she said.

'It's long enough if there isn't anything to stay for,' he answered. He pushed a cracker laden with cheese and pâté into his mouth and, as he ate, Melody felt a piece of herself die inside. *Nothing to stay for.*

Mrs Galespie mumbled something undecipherable under her breath about banging heads together and she stubbed her cigarette out so forcibly that it splayed and spilt the last of its tobacco into the ashtray. 'I'd say it's time we called it a day,' she said, heaving herself up from her chair and nudging Colin with her fist. 'Some of us need our beauty sleep.'

As Joe and Melody stepped into the cold night air and

Mrs Galespie shut the door behind them, Joe pulled his collar up and shrugged into his jacket. 'It's a cold night,' he said.

'Freezing,' Melody replied. She pretended to shiver and wrapped her scarf around her neck, shoving her mittened hands deep into her coat pockets.

'I'll walk you home.' Joe looked down at her and their icy breath pluming from their mouths mingled in the air between them.

'I'm fine, thank you,' she replied. 'I walk home after my shift at the pub much later than this sometimes.' She wanted to change her mind. To say something different. To ask him to walk her home and stay with her forever. But he was leaving Exmouth and there was nothing she could do about it. She looked down at the ground before the moon unveiled itself from a cloud and shone its bright, silvery light on her feelings.

'Night, then,' Joe said. He hesitated and, for one delicious moment, she hoped he was going to kiss her again and perhaps change his mind about going to Rotterdam. But then, just as she was about to raise her face towards his, he turned away from her, making his way home.

Melody, her soul in her boots, headed down Camperdown Terrace in the opposite direction, calling softly over her shoulder, 'Night, Joe.'


New Year's Eve, for the second year running, arrived with a desperate feel to it.

Melody was at work at the pub and it was full of dock workers saying their goodbyes. Goodbyes not just to the year 1989 but to an entire decade. A decade the likes of which many had never lived through before. Economic hardships and technological breakthroughs had marked each year. Greenham Common and women's rights, the Falklands war, the coal miners' and ambulance strikes, all had raged for victory among the uprising of fashion, music and technology.

Despite the alcohol that flowed and the party that was had, there was a terrible sadness in the air that the decade had also brought about the loss of many small working docks and communities like theirs. The gathering of locals for New Year was more akin to a wake than a celebration of their future.

For most of the day and well into the night, Melody, her heart heavy, pulled pints and poured spirits to the sound of the piano keys being hammered within an inch of their lives by anyone who could play a tune. Songs were sung, or yelled, at the tops of voices, hands were shaken, backs were slapped and many tears were shed. Sprigs of mistletoe were tied to the ceiling and men and women planted kisses on the cheeks or lips of anyone who passed underneath it, knowing that they may never get the chance again.

Big Joe Wiley was there circling the crowd and Melody watched him out of the corner of her eye. When a woman with dark hair and fascinating eyes pulled him under the mistletoe, Melody was unable to look away. The woman wore a thick woollen jumper with harem pants and leather sandals and she had a tattoo which formed a perfect Celtic circle around her arm. Melody had seen her around before. They'd even shared idle chit-chat from time to time but now, as the woman kissed Joe under the mistletoe, Melody felt the beast of jealousy grow green again. She wished she wasn't so busy working because so far she'd only been kissed by the landlord, the other girl behind the bar and Mrs Galespie!

When 'Auld Lang Syne' was sung, just as the midnight bells sounded, the whole atmosphere in the pub changed. As with last year, Melody could see that no one knew more than the first well-known verse and, with her throat choking with emotion, she couldn't help but remember Old Albert and how proudly he had known and sung every word. This ballad, an ode to days gone by, could not have been more fitting and, as everyone crossed arms and linked hands, they all sang their hearts out. There was not a dry eye in the house.

# 33

In the morning, the first day of a new decade, Melody, and as many people whose hangovers would let them, stood solemnly on the wharf of the dock. A steady drizzle fell from an iron-grey sky as they watched the *Star Libra*, an old lady of the sea, become the very last cargo ship to ever leave their dock.

Melody was glad Milo wasn't here to see this. He'd always loved to watch the huge ships steering in and out and the cranes coming to life, the lorries and trucks lining up ready to pick up incoming cargos. Today, the air was heavy with gloom. Bitter feelings showed in the thin lines of mouths and the clenched fists of the working people, their emotion clear in every line of their faces as the *Star Libra* started her engines. Slowly and with dignity she performed balletic moves to turn in the dock basin and nose her way out through the dock and out to sea.

Melody and all the others who were there followed the final journey of the *Star Libra*, flanked by the harbour master and his pilot boat. The *Star Libra* blew her horn all the way along the entire shoreline of Exmouth, the skirts of her iron hull rolling and dipping with the swell of the sea as she made her final courtesy. Lights were flicked on and off in buildings and cars and people lined the esplanade each hooting and waving their final salute.

It was the first time Melody had ever seen Big Joe Wiley cry. His eyes had watered last night in the pub during the mass rendition of 'Auld Lang Syne', but so had everyone's. This was different. This was raw. As the *Star Libra* disappeared from view, his hands were balled into tight fists and, as he brushed past Melody, she saw that his shoulders were hunched and his face was streaming with tears. She called out to him but he didn't hear.

Melody spent three hours sitting by the empty and desolate dock, debating with herself as to whether she should go to him or leave him be. Several times she'd walked towards his boat and several times she'd walked away again, knotted up with the agony of her indecision.

'I don't want you to leave,' she said silently. 'But I don't know how to make you stay.'

The next day, Melody carefully sieved a light dusting of powdered sugar using a doily as a stencil. The result was an intricate pattern of sugared lace on the top of a freshly baked Victoria sponge. She eased it into Flora's old cake tin lined with baking paper and held the tin towards the open window of her kitchen.

'Do you think he'll like it?' Two pigeons had taken to landing on her windowsill for scraps of anything she may leave out for them and this morning they were back again dipping and bobbing along the ledge. She'd called them Dip and Bob.

'There will be none of this for you today, this is a very *important* cake,' she told them, scattering, instead, the crumbs of a biscuit onto the ledge. The drizzle from yesterday had frozen overnight in their water bowl and so, melting the ice and refilling the bowl, she carried on chatting to her feathered friends. 'I need a reason to visit him,' she confessed.

The winter wind whistled across the rooftops of the surrounding houses and through the open window, turning Melody's nose pink with the cold. But, as someone who had lived next to the sea for all of her life, she was hardened to the weather. Kneeling on the floor, next to the window, she rested her chin in her hands, watching Dip and Bob pecking at their breakfast. She tried to work out what she might say to Joe when she saw him. She smiled when the two birds jounced their heads as she talked to them, as if trying to understand what she was saying. 'I only know that I don't want to lose him from my life and I'm going to do something about it.' Glancing at the time on her tangerine clock, she stood up and closed the window, watching her two friends fly off to land again on the ridge of a slate roof.

Making her way towards the dock with her cake tin in one hand and her nerves in her throat, she was surprised to see a flash of colour out of the corner of her eye at the end of a side street. She recognised it as the bright wool of a Nepalese jacket, woven with multiple colours. It belonged to Joe. Hurrying down the side street she saw him walking past the rugby fields towards town. He also had a huge rucksack on his back and his guitar slung over his shoulder. Her heart beating fast, she watched him disappear around the corner and guessed, with a heavy heart, that he must be heading in the direction of the railway station.

With her breath coming in short bursts and catching in her throat, she followed him, coming to a standstill at the entrance to the station. Doing her best to compose herself, she took deep breaths and made her way inside where, just as the Exeter train pulled into the station, she saw him.

'You're leaving?' She caught up with him just as he put his hand on the door of the train's carriage. Turning sharply he looked visibly surprised.

'I'm leaving,' he echoed. 'For Rotterdam.' He opened the door to the carriage and, climbing inside the train, he pushed down the window and looked out at her.

'But remember what Mrs Galespie said – there's still fishing work and boat trips for tourists. Couldn't you do that, instead?' She looked up at his face and *willed* herself to just come out with it and say what she really meant. She *willed* herself to beg him to stay.

'I would, but…' He started to say something else but the guard blew his whistle right next to Melody and the shrill sound of it made her jump.

'Would what?' she asked.

He reached a hand down towards her through the open window and she took it, seeing a look of such sadness come into his eyes that she felt confused by it.

The guard blew the whistle again and walked the length of the train, slamming shut any doors left open. 'Goodbye, Melody,' Joe said softly. The train began to move and he let go of her hand. She took a step, then another. Then, taking a deep breath, Melody started to run. A winter sun was glinting on the windows and she couldn't see Joe any more. The carriages were beginning to curve along the track, but still she ran. Even if he didn't feel the same way, at last she'd found the courage to voice her feelings for him. 'I LOVE YOU, Joe Wiley,' she shouted.

At that precise moment, the train sounded its horn, blasting her words clean out of the air.

# 34

## Cheltenham, Gloucestershire

1990, FEBRUARY

The emptiness of January had worked its way inside Melody and burrowed there, as cold and bleak as the weather itself. Even Juliana's phone calls, shifts at The Beach pub and the mountain of craft things she should be getting on with couldn't fill the desolation she felt.

Day after day she'd taken her wicker basket and combed the beach trying to rediscover the familiarity and simplicity of her old life. Early mornings became her friend again. The sea mist lay across the water like spun sugar, enshrouding boats and yachts as she stepped a solitary path along the shore. She would return to her flat, her basket filled only with a plastic bottle or tangled crab line, or an inflatable beach toy, burst and lifeless and abandoned.

It hadn't taken much persuasion to accept an invitation by Gordon and Isobel to go back to Cheltenham for a visit. Melody suspected that it was because it was February and Milo's birthday. This year he would have been thirty-three years old.

Stepping off the train, she was met by the familiar beeps of Juliana's car, her open arms and usual comment about how lightly Melody had packed. They drove along the leafy lanes and past the patchwork fields of the countryside, past the same Cotswold stone houses and ancient dry-stone walls. As they chatted, Melody began to realise that she was learning to love this part of the country. The familiarity and the beauty of it. And most of all, to look forward to the growing bond with her family.

As soon as Juliana drove up to the Regency house in Cheltenham and beeped her car horn twice, Gordon and Isobel appeared at their front door smiling and waving. As they hurried their way towards them Melody could see how similar Isobel was to Flora. The shape of Isobel's face was so similar, her warm smile, the curve of her lips and the depth of her brown eyes. The only thing that stood them apart was the fact that, at middle age, Isobel's hair, now styled in long layers, was flecked to silver.

Embraces were given and hands were held as Gordon, smiling with his twinkling eyes, ushered them both up the steps and into the house. 'Come in, come in,' he cried, taking their coats and hanging them on large brass hooks.

Their home, opulent and huge, a place that had been so intimidating, was now so welcoming for Melody. It was a grand house but one which had been lovingly furnished. She felt calmed by the soft heather-coloured paint of the walls and the vases of flowers and how quirky, colourful ornaments adorned every corner of every room. More photographs had emerged since her previous visit. Photographs of her with Juliana when they were young, playing on the beach together or posing for the camera with ice-creams in their hands. Milo, too, smiled at her from a big silver frame.

This time, when she saw the baby grand piano by the Georgian doors leading to the garden she went over to it and put her hand on its glossy white lid. She remembered how Juliana had told her that as a child she would play the piano when her parents held soirées and yet she had never heard her play. 'Play something for me,' she asked Juliana, noticing how Isobel's eyes lit up at this request.

'Oh yes, how lovely. Go on darling, play something. I haven't heard you play for so long.'

Juliana obligingly opened up the piano stool and rifled through the music sheets until she found what she was looking for. She grinned conspiratorially at Melody and propped the sheet on the music desk. '"Scenes of Childhood", by Schumann,' she announced. 'This second scene is called, "A Curious Story". Mummy, Pops, this is for Melody, our very own storyteller by the sea.'

Gordon beamed and Isobel reached for Melody's hand and, after so long on her own, Melody's heart was fit to burst. She finally belonged to a family again and her amazing, talented sister was playing sweet, beautiful music just for her.

'Melody, darling, tell us everything you've been up to,' Isobel said when, finally, Gordon was pouring the usual sherries and they'd all sunk into the enormous feather-filled sofas. Melody mulled the question for a moment. There was so little and yet so much to say. She hadn't meant to come out with it though, not then anyway, but she found herself blurting it out anyway. 'I had a friend,' she began sadly. 'You may remember him. His name is Joe Wiley.'

They listened to the tale of Melody's broken heart, clucking and tutting as if Joe Wiley were a prince lost to a princess, and if Melody had thought that Isobel would judge her or feel that a beach dude was no fitting partner for her, she didn't. Her face was a picture of sympathy. It didn't change anything for Melody to share her woes with her family, but it helped. Theirs was a family that would never again have secrets between them.

# 35

## Exmouth, Devon

Melody walked over the swing bridge looking at a line of small boats moored in the dock along with whalers, rowing boats, oystering boats and spaces for the trawlers that had left for a day's fishing at sea. How silent everything was compared to just a few months ago. How sweet it smelt by comparison, with only salt and seaweed and boat petrol to fill the air. The huge old grain silos had already gone, leaving an unfamiliar gap on the landscape. She stepped past the piles of fishing nets and lobster pots and stared in wonder at the place she used to call home.

The land was up for sale again and more buildings had gone, and as she made her way along Shelly Road the scenery grew more desolate. One or two bungalows still remained but most had gone or had tumbled down like a house of cards. A single brick chimney stack pointed towards the sky, skirted by a pile of concrete and bricks that had once been someone's home. An abandoned digger nestled within piles of wooden panels, ridge boards and broken window frames.

Making her way into the carcass of Spindrift, Melody noticed that Daniel's boots had gone and that the wind was blowing through from the double doors in the sitting room, now ripped off their hinges. As with the whole of Shelly, there was debris everywhere. She ran her hands along the wall in the hallway and stood in the doorway to Flora's bedroom. Someone had thrown her dressing gown up into the light fitting where it dangled from the ceiling, dirty and damp. She took it down and hung it carefully back on the hook behind the door. 'Are you still here, Mum?' she whispered. She pressed her face into the old yellow towelling of the gown, searching for the scent of her. But there was none.

In Milo's room, she tried not to mind that the shelves that had once held all his beach treasures had been pulled down. In the sitting room, his wheelchair had gone, played with, no doubt, by whoever had been in there since. The giant shell was nowhere to be seen. She hoped that Milo no longer needed it to listen to the ocean, any more than he needed the wheelchair – that now he had the freedom to be wherever he wanted to be. Juliana had said once that she lived with ghosts – and maybe she did. Maybe she always would.

Crunching her way over broken glass she walked through the damaged double doors and righted the two sun chairs that were now on their sides. Her toilet had somehow found its way from the bathroom and was now smashed on the terrace beside her. Looking around at the husks of the little seaside homes she felt as if she could still see Old Tess and Old Albert sitting outside their bungalow with a cup of tea. They waved at her and she waved back. Enid Johnson was hanging out her washing. The Franklins were watching over their grandchildren playing on the sand, their dog running in and out of the water barking at the waves. Mrs Galespie was having a cigarette on her terrace, chatting to anyone who would listen. She imagined Big Joe Wiley pulling *Wild Rose* onto the beach from the sea and wondered how he was doing in his new life.

Resting her hands on the white peeling paintwork of Spindrift's old fence, where her gate now swung from its hinge, she allowed the sea breeze to play with her wistful thoughts. She didn't know how long she'd been there. And she also didn't know how long she hadn't been alone. She only knew that the hand that softly lay upon her own hand was weathered by the sun and the sea and from years of hard work.

A tendril of pale hair caught in the wind and tangled with her own. Melody could barely breathe. The weathered hand cupped her own and pulled her gently around until she was facing him, looking into the clear blue eyes of Big Joe Wiley.

He wasn't smiling. There was no lazy grin to reveal a feathering of laughter lines but instead there was something much deeper in his expression, a haunting, searching look.

'You came back.' Her words were barely a whisper, as if the moment might burst and disappear if she said them too loudly.

'I came back to tell you something,' he said, softly.

Resting her gaze upon his lips she waited, ripped apart by agony and hope, for him to tell her what he had come back to say.

'I came back to tell you that, for as long as I can remember, I have loved you. I loved you when you were all spots and bruised knees, hanging off rocks to catch buckets of crabs. I loved you for how deeply you cared for Milo. For giving up college, saying it wasn't for you when all along you did that for Milo and Flora. I loved you when I watched you wandering the beach every day with your basket saving the ocean from broken fishing lines or plastic bottles. I loved you when you lugged seaweed off the beach and rowed it out to sea with me, when you swam with me, when you propped up the bar drinking pints with me and especially...' He paused and a hint of laughter lines splayed across his temples. 'And how could I ever forget our drunken kiss?'

Melody stared up at him. Her thoughts were jumbled and upside down and she couldn't find the words to tell him what she so wanted to say. Bubbles of pure emotion filled the empty space inside her with such intensity that she could feel them fizzing through her veins.

The glint in his eyes shone like the blue skies of a Devon summer and his breath was sweet with beautiful words. She curled her trembling fingers around his and he looked down at her hands, so small against his. All the missed moments over all the years were right there inside their palms and she knew she never wanted to let him go again.

'I love you, too, Joe,' she whispered. 'I always have.'

She kissed him then, gently and lingering, tender with everything she had ever wished she could say. A seagull laughed its call in the sky above them and the wind chime, still hanging on the eaves of Spindrift, jangled its blessing in the wind. When the March chill blew in from the sea, Joe wrapped Melody inside his warm jacket and enveloped her within his arms, resting his chin on the top of her head.

'I have to go back to the Netherlands,' he said hesitantly. 'It is a city but it has waterways, parks, cafés and the old port is lovely.' He squeezed her a little tighter and talked into her hair, telling everything all at once. As he described it, Melody tried to imagine Rotterdam – such a different-sounding place from Shelly. 'Come back with me, Melody?

It wouldn't be forever, just until I finish my contract then we could come back, set up home here in Shelly again… together.'

The wind chime jangled again and Melody thought about Milo and how he had to live his life through her stories and how much he would have loved to go on a real adventure.

She didn't hesitate. 'Yes, Joe,' she whispered. 'I'll come with you.' And as he lifted her off her feet and spun her around, she shouted into the salty wind to all her ghosts, to Flora and Spindrift but mostly to Milo, 'I am going on an *adventure*!'

When he put her back down on her feet and kissed her firmly on the lips she had one more thing to say. 'We will need to come back for Christmas, though, because I've promised that this year I'm going to spend it with my parents.'

'Your parents?' Joe looked surprised and a confused frown played above his lovely blue eyes.

'It's a *very* long story,' Melody laughed.

# PART 4

# 36

## Exmouth, Devon

Melody sat out on the decking listening to the sound of the waves rolling against her beach, a straw hat shielding her face from the sun, the sea breeze whispering through her silver hair.

A little boy wearing red wellington boots and a blue and white striped towelling sweatshirt was playing in the sand below where she sat. It was summer and he didn't need wellington boots, he just liked to wear them and Melody knew that if he could, he would wear them to school or even bed. He climbed into *Serendipity*, beached upon the sand, and pretended to fish over the side.

As she watched him, and his delight in everything to do with the seaside, he reminded her of Milo. How different things would have been for Milo had he grown up in this modern world. Flora and Daniel would never have received a despicable letter deeming him *ineducable*. He would never have faced the possibility of life in an institution, or been condemned to a lonely existence in his own home instead of going to school. In this modern world, Milo would have worn a uniform and had a little rucksack with his water bottle and lunch box inside. He would have had friends to play with and professionals who understood his needs. He would have had a full diagnosis, a prognosis, adaptations, independence and quite possibly the kind of care and attention that meant he would have lived a lot longer. How hidden away he had been from the joys of life. How lucky they were that Flora had been such an amazing mother in an era that still understood or tolerated so little about people's needs.

As Melody reflected on the twists and turns of the decades that had gone before, she also knew that if life had been kinder to sixteen-year-old Isobel all those years ago, she wouldn't have lived with Flora or Milo at all. She wouldn't have grown up in Spindrift with the coastal air in her lungs. She may never have met Joe Wiley. She may never have gone on an adventure to Holland or returned and bought their beautiful new home in Shelly.

The terrace of their ground-floor apartment was big enough for a swing couch and pot plants, with ground space to store *Serendipity* and *Wild Rose*, both boats lovingly maintained by Joe. There was a big cupboard in the entryway to the apartment for all the buckets and spades and fishing nets a child could ever need and inside there were four bright and airy bedrooms, plenty for guests, plus a big, modern kitchen complete with dishwasher. Three comfortable sofas were set in the sitting room facing the huge, windowed doors that opened out onto the terraced area.

They had bought the apartment on a blazing hot day in summer when the sea was azure blue and dancing with the coloured sails of yachts and kite surfers. 'Do you have children?' the sales manager had asked. Melody had run her hand over the new little person curled up inside her.

'Nearly,' she'd smiled.

'This area is a wonderful place for children and adults alike,' the sales manager had enthused. 'By the time the regeneration is finished the whole of Shelly will be simply beautiful.'

Melody then signed her name next to Joe's with a flourish and looked the sales manager directly in the eye. 'Shelly has always been beautiful. But now it will just be a different kind of beautiful.'

'When can I go fishing?' the little boy called plaintively, breaking into her thoughts. He had a garland of bladderwrack seaweed around his neck and was popping the bubbles of it. It was the third time in an hour that her grandson had asked this question and he looked up at Melody, imploring her as if he hadn't been out in the boat only yesterday, or the day before that.

She smiled at him. 'When Mummy and Daddy get back from their walk, Frankie,' she answered, also for the third time in an hour. She scanned the promenade which edged Shelly beach, or Pirate's Cove, as it was known now. It was a little smaller than it used to be when Spindrift was there and was now flanked by apartment blocks but the beautiful view was still exactly the same as it had always been.

Holding a hand to her brow to shield her eyes from the glare, she looked for sight of her son Craig and his wife Abby pushing the baby in his pram to get him to sleep. He'd been yelling blue murder when they left and Melody had heard him even after they'd rounded the corner towards the marina. 'They won't be long,' she called to her grandson.

'You said that a gazillion years ago,' Frankie complained. He frowned for all of two seconds before spotting a large dried-up crab by a rock, his face breaking into delight. 'Wow, Nanny, look at this,' he cried. He pushed his hair, long and wild and dark as autumn chestnuts, off his face and held the crab up for her to see. She laughed to herself as the body of the dead crab dropped down onto the sand and Frankie, who was oblivious to this, was left holding up a single crab leg in his pudgy hands.

'What have you got, little fella?' Joe came out of their apartment and leant over the railing to inspect the find just as Frankie whooped and dropped the crab leg, running up the slope of the cutting towards his parents, shouting, 'They're back!' He sang at the top of his voice, 'Daddy's going to take me out in *Serendipity*, Daddy's going to take me out in *Serendipity*.'

Joe lowered himself onto the swing couch next to Melody and, while they waited for Craig and Abby to reach them, he rocked it gently. He tucked a lock of his hair behind an ear, shorter now and completely silver, but, at seventy-three years old, with his sun-kissed skin, weathered deck shoes and cotton shorts, he was still very much Big Joe Wiley.

She had married him in the old stone church in Exmouth on a day when fat clouds lumbered across a blue Devon sky and the graves of Flora and Milo, decorated in wedding flowers, looked on. She had made her wedding dress from simple ivory linen adorned with a row of tiny clam shells found on the beach and sewn down the back seam. Isobel had wrapped a shawl around her shoulders telling her that it was a gift from Flora. Flora had made it for Isobel's own wedding day out of gossamer-thin voile, hand-embroidered with daisies in ivory silk thread. The day that Joe Wiley had become her husband she'd kissed him on the steps of the church with Milo in her heart, her sister behind her carrying a bouquet of sunflowers, her father by her side, her mother crying with joy and her other mother wrapped around her shoulders as soft as a sea mist.

'Have you had an update on when the folks are getting here?' Joe asked.

Melody checked her mobile phone to see if there was a message from Juliana but, just as she did, it rang. She put it to loudspeaker and they both leant in so that they could hear what she had to say. 'We're only about an hour away, Mel, and the others are following behind,' Juliana said, her voice raised over the sound of their car travelling on the motorway towards Exmouth. 'Say hi to Melody and Joe, you two.' Melody and Joe listened for the sound of Gordon and Isobel's excited greetings coming down the phone from the back of the car and they smiled.

'Craig and Abby are here now with Frankie and the baby but Frankie and Craig are going out on *Serendipity*. They should be back by the time you all get here. The table's booked at The Beach for supper and I'll put the kettle on for you all. Oh, and there's cake!' She turned the call off and took a photo of Frankie with her phone. She had never thought she would get a mobile phone but not only did she have one, she used it all the time – for photos, texts, videos and FaceTime calls and sometimes even to make calls to Juliana while she was in the bath. Frankie, who had already put his life jacket on and was impatiently holding a bamboo pole with a net on the end, gave a silly smile for Melody as she sent two pictures of him to Juliana.

'Great-Aunty Jules and Great-Uncle Richard are nearly here with Great-Grandad Pops and Great-Granny Izzy,' she called to Frankie. 'When you get back from your outing they'll be here with everyone else.' Frankie whooped again so loudly that the baby made a squeaking sound and Melody reached over to rock his pram.

Within the hour, Melody and Joe heard two beeps of a car horn and Richard's huge four-by-four car pulled into the parking space next to Joe and Melody's car. Behind them, two more cars pulled up with their daughters, Claire and Tammy, their partners and children. Richard set about getting Gordon's wheelchair out of the boot of the four-by-four while Joe greeted everyone else and Melody and Juliana helped their parents out of the car. And while the children spilt from their cars and ran to greet everyone, Isobel reached her shaky, speckled hands out for a hug and Melody wrapped her arms around her. 'Hello, Mum,' she said, planting a kiss on her cheek. 'Hello, Dad.' She bent to kiss Gordon, feeling the softness of his snow-white hair against her cheek. 'Come on everyone,' she beckoned, 'there's a pot of tea and lots of cake waiting for you all.'

Inside, she made her parents comfortable on the sofas in front of the huge windows overlooking the sea while Craig and Abby pulled dry shorts and a tee-shirt on Frankie who had accidentally on purpose fallen in the sea fully clothed when they came into shore. Joe brought Flora's old tray out of the kitchen complete with the ancient china tea set, a jug of orange juice and a platter containing the huge coffee and walnut cake plus several vanilla muffins made only that morning. 'An act of love,' Joe had said, when he'd gone into the kitchen, inhaling the aroma of fresh baking and swiping one, then darting away before Melody could flick him with the tea towel.

'How is the latest book going, Mel?' Juliana asked, wrapping an arm around Melody's waist while the children pulled off their socks and shoes and ran like wild things out onto the beach, holding vanilla muffins in their hands.

'It's good,' Melody answered. 'I'm halfway through writing it. I'd say things are going very well indeed.'

On a shelf on the wall, below Flora's painting of them when they were children and above the cupboard where Noah's Ark was kept, was a row of published books. Each book had *by Melody Wiley* on the cover. And each book told a children's story of adventures by the sea. All the wonderful characters Melody had ever known who had lived and died in Shelly were woven within the lines of them. Storybooks that brought Flora and Milo, Old Tess and Old Albert and the wonderful Mrs Galespie to life again within their pages. Storybooks that were available in audio and braille, too, so that all children could enjoy them.

'What is this latest one about?' Juliana asked.

Melody squeezed her sister's waist and leant her head over until their silver hair was touching. 'It's about someone who lives by the sea and who collects treasures from the beach and turns them into stories.'

When it was time for supper, Juliana took Isobel's arm, Craig pushed his grandfather, Gordon, in his wheelchair and Melody pushed the baby in his pram along the smooth modern paths around the apartments. The whole family, lock, stock and barrel, followed, chatting and laughing with each other.

They all made their way over the dock bridge where the marina was full of glamorous boats of blue and white and an opulent line of yachts competed with each other for the tallest masts. A line of people waited for the ferry to Starcross and a row of seagulls sat on the railings of The Point café by the dock bridge. The family made their way past the site of the Pier Head Stores which was now an apartment block and onwards to where the ground of the old Pier Café had long since been turned into a seafood restaurant.

'How's the shop going, Mum?' Craig asked.

'It's doing brilliantly, thank you, my love. My sea treasure craft pieces are selling well and so are Dad's driftwood creations.' A little building to their right was crammed full of artwork and wonderful ethical products and Melody looked through the window of her and Joe's shop as they passed it. She loved that, in addition to their own pieces, they were selling many more beautiful, repurposed items made by other people.

'Are you *ever* going to slow down?' he asked.

Melody laughed with pleasure as she pushed her little grandson towards the pub entrance. 'No! Not while there are children who need stories to be told and an ocean full of sea life to protect!'

The pub interior was also much changed. There was no carpeted side for captains and pilots or a side for dock workers and no longer any grubby boots outside the door. There was simply the inside of a lovely pub with tables and chairs, each decorated with a little vase of yellow roses and white gypsophila.

When Craig pushed Gordon in his wheelchair into the pub, Melody was reminded of how, on Milo's eighteenth birthday, Flora had determinedly pushed him all the way there for his coming-of-age beer. She remembered how Flora had to get him along the bumpy road, up and down the pavements and over the dock bridge before lugging him into the pub across the steep threshold. How she'd ignored the stares and the ignorant comments of people. How boldly she had held Milo's beer for him and wiped away the dribble from his chin.

As Craig pushed the tables together and their very big family sat down, Melody cast her gaze around them all.

Isobel rocked the baby's pram and Frankie was pretending to fall off his chair, making the children all burst out laughing, when Richard brought their drinks over from the bar to the table. 'I'd like to propose a toast!' Melody said, standing up from the table. 'To the future, the present and the past because it makes us who we are!' She would always live with ghosts, she knew that, but she was also living life with her family and, right now, they were all there. Four generations of her family all gathered around her.

# Epilogue

## Cheltenham

ISOBEL

Isobel dusted a photograph of her sister, her speckled hands shaking with age. Flora's face, so similar to how Isobel's own had once been, smiled at her through the frame, her eyes still bright, her skin still young.

'We were in Exmouth again yesterday, Flora,' Isobel said out loud. 'It was so lovely. The whole family was there, but I expect you know that. And you probably also know that Melody is writing another book which will be as wonderful as all the others. She says that this one is about a girl who collects treasures from the beach which, I expect, is about her own life, don't you? I really can't wait to read it.' She glanced over at a bookshelf where a row of books by Melody Wiley took pride of place and her heart swelled with pride. She knew that if Melody had been hers to keep, she would have weaved the threads of her life differently, bound them in a way that Flora hadn't. She knew that Flora had enabled her to be as free as the gulls that wheeled in the sky and had given her the music of the sea in her soul.

She kissed her sister's photograph and placed it back on the shelf next to Melody, Milo, Gordon and Juliana's photos and all the other photos of her very large family. Then, walking over to the huge Georgian windows in her living room, she looked up at the ever-changing sky. 'I will forever be grateful to you for your kindness and understanding over how I felt about Melody. How I could never hug her, knowing how fearful I was that, if I did, I would be unable to ever let her go again. Did you plan for her to discover the truth, Flora?' A cloud tumbled into curls then frayed at the edges among a texture of blues and she listened for answers knowing that, even in the silence that always followed, she could hear them. She smiled at the cloud and blew a kiss into the air.

'All those years ago, I gave Melody her name. My music, my song. But I know the answer to my question, my dear sister. You gave her back to me.'

# Acknowledgements

For my wonderful sister, Pam, her keen eye and endless patience in supporting me every step of the way with the writing of my books.

For Broo, my fabulous agent, for your supportive phone calls and lovely chats over a glass of wine.

For Aria, Head of Zeus, and all the brilliant team there for their ongoing support.

Thank you to my life-long friend, Della, for spending a happy weekend with me in The Old Dairy, Lympstone and walking the path along the River Exe to Exmouth seafront. And to her darling brother, Michael, who smiled through life's adversities.

For Jill Mansergh (Weeks), Gillie Newcombe and her brother Rick Newcombe. Thank you Jill for inviting my sister and I plus everyone including Keith Graham, (ex Harbour Master) to your seaside home in Shelly (Pirate's Cove) for a reunion. And for providing us with tea and cake while we looked at the beautiful sea view and talked about our wonderful memories of this darling little town.

For Keith Graham, ex Harbour Master, for joining me and

Jill in going down Exmouth's memory lane and for sharing your stories and your photos.

Thank you to Andy Herbert and Derek Allen for spending a brilliant afternoon (and a few beers) in The Beach Pub with me and for sharing your years of knowledge and your Exmouth photo albums.

Thank you to Maisie Dawson, landlady of The Beach pub, for your enthusiasm for my book and for keeping it a fantastic pub on the edge of Exmouth Harbour.

For Dr Sue Shepard and your help regarding past and present progress for inclusive education. The tea, cake and glasses of warm mulled wine were most welcome.

Thank you to Jules and Den for your warm hospitality at The Old Dairy, Lympstone and for having just the loveliest B&B.

Thank you to Exmouth Museum for chatting with me about all the wonderfully interesting artefacts you have for Exmouth.

And last, but not least, thank you to my good pal Jacqueline Kingsbury for your invaluable and ongoing support.

# About the Author

PHYLLIDA SHRIMPTON obtained a post graduate degree in Human Resource Management, a career choice which was almost as disastrous as her cooking. Thankfully her love of books and writing led her to a new career as an author. Her young adult novel *Sunflowers in February* won the Red Book Award for YA Fiction in 2019. Having lived in London, The Netherlands and the Cotswolds with her husband, daughter, giant Saint Bernard and grumpy old terrier, she now lives on the Essex Coast in a place she likes to describe as being where the river meets the sea.